INTENTS OF THE HEART

INTENTS OF THE HEART

Volume I

Provoke Not the Children & Tables of the Heart

Lezlie A. Word

Writers Club Press

San Jose New York Lincoln Shanghai

Intents of the Heart
Volume I

Writers Club Press
an imprint of iUniverse, Inc.

For information address:
iUniverse, Inc.
5220 S. 16th St., Suite 200
Lincoln, NE 68512
www.iuniverse.com

ISBN: 0-595-23703-7

Printed in the United States of America

*This series of novels is dedicated to all of the children,
both the survivors and the victims,
who have lived domestic nightmares.*

*A special remembrance to those who shared their experiences with me
so that this story could be all the more realistic.*

*Many thanks to all of the early "readers" who encouraged the completion
of this story and to Debbie Jobe for her editing skills
and insightful observations without which this volume would not be possible.*

*As always, this work is presented in honor of my Lord and Savior,
Jesus Christ, who promised,
"These things have I spoken unto you,
that in me ye might have **peace**.
In the world ye shall have tribulation:
but be of good cheer;
I have **overcome** the world."*

*John 16:33 KJV (**emphasis mine**)*

"For the word of God is quick, and powerful,
and sharper than any two-edged sword,
piercing even to the dividing asunder of soul and spirit,
and of the joints and marrow,
and is a discerner of the thoughts and *intents of the heart.*"

Hebrews 4:12 KJV
(*emphasis* mine)

Provoke Not the Children

"And ye fathers, provoke not your children to wrath:
but bring them up in the nurture and admonition of the Lord."

Ephesians 6:4 KJV

For our wonderful parents,
Norman & Patricia Word and James & Ocie Tyson
Thank you.

(Richard and Lezlie A. Word-Tyson)

CHAPTER 1

*R*ex stood scowling in the doorway.

His figure, though of small stature, lurked menacingly huge to the terrified boy of six who awaited him. There was no movement. No sound, aside from his breathing, penetrated the still air.

The silence was nearly maddening.

Young Darren sat on his bed, fearful of the punishment that lay ahead. His light brown, almost blond, topped head bobbed ever so slightly with nervousness. His pale blue eyes peered up into his father's face. He quickly averted them from the frigid stare he received and surveyed the floor. He fought to keep the large sob in his throat from escaping. But, he knew better than to cry.

The disaster had been discovered at supper. Rex worked the night shift, so he had slept all day and just eaten. And, now, before he left for the factory, he came to Darren.

Rex slowly entered the room, the darkness of the evening closing in behind him. Darren's heartbeat thudded in his ears. Moisture formed on his hands that were clenched tight. With a quick glance, he saw that Rex's waist was bare; the belt was dangling from his father's fist. Small tears found their way to his cheeks. Fortunately, his father had not noticed them…yet.

"Best get ready, boy," Rex spat, motioning with the strap. "You gonna get it good for—"

"Daddy, I'm sorry 'bout your radio—" Darren began to plead.

"Sorry ain't good enough!" his father said. "You shoulda been more careful. Now, get your ass bent over that bed like I told ya." Darren reluctantly obeyed. "You'll think twice 'fore you go messing with my things, again, won't ya?" He accented his question with the first lick, the snap of it echoing in the small room.

Darren fought his impulse to jump and choked out, "Yes, sir." Rex, unsatisfied until Darren lost control of his tears and cried, berated him for his weakness. "Don't you cry, boy," Rex screamed. "No son of mine cries like a damn sissy! D'you hear me?!" Again, the blows came.

"Yes-s, s-sir," Darren stammered, drying his eyes with a shirtsleeve. He coughed and choked back his sobs. When the beating ceased, Darren stood upright and turned to face his father. He watched as Rex slipped the warm leather belt through the loops of his trousers. The boy's lip trembled, but he did not cry, again. Rex turned, pleased, and left for work.

Darren crawled atop his bed and, now alone, muffled his cries in the pillow. He hadn't meant to break the radio; it had fallen from the table accidentally. But for his father, there was no acceptable explanation.

Rex Mitchell had lived in Hadesville all of his life. In fact, his own father had worked at the same Matherly Parts Factory until his death a few years before. Rex's father, a huge man, was one who used his size to cower those under him. Rex Mitchell had lived with abuse all of his life and knew no other way to live.

Darren still lay on his bed when he felt a tap on his arm. Startled, he turned to peer into the tearful midnight blue eyes of his four-year-old sister, Lauren. Her platinum hair was awry and her lips quivered as she talked. "Are you okay, Darewin?"

"Yeah, I'm okay," he answered softly. Noticing her tears, he suddenly felt a pang of fear. "Why are **you** cryin', Lauren? Did he—?"

"No," she said, wiping her nose with her hand, "I was cryin' cuz I heard you. I'm sorry."

"Thanks, Lauren." Darren grinned. "I love you, too." He winced as he stood. Tall for his age, he bent to embrace his sister. She smiled in return and they found a game to play.

For a time, their nightmare was over.

CHAPTER 2

*I*t was powerfully hot, a perfect July in the year 1949. Rex and Helen Mitchell, now in their late twenties, had been married for nine years. They rented a small house in the town of Hadesville with their two children, Darren and Lauren.

Rex was fairly handsome (when he wasn't wearing his usual frown), blond, blue-eyed, and wiry. Although only five-nine in height, he was incredibly strong and possessed a dreadful temper. His wife and children feared him with good reason.

Helen, whom he met at a county dance in her hometown of Edenton, was two years his junior at twenty-six. Slightly shorter than her husband, she had chestnut hair which complemented her deep-ocean-blue eyes, a trademark of her mother. She would have been an attractive young woman were it not for her years with Rex and the children.

Rex's job at the factory was especially hard on the children. Since he worked the night shift, they had to avoid waking him during the daytime. Thus, they spent most of their summer playing in the yard.

It was on one of these days that they decided to walk to the corner store to spend the few cents they had saved from their birthdays that were in May and June. They received permission from their mother and left, hand-in-hand. It had not really occurred to them that their father would not approve of their walking alone to town, although it was not even a mile to the store. Helen had not taken the time to consider the matter and allowed them to go. She later wished she had not.

Rex, dressed only in his briefs, emerged from the bedroom, stretching. It was four o'clock in the afternoon, and Helen was just about to put the chicken in the skillet. Darren and Lauren had been gone for over half an hour. "Sleep good?" He grunted. "'Bout to put th' chicken onto fry. Be ready by the time you clean up." Turning, he walked to the bathroom the landlord had installed the year before.

Fifteen minutes later, Rex stood at the icebox searching for a cold drink. He pushed a jar of mayonnaise aside and pulled one from the shelf. Helen, sweat pouring down her forehead, stood in front of the hot stove. She swabbed at it with the tail of her apron; the two window fans were hardly enough to combat the blistering heat.

"Where's th' damn bottle opener?" Rex growled as he yanked the junk drawer open. "Can't never find nothin' in this house!" He rammed his hand into the utensils and scoured for the device. "How th' hell d'you get—"

"It's in there, Rex" Helen said wearily. "Jus' keep lookin'." She turned the chicken as grease popped in her face. She frowned, trying to avoid the blasts.

Rex grunted, holding the bottle in one hand and searching with the other. "Oh, shit!" he screamed, jerking his hand from the drawer which went crashing down. Helen jumped as the contents fell in all directions. Rex set the bottle on the counter and grabbed his bloody hand that dripped onto the linoleum. He had forgotten about the broken knife he had dumped in there months ago. His face flushed with anger and he cursed under his breath.

Suddenly, he remembered his wife. He looked at her, daring her to laugh. Emotionlessly, she began to clean up his mess, and he went to the bathroom to clean his cut. After replacing the drawer, she went back to her chicken. It was not until after Rex had dressed the wound and returned to the kitchen that he missed the children. "Where's th' kids?"

Helen turned. "At Musser's. Wanted to buy some candy, I think."

"Where?" Rex's tone turned vicious. "You know I don't like them goin' down there. They knew better." He stomped from the room and began to lace his shoes.

Helen followed him from the kitchen, a look of concern on her face. "Where're you goin'? Not to get 'em, I hope." He didn't answer as he stood, walked to the door, and slammed it on his way out. Helen checked her chicken.

Darren and Lauren paid for their licorice and peppermint and stuffed it into their pockets, smiles erupting on their faces. As they turned toward the door, however, they froze. Rex was staring at them. Their faces fell. Darren instinctively grasped his sister's hand, and they stepped backwards. Their father moved toward them, his anger masked from curious onlookers. Lauren began to cry, and Darren whispered for her to stop. He knew it would only make their father more furious.

"I can't, Darewin, I c-can't," she cried, the tears now dripping from her face. "I'm s-scared."

"Don't worry, Lauren. I'm here," he assured her. "He won't whip us in front of these people. Jus' keep movin.'" They took another step away from him.

Rex's temper rose; he placed his hand at his waist on the buckle. His message was received, and the children halted. "Time to go home," he said with barely-controlled anger. They obeyed without question.

The walk home was in silence. Darren and Lauren still clutched hands, and tears blurred their vision. The sun seemed to mock them with blazing heat, making the distance feel twice as long as before. Both could feel the sticky candy in their pockets.

When they reached home, he instructed them to go to their room. They had twin-sized beds and a dresser and chest to share. Climbing atop their beds, they emptied the candy on the sheets. Darren took it all and quickly hid part of it under the bed in his special box. He whispered to her that it would be safe that way. He'd barely shoved it into place when Rex came to the door.

"Give me that candy you bought." The children sat silently. "Give it to me."

Darren mustered all of his courage. "We, we jus' got some peppermint. We didn't have time to—"

"Give it to me!" The boy reached into his pocket and pulled the handful of candies they had paid for. His father snatched it from him with a sneer. "Where's the rest of your money?" Sorrowfully, that, too, was forfeited. "Told ya'll not to leave the yard, didn't I?"

"Yes, sir, but Momma said we could—"

"*I* told you not to go! You listen to *me*. You understand?!" They nodded. Lauren's tiny face twisted with fear. Her tears had returned. "Stop that wailin'!" Rex reached across the bed and slapped her in the face. She screamed and rubbed the tender spot.

Raising his hand to hit Darren, he noticed the anticipation and clenched jaw of the boy and stopped, mid-air. He swallowed hard. "Ya'll knew better than to do this." Lauren's sobs quieted, as she feared for her brother. "I better not see you outside this room tonight. D'you hear me?" His eyes, filled with fury, pierced them before he walked from the room and closed the door.

Darren and Lauren waited until after eight o'clock when Rex had gone to work before making their move. The young boy clambered from the bed and stuck his head under the covers. Pulling the box from its hiding spot, he smiled at Lauren.

"Whatcha doin', Darewin? Huh?" She peered over the side at him. "Whatcha up to?" He put his finger to his lips to silence her. In a moment, they were munching on long strings of black licorice…their favorite.

CHAPTER 3

*H*elen Thomas Mitchell was sixteen, young, impressionable, and unhappy at home when she met the handsome senior at the dance in the year 1939. There was talk of the war in the air, and the blond, blue-eyed angel that she saw was full of the war spirit. She believed Rex Mitchell would be her dream soldier.

Rex had lived his life, taking all sorts of abuse, just living for the day he could join up—the United States Navy. He'd heard tales from his father of the Great War in Europe and all of the women who threw themselves into the arms of the lonely American soldiers so far from home. Rex had longed for the chance to escape the hell he lived and give it to someone else for a change.

Rex and Helen met in Edenton, her hometown, and were immediately attracted. He learned of her eagerness to leave home and the stepfather she despised and sensed her willingness to be submissive to him. And, by the time she saw his aggressive, cruel nature, she was easily manipulated by her love for him. In only a few months, Rex Mitchell could have led her anywhere he pleased.

To Rex's dismay, he was unable to join the Navy at eighteen. Instead, he reluctantly agreed to support his family for a year because of his father's illness. Helen waited impatiently for him as she completed her junior year of high school. So, by the next summer, Rex's younger brother was old enough to go to work for his folks and he could take advantage of the situation and propose to Helen. She accepted, and they eloped on the tenth day of September in 1940. Of course, she dropped out of high school, and he registered for military service. The young couple found a small apartment in Hadesville that he would be able to afford on his seaman's salary. The furnishings were scarce, and life would be hard for them...and would get harder.

Rex received a letter from the recruiting office requesting his physical examination. Absolutely thrilled, he left the house in an unusually good mood. Helen hoped that all would go well for him. But, he returned home in bad temper. Rex carried a bottle of whiskey and sat on the one chair they had in the living room. He hadn't spoken, and Helen dared not ask what the result had been. She would learn, two days later once he had awakened from his drunken stupor, he had been denied due to his hearing. Injured as a child by his father, Rex was deaf in his left ear. It had not escaped the physicians.

Rex was depressed beyond measure. His only goal in life—his objective—had been crushed in one swift blow. To cuss like a sailor, if only a wishful one, took on new meaning for his scared, timid wife. She simply allowed him to deal with the disappointment in his own way, even if it meant taking the brunt of the aggression. She stood by her man.

Eventually, Rex's anger simmered into a quiet rage, and he applied for a job with the parts factory for which his father had worked, forcing him to take back his vow, never to darken its door. He was called within a week and went with a heavy heart. Dismayed further by the involvement of the U.S. in World War II after Pearl Harbor, Rex was limited to listening to the radio for updates, and his work in the factory was his only contribution. The tides for him, however, were soon to change.

In December of 1942, Rex received his Christmas present in the mail. He had been called to the service despite his handicap. He could fulfill other duties, such working in the galley. To Rex, his position meant nothing; the importance was in his going. He was ecstatic and left in January for his twelve weeks of boot camp training before he was sent to the Pacific.

Helen had only received one letter from him when she made an important discovery. She'd not been feeling well for several weeks before his departure, and now she knew why. She was two months pregnant.

Helen wrote her mother and Rex on the same day. The Thomases (her mother and stepfather) had moved to Texas and sent her a check to begin buying baby clothes and other necessities. Her mother offered to come, but Helen refused her. It would be summer before the child arrived.

Rex's reaction was quite the opposite of the elated mother. He ranted and raved, cursing all creation throughout the barracks. He had planned to stay in the Navy, now that he was enlisted, and make a career for himself, if possible. Now, he knew he could not; he did not make enough on his seaman's salary to provide for both wife and baby. He would have to return home as soon as the war was over. Rex despised the child from the moment he was informed of its existence.

Rex left for the Pacific in March 1943. He had written Helen only twice, telling her of his plans to return to his job at Matherly Parts. She was disappointed for him, but secretly pleased that he would be coming home for the child.

It was during this tough time alone that Helen for the fist time questioned whether or not she had been wise in eloping with her difficult husband. Although she did not doubt her love for him, despite his many faults, she did wonder if she had made her decision too soon in their relationship. Was it this love that she clung to which had driven her, or was it that she was miserable at home and wanted only to escape?

It is important to note that Helen came from a family one could hardly call permissive, but never would it have been characterized abusive, either. Her natural father, a ruddy, red-haired Irishman, was a hard-worker and caring man. Though he had been quite strict with the older girls, Eliza (who would die in childbirth in 1946) and Carolyn who still lived in Edenton, he'd had difficulty disciplining the youngest, a surprise arrival. That grim task (when he allowed her to go through with the punishment) he left to her mother, Caroline, which had, unfortunately, driven a wedge between them over the years, between both mother and daughter and Helen and her envious sisters.

When Henry Thomas died so young, Helen could hardly stand it. Despite the kindness of her new stepfather, Billy, she resisted his guidance and became difficult to control. Not having her father around to protect her anymore, she resented the restriction and sought freedom from them. It had been then that Rex had entered into her life, and, she believed, become her savior.

Now, though, doubt crept in and she feared she'd made the mistake of a lifetime. Thinking that her family would never accept her, even if she were to be brave enough to seek them, she resolved in her heart to endure the situation of her own making. Many, many times would she question the wisdom of that decision.

Darren Lee Mitchell was born on June 30, 1943, a few weeks earlier than expected. Helen's mother who had come in May to help took her to the hospital. The telegram reached Rex in a couple of days aboard his ship where he was a third class seaman. Although happy at being the father of a healthy boy, he nonetheless blamed the infant for his spoiled plans. Unfortunately, it was a burden that would follow the boy all his life. Rex crumpled the note, discarded it, and continued with his work in the kitchen.

Little did either of the young parents know that in a short year, they would be reunited as a family. Rex's ship was hit by enemy fire, and he returned to the States with a minor injury. It was June 1944, and the war's end was close at hand. Rex came back to Hadesville with a few broken bones and a crushed spirit.

Greeting Rex at the train station were his wife and son. Dressed in his Navy whites, he was quite handsome despite his sour disposition. He refused the reaching arms of his tiny son and limped across the parking lot with the aid of his cane.

The months ahead were difficult ones, indeed. Angry at the world for his misfortune, Rex found himself a twenty-three-year-old injured veteran of a world war, a husband, father, and worst of all, the employee of a factory that he hated almost as much as he hated himself.

It was in the fall season of that same year that Helen again found herself with child. Rex cursed the Japanese for this new *surprise*. He reasoned that if his ship had not been sunk, he would not have been home to cause this disaster. Somehow, he could always find someone to blame for his *problems*.

He was not the least bit supportive of Helen during her pregnancy, though they did move to the small house they still rented. In her condition, she'd had her hands full with the tireless Darren, but Rex was blind to her discomfort. Yet, she always found a way to forgive him.

Lauren Ann Mitchell was born May 4, 1945, to a beaming mother and scowling father. He had insisted that she get herself *fixed* so there would be no more mistakes. Although Helen had always hoped for a large family, she consented to his wishes, as always.

Time passed, and the children grew faster than Helen could have imagined. She showered her love for them when she found opportunity. Rex continually accused her of spoiling them, but she knew, even if she would not have admitted it, those children would never be spoiled as long as their father lived. So, she did what she dared under his watchful eye.

Rex was home each night, while working days, which she enjoyed. She felt safer when he was there to protect her; Rex was her security, and she needed him. However, that period of peace was ended abruptly when Darren was four and Lauren two; Rex moved to the night shift.

It was then that the trouble at home began to worsen. Attempting to sleep during the daytime, their father was unforgiving of their noise and interruptions. They soon learned that Daddy was someone to fear and Momma was no refuge for she always answered them, *Do as your Daddy says.*

Helen gradually became very nervous at night, and finally, unable to sleep at all. She was but twenty-four, yet aged by her family. She saw a doctor about the problem and was prescribed a sedative.

Soon, it became her nightly ritual, and her addiction began to take hold. The children were aware that whatever it was that Momma took, it made her very tired and unable to help them if they needed her. Even as bad as it seemed then, it was only to grow worse in time.

CHAPTER 4

*T*he hot, sticky days of July gave way to the muggy ones of August in 1949. One such afternoon, Rex had been asleep since his head hit the pillow at eight o'clock that morning. Helen moved one of their floor fans to their bedroom so that he would not fuss so much about the heat.

Darren and Lauren had spent so many hours in the sun that they both were baked a golden brown. Their sparkling blue eyes shone under dark lashes as they romped from daylight to dusk, playing all sorts of games, living in the world of make-believe.

Both of the children were saddened that school would soon start even though Lauren had not yet begun, and Darren was a good student. It was their separation that troubled them, especially Darren. He dreaded leaving his sister unprotected during the day. Loving his sister to distraction, he watched over her as a mother hen does her chicks; he trusted no one else to do it properly.

That particular afternoon, Helen was in the kitchen putting the finishing touches on her tuna casserole. Having cleaned all day, she had left the children to themselves. Her cotton dress was drenched with sweat as she put the dish in the oven and disappeared to take a quick bath.

Several minutes later, Rex awakened and stretched. "God, it's hot!" he exclaimed, clicking the fan speed to high. He stood for a moment to let the cool air flow through his prickly spiked hair. He stretched, again, and walked slowly to the bathroom door. He found it locked. "Who's in there?"

"Me, Rex. Jus' a minute!" Helen called back.

"Minute, hell! I've got t'piss. Open th' door!" He pounded his fist to emphasize the point. "I said, open it!"

It flung open wide; Helen was standing in only her bra and panties, flushed and angry. Rex grabbed her arm, slung her out into the hall, and closed the door behind him. His wife stood, exposed, and brushed small tears as they escaped her eyelids. She hated when he was like this, and it was becoming far too often.

Darren and Lauren ran into the house, catching their mother in the hallway. Quietly, they dropped their heads, went to their bedroom, and sat on their beds to wait for supper. Daddy's mood was obvious.

Rex finally emerged from the bathroom and went to the refrigerator for a beer. Helen hurried into the small room to dress. She had barely finished when she heard Rex's curses. The children nearly collided with her as they all rushed to see what the commotion was.

Smoke was pouring from the oven door Rex had opened. Helen screamed, realizing that it was her casserole that was burning. "Oh, my God," she whispered, "our supper!" She donned oven mitts to retrieve the blackened mess.

"I'll be damned!" Rex swore, turning to his weeping wife. "What am I gonna eat, Helen? Huh? I've got t'work! I can't go without somethin' t'eat!" He glared at her before slamming the back door shut which he had opened to release the fumes. "What th' hell are we gonna do, now?" His eyes danced with fury.

"I-I'll fix somethin', Rex," Helen stammered quietly. "Jus' go cool down."

"Cool down?! In this heat? Like hell!" He stormed out the door and strode to his small tool shed.

The children stood like two statues, terrified even to race to their room. Helen's sobs broke the silence, and they put their arms around her. "It's all right, Momma," Darren whispered. "It's all right." Lauren kissed her on the cheek. Helen swallowed her fear and smiled through her tears. She found some lunch meat for sandwiches.

Lauren began to cry when Darren informed her later that evening that school started the next morning. "Please don't leave me, Darewin, *please*." Helpless, Darren simply hugged her and promised to hurry home each day.

The four-year-old's fears were realized the very next day at lunch. Helen had made a pimento cheese sandwich for Lauren, forgetting that it was Darren who loved them so. She could not be coaxed into even trying a bite of it; the more her mother insisted, the louder she protested.

Finally, their argument reached the ears of the unconscious Rex. Awakened from his sleep, he rose…thirsty for a victim. Lauren's cries whimpered to a stop when she spotted his shadow in the doorway. Her mother turned in horror as the father moved toward the younger.

"What're you cryin' 'bout, Lauren? Huh? Why you wakin' me up?" he screamed as he raised his hand and slapped her across her tender face. Lauren shrieked and began to wail.

"Rex," Helen interrupted, "it's all right. She jus' don't like pimento—"

"I don't give a damn what she don't like! I'm tryin' t'sleep, an' she better keep her mouth shut, or I'll really give her somethin' t'bitch about!" The child's sobs quieted. "You hear me, Lauren? Huh? Do you?!"

Lauren tearfully nodded, and Rex stomped back to his bedroom. She soothed the stinging spot on her face with her tiny palm. Helen turned to her, her heart breaking, and whispered, "Eat your sandwich, Lauren."

The child choked it down and regurgitated it ten minutes later.

CHAPTER 5

*A*s the school year dragged on, little Darren feared more and more for his sister's safety. Though Rex was equally cruel to them both, the extra time she had to endure each day with him increased the likelihood of his finding fault in her. Never did she do anything that pleased him.

Helen chose to ignore the pain she saw etched in the faces of her children, instead drowning herself in self-pity and her precious medication. She tried to keep Lauren out of Rex's way by letting her spend countless hours outside when he was home, but by sheer probability she would eventually cross his path.

Even as young as she was and craving the attention she only got from her brother, Lauren learned to find some solace in the peaceful surroundings in the small yard in the back of their house. It became her only joy, outside of the tender protection of her big brother. She simply couldn't wait for him to be home for the summer.

There were few pleasant experiences the children would be able to recall in the years to come, but Halloween that year was one of them. A package arrived by post for the children on October 28, 1949, from Texas. Receiving presents being such a rare occasion, they hardly knew what to do with themselves. Though Rex was still asleep when it came, their mother allowed them to open it. Inside was a note from their grandparents, Billy and Caroline Thomas. They sent their love and a surprise. Two boxes, inside of the larger one, were tagged—one for each of them.

Darren opened his first. He found a complete cowboy outfit. The hat, vest, guns, badge, and even boots were there. With a grin no one could erase, he quickly put them on and modeled for his mother and sister. Lauren giggled with delight, and Helen reminded them not to wake their father.

"Open yours, Lauren," Darren whispered as he pulled his gun from the holster. "C'mon. See what ya got."

Lauren snatched the wrapping paper from the box and opened the lid. Inside she found a ballerina costume. Helen helped her into the tights, tutu, and shoes. She twirled for them until she was so dizzy she couldn't stand up. Both children fell laughing on the floor.

Many, many years later, they would remember that night and smile.

✤   ✤   ✤

When Thanksgiving came that year, the Mitchells went to Edenton for the first time since the invitation had been offered. Helen's sister, Carolyn, lived there with her husband, Malcolm, and their two children, Kathy and Todd. He was a lawyer in an established firm and hoped to begin his own practice very soon. His wife chose to stay at home with the children.

Helen and Carolyn had really never been close, even as youngsters, but the years and Helen's elopement had distanced them further. It was after their mother and stepfather moved to Texas that the elder decided to renew their relationship and sent the invitation when Lauren had been but a year old. Rex had never agreed, until now.

The Prestons lived in a large, old farmhouse on a spacious piece of property in the outskirts of town that he had inherited from his grandmother. Malcolm had stocked it with both cattle and stables with a few horses. They were not wealthy, but far removed from the daily struggle the Mitchells experienced.

Rex, of course, did not want to attend. A decorated soldier and officer and the youngest member of his family, Malcolm had been the only one of four brothers to return home from the battlefield. It gnawed at Rex that his brother-in-law had served in the army for the duration of the war *and beyond.* In fact, he had remained in Europe and had only returned home to complete his schooling three years before.

Helen, though, was delighted in the prospects of the trip. She had no other close friends in Hadesville and never got the chance to see her niece and nephew. After much coaxing, she convinced her husband that the train tickets were worth the aggravation. After all, the least they would gain would be a great meal, and Lord knows, they saw few of them.

Malcolm met them in Edenton at the train station on Wednesday night. His chocolate brown hair was cut short and brushed back from his forehead. He had dark eyes, as well, and a winning smile. He was quite handsome and distinguished, a few inches taller than Rex at six-one. The two men retrieved the luggage and carried it to the car followed by Helen and the children. The ride to the farm was a silent one.

Carolyn and her children awaited them at the front door. "Oh, Helen," she said softly as she hugged her little sister. "It's so good to see you. And the children! My how they've grown!" She embraced both Darren and Lauren who were limp in her arms. They were not accustomed to such affection. "Hello, Rex," Carolyn offered with a hard smile.

He just nodded in her direction. "Where do you want these?" He motioned to the baggage. Carolyn frowned and led them to the guest room.

Carolyn and Helen favored one another in appearance. Both were of average height and possessed their mother's deep ocean blue eyes and their father's smile. The younger had light brown hair whereas Carolyn's was deep auburn with copper streaks.

Kathy and Todd Preston were eight and two, respectively, that year. Bashfully, they said their hellos and were soon ushered to bed. The young Mitchells were tucked in, as well, in rooms with their cousins.

CHAPTER 6

❈

*E*veryone was busy the next morning either in work or at play. And
when the feast was ready, all gathered around the large table in
the dining room. The children were seated at a smaller one in the
adjoining room. Helen and Carolyn prepared their plates and then
their own. Darren and Lauren eagerly picked up their forks and
began to eat the turkey and dressing nearly as soon as it was placed
before them. Kathy sat in amazement and finally spoke. "We ain't
said the blessing, yet."

Darren stopped, fork in mouth. He looked at Lauren who had put
a black olive on her finger. She peered back and then glanced at her
cousin. Darren swallowed. "Huh?"

"We ain't said the blessing, yet," she whispered. "We do that first."
Darren still sat unmoving. "Put your head down. I'll do it." She demonstrated, and Darren followed. Lauren did as her brother. "God is
good, God is great, thank you for the food we're about to eat. Amen."
The two confused children shrugged their shoulders and joined her
as she ate. The adults had not fared much better. Rex, too, had been
eating when he was reminded. He threw down his fork in controlled
anger and lowered his head, thinking anything but a blessing.

The meal was the largest the Mitchells would see in the year. All
ate as if it would be their last, even Lauren. She felt more relaxed at

her aunt and uncle's home. She couldn't have put words to it, herself, but it was the security and safety that she sensed and loved.

During the meal, the children talked continuously. As Carolyn checked on them, she noticed that Kathy's glass of milk was too close to her arm. "Move your glass before you knock it over," she instructed. She returned to the adults with dessert. Unfortunately, the young girl did not heed the warning. She was engrossed in her story to Darren about her new kittens. Catching it with her elbow in one of her excited motions, she tipped it over, spilling the milk onto the floor. The squeal, quickly silenced, was heard by all in the adjoining room.

Malcolm left the table to see what had caused the commotion. Kathy was quietly cleaning the mess with her napkin. He handed her a towel, took her glass, and refilled it with water. "Kathy, be more careful next time. Listen to your mother."

"Yes, sir," she replied as he patted her on the shoulder, smiled at the children, and returned to his seat. Lauren exchanged a long look with Darren. Fearing for her cousin, she had tears in her eyes. She had not expected her uncle's reaction. Her brother smiled, reassuringly, and they continued with their conversation.

After all had eaten their fill, they moved to the den. The adults had eaten so much that they were only able to grunt in response to each other's questions. The children stretched out on the floor and were soon asleep.

Several hours later, however, all had recovered and were ready for some action. Malcolm invited Rex to a walk through the pasture and to see his cattle. The women moved to the kitchenette to catch up. Todd amused himself quietly in the playpen. Once again, the older children romped to the outdoors. Kathy was anxious to show them her new kittens and eager to allow them to have one to take home to Hadesville. They knew better than to ask; Rex hated pets of any kind, especially cats.

To Helen's surprise, the visit had gone well thus far. Her husband had been fairly agreeable and allowed himself to relax a bit. She had truly enjoyed herself, as well, and knew that their children had. But, seeing little Todd made her wish for the infant she would never have. Of that, among other things, she envied her sister.

It was evening before it happened. It was what everyone was waiting for, the event that would send Rex home in a rage, vowing never to return. The children were in the yard playing with the kittens when Rex called for Lauren. She ran to him; the others stood and brushed the cat hair from their clothes. Her father was standing beside of the corral waiting for her. Malcolm had stepped inside of the barn to get a saddle and bridle for her to ride the pony. She was nervous, but tried to act brave in front of him.

"Malcolm wants you to ride the pony," he called from a distance. She smiled gleefully as she rushed to his side. He looked down and his face twisted into an evil expression. "What th' hell have you got all over you?"

She peered down at her dress. "Oh, it's from the kitties," she said softly as she began to brush it from her.

"God, Lauren, you know I'm allergic to cats!" He sneezed once and then several times before he stopped. "You know not to go near 'em! I've told you over and over. Haven't I?" Again, he sneezed. "Damn! How many times have I told you? How many?!" He reached and caught her arm just as she started to run. He had only just begun when Malcolm emerged from the stable, the equipment in tow.

"Daddy, stop, no-o-o!" Lauren was screaming. His belt snapped against her bare legs. "I didn't mean to get the kitty hair on me! Please, Daddy, stop!" She yelled, "Darewin, *Darewin!*"

Her brother heard and ran around the corner. He stopped in amazement and Kathy, who was on his heels, crashed into him. Malcolm felt his blood pressure rise. "Rex!"

Rex turned to look at him, and Lauren wrenched free. She ran to her uncle, who had dropped the saddle, and grasped his legs. She was crying uncontrollably. Darren and Kathy quickly joined them.

"Come 'ere, Lauren," Rex gritted between his teeth. "*Come here to me.*"

"Now, Rex—" Malcolm started.

"Malcolm, she's mine. Lauren, come 'ere!"

"Rex, I'm not going to let you hit her, again. Not as long as you're at my house. She's had enou—"

The angry man interrupted, "Don't worry, Malcolm. We're **leavin'.**" Rex turned and saw his son. "Darren, get in the car. Malcolm's taking us to the station." He strode angrily to the house and ordered Helen to get their things. She asked for no explanation and did as he ordered.

Carolyn did not know what had happened until after they had gone, and Kathy told her the grim tale. Together, they offered a prayer for their troubled relatives, the children, most of all.

The Mitchells arrived home at midnight. Helen unpacked the suitcases; Darren sat quivering in a corner of the living room. Lauren was in their bedroom receiving her punishment for disobeying her father while at the farm. She had made a fool of him, and nothing could have spared her. Later, Darren tried to comfort her, but only time could erase the bruises on her body; and nothing in his power would be able to heal the wounds to her spirit…for they were deep.

CHAPTER 7

The eggnog was quite potent; Rex had brought it himself. Helen drank only a couple of glasses, but Rex was not as cautious. His speech was slurred, and he lay on the couch. Darren and Lauren had been given some of the beverage by their father despite Helen's protest.

It was Christmas Eve.

"Oh, hell, Helen! Won't hurt 'em," he had said. "Come 'ere, boy. I'll make a man of ya."

The children sat quietly on the floor. Their eyelids drooped from the sedative, and only the pleasant thoughts of the morning to come kept them awake. The alcohol had made their father very talkative; many things would be revealed that evening.

Wild Navy tales of exotic women and drunken parties were told. Helen tried to shush him, but it was useless. He showed Darren the anchor tattoo on his bicep. His son was curious, yet apprehensive. "See that, boy? That's the mark of a real man, there." Darren dutifully nodded. "Yep, the Navy was th' only place for me." Helen sat very still. She feared the direction of the one-sided conversation. What was he leading up to?

Rex's face became tight and drawn. He frowned and turned to the boy sitting beside of him. "Yeah, it was my life 'til the accident."

Helen drew in her breath. "Rex, *don't*."

"Don't what, woman?! I was jus' talkin' to th' boy." His tongue was heavy. "Mind your own damn business."

Darren's pulse quickened. He looked at Lauren; she had fallen asleep. Her angelic face was so peaceful. He was thankful that she could rest. Rex jerked his arm, forcing him to his gaze. "Boy, you listen to me when I'm talkin' to you. You hear me?" Darren nodded fearfully; Rex grinned. "Yeah, everything was great. I was enlisted and on my way to the war. Your momma and me had it all planned. The Navy would be our livin'." He paused. "Then, *it* happened."

"What, Daddy? What happened?"

Helen's eyes had already filled with tears. She pitied the poor child. She had never intended for him to know.

Rex looked into the wide, expectant eyes of his son. "*You*, boy. That's what happened. You were *born*." The viciousness of his voice made the boy cringe. Tears welled up in his eyes. He wrenched free of his father's grip, ran to his room, jumped on his bed, and cried into his pillow.

Helen turned on her husband. "How could you? How could you tell him that, Rex?"

"It's th' truth, ain't it?" Rex sipped from his mug. "Boy's got to grow up someday." Helen controlled her anger and stood. She carefully carried Lauren to her bed. When she returned to the small living room, Rex was unconscious.

Sunlight had only begun to peep through the curtains of the children's bedroom when Darren finally awoke. He silently slipped from his covers and tiptoed to his sister's bed. "Lauren," he whispered. "*Lauren*!" He gently shook her arm. The tired child yawned and slowly opened her eyes.

"Darewin?"

"C'mon, Lauren," he urged, "It's Christmas!"

Lauren's eyes popped open. Now, she remembered. "Santa Claus!" Darren nodded with a smile. The two quietly crept to the door and opened it cautiously. They entered the hall and then the living room. Their mouths hung open in surprise.

A small tree stood where a chair had been. Helen had hurriedly decorated it during the night. Underneath, there were a few packages, all Darren hoped, with their names on them. Lauren still held to her brother's hand. He put his finger to his lips to keep her from saying anything. He led her to the tree and stopped, smiling broadly.

A red wagon with *Radio Flyer* on the side was pulled to the base of the tree. Inside was a doll for Lauren. She squealed and grabbed the "baby." Darren laughed at her and moved to get a better look at his new toy.

The stockings were half-filled with candy and fruit. Darren was tall enough to get them from the nails. Their mouths were ringed in chocolate by the time Helen found them. She sat down smiling as they played; Rex stayed abed. She reminded them to be quiet as she cooked breakfast.

After all had eaten, they went to the living room, again. Grouchy Rex, ill from a hangover, sat with a scowl. Helen handed them their two presents. Darren and Lauren each received a new winter outfit. Theirs had become too small, and they needed something fancy on occasion. Darren got some toy soldiers (Rex chose them), and Lauren received a set of plastic dishes. They played all day and thoroughly enjoyed themselves. The horror of the night before was momentarily forgotten.

❀   ❀   ❀

In January 1950, Rex took Darren for a haircut one Saturday afternoon. He explained on the way to the barber that it was time he started his training. He had big plans for his son, plans that Darren was just about to discover. When they returned, Helen's mouth fell agape at the sight. Lauren ran up to her brother. "Darewin! Where's your *hair*?" She laid her hands on his crew cut, allowing the hairs to prick her.

Rex sat in his chair. "Darren got 'im a good *military* haircut. Better get used to it." Darren kept the tears from escaping his eyes. He hated the new look, but his father did not understand. After all, why wouldn't a boy of six look forward to a military career?

Lauren suspected how he felt, though. Her hair was long, shiny, and just below her shoulders. Every night Helen combed it while Darren looked on. She could only imagine the horror of losing her own platinum locks.

❦   ❦   ❦

Rex surprised the entire family on Valentine's Day. It was Saturday morning, and he left early. Helen had prepared breakfast, but he had refused. She fed the children and then herself.

It was afternoon when he returned. He yelled for everyone to come to the living room. Helen and the children slowly responded. They were apprehensive, at best. Rex held a large sack in his hand that he laid on the couch. He motioned to his wife and she walked to him. "Rex, what's the matter?"

"Can't a man bring his wife some candy on Valentine's without everyone bein' so suspicious?" He smiled as he pulled a cardboard heart of chocolates from the bag. Helen was speechless. She finally hugged and kissed him.

"Oh, Rex," she whispered. "This's so wonderful. Thank you."

Rex rarely smiled, so this behavior was quite unusual. He grinned and reached into the sack, again. He retrieved two plastic containers filled with candy hearts. He handed one to each of the children.

"Thank you, Daddy," they replied in unison. "Thank you!" They peered up into his face and smiled. His motive was a mystery no one would ever solve.

It was the only remembrance of kindness that they would ever be able to recall.

CHAPTER 8

Wisps of green grass peeked out from the dead stalks of winter. Buds on the trees signaled the arrival of the new season. The brisk winds of March had everyone suffering from spring fever. The Mitchell children were as excited as the rest of the world and yearned for a kite to test their skill against Mother Nature. They saved their pennies, keeping them in Darren's special box. Finally, they were able to purchase one from Musser's in mid-March.

Darren selected the *Super Deluxe Flying Dragon*. It was red and orange, the biggest one he could find. He and Lauren spent their Saturday morning trying to assemble the monster. Helen checked on them a couple of times while Rex slept.

Lauren's blond head bobbed in delight as she skipped around her brother. She was so anxious for him to get it ready. He was covered from head-to-toe in paper and string. "Lauren, watch out! You're steppin' on my stuff!" he called in an excited tone. "Be careful!" His face flushed red and he gave her a stern look. Lauren's tiny features twisted into a frown. Tears welled up in her ocean-blue eyes. She quietly began to walk toward the house, dragging her bare feet. "Sorry, Darewin."

Darren bowed his head in concentration. He detected the quiver in her voice and then, sobs. He swallowed hard. "Lauren," he called in a hushed voice. "Come back, Lauren. I'm sorry." He raised his head to meet her gaze. She smiled and sauntered to him. She sat, Indian-style, and watched him work in wonder.

It was midday, almost lunchtime, when the kite was together. Standing on end, it was taller then Lauren, and Darren had to stretch to hold it up. She clapped with glee and he smiled with pride. It was beautiful.

Just as Darren had explained the procedure to his sister, Helen called them in for a sandwich. Reluctantly, they obeyed. Their father had awakened and sat with a scowl. He informed them of his plans to go to town, and all released a sigh of relief—an afternoon without his ever-watchful eye was indeed a glorious treat.

The children watched as their father walked to the corner by Musser's store. Slowly, the bus chugged to the curb and he boarded. They stood in the springtime sun and saw it pass. Finally, they were alone.

Darren carefully took the precious kite in his hand. He held the string in the other and explained it to Lauren. She stood by as he began to run and the kite lifted behind him. To their dismay, it hit the ground with a thud. Darren stopped and scowled. His face grimaced as he wound the string back on the spindle. Lauren ran to him. "What happened, Darewin? Huh? Why didn't it fly?"

"Don't know, Lauren," he answered. "We'll keep tryin'. Don't worry; it'll fly." He smiled and she did, too.

Two hours later, the initial failure was only a fading memory. Their dragon had taken flight, after all, and was soaring up above. Darren had even allowed Lauren to guide it for a while. They held their hands to their foreheads to shield the scorching rays.

It was nearing suppertime when disaster struck. Lauren, knowing that Helen would call for her soon, asked to hold the string once more. Darren reluctantly agreed. "Okay, Lauren, but be careful," he warned. "Don't let go." He placed the tube in her hands and she held tightly. The wind pulled the kite higher and higher and she let it have more string. It rose some more. Darren turned and saw what she had done. "Lauren! Pull some back in! It'll fall!"

The child began to reel the kite back toward her, but it was too late. The wind had died, and the kite was plummeting to the ground. Darren grabbed the tube from her hands and tried to turn it around. He pulled this way and that, but to no avail.

Then, it happened. He caught a wind current and it soared once again. He smiled and yelled to Lauren. "Look, Lauren! We saved it!" She jumped up and down happily. It sailed to and fro and then took a dip. The Super Deluxe Flying Dragon dropped just below the power lines and then wound around them. As the children watched in horror, their red and orange monster wrapped itself around the electric lines and pole.

Darren and Lauren stood with their mouths open to their chests. What had happened? What had they done? They were silent for a long moment. Then, Lauren began to whimper. Her brother ran to her and held her tightly against him.

"Darewin, what're we gonna do?" she asked through her gasping sobs. "What's he gonna say? What's he gonna do?" She wailed so that Darren held his hand over her mouth.

"Shh, Lauren. Momma will hear you." She choked on her tears. "We've gotta get it down, that's all." He knew that Rex would be furious and that for his sister's sake, he had to retrieve it.

They tried everything. They pulled, yanked, struggled—nothing would free the dragon. It would require an adult to remove the kite from the lines. Darren knew that it was dangerous, but seeing his sister's face made him brave. He was just about to get the ladder when they heard the noise. The old city bus was returning. Both knew that Rex would be aboard.

Without a second thought, Darren grabbed Lauren's hand and ran to the tool shed. They hid under an old tarpaulin their father used occasionally. Darren again held his hand over Lauren's mouth.

He could feel her tiny body shaking, and he whispered comforting words to her.

Rex climbed from the bus and stepped onto the sidewalk, walked inside, and entered the living room. Helen was in the kitchen frying some fish she'd bought from a neighbor. She didn't heard him enter. Rex walked to the doorway. "Where's the kids?" Helen screamed. "What the hell's the matter with you, woman?!" Helen clutched her heart that was pounding. "My God! I can't walk in my own house without people screaming at me."

"Oh, Rex, you scared me, that's all," Helen answered with a weak smile. "Don't be that way."

He turned without comment and got a beer from the icebox. He took a long gulp before turning to his wife. "So, where are they?"

Helen flipped her fish and took some fries from the cooker. "Oh, outside. They've been flyin' their kite. Took 'em all mornin' to get it together. You should've seen 'em." She smiled. "Got it up real high, too."

Rex finished his drink. "Them kids got no business flyin' kites out there. Might get into somethin'."

"Oh, Rex, don't be silly. They were just—"

"Better watch your mouth, woman," he said between gritted teeth, his hand gripping her arm. "You hear me, Helen?" His pale eyes glared into hers.

Helen swallowed. "Rex, you're hurting me. Let me go!" She jerked her arm from his grasp.

"Just you remember that," he spat as he turned quickly and stepped out the back door.

The children still sat under the hot covering waiting for something to happen. They didn't have a plan, aside from survival. What could they do? They simply waited and hoped for deliverance. Lauren had stopped crying and sat silently. Every once in a while, Darren would squeeze her hand to reassure her of his love.

The moment Rex stepped from the house, he saw the dragon. He walked to the pole and gazed at the mess. Blood rushed to his face and he clenched his fists. "Darren! Lauren! Come 'ere!" he screamed. The two children sat without a sound. "Do ya hear me? Come 'ere!" Again, he waited and no one came. "You're gonna be real sorry if I have to come after you! Come 'ere!"

Rex's patience was fading fast. He could feel the anger filling his body, sweeping his entire figure. He was determined that they would obey him. A full five minutes passed. He waited. Nothing moved; not a sound escaped their lips.

Finally, he could stand no more. He walked briskly to the side of the shed. He retrieved the ladder and took it to the light pole. He climbed and using his knife, cut the Super Deluxe Flying Dragon from its final lair. His task completed, he returned the ladder to its reclining position by the building.

Standing in the open yard, he tore the kite into several pieces. No amount of glue would ever restore the creature; it had flown its last. Bits of red and orange paper flew into the wind, never to be seen by the children again.

Time passed, and Rex waited for them. Helen emerged to call him to supper. She saw the torn kite and knew something terrible had transpired. She finally coaxed him inside, and he sat at the table. Helen learned of the whole story—the twisted kite and the hiding children. She ate silently, allowing Rex to rant and rave as he saw fit. She knew better than to try and reason with him.

"Think they're safe, eh?" he asked, as much to himself as to her. "Well, they'll find out different. They're gonna answer to me." He swallowed a large part of a hushpuppy. "No child o' mine is gonna make me stand and call for 'em and them not come. No, sir, they'll find out different."

Helen ate sparingly, worried about her children. When Rex paused, she asked, "Where do you think they are, Rex, in town some-where?"

He slammed his fork on the table. "You dumb ass, no, they're not at town! God, you ain't got no sense." Rex stood, hovering over her. She cowered. "I *know* where they are; they're in the damn shed! That's not the point!"

Rex stomped to the kitchen for another beer. "Helen, no kid o' mine is gonna make a fool of me." He took a gulp. "They'll come out. They gotta. It'll be gettin' dark soon, and they're gonna get mighty scared out there all alone."

He strode to his wife's figure. Leaning over her, he looked her straight in the eye. "And, that's when they'll come cryin' to th' door wantin' to get in." He smiled and took another sip. "And, that's when they'll have to answer to me." He slowly walked to the living room and stretched out on the couch.

Helen quietly began to clear the table.

CHAPTER 9

The soft breeze blew through the dark night and made the children shiver. They sat in the shed, embraced against the inevitable attack by their father. Lauren had stopped crying and rested her head on Darren's shoulder. Amid the silence, Darren's stomach growled. He hadn't eaten in hours. His sister, who didn't eat much anyway, wasn't as affected by the fasting. She would have only thrown it back up.

Rex fell asleep on the couch. Helen cleaned the supper dishes and wrapped up the leftovers. She quietly went to their bedroom to try and sleep. She found, however, that she was much too upset and cried for an hour. She finally took some of her medicine and collapsed.

It was deep into the night that Lauren awoke and voiced her desire for something to eat. Darren tried to convince her otherwise. He whispered, "Lauren, we can't. He's in there."

"I know, Darewin, but I'm hungry. I feel sick," she whimpered. "I *got* to have somethin' to drink. *Please.*"

Darren swallowed. "Lauren, please don't make me go," he pleaded. "Daddy's in there. He'll catch us. You know he will." He pulled her closer to him. "C'mon. Try to get some sleep. You'll forget 'bout bein' hungry. Trust me."

The four-year-old would not give in so easily. Her lip trembled and the tears rolled. "Please, Darewin, please!"

Darren had taken all he could. "All right, Lauren, all right. Stop that cryin'." He gently moved her aside and stepped from the tangled plastic that had hidden them earlier. "Now, be *quiet*. I'm gonna try to get inside and back out without wakin' anybody up. Okay?"

The tiny head bobbed accordingly. "Thanks, Darewin."

The boy moved stealthily along the walls of the shed in the shadows. He peered nervously around him, expecting an ambush. He crept slowly, trying to be as quiet as humanly possible. Darren stepped onto the concrete blocks that served as back steps. He figured that their mother had left the remnants of supper for them somewhere. He cautiously grasped the handle to the screen door and tried to open it. The lock held.

For a moment, he stood in amazement. His parents never locked their doors except for a trip away from home. They never fastened them, even at night, and especially when the children were outside. What was going on? He tried again and again, unable to accept the reality. In desperation, he ran to the front door, but it, too, was shut tight.

When Darren returned with nothing, Lauren began to cry. He explained that he couldn't do anything and she might as well endure it. He sounded confident, but his insides were shattered. If their father was angry enough to lock them out, what would he do when he found them?

❧   ❧   ❧

Helen awoke early that Sunday morning, but stayed in the bed until late. Nightmares had prevented her from sleeping soundly; she envisioned her children cold, hungry, and alone. The mere thoughts made her shiver. When she entered the living room, her husband was still asleep on the couch. She took the empty beer bottle from the end table and threw it in the trash. She decided to cook breakfast quickly for him; perhaps, it would put him in better spirits.

Rex awoke to the scent of sizzling bacon. He stretched his sore muscles from sleeping on the soft couch. His head was pounding. Slowly he walked to the bathroom, trying to focus his fuzzy vision. When he emerged, he went into the kitchen. Helen turned to face him. "Sleep well, Rex?" she asked, a bit sarcastically.

He scowled. "Damn you, you know I didn't sleep good on that damn couch. Hell, I can barely walk!" Remembering the children, he slammed his fist on the counter and walked quickly to the their bedroom. "Where are they?!" She quickly met him in the living room. "Huh? Where th' hell did they go?"

Helen stammered, "The ch-children?"

Rex's eyes blazed with his rising temper. "Who th' hell else would I be talkin' about? Huh?" He stepped back and put his hand on his forehead. "Who else, Helen? God!"

His wife dropped her head. "I'm sorry, Rex. I didn't know," she whispered. "They're not here; they didn't come in. You locked the doors, remember?" She looked at him accusingly.

Rex's blond hair was sticking up in a crew cut, his ice blue eyes stared forward, and his face was emotionless. He was so angry with himself that he could have died—not because he had locked them out, but that he had missed them when they'd tried to get in. Without a word, he strode to the bedroom. Donning shirt and shorts, he emerged in sock feet. "Where's my damn shoes, Helen?!"

"What you need 'em for, Rex?"

"What th' hell does it matter? Where are they?" he screamed. She pointed to the couch. The tip of his work boot peeked from the tattered drapes. He laced them and stood for a moment staring at his frightened wife.

Tears glistened in her eyes. Her hair, pulled in a ponytail, made her appear younger than she was. She looked like a child, herself, pleading silently with the enraged man. "Rex, please don't do this. *Please*," she begged.

"Get outta my way," he spat viciously and pushed by her to get to the kitchen. He unhooked the screen and stepped off the back steps. Helen collapsed in the chair and wept.

Rising blood pressure had caused Rex's face to flush fire engine red and his hands were clenched tightly at his sides. His head pounded, yet he felt filled with energy. Walking swiftly to the back of the tool shed, he picked up an old board from the pile of kindling.

The doorway darkened with the father's shadow. His face was drawn tight with fury and his teeth were gritted shut. He stepped inside and saw them. The children were lying on the old tarp still asleep. Lauren's head was atop Darren's chest. Their blissful faces were peaceful and unaware of what was about to befall them.

Rex gripped his makeshift paddle in his left hand and reached for Darren's arm with his right. He jerked the boy from his slumber; Lauren's head bounced and she awoke with a start. "Darewin!"

Darren was awake already and pawing to free himself. His father held him tightly as he brought the board around for the first of many licks. Lauren's face pinched into a terrible scowl, and she began to wail. Darren yelled for her to run, but she couldn't get her legs to move.

Rex yelled curses as he struck. He was furious at their disobedience and possessed no mercy. Darren's face was red and he bit his tongue in pain. Tears poured down his cheeks, but his father was too busy to notice.

"No, Daddy! No!" Lauren screamed in terror. "We're sorry! Please don't hurt Darewin, please!" Her tiny body trembled and she wanted to close her eyes, but she couldn't. Darren was exhausted and almost faint when Rex finished with him. Taking his son by the collar, he threw him outside into the yard. The boy lay still.

Rex then turned to Lauren who was already sobbing as he neared her. Again, she yelled out, hoping her mother would come. Her father proceeded to give her the same treatment he had her brother. Darren did not move to help her; he only cried as she called for him.

When Rex had finished punishing them, he threw the board in the shed, knocking tools from the wall. Lauren lay on the floor, her nose bleeding from a stray blow that had caught her in the face. "Ya'll like it so well out here, stay for all I care," Rex said slowly between long breaths. "I don't want to see either of your faces in that house today. Hear? *I don't want to see you.* Understand?" They nodded. "*You better.*" He strode across the lawn and into the house.

"Darewin?" a weak voice called. Lauren lay on the hard floor of the shed, tears mixing with the blood that poured from her nose. "Darewin!"

"A minute, Lauren, gimme a minute," he called back. He hadn't moved from the lawn for fear of further blows from his father. Now, he forced himself to his knees as he grimaced in pain.

"Darewin, I'm bleedin'! Help me…"

The boy slowly stood. He turned his face toward Lauren who had also gotten up and felt his pulse quicken. A light bruise had formed around her left eye, and the blood that covered her mouth and chin had begun to dry. Blond wisps of hair fell into her face. "Are you okay, Lauren?" he asked, walking to her. "Huh?"

Her sorrowful blue eyes gazed up into his. Her lip trembled as she tried to speak. "He hurt me, Darewin. He hurt me real bad," she whispered as her head fell to his shoulder with her sobs. He placed his tired arms around her and held her for a long time.

Helen was still crying when Rex entered the house. He only glared at her as he sat in his chair. Face still crimson from the exertion of the beatings, he breathed heavily. "Damn!" he swore. "Helen, get me a needle." She quietly obeyed him. "Come 'ere," he motioned. "Get those splinters out." She looked at him strangely and then took his hand in hers. His grasp of the broken board had driven slivers into his fleshly paw.

Rex looked up into her fearful eyes. "You'd best be careful, woman, how you use that thing. Understand me?" She nodded as she turned to her patient.

❧   ❧   ❧

Darren and Lauren finally moved back into the shed. They closed the door despite the heat and pushed a bucket to hold it shut. This time, they'd hear him coming. Darren pulled the chain that lit the bulb hanging from the ceiling. The dim light shone on the two of them. When Lauren refused to lie down for a while, the boy prepared to check her. He found an old rag and dampened it in the pail of water left by his father a couple of days before. She whimpered as he pushed against her bruised cheek and eye. He assured her that he was being as gentle as possible.

When he had finished with her face and the scratches on her arms and hands, he informed her of his intentions. She protested, but he convinced her of the necessity. He had to know the extent of the damage before he could do anything to help. Darren carefully grasped the sides of Lauren's knit shorts and pulled them down to her ankles. She asked him to be careful; he reassured her that he would. She stood like a statue as he removed her panties.

Dark bruises, blue and purple, covered her where Rex's instrument had struck. Faint lines of the board marked the exact spots in some places. Most, however, were blended by the numerous blows she had taken. Even Darren's light touch brought screams from the child. He swallowed hard as tears of pity flowed down his cheeks. "Lauren, I can't do nothin' to help you."

"What's wrong, Darewin?" she asked. "How come it still hurts?"

"Uh, well, Lauren, I don't know how to 'splain it," he stammered. "You 'member last month when you tripped in the yard and bruised your knee?"

"Yeah."

"It's like that," he replied with a sigh. "'Cept it's worse. Lots worse."

"Oh," she answered softly. "What 'bout you?"

Darren shuffled his feet and pulled her underwear and shorts back into place. "Same, I guess."

"Oh."

They spent the night lying on their stomachs upon the old tarp that had shielded them. Their mother came the next morning and hid them from their father until he went to work. It was a full week before either rested comfortably.

❦   ❦   ❦

The horror of March was forgotten—at least for a time, and Helen allowed the children to help her dye eggs on Good Friday. She set up old coffee mugs on the counter with food coloring, vinegar, and boiling water. Wide-eyed, they awaited the precious moment when she would let them mount the two stools and begin.

Numerous arguments arose over who had the prettiest color to watch or the number of eggs to be done. However, nothing could have prevented their joy of the evening. Their father had long since gone to work to earn double-time on the holiday.

Sunday was a special time as well. The Easter Bunny brought two small baskets, blue and pink, filled with goodies. Each contained a tiny wind-up toy that would bring many happy hours for them.

CHAPTER 10

*L*auren was elated when the package arrived. It was addressed to her from Uncle Malcolm and Aunt Carolyn. She wondered what the cardboard container concealed. It was a present for her birthday that was only a couple of days away on the fourth of May. She would be five-years-old and anxiously awaited kindergarten. On the special day, Helen baked a carrot cake for her youngest. It was Lauren's favorite and cooked to perfection. Five tiny candles were carefully placed, and she squealed with glee.

Darren stood beside of her as they waited for Rex. Helen had called for him, but he ignored her. Impatient, Lauren climbed atop one of the dining room chairs and took a deep breath. Wish in mind, she blew out every one. Her brother grinned and she hugged him.

Helen cut each of them a piece of cake and served the ice cream. Rex entered with his usual scowl. He popped the top of a bottle of Coca-Cola and took a long gulp. "Ah, that's good." He turned his attention to the table. "What ya'll doin'?"

Helen blushed. "Rex, you know why. It's Lauren's birthday! I called for you." She tried to smile; the children sat emotionless.

"Oh, yeah," he grumbled. "I forgot." He pulled out his chair and sat. "How long's it been, now?"

"She's five, Rex," Helen answered in a low tone. "Remember?"

"How th' hell could I forget?" He grinned. "That's my Tokyo Surprise right there."

"Oh, Rex, no!" Helen gasped. "Don't start that, please!" She paled. It was not the first rendering of this story she'd heard. "Please, Rex, not today."

"Why not today, woman? What's it matter?" He swallowed the last of the pop. "Everybody knows about it. No secret."

"Oh, Rex, that's not true," Helen pleaded. "Please, just drop it."

"Aw, hell, Helen, give it a rest. If the damned Japs hadn't hit my ship, she never wouldda been here and you know it." He pointed his thumb at the wide-eyed five-year-old girl. Darren was stoic.

"Rex, just drop it," she begged, again. "Please, drop it."

Rex growled, "I'm goin' back outside." He stood and grabbed a piece of cake from the stand. Opening his mouth, he pushed half of it in. As he chewed, he stepped past his wife and out the back door.

"D-Daddy d-doesn't w-want me, does he?" the child asked with tears in her eyes.

"'Course he does. C'mon, now. Let's see what Aunt Carolyn and Uncle Malcolm sent you." Her mother forced a smile and retrieved the package from her bedroom. Lauren sat on the table and carefully pulled on the paper. She unwrapped the mailing covering and then the tissue. Helen used a knife to cut the tape and handed it to her daughter.

The girl's eyes widened as she pulled the object from the box. It was a porcelain doll clothed in a red and white polka dot dress trimmed in lace. She held it to her chest and rocked back and forth. Its name would be Macy.

❦   ❦   ❦

The long, hot days of summer stretched out before them. The children, so excited at first, were slowly becoming bored. Darren finally succumbed to Lauren's urgings to play "house".

"Okay, Darewin, you're the daddy and I'm the momma," Lauren explained, holding the rag doll under her arm.

"How else would we be?" Darren shot back, exasperated. "Gosh, Lauren. I'm not stupid."

She did not respond to his sarcasm. "And this is our baby," she stated as she presented the doll. "Got it?"

Darren exhaled, *loudly*. "Yeah, Lauren. Let's get on with it." She smiled. Despite the rocky beginning, their role-playing turned out to be quite successful. Darren pretended to go to work and returned to fuss at her and demand supper. Lauren was rough with the "child" as she sat her at the table.

It was about that time that Helen sought the children. She heard their voices and approached quietly. She stopped, out of sight, and listened for a moment. Darren was yelling at the doll and slapping her at the table. Lauren was yelling at him. But, it was not to stop him; she wanted her fair share.

"Darewin! No, let me, now! You've already hit her once. Let me!"

"No, Lauren. You told me I was the daddy!"

"No, let me. It's my turn!" Lauren yelled back.

Helen stood stock still, straining her ears to hear clearly. Tears formed in her eyes and spilled onto her cheeks. She had finally realized that they were fighting over who was to punish the baby. She choked back her sobs as she heard the blows being administered around the corner.

Running back into the house, she stumbled into her bedroom. Gasping from her guilty sobs, she fumbled for her pills, quickly swallowed two, and collapsed on the bed. It was only a short while until she was asleep.

❦   ❦   ❦

Darren turned seven on June 30, 1950. He blew out the candles on his cake in the presence of his parents and sister. He received a small pocketknife from his Uncle Malcolm and Aunt Carolyn.

Rex bought their present for him, himself. The boy excitedly tore the paper from the large box. Inside were a baseball, bat, and glove. Darren's face broke into a wide grin. He looked, unbelieving, at his father. "Thank you, Daddy."

Rex tried to hide his pleasure. "Got to get you in a sport, boy. You need to be in good shape. We'll start your trainin' tomorrow." Darren and his father left early the next morning with the equipment in tow. It was quite unusual for the boy to spend a day with his father at the park—or anywhere else, for that matter.

Lauren felt deserted without her brother as playmate. Helen suggested she play with her dolls. The child reluctantly agreed and spent the day in her room.

❦   ❦   ❦

The sun was at its height pouring down hot rays on the children. Darren and Lauren sat on an old blanket in the yard. Helen was taking a nap; Rex was fishing. It was the Fourth of July.

Darren wiped the perspiration from his forehead and adjusted the ball cap on his nearly bald head. Rex had taken him for a haircut just the day before. His eyes squinted as he looked at his sister. Helen had dressed her in a pair of terry-cloth shorts and a halter to match. Her bare feet shifted on the soft quilt. She, too, was quite warm.

"Wish I had somethin' to drink," Darren said longingly. "Maybe a RC from Musser's or a popsicle. How 'bout you?"

Lauren nodded quickly. "*A cherry popsicle?*"

"Yeah, any kind you want," he replied with a grin.

"Can we?"

Darren thought for a minute. Slowly, a smile tiptoed across his face. "Don't see why not. C'mon!" He jumped to his feet. Lauren followed. The seven-year-old motioned for his companion to be quiet as he ran toward the back door. When he returned a few minutes later, he held out his hand. Two shiny nickels twinkled in his palm.

"Saved 'em," he said, "for just the right time. All right, Lauren, listen to me. We can't tell anyone about this, you hear? *Nobody*." She nodded slowly. "We're gonna run down to Musser's, buy our popsicles, and hurry back. We'll eat them on the way. Okay?" Again, she nodded.

The children raced along the side of the road. It was scorching hot, a perfect July day. They were breathing hard when Musser's finally came into view. Darren chose their treat and paid for them. He carefully unwrapped each and handed one to his little sister. They quickly began to devour the frosty substance and hurried home. No one was ever the wiser.

❦   ❦   ❦

Saturdays were reserved for baseball. It had become an obsession for Rex and his son. Although his father was a difficult coach, Darren enjoyed the sessions. It felt so good to hear an occasional word of praise from Rex that he was willing to try just about anything.

Darren was learning to pitch and field some. He had a natural ability for speed, but was learning control. By the next season, he would qualify for the little league, and Rex was determined that his son would be on the first string despite his youth. It was fortunate that Darren was talented on the baseball field for it was the boy's only accomplishment that his father would ever take pride in.

Lauren would never be so lucky.

CHAPTER 11

$\mathcal{D}$arren led a terrified five-year-old to school on the first day. Lauren, although excited beyond measure, was also afraid of what awaited her. She clutched her brother's hand and tried to keep up with his quick pace.

Rex had warned her the evening before that she'd better behave in school. Those teachers won't "put up with your bullshit", had been his exact words. He had frightened her with all sorts of horror stories from his own school experiences. Thankfully, Darren had spoken to her after their father went to work, and it comforted her somewhat.

Now, the morning had come and she was to discover for herself what this thing called school was all about. Darren had practically shoved her out the front door. Helen waved goodbye with tears in her eyes; Rex was still asleep.

The children walked to the elementary school in silence. Both were nervous; neither knew whose homeroom they'd be in. Darren was hoping for Mrs. Sharp, the kind woman he had seen in the hall.

Darren led his sister to the kindergarten rooms and stopped to say his farewell. "Now, be good, Lauren. Do what she says," he spoke slowly, gazing into her big, bright eyes. "You got Mrs. Smith—that's good. You'll like her," he added in a whisper.

"Darewin, please don't leave me," she begged. "Please." She tugged at his sleeve and pleaded with her eyes.

"No, Lauren, I can't stay. You know that," he spoke with a reassuring grin. "C'mon, we've talked about this. You'll be okay. I promise."

"Cross your heart?"

Darren laughed aloud. "Cross my heart," he said softly as he made the motion with his finger across his chest. She smiled and he hugged her tightly before he turned down the long hallway. Lauren watched him until he disappeared into a classroom. She fought back the sob in her throat and wiped the small tears in her eyes. She took a deep breath like Darren had taught her and walked into her own classroom.

Her eyes opened wide in amazement. Brilliant colors covered the walls. There was so much to see that Lauren secretly wondered if she would ever take it all in. Her mouth hung in surprise. Darren had never told her how beautiful school was!

Though the day seemed to fly for Lauren, it dragged for Darren. He had not been as lucky as his sister. He had gotten old Mrs. Raven who was at least a hundred (according to the students) and mean as they come. Darren was certainly glad that his sister had fared better. In fact, he wished to high heaven he could join her.

❈   ❈   ❈

Lauren sat quietly in a corner of the room although it was playtime. She was startled by a young girl who sat beside her. "Hi," the girl said softly.

"Hi."

"What's your name?"

"Lauren."

"Do you live on Berry Street?"

Lauren turned to face her companion. "I don't know. Darren walked me here."

"You got a brother?"

"Yeah," Lauren smiled, thinking of him. "He's in the second grade."

The girl looked impressed and a little sad. "Wow," she said with admiration. "I don't have a brother or a sister."

"You don't?" Lauren asked in surprise. She thought everyone had siblings. "Don't you have a momma and daddy?"

The girl grew solemn. "My parents got killed in a car. I live with my grandparents. They take care of me."

Lauren sat in deep thought. She didn't know that parents could die. She thought that only happened to puppies that got run over. "Did you like them?"

"My momma and daddy?" Lauren nodded. "I guess I did. I was real little."

"Oh," Lauren said with a sigh.

❦   ❦   ❦

By September, Lauren had adjusted to the new routine. She was learning so many new things, including her friendship with the young girl, Kim, she had met the first day. Though she never revealed her terrible home situation, she was able to find comfort in her new experience.

Darren had not been so fortunate. He and his teacher had had several confrontations already, and the year would produce more. She just did not understand why attention and acceptance of his peers was so important to the young Mitchell. If she had only known what life with his father was like. Their wounds were not always emotional; too often Rex left physical evidence of his cruelty. Though both did a good job of covering for him, sometimes they were questioned.

"What happened to your arm, Lauren?" Kim asked with widened, chocolate eyes. Her long, shiny hair was pulled back from her forehead in a barrette, making her eyes penetrate Lauren's very being. The girl squirmed, trying to think of an excuse. Lauren knew not to tell how Daddy had grabbed her roughly the night before at dinner.

The bluish bruise had formed almost instantly. It was still encircled by a reddish color. Covering it with her sleeve had failed.

Kim's eyes waited for an answer. Lauren felt them and finally choked out a response. "F-fell off my b-bike. Not used to it."

"You got a bike? Wow! Can I ride it sometime?" her friend eagerly asked.

Lauren was now in a mess. It was her first lesson in lie-cover-lie to which she would grow too accustomed. "Uh, well, it's broke. Daddy threw it away."

"Oh."

Lauren breathed a sigh of relief when the teacher's voice called recess to a close. Her pounding heart echoed in her ears as she took her seat. She tried to remain calm, but soon found herself in the bathroom, vomiting.

❧   ❧   ❧

Early November brought the first wave of cooler weather. Yellow, orange, and red leaves lay over the lawn like a rough, colorful carpet. Rex neglected his duties at home while working overtime.

Despite his willingness to work, the Mitchells were in dire straits financially and needed the boost. In fact, it was this situation that drove Helen to the conclusion that she should go to work. Helen had been considering this option for quite some time. She felt certain she could get on as a clerk in the department store in town or maybe at Musser's. However, she had been reluctant to discuss it with her husband and with good reason.

Rex Mitchell had no management skills whatsoever. Despite his wife's worries, he had taken his earnings and a trifle he had saved to purchase a television set. It was small, but a luxury just the same. "Rex, what in the world—!" Helen asked in disbelief.

He sat in the living room with the set on a nearby table. His feet were propped on a footstool they had gotten as a wedding present from his parents. He slowly ran his fingers through his short, blond hair and peered up at her distraught figure with pale blue eyes. "Helen, I earn the damn money. I guess I can spend it like I want."

She exhaled in an attempt to control her temper. "Rex, it's my money, too," she explained to him. "And what 'bout the children? What do we tell them when they're hungry? Huh? Daddy wanted a TV?"

"Dammit, woman, you can bring up more shit." He rose from the chair and crossed the room. "They're not goin' hungry, Helen. God! You think I'd let 'em starve?" He reeled and faced her. "Huh? What kinda shit is that?"

Helen knew that now she was in for a battle. "Rex, I didn't say that," she said, cowering. "It's just awfully expensive. We need the money for—"

"Money! Since when do you give a damn about money? All the time we been married you never gave a shit 'bout money. Why th' hell do you care, now?" His anger intensified as the argument progressed. "God! What's gotten into you, woman? You act like I bought a car or somethin'!"

Rex's face flushed crimson. He did not respond well to criticism whatever the situation, never had. He flexed his hands in and out of fists trying to control himself. Small tears formed in her eyes. "Rex, please, listen to me," she pleaded.

"I'm listenin', woman! Go on!"

Helen cleared her throat. "Rex, I've decided to get a job. Maybe just part-time for a while. You know, 'til things get better." She mentally braced herself.

"Well, I'll be goddamned!" Rex exploded. "What th' hell is goin' on here?" He took a step toward her and she instantly backed up a bit. "A job! What th' hell would you need a job for? Huh, Helen? You know who wears the pants around here!"

"Just for a while, Rex," she begged. "For some extra money. That's all."

Rex stood for a long moment. The children had long since hidden in their bedroom. They could smell the storm coming and went for shelter. As young as they were, they knew that Helen's vessel would be a shipwreck before the hurricane blew over.

Helen stood stock still, awaiting the blast of hot air. She was filled with fear, yet she appeared calm. Her long ponytail had fallen and was laying on her shoulder. Her youthful face was drawn tight, exposing the premature age lines. The eyes of her husband sent shivers up and down her spine. She was all-too-familiar with his expression. His lips were thin and white with anger.

"Listen to me, Helen," he started slowly. "No woman of mine is goin' to work—*ever*. I'm the breadwinner for this fam'ly and I don't need no damn woman keepin' me up. You got that?"

"But, Rex, we need the money! There's nothin' wrong with me goin' to—"

"No!" he shouted. "Dammit, Helen, forget it! You're stayin' at home like a woman's supposed to. Like my Daddy always said, the kitchen and the bedroom, Helen, the kitchen and the bedroom!"

She visibly stiffened. "Rex, don't say that again. You know I hate that."

Rex's lips curled into an evil expression. "Kitchen and the bedroom, Helen. Man first, then woman. That's God's order."

"*God's* order?!" she shouted. "How dare you, Rex Mitchell, speak of God's order? You haven't seen th' inside of a church in years!"

"Neither have you!" he shot back. "But, don't you go throwin' that up to me, now." His smile had vanished. "I didn't go to church when you married me and you knew it."

"Well, don't you go sayin' those things to me, neither, Rex! Fair's fair, you know."

"Damn, Helen, it's like arguin' with a street sign." He stepped to within her reach. "No," he added, "a sign would have more sense." Helen prepared to strike him. Oh, how she wished to knock that smile from his face! She stopped her hand, however, just before it struck.

Rex's eyes were wide. He couldn't believe she had almost smacked him. He recovered quickly, though. "Th' day you hit me, Helen, will be your last. Got that?" She nodded. "Now, no more of this job shit. I'm sick of hearin' it." He sat in his chair. "Get me a beer. The fight'll be on soon."

Helen did as he asked and even turned the channel for him. As she bent to retrieve a coaster from the floor, he slapped her behind. She gave him a sour look, but he only laughed. She retreated to their bedroom.

CHAPTER 12

*T*ime passed for the Mitchell children much as it always had. More than a year was gone, and another trip to the Preston farm was, this time, successful. It was the one joy, besides having each other, that the youths possessed. For reasons they did not understand and couldn't explain, they loved the farm and the family who lived there. It was worlds apart from their sad existence and they longed for Thanksgiving and the hope it brought with each passing year.

Helen sat at the kitchen table reading a letter she'd just received from her sister when she wiped a tear from her eye. "What's th' matter with you?" Rex asked, one eye on the television in the living room and one on her. "What you cryin' about?"

"Carolyn's going to have another baby," she said wistfully. "Isn't is wonderful?" Rex grunted. She decided not to share all of the good news with him; she knew how he felt about her "goody-goody rich relatives", as he called them. After all, why would he care that Malcolm had gained control of the old Derebourne Law Firm for which he and his late grandfather had worked and renamed it after himself? It would only remind him of his own failure.

It was about the time Helen was considering this when Rex exploded right beside of her. He had just heard the news. General MacArthur was fired by President Truman. "That goddamned son-of-a-bitch!" he yelled as he jumped up and stomped to the counter in his agitation. "Can you believe that? That dumb ass fired the greatest soldier that ever lived!"

Helen, wearing an apron, got up and walked to the stove. She turned her head slightly to acknowledge him. She sighed. "No, Rex, I can't."

"Damn, I can't believe it." He slammed his fist on the counter. Glasses in the drainboard tinkled as they vibrated against each other. He got a beer from the icebox and took a long gulp.

"What's the matter, Momma?" Darren asked as he peeked inside the door. He'd not known his father was still in the house.

"Come 'ere, boy," Rex demanded. Darren froze, then thawed himself enough to move toward his father a few steps. "Come 'ere!"

Darren's light brown locks were messy and wet. He had been playing with Lauren for several hours. His blue eyes met those of his father, and he swallowed hard. "Let me tell you, son," Rex began in a calmer voice. "General Douglas MacArthur is the greatest man who ever walked this earth. He was the best damn commander in the Pacific back in the war. You know, when I was in the service." Darren dutifully nodded. He had learned that his father's pride in his navy years was the key to keeping him happy. He never disappointed Rex in appearing awed. "And, now, this goddamned president of ours has fired him! Hell, what was he thinkin'?" His anger resurfaced. "You see what I mean, boy?" Darren nodded quickly. "All right, you go on. Leave me alone, now," he said as he roughly shoved the boy to the living room. Helen returned to her cooking.

❧   ❧   ❧

It was October 1951. Lauren was doing well in the first grade, bringing home her "reader" with pride and reading aloud to her brother each night. He was so proud of her that he could barely stand it. They had just finished their nightly lesson when they were called to the kitchen.

Helen was late with the meal, and they were going to eat from the stove. A line formed: Rex, Darren, Lauren, and Helen. Her father had already seated himself and began to hurriedly eat the fried chicken when Lauren stumped her toe on the leg of one of the chairs and lost her balance on her way to the table.

Darren turned just in time to see the plate fly from her hands, landing with a thud on the linoleum, splattering the contents. Luckily, none had landed on her father. Immediately, she threw her arms to her head to protect herself from the oncoming blows. Rex hit her several times before she began to scream and then, cry. Helen rushed from the kitchen to see what had caused the commotion.

"Damn girl, you're clumsy as an ox!" His face was flushed. Darren sat solemnly waiting for the conclusion. The mother stood, hands-on-hips, with tears in her eyes. "Well, stop that damn cryin' and clean it up! What th' hell are ya waitin' for?!" Another blow.

Lauren scrambled to her feet, heaving with sobs. "I-I'm s-sorry, D-daddy," she sputtered. "I'm s-sorry." She got a wet dish rag and dry cloth from her mother. As the rest of the family sat down to eat, Lauren cleaned up the mess. She went to bed without her supper and cried herself to sleep.

The next morning, she rose early and brought his paper inside for him and helped her mother serve breakfast as a self-imposed penance. Her father did not acknowledge her presence, much less her apology. No matter how she tried to please him, Lauren always fell short of the mark.

CHAPTER 13

It was Thanksgiving, again, before they knew it. Darren and Lauren happily helped their mother pack their small suitcase for the weekend. The train arrived at Edenton Station almost an hour late. An unusual cold spell had brought an untimely bit of snow and ice. It was quickly melted, however, and they were only delayed for a short while.

Malcolm and Kathy sat in the terminal. The young girl of ten was asleep, her head resting on her father's chest. He gently nudged her awake when he saw Rex and his family approaching. "Sorry 'bout the wait, Malcolm," Rex said, hesitantly. "Had to melt the ice on the windshield, I think." He laid the large suitcase on the floor.

"Quite all right," his brother-in-law answered with a sleepy smile. "We've gotten a good nap of it, eh, Kathy?"

"Yes, sir," she replied, wiping her eyes. "Hello, Uncle Rex, Aunt Helen." They exchanged pleasantries with the child and the cousins did, as well.

Malcolm gestured and all trudged from the depot. "Carolyn's been dying to see all of you," he added. "She's been real tired, expecting and all." Helen nodded with a sad smile.

When the Mitchells arrived at the Preston farm, Carolyn had already put Todd to bed. She was well into her pregnancy; the child was due in late December. Exhausted as she was, she stepped onto the porch to greet them.

The next morning, Darren and Todd went exploring outside. They donned caps and jackets and left with grins on their faces. Darren, the elder at eight, led the excited four-year-old by the hand. Todd's smile was adorable with the space between his front teeth. Kathy coaxed Lauren into staying with her in the house. She produced her new doll, and Lauren ran to retrieve hers from the suitcase. She always carried Macy, the birthday present they'd sent her years before, with her wherever she went. The girls played all morning as the mothers prepared the meal and the fathers rode horses.

It was almost time for the Thanksgiving feast when Carolyn found opportunity to confront her sister. She quickly looked around her to assure they were, indeed, alone. "Helen, I want to talk to you," she said softly as she wiped her hands on the dishtowel.

Helen turned to face the elder. "Is, is something the matter?" she asked.

Carolyn pulled a chair from under the kitchen dinette and sat; Helen followed suit. She folded her hands and wrung them. Her deep blue eyes peered into those of her sister. "Helen, I'm worried about you."

"Worried about me?" Helen's face was ashen. "Why, what do you mean? Why would you be—?"

"I'm worried about you," she replied slowly, "and the children." Carolyn's heart pounded; she could sense the fear in her sister's face.

"The ch-children?"

"Yes," Carolyn nodded, "*especially* them. After year-before-last I've not been able to—"

"Now, I can explain that," Helen began. "It was the cat hair and Rex's allergies and he—"

"He was terrible," Carolyn finished for her. "But, my concern goes far beyond that, Helen. It's much more than that incident." She paused, waiting for a response. She got none. "It's the way you are with him. You act as though he is the only thing worth living for—like you're nothing!"

"I-I don't know what you m-mean," Helen stammered. "You do the same for Malcolm. He's—"

"The love of my life," her sister finished for her, "but I don't jump every time he speaks. Helen, you're different than you used to be."

"I've not ch-changed, I'm just like I always was—"

"No, you're not," Carolyn stated emphatically. "This is not the sister I knew." Silence reigned for several moments. "Helen, I know how hard it was for you after Papa died. He was everything to you—"

"I got over that a long time ago, Carolyn," Helen broke in quickly with a sharp stab of pain to her chest. "Papa's been gone a long time, now."

"And, then Momma and Billy were killed last year in that car accident…it hasn't been easy for any of us." Carolyn wiped a stray tear from her eye. "Even though you never got along with our stepfather, he *did* care for you. You know that, don't you?"

Silence.

"Helen, listen to me, please. We've got to stick together, now. We're all we have left." Her voice cracked as she thought of their elder sister, Eliza, who had died in childbirth during the summer of 1946. Even now, the pain sliced her heart. Swallowing the lump in her throat, she continued. "I love you, Helen, and the children. I don't want to see you mistreated."

Helen found her voice and forced it to be steady. "We're not mistreated, Carolyn. Rex loves us."

Carolyn sighed, knowing that it was useless to pursue it any further. "All right, Helen, all right." She slowly stood and then laid her hand on her sister's. "But, please, if you ever need me, just call. Promise?"

"Promise," Helen answered as she felt the tender squeeze. Though she never intended to cry for help, she was comforted to know that there would always be a haven for them.

Dinner was served around noon. All gathered around the table—the adults in the dining room, the children in the kitchen. The blessing was offered and everyone ate his fill.

❧   ❧   ❧

It was after breakfast the following morning that Lauren confronted her cousin in the bedroom. "Kathy, who are you talkin' to when you say the blessin'?" Her blond locks fell about her neck and shoulders, highlighting her sparkling blue eyes.

Her dark-haired companion just stared for a moment. "Talkin' to God, Lauren," she finally mustered. "Didn't you know who you was prayin' to?"

"Prayin'?" Lauren's eyebrows lifted. "What do you mean prayin'? You was jus' talkin'."

"That's prayin'!" Kathy exclaimed, exasperated. "Don't you *pray*?"

"I don't even know what you're talkin' 'bout, Kathy," Lauren answered, tired of trying to explain herself. Her young cousin was justly confused. She had never had to explain *praying* to anyone before.

"Oh, Lauren," she began as she sat on the floor. "It's easy. See, God is up in heaven and—"

"Who's God?"

"*Who's God*?!" Kathy repeated. "Why, Lauren, He's the Lord! He made everything, even us. Don't you know who God is?"

Lauren sadly shook her head that she didn't. Well, except for hearing His name called in vain by her father. That was the only God she knew.

"Don't you go to church?"

"What's church?" Lauren asked, puzzled.

"It's where you go to worship God!"

"But, *who's God*?" Lauren asked, again.

Kathy paused, gathering her thoughts. "Okay, Lauren. Let me think about this." She paused. "Well, God is *everywhere*. He sees *everything*. He sees us here, now. He *knows* who we are."

Lauren fearfully looked around them. "He does? Where is he?"

Her cousin laughed. "You can't see Him, Lauren. He's invisible. But, He's here just the same." Again, Lauren peered around; fear was etched in her features.

"Don't be afraid," the elder consoled. "God loves you. He loves all of us. He *is* love." She moved to get closer to her cousin. "See, Lauren, when we pray, we talk to Him—just like I talk to you. And, He listens, too." Kathy smiled.

Lauren's mind attempted to take it all in. It was so incredible. Was there really such a being? One who loved her? One who would listen?

"We say the blessin' to thank Him for it, Lauren. It's our way of talkin' to Him," she explained. "Except, we can pray any time we want, not just when we eat. He's always there. Get it?"

Lauren nodded that she did, although she wasn't quite sure. There were still so many questions left unanswered. "But, what's his name?" she asked. "What do you call him? Just, *God*?"

Kathy thought for a moment. "Well, He *is* God," she said. "But, Daddy always calls him Lord. It means the same thing," she hastily explained. "Oh, but Momma calls Him *Father*," she added. "She says He's like a daddy to us and we're like His children."

Kathy rose from the floor and motioned for Lauren to follow. She had no idea what she had just done. Little Lauren did not want another daddy.

Rex Mitchell was quite enough, thank you.

❧   ❧   ❧

On January 6, 1952, Marilyn Preston was born to beaming parents. Rex and Helen received the telegram the next morning. Darren and Lauren begged to go see the baby, but it was not possible. Rex had been laid off from work for two weeks.

CHAPTER 14

*H*elen rushed to her daughter's side despite Rex's cursing. She examined the leg first, which had begun to swell and was already quite painful to the touch. She carried the girl to the bedroom and laid her carefully on the bed with a light kiss to her forehead.

Darren still sat in the floor where he had been before the beating began which ended with the vicious kick of Rex's booted foot. He felt so utterly guilty; he'd lied to his father in blaming her for his own mischief, thus his frustration with her became his father's fury. He had been forced to watch her take the whipping that he could have—and should have—endured. His tear-stained face sought her eyes as he crept to the side of her bed. His hand landed softly on her arm. She turned and gazed at him, a stranger.

Darren's lip trembled as he spoke to her. "I'm s-sorry, Lauren, so s-sorry." He fought the urge to bawl. "It's all m-my fault. I lied to him and he hurt you. I'm s-so sorry. I'll never do it again."

In his eyes she saw pity; in his voice, she heard repentance. She knew she could forgive him anything. "It's okay, Darren. I'll be all right," she spoke softly.

"Sure you will," he assured her with a forced smile. "Sure you will. I promise."

The next morning, Helen took Lauren to see a doctor at the health department. The X-rays revealed a small fracture. They placed the injured limb in a cast to protect it from other harm. Lauren was very brave through the whole ordeal, and the doctor told her so. "Well, there you go," he said as the finishing touches were made. "You're ready to go, miss." The young girl smiled at the kind man. Helen sat very still, fearful of any questions that might be posed about the incident. She jumped when it finally came to pass. "So, little miss, how exactly did you get that nasty fracture and those bruises?"

Lauren's smile faded. She looked into her mother's eyes. "Uh, I f-fell on the ice," she explained.

"I see," answered the doctor knowingly, "I see." Nothing more was said or done.

Helen helped both her children onto the old city bus for the ride home. She wanted to get there before Rex got up to eat. She didn't have anything prepared, and she would avoid any other incidents if she could. But, Helen Mitchell was no fool; she knew that the situation was growing worse. She realized that her children, if not herself as well, were in danger. However, she remained adamantly at Rex's side despite the fact that Lauren had lied to the kind doctor. After all, it had not rained or snowed in a week or two.

There was no ice to fall upon.

❧   ❧   ❧

Lauren Ann Mitchell turned seven-years-old on May 4, 1952. School ended a couple of weeks later and she was promoted to the second grade. Her leg had healed nicely, and she romped with her brother in the yard.

The summer sun grew hotter by the day and the children grew bored with the laziness of it. Neither was allowed to venture out of the yard, and it proved lonesome. Lauren cared little for Darren's baseball and he thought even less of her doll. Both, it seemed, grew independent in play.

One afternoon, later than usual, Rex awoke and groped his way into the kitchen. Helen was already working on his supper for he was due at the factory in a bit more than an hour. He quickly showered and came to the table. Helen called the children in from the yard. They washed their hands and sat quietly, trying to judge their father's mood. Supper was a silent affair.

Rex hurriedly ate and walked to his chair in the living room to put on his shoes. Lauren's doll, the porcelain one she had gotten from the Prestons, had been left in it by mistake. "What th' hell—?" Rex murmured as he reached beneath him and grasped the fragile figure. "Oh, that damned doll!" he exclaimed.

All turned to see what had upset him. Lauren gasped in horror. Her father was holding Macy, her favorite. Rex's cold stare met his daughter's fearful blue eyes. Silently, they pleaded with him. "Lauren, I've told you about leavin' this shit out! Haven't I?"

"Y-yes, s-sir," she choked as she stumbled to her feet. "I'll m-move it," she said as she started toward him.

"Come get th' damn thing," he snarled as his flung it down. The doll's head, hand-painted, shattered into the maple coffee table at Rex's feet. Shards of porcelain were everywhere.

"N-o-o!" Lauren screamed as the horror of it registered in her mind. Tears welled up in her eyes and overflowed. Her lips trembled as she began to whimper.

Rex tossed the headless body to the floor. "Pick up this shit, Lauren," he mumbled as he stepped into his shoes and laced them. In a moment, he had gone.

Lauren tearfully swept the broken pieces into a dustpan and discarded them. She carried the doll to her room whispering, "Macy…poor, poor Macy…" Damaged beyond repair, it was still a prized possession she refused to give up. Placing it on her pillow, she wept anew.

❦   ❦   ❦

With March came spring, and with spring, baseball. Darren played for the Cardinals in the Hadesville Little League. He played outfield some, but was their star pitcher. Even the veteran coach was amazed with his ability.

Darren put all his energies into the sport. He practiced each day with a friend who lived down the street and then with the team. Although his father had many reasons to be proud of Darren, Rex always found areas to criticize his son. Darren was not perfect, and his father told him so in no uncertain terms. He was fortunate in that he did receive some praise; Lauren never did.

Lauren spent her birthday alone in early May. She was eight and her brother would soon be ten. Both Darren and their father were at the ballpark because Darren was pitching an important game. They didn't have the money for Helen or her to attend.

Despite Darren's busy baseball schedule (they were champions that year), he found lots of time to spend with his little sister. They made several secret missions to Musser's that summer quite undetected. Out of sad necessity, they were getting better at deception.

❦   ❦   ❦

It was soon November and time for the annual trip to the Preston farm in Edenton. Lauren and Darren were so anxious to see their relatives that they could hardly wait. Both helped Helen pack their few essentials and a couple of toys. The evening before Thanksgiving, the Mitchell family left the train station. All boarded and rested during the hour trip. Rex and Helen sat quietly as the children dozed.

Meanwhile, the Prestons sat at their large table eating supper. Their eldest, Kathy, was in a glum mood. She had just been grounded for leaving Todd and Marilyn alone outside when she had been told to watch over them and, therefore, would not be allowed to play outside with her cousins when they arrived. She pouted, but to no avail.

Malcolm hurriedly ate so he could be at the terminal on time. Carolyn kissed him on the cheek as he stepped from the front porch. She urged the children upstairs to get their baths and be ready for bed, carrying the nearly two-year-old Marilyn on her hip as she followed them.

※   ※   ※

Darren awoke the next morning to the scent of bacon frying. He climbed from the small bed and glanced at Todd who was still asleep. As quietly as he could, he dressed and hurried from the room. Skidding into the kitchen, he came to an abrupt halt in front of his aunt. "Well, Darren, are you hungry?" she asked with a grin.

Darren dropped his head in embarrassment. He could feel the warmth moving up his neck into his face. "Y-yes, ma'am," he answered bashfully. "I g-guess so."

Carolyn laughed brightly. "Nothing to be ashamed of," she said, wiping her hands on a dishtowel. "To tell you the truth," she began as she took his chin in her hand and lifted his face to hers, "I've been snitching some myself. I had to cook more." She grinned, again.

Darren's face lit up with a smile in return. "Smells good," he agreed.

"It is," she replied as she grabbed another bite and popped it into her mouth. She handed a slice to Darren and he, too, ate it hungrily. "I won't tell, if you won't." She placed her arm around him and hugged tightly.

The rest of the family joined them shortly. The blessing was said, and they began to eat. Darren searched his aunt's face and she winked. He hid a grin behind his biscuit.

CHAPTER 15

$\mathcal{M}$rs. Williams, Lauren's third grade teacher, stood before the class one breezy March day. "Now, class, I have some special news for you." She smiled as the faces of her students lit up with excitement. "It is coming time for our field trip." Squeals of glee escaped the lips of everyone in the room, especially when they were informed that it was to the zoo they were going.

Lauren had heard of zoos at school but certainly had never been to one. She was thrilled. Her hopes were soon crushed when it was announced that the trip would cost each student one dollar. Lauren knew that her father would never give her any money. She sat with a frown until her savior continued. "For those of you who do not have a dollar, the school will help. All right?" Lauren's face beamed. She would get to go, too.

* * *

"What in th' hell do you mean the school will pay for it, Lauren?!" Rex screamed as he slapped her in the face. She whimpered in his shadow. "Huh? What do you mean by that shit?"

Helen stood silently in the corner of the room. She had asked Rex for the money. When he refused, Lauren had unwisely informed him of the waiver. "That's what the, the teacher s-said," she stuttered as she wiped the tears from her cheeks. "She t-told us."

"Goddamn!" Rex exclaimed as he paced a few steps. "Since when do I need a handout from th' damn school? They sure as hell didn't help me when *I* was there. I don't know why they'd be s'damned concerned now!" Darren peeked from behind the door to his bedroom. His heart ached for his sister, but there was nothing he could do. He hoped she would be all right. "What's the matter, Lauren? Think your old man can't take care of ya? Huh? That what you think o'me?"

"N-no, s-sir," she whispered. "N-no." She began to sob.

"Yes, it is!" he yelled in her ear. "That's what you think, ain't it? I got to have a damned handout from the school! Ain't that what you thought, Lauren?"

His face was crimson; his blood pressure rocketed. Lauren's blond hair fell about her face, half-hiding her expression. She peered up into the pale eyes that were identical to hers. "No, s-sir," she whimpered.

Rex grabbed a handful of her hair as he jerked her face toward his. She squealed. "Damn you, Lauren, don't lie to me!" He shook her hard. "I'm talkin' to you, goddamn it. Listen to me!" Lauren was crying uncontrollably, now. Sharp pain flew from her head where he still held her long locks. She tried not to move, but he pulled her to attention. "Listen to me, Lauren. I don't need no handout from anyone. You hear?" She nodded. "You tell that damn teacher I don't need her help. Understand?" Again, she nodded.

Rex released her and pushed her from him. She stumbled backward into the coffee table and then regained her balance. He stood for a moment, motionless, then turned to her with a start. "Who's your teacher? What's her name?"

"It-it's Mrs. W-williams." Tears fell from her chin, staining her yellow sundress.

Rex stomped to the telephone and threw the directory toward his wife. "Find that damned teacher's number."

Helen picked the book up from the floor and searched for the name. Luckily, she knew the husband's name and found it quickly. She dictated it to Rex who dialed the phone. Lauren sat on the floor crying as her father cursed the poor woman to high heaven. He used language even she had not heard him utter. She held her head in shame.

The next morning, Lauren returned to school completely humiliated. She dared not look into her teacher's eyes for fear of discovery of her guilt. She remained silent all day. Her friend, though, returned with a dollar in tow. Kim questioned Lauren about hers. The distraught girl explained that she was not getting to go. Her friend was quite sad about having to go alone on Friday.

So, the following school day, Kim came to Lauren with a huge smile on her face. When Lauren inquired, her best friend produced a crisp new one-dollar bill. She explained that her grandparents had given her an extra one to give a friend who needed it. She comforted Lauren by saying she had not told them who it was for. Lauren tossed the idea around in her head. Finally, she made her decision. She took the dollar and marched up to her teacher.

"Mrs. Williams?" she asked. The woman turned to her with a heavy heart. "My daddy said to tell you he was sorry about the other day. Here's my dollar," she lied.

The teacher was surprised. "Thank you, Lauren," she answered. The girls walked back to their desks and the money was collected from the others.

Friday was a special day to Lauren. She often thought back to that sunny day she and Kim had strolled, hand-in-hand at the zoo, gaping at the animals. She felt so good, so free. She thanked her friend and walked home alone that evening. Darren was at baseball practice.

When she entered the house, however, she knew something was wrong. Helen was sitting quietly in the living room; Rex was hot with anger and smoldering in his chair. "Lauren!" he called viciously.

"*Come in here.*" She swallowed the lump in her throat and walked to meet him. She was soon to discover that her teacher had called to thank them for allowing Lauren to attend the field trip.

Lauren did not return to school on Monday. Her face was bruised and swollen from the numerous blows she had taken from her wicked father. She lay, silent, in her bedroom. Helen attended to her while her husband slept.

❦   ❦   ❦

In October of that year, 1954, Helen became Rex's physical abuse victim for the first time. He had stopped by a bar on his way home from work and was quite drunk by the time he arrived. He staggered into the living room. "Rex, I've been worried," she said softly.

"Whatcha worried 'bout, Helen? Jus' a few beers," he slurred. "Wh-what's wrong with that?" His eyes gleamed glassy under the dim lamplight. He stumbled to his chair and sat with a thud. He pushed one shoe off with the other and lay back with a sigh. He dozed for a few hours. Thankfully, the children were at school.

When Rex awoke, his energy had returned. He sneaked up on his wife who was busily washing the dishes. Grabbing her by the arm, he pulled her toward the bedroom. Helen protested, but to no avail. He shoved her onto the bed and closed the door. "Rex! What's wrong with you?"

"Nothin', Helen, nothin'," he answered with a sloppy smile. He unbuckled his belt and let his pants drop to the floor. She felt her pulse quicken.

"Rex, what's goin' on?" she asked, the fear evident in her voice. He only smiled as he removed his smelly t-shirt. By then, she knew exactly what he had in mind. "Now, Rex, no," she began as she backed away from her husband, "not today. You're drunk." He ignored her pleas and stalked her as she moved off the bed and made a run for the door.

Rex's arm caught hers just before she turned the handle. As she tried to escape his grasp, he slapped her in the face. Screaming, she took the blows he offered. Eventually, however, she resisted no more and he threw her, once again, to the bed. During the fearful moments that followed, Helen Mitchell was raped by her own husband.

❧   ❧   ❧

Lauren became disturbed in April of that year. She was quieter, even than usual, and her brother was worried. One evening, after their father had gone to work, he could stand it no longer. He marched into her bedroom (she had her own, now) where she was working on math homework. He made her climb onto the bed, and he sat opposite her.

"Lauren, I know something is the matter with ya," he spoke firmly, perhaps even more severely than he'd wanted. "So, you might as well tell me. I'm not leavin' here until you do." He stared into her midnight blue eyes filled with tears.

Lauren's chin quivered. She held her face in her hands and wept bitterly. "Oh, Darren," she wailed. "I'm dyin'!"

Darren was stunned. He'd not expected that. "Lauren," he asked gently, "what makes ya think you're dyin'?"

She cried louder. "Oh, Darren, I'm bleedin' somethin' awful!"

Darren quickly looked her over and saw nothing that resembled blood. "Where, Lauren? Where are ya bleedin'? I don't see nothin'!"

Her tiny head bobbed with her weeping. Her face turned crimson. "When I go to the bathroom, it's on my panties," she whispered.

For a moment, the boy was silent. Then, slowly, a smile crossed his face. He laughed, and she looked at him as though he'd just landed in a UFO. Fine thing, she thought, I'm dying and he's laughing! "Oh, Lauren," he gasped. "You're not dyin'." She looked at him with interest. "You're growing up," he said, "that's all."

Lauren listened attentively as her eleven-year-old brother explained the miracle of menstruation. He tried to be as simplistic as possible. When she realized that she was to remain in the land of the living, she hugged him around the neck. He took her to Helen so she'd get some feminine supplies.

❧   ❧   ❧

Darren turned twelve on the thirtieth of June, series championship day. Rex yelled from the stands while Helen sat, hands folded, praying for a victory. Lauren sat restlessly by her mother. Darren was pitching, and it was in the bottom of the ninth; his team led 2 to 1. The count was two balls, two strikes and a man was on first. He felt the sizzling sun on his neck and ran his fingers across his crew cut. His hair, bleached almost blond by the rays, was hardly a stubble. Blue eyes gazed at the catcher; the view to the plate was hazy.

The young pitcher went into motion and released the pitch. His heart sank with the crack of the bat against the ball. He turned and watched it sail over the back fence. A home run, and just that quickly, it was over.

The walk home was silent except for Rex's occasional burst of emotion. He had already ranted and raved at the boy for his incompetence. In fact, it had been his father, not the coach, who had stormed onto the field to berate him. Darren's eyes were filled with hot tears as he trudged behind his father.

CHAPTER 16

*L*auren noticed the Milton boy in September of 1956. She had seen him before, naturally, but not in quite the same way. Eleven and in the sixth grade, she had her first crush. Long, blond locks fell to the middle of her back, and she pulled them up into a ponytail. She wore a skirt that day with a quarter-length sleeved blouse with ruffles at the neck. Her eyes danced, blue as the deep sky.

Tom had been watching her for weeks. He was mesmerized by her quiet nature and blushing nods. Barely as tall as she and a bit on the plump side, he had dashing brown eyes and hair. He wasn't as good-looking as Darren, she thought, but handsome just the same.

Lauren's best friend had suspected the "unspoken" relationship for a long time. She teased the Mitchell girl often about him and threatened to let him in on the secret. Lauren had been able to keep her at bay for three weeks when it happened.

Tom wrote her a letter.

Lauren sat on the playground, her heart thumping in her chest. She pushed her bangs back from her head and took a deep breath. Her friend's neck craned over her back to get a peek. It was very sweet. Tom expressed his affection and asked the all-important question. *"Will you go with me?"* Lauren already knew her answer.

Yes! Yes! Yes!

The couple kept in constant contact through their love notes. She wrote him at least twice a day, and he returned them. Both were very happy. In fact, they had just celebrated their three weeks anniversary when their relationship came to a quick end.

Rex found the note that Lauren had carelessly dropped out of her schoolbag that morning. Helen tried to reason with him, but nothing would do. He was waiting for her when she and Darren entered the house that afternoon.

Helen motioned for Darren to follow her to the kitchen. He did so, silently wondering what was going on. Lauren swallowed hard as she set her books on the table. Rex stood in the living room. His face drawn tight, the blood rushed to his head. His fists were clenched at his sides; one held the letter.

"Sit down, Lauren," he said, anger controlled for the moment, and motioned to the couch. She obeyed him; her pulse pounded in her ears. "What th' hell is this?!" her father suddenly shouted, making her jump.

Lauren saw the paper in his hand and nearly swallowed her tongue. "It's, it's m-my l-letter!"

"Dammit, I know it's your letter!" he shouted. "What are you doin' writin' 'em?"

She stammered, "H-he's my b-boyfriend—"

"Boyfriend, hell! You're not old enough to date!"

"Not date, Daddy," she explained softly, "just go with."

Rex crossed the room and then turned to face her furiously. "Go with," he repeated. She nodded fearfully. "You want to go with someone?" She did not answer and he grabbed her by the shoulders and shook. "Answer me, dammit! Do you?!"

"Y-yes," she replied, not understanding that her father implied much more than her simple explanation of courting. Rex's palm met her cheek in a blinding flash and she squealed.

"Not anymore you're not," he spat. "I'll not have a little slut in my house." He released her with a shove and grasped the telephone receiver. "What's his damn number?" When she did not answer him, he screamed, "What's the bastard's number, Lauren!?!" She mumbled the digits and he dialed.

As she listened, tears fell down her cheeks. Rex cussed Tom's father and threatened him with bodily harm if his son ever even so much as spoke to his daughter again. When he had finished, he slammed the phone into the receiver and turned to her.

"Come 'ere, you little whore," he sneered. "Come t'me!" Lauren's whimpers grew to sobs. "Come 'ere!" Not waiting for her to respond, he lunged for her arm, dragged her to his bedroom, and threw her on the bed.

"You won't want to go with anyone when I get through with you," he spoke menacingly as he removed his worn belt. He snapped the ends together. "Got to get this urge outta you before I got a baby on my hands. You hear me?" The first blows came.

Lauren mustered a weak, "Yes, sir," still not understanding how her courtship with Tom was so dangerous, or how a baby could be the result of their note writing. Rex continued to lash her as she called for Darren. He sat in the kitchen, his head in his hands, weeping silently. Although as tall as his father, he knew that he was no match for Rex Mitchell. He was powerless to stop him.

When it was over, Lauren walked stiffly to her own bedroom. Her face was flushed and swollen from her crying. She was so angry, she couldn't even speak. She closed the door. With all of her might, she beat her rag doll, wishing it were real.

Tom Milton never spoke to her again. He looked with longing eyes, but said nothing. She knew better than to try and mend the relationship.

It was over.

CHAPTER 17

*T*hree years passed…and the children became teenagers. Sports kept Darren's sanity and for Lauren it was her brother's loving care. He got a part-time job at Musser's Grocery the summer he turned sixteen, 1959. He saved his money and bought clothes and school supplies that were worthy of an athlete of his distinction. He was quite popular, despite his background, and endeavored to remain so.

Lauren went to high school that next August with anticipation of a new beginning. It had been difficult for them the past two years that they had been separated. Now, she would be a freshman and the event was commemorated.

Darren bought her a silver locket that held pictures of them. He told her it was a good luck charm; it was a way for him to always be with her. She never failed to wear it—a true treasure.

Darren returned home at one o'clock, two hours past his curfew, one night in October. He quietly opened the back door and stumbled inside. Stealthily, he made his way toward his bedroom and reached for the knob. It wasn't there.

Standing where the door should have been was his father. Without a word, Rex grabbed him by the collar and dragged him to the living room. Flicking the light switch on, he momentarily blinded his errant son. "Where th' hell you been, boy?! Huh? Where've you been?"

Darren stared down into his father's face with bloodshot eyes. He stood five inches over Rex and he shuffled his feet. "Uh, out with friends," he stammered with a heavy tongue.

Rex sniffed. "Damn, boy, you're drunk!"

Darren shook his head. "Uh, no, sir," he lied. "No, sir."

Rex slapped him full in the face. Darren was stoic. "Don't you lie to me, boy. You're drunker than hell." He watched his son teeter and then regain his balance. "What've I told you 'bout drinkin', Darren? Huh? What've I told you?"

"Nothin'," Darren replied, eyebrows furrowed. "I don't remember nothin'."

Rex quickly grabbed his drunken son and had him easily on the floor. Darren choked as the elder's boot fell on his neck and pressure was applied. He could see Rex's snarled expression and gurgled. "This ain't never goin' to happen again, Darren. You hear me?" The young man nodded as best he could with a shoe on his Adam's apple. "You better." Rex released him and watched him stagger to the bedroom and collapse. He looked at the table by his elbow and gazed at his own empty beer bottle.

❦   ❦   ❦

November brought political news like the U.S. had never seen. The Presidential elections were held, and John F. Kennedy won. "That Yankee bastard!" he exclaimed. Helen was sewing nearby. "Th' damn Catholic won!" He went to the kitchen and got a beer. "You know what that means, don't you, Helen?" She gave him a blank look. "Th' Pope'll rule us, that's what."

"Oh, Rex, you're overreacting," she said softly. "I kinda like him. I love to hear him talk."

Rex sneered. "Just like a woman. Like to hear him talk." He released a long breath. "God, Helen, there's more to politics than talkin' and looks. Damn, but you are a dumb ass if I ever saw one." He took a long gulp. Helen wiped an escaping tear from her eye.

"Maybe so, Rex," she answered softly as she continued to mend his work clothes. "Maybe so."

❁   ❁   ❁

The school year rounded out in good fashion. Darren received local recognition in both basketball and baseball, the latter yielding the best results. He would be a senior in the fall and was quite excited. He knew that even if he could be the class valedictorian (which he was vying for), he could not attend college without an athletic scholarship. He hoped for his best season ever.

Lauren was fifteen on the fourth of May and celebrated with her mother and brother. They ate large slices of carrot cake, and she opened presents. She received a new blouse and purse. She thanked them both and ignored her drunken father.

CHAPTER 18

*I*t was Thanksgiving, 1960. The Mitchells, for the first time, drove themselves to Edenton. Rex had managed to save some and bought a 1956 Chevrolet. They rode in customary silence. Rex and Helen were seated in the front, thirty-nine and thirty-seven, respectively. The teens were slouched in the back.

They arrived at the Preston farm just as Kathy did. She was nineteen, now, and a freshman at Edenton University. Like her father, she studied law. Even though the commute would have only been forty minutes, she had opted to stay on campus and strengthen her independence.

Kathy's dark brown hair was to her waist, straight as a stick. She kept it pulled back in a large barrette. Her chocolate eyes danced with excitement. It had been a month since she'd been at home, and she smiled as she emerged from her car. Both Darren and Lauren greeted her.

Todd stood on the front porch. Quite tall for his thirteen years, he was the picture of his father. He cut his dark hair very short at the neck, complimenting his eyes and winning smile. Like his elder sister, he was intelligent and had a bright future. Darren immediately talked with him about sports; basketball season had already started. The younger wanted some private coaching over the weekend, and Darren was happy to oblige.

On the other hand, Lauren stood silent. Her lengthy, platinum hair and shimmering blue eyes made her stand out among the others. Though Darren's locks were sunbleached, it was hardly noticeable cut as short as it was. The two of them looked nothing like their first cousins.

Malcolm and Carolyn, forty-three and forty, greeted the adults. She hugged her sister, and he shook hands with Rex. Pleasantries were exchanged though the tension that always existed between the two couples was obvious to both.

Oh…and there was Marilyn, the youngest. She was nine, a fourth grader. Her temperament was quite different from her older siblings. She was small for her age and often bossy and belligerent. With auburn hair the color of her mother's and penetrating hazel eyes, she was constantly on-the-go. She peeked at the crowd from behind the living room curtain.

The entire family conversed in the den that evening. Kathy had much college news to share, and Rex bragged of Darren's athletic accomplishments. Though Helen beamed at the unusual praise, her son was embarrassed by it. He knew not what to make of it. Lauren, of course, was never mentioned.

Carolyn did her best to remain cheerful, though her mind worked furiously at what she saw. Her niece, going-on-sixteen, was withdrawn and so much unlike her Kathleen had been at that age. The elder had always been serious-minded, but never as devoid of emotion as the young Lauren. She said a silent prayer for her.

Malcolm invited his brother-in-law to a ride the next morning, and his offer was accepted. Todd and Darren would meet on the basketball court (a small area beside of the detached garage) and their sisters would help with the preparation of the meal. Marilyn was the only one without a task or diversion. Shooed away by the boys and left behind by the men, she pouted in the barn. After all, she wanted nothing to do with the kitchen.

Kathy and Lauren were given the job of setting the table and straightening the other rooms of the house. The college student tried to draw her cousin into lively conversation, but it was difficult. Though they had played together nearly every year of their lives, it had always been apparent that they lived in different worlds. The years had only driven a thicker wedge between them.

❀   ❀   ❀

It was during the meal that the youngest of the cousins became a true nuisance. The adults allowed the two eldest children to eat with them in the formal dining room while the others were at the dinette in the kitchen. Marilyn, who had been angry and jealous all morning, continued to talk to Lauren even after her father announced that the blessing would be said. When he repeated himself, louder and slightly irritated, she quieted and then bowed her head, a smile on her face.

A few minutes later, she began to argue with Todd. "No!" she exclaimed as he poured her a glass of milk. "I don't want any."

"But, you just said—"

"I don't want it, *now*. I want water!" she screamed back at him.

Carolyn's voice interrupted the discussion. "Marilyn, Todd, please lower your voices and get along." They nodded even though she couldn't see them. Todd drank the milk he had given her and got a glass of water from the tap.

"I want milk," she said simply, giving him a devilish look.

Todd had taken a deep breath and gotten ready to attack her, when he saw his father. Malcolm stepped behind his youngest. "Marilyn, I think you need to eat elsewhere."

She turned with a start. "But, Daddy—"

"Now, Marilyn," he spoke firmly as he motioned to the living room. He retrieved a TV tray and brought it with him. She sat on the couch and he pushed it up to her. "I don't want to hear any more of your stubbornness, young lady." She stared up at him. He set a firm grip on her shoulder, gave a small squeeze, and then returned to the table.

Not five minutes passed before a loud clang erupted from the adjoining room. All at the large dining room table jumped and turned their heads toward the noise. Carolyn quietly stood and motioned for her husband to remain seated. He gave her a questioning look, but she assured him with a wink and exasperated expression. He diverted the attention of the guests as his wife walked slowly to their daughter.

Bits of turkey, dressing, cranberry sauce, and other remnants of her dinner were on the floor. The tray was upturned and the plate was broken. Marilyn sat with her glass of water in her hand. Carolyn surveyed the damage to the linoleum and met her daughter's stare. "What happened?" she asked sternly.

Marilyn's hazel eyes gleamed. "Fell over," she replied with an ill-timed smirk.

"I can see that," Carolyn went on with controlled anger. "How did it fall?"

"Guess when I pushed it," she boldly admitted.

Taking a deep breath and feeling her pulse quicken, Carolyn held out her hand. "Let's go, Marilyn."

"No, I want to stay here!" the child replied as she drew away.

"Come with me," her mother stated firmly. Once again, the girl shoed away and shook her head negatively. Then, as the elder stepped to grab her, Marilyn raised her hand and threw the glass of water into her mother's face.

Stifling a squeal and sputtering in fury, Carolyn had her in an instant. Though the nine-year-old struggled, she was dragged up the stairs, down the hallway, and into the master bedroom. The cries of the daughter filtered into the merry feast, but Malcolm ignored them and broke into fresh conversation.

The door closed behind Carolyn and she retained her grip of Marilyn's wrist as she crossed the room. Her daughter, now pleading for mercy, was unheard. The mother opened her closet and sought the adequate instrument before addressing her child.

"I cannot believe that you would show such disrespect for me, Marilyn," she said. "You knew better than to act like that and certainly to throw water on me. That was a poor decision, I must say!" She roughly sat her daughter on the bed and brandished the supple switch she had used only the day before. "Now, young lady, you may think that you can do whatever you want, but I can assure you that you'll not be allowed to do so as long as you live with your father and me. And, if it takes a good whipping to remind you of it, I will more than oblige you!"

"But, Momma, please—"

"Marilyn—"

"I'm sorry, Momma—"

"I'm certain you shall be." There was a pause. "*Now*, Marilyn."

Carolyn's voice showed clearly her agitation and the expression on her face mirrored it, as well. She started to grab the young girl, again, when her daughter obeyed and prepared to take her punishment. It was over in just a few minutes.

Malcolm was surprised to see his wife return so quickly to the table. She seemed quite calm to the guests, though he knew her rather well; it would take her an hour, maybe longer, to recover from the confrontation. She forced a smile and offered dessert.

Meanwhile, a repentant Marilyn was snubbing and cleaning the floor of the mess she had made. She wiped her runny nose with the back of her hand as her empty stomach growled. It would not be satisfied for many hours; she was denied the dinner she had ruined.

The rest of the holiday passed without major incident. The Mitchells returned home not knowing how soon all of their lives were to be shaken. In fact, no one would ever be the same ever again.

CHAPTER 19

*M*ay 4, 1961, would be a day Lauren Mitchell would never be able to forget. She was sweet sixteen and had a date that evening with Chris Forren, a junior. Her brother had given her a new dress for the occasion, so all in all, it was to be a beautiful day. The scent of budding flowers was in the air; Lauren relaxed in the backyard under an old elm tree. Final exams were coming up, and she hoped the best for Darren. His class rank would depend upon them.

Her father returned home late in the afternoon. He had driven his son who would not return until late the next day to the school for the out-of-town game. He got a beer from the refrigerator and turned on the TV. Later, in his drunken state, he would be awakened by the ringing telephone. He yelled at Helen, but she was outside. Stumbling to the table, he grasped the receiver. A few minutes later, he threw it across the room, pulling the cord from the wall. He screamed curses at an invisible audience. He had just been laid-off from work for the next two weeks, and there would be no money.

When six o'clock rolled around, Lauren emerged from her bedroom. She was wearing the pretty sundress Darren had worked so hard to buy for her. She borrowed her mother's watch and placed the precious locket around her neck.

Helen smiled with obvious pride; Lauren was so beautiful. Her lengthy blond hair was braided and shimmered like gold. The midnight blue eyes sparkled in the lamplight. Rex sat with a scowl, as usual. He was nearly drunk, still, another bottle of beer gripped in his hand. He hadn't spoken another word since the news from Matherly Parts. Lauren stood, blushing. For the first time in her short life, she felt worthy of admiration. She bathed in her mother's abundant compliments and tried to ignore her father. She had grown accustomed to his indifference.

The horn made her jump and she suppressed a squeal. Kissing her mother goodbye, she ran out the front door to meet Chris. She certainly did not want him to see her father; he was such an embarrassment. Smiling broadly, she got into his car and they drove away.

Several hours later, Lauren was not so thrilled. Chris walked her to the front door after helping her from his dazzling car. It was two in the morning. "Are you sure you'll be okay?" he asked, concerned. "I mean, I could tell them what happened," he offered.

"No," Lauren replied nervously, her heart pounding. "It's okay. I'll tell them. It wasn't our fault the projector broke and then we couldn't leave because our car was blocked in and everybody else waited for them to fix it. They'll understand."

"Well, okay," he answered, gazing into her tired eyes. "I guess I better go. My folks will be worried, too." He smiled and kissed her on the cheek. She felt the chill down to her toes as his hand slowly slipped away from hers. In a moment, he was gone.

Lauren paused, her hand on the knob. She knew there would be a battle if her father were still awake. He would never believe her story, she thought with a shiver. But, she had to go in, ready or not. If only he had passed out would she be safe.

Lauren quietly stole into the house, creeping on tiptoe to her bedroom. She removed her dress and slip and laid them on the bed to smooth the wrinkles before placing them on the hangar she'd left there.

It was then she felt the presence.

Standing in the dark, naked save for her underclothes, her whole body tensed with the sound of his breathing. She was afraid to turn and face the truth, but she swallowed hard and found the strength to do so. His pale eyes met hers in the darkness. His breath came in short spurts; the stench of alcohol wafted to her. Dressed only in his blue jeans, Rex's face was contorted with rage. "Daddy, it wasn't my *fault*. The theater projector—"

"Shut up!" he interrupted with a snarl. "I don't want to hear none of your damn lies, Lauren. Not your *damned lies*." He took another step and closed the door behind him. For a moment, the pitch blackness of the room swallowed them. She stood, terrified and waiting. The lights, now blinding, came on as her father hit the switch. She blinked and his face came into focus.

"Daddy, please, *listen* to me—" Her plea was interrupted by Rex's hand cracking against her cheek. She released a short scream and covered her face with her hands. Tears immediately formed in her eyes. "*Please, Daddy*—" Another blow knocked her to the bed and her next scream brought Helen to the door.

"Rex," she gasped, "what on earth—?"

"Get th' hell outta here, woman. This is my affair," he slurred. "Get out, I said! *I'm gonna take care of this*."

Helen didn't move. "Rex, what are you doing?"

Rex reeled and shoved her through the doorway. Helen landed with a thud in the hall. "*I said, get out*," he spoke through gritted teeth. "I'm gonna teach your little whore who's in charge here."

Rex turned to the frozen girl who now sat on the bed with wide eyes. "She's gonna learn that stayin' out all night with a boy and lyin' to me ain't gonna work." A smile crossed his face. "That's a promise." As Helen got to her feet, he grasped the handle of the door and swung it shut. By the time his wife was to it, the lock was in place. She pounded with her fists, but he ignored her.

Lauren's blood pressure rocketed. Never had she been so terrified for her life. All she could think of was that Darren was miles away…no one could help her. She had risen from the bed, but now tensed with his approach. He unbuckled his belt and unzipped his pants. His daughter's mind reeled with the implications, too stunned to speak. He stepped toward her, and she backed into the side of her bed. Her eyes pleaded with him to stop.

"You little bitch," he growled, "you jus' don't know what's good for ya, do ya?" He licked his lips in anticipation. "You want this?" he asked, grasping himself with one hand, taking hold of her hair with the other. "Huh? This what you want?!"

"No," she whispered. "Please, no, Daddy—"

"Is that what that boy gave you tonight? Huh? Is it?!" He pulled her hair so hard that the tears welled in her eyes. She tried to shake her head to answer him, but he held it too tightly. "That's what I thought." With a shove, he threw her to the bed, facing him. He wet his lips, again, his mind whirling in every depraved direction. "Well, now, I guess if I gotta feed another mouth 'round here, it might as well be one o' mine. That's my thinkin'." He smiled and put a knee to the bed between her legs.

Lauren found her voice. "Momma! Momma, *help me!*" she screamed. "He's gonna ra—" Rex lunged for her throat and silenced her.

Helen's pleas could be faintly heard on the other side of the door. She pounded her fists against it and demanded entry. Rex only turned and threatened, "Keep it up, woman! You'll only make it worse for the little bitch if I hear you!" Helen's cries were quickly silenced. Helpless and defeated, she ran to her room and swallowed two of her pills. In a matter of a few minutes, she slept fitfully amid her daughter's screams for mercy.

Rex ripped his daughter's underwear from her thrashing body and tossed them aside. Despite her struggle, he was able to pin her arms above her head and get himself into position. Even as he prepared to enter her, however, something stilled him.

Looking into her terrorized eyes, he saw not a woman to be taken, but a child. Her face, so youthful, was contorted with pain, but still that of his daughter, not his wife. Even as cruel a man as Rex Mitchell was, something deep inside would not allow him to commit the unthinkable.

Furious both with her and himself, he struggled to his feet. For a brief moment, his daughter thought she'd been spared by unprecedented mercy. She was soon to discover, though, that Rex had every intention of punishing her…and making her regret she'd ever been born to him.

He retrieved his jeans and pulled the wide leather belt from the waist and held it in his paw. He let it jingle ever so slightly, making her shiver. He motioned it toward her with the words, "Get ready, little girl. You know what's comin'." His voice was weak and scratchy.

"Please, no," she begged, again. "*Daddy, please, don't.*" Her whimpers resembled those of a three-year-old. The pleasantry of the evening had long since departed from her. Rex grasped Lauren's legs and roughly spun her onto her belly, exposing the young woman to the father's cruel eyes. Without pity, he lashed her until her screaming, pleading voice failed.

When he had punished her, Rex left and locked the door behind him. He collapsed on his own soft bed beside of his dozing wife. The bloody belt lay at his feet.

Darren entered the house a hero. His team, the Hadesville Hornets, had won with his no-hitter performance; the hand his father had broken earlier in the year had healed perfectly. He burst into the door and searched for his sister. "Lauren! Lauren!" he called excitedly. There was no answer. He called, again.

Helen appeared from the kitchen and motioned for him to be quiet. He walked to her, worried, and she took him outside. While his father slept, Darren learned of what had occurred the evening before. And, though he begged to see her, Darren was denied. Rex had fastened a lock on her bedroom and wasn't allowing anyone in or out. He, himself, had set a five-gallon bucket just inside the door for her use and a plate of food with a jug of water.

No sound came from within and for two days, Darren was forced to wonder about her in silence. But then, he got a glimpse of her stretched out on her bed, the same day Rex called the school and informed them that his daughter would not be returning due to an illness. Determined to teach her a lesson once and for all, her father became her jailor, and her mother, not much less.

Lauren merely survived behind the locked door. She tended to her wounds as best she could with the meager supplies she had. The water given her was used to keep the cuts clean and she spent most of her time lying on her bed, quiet and still. What she had ever done to deserve such an existence, she was sure she didn't know.

The school year was drawing to a close for the Mitchell senior, but he was far from elated. Darren's mind, unable to concentrate on his studies, worked constantly to find a solution to the problem they now faced, more terrible than ever, with their father. He would be eighteen in six weeks, and he could leave. But what about Lauren? Going was not an option if he couldn't save her, too, yet he could not do it alone. Thus, he found the courage to make good on an offer he had been given not too many months before, one that would change their lives forever.

CHAPTER 20

*D*arren graduated as salutatorian of his class in mid-May. He had performed well on his exams, despite the trauma at home. Only his mother attended the ceremony; the jailer and his prisoner were at home. Continuing to work past graduation at Musser's store, he gave most of his earnings to Rex for the family, but he was able to keep enough for their special cause. He told his sister of the plan only the day before he put it into action. It was June 30, 1961, his eighteenth birthday.

Helen wished him a happy day before departing for town to do the shopping. Darren had been paid, and the kitchen was empty. Rex had not returned to work, and it was evident that times were truly hard. Meals were meager and few. He sat in his chair watching television—one eye on the door to Lauren's bedroom. Sent to the kitchen to retrieve a beer for his father, Darren took a deep breath as he removed the pills from his pocket that he had taken from his mother's bed table. He was expressionless as he crushed the tranquilizers and dissolved them. He served the potent drink with an inward smile and waited.

Within the hour, Rex drifted into a deep sleep. His son watched him carefully before deciding that it was safe to proceed. He tried to shake his father awake; it was useless. He searched his father's person and grasped the key to Lauren's bedroom. He rushed to it, now, and unlocked it. As the door swung open, he saw her standing there in the dress he'd bought for her birthday, and the locket hung around her neck. They embraced, and she clung to him for a long time.

"Lauren, take your bag to the front door," he instructed. "I'll be there in a minute." She obeyed him, trusting in his judgment. He soon joined her with his own baggage and then, with a reassuring smile, left her, again. For a moment, Darren stood in the living room and took a deep breath. It was time; time to leave everything he had ever known. And, then he glanced at the sleeping monster and revulsion filled him.

With deliberate steps, he walked to the bedroom they had shared growing up, the one which had been only his for five years. He reached underneath the bed and pulled his secret box from its hiding place. Soft scents of old peppermint and licorice came to him. He smiled as the tears welled in his eyes. There were old notes, love letters, and keepsakes. He closed the lid and took it with him.

Getting some twine from the kitchen drawer, he listened for Lauren. He strode to the entrance and handed her the box. "Put this with my stuff," he said softly. "I'll be back in a minute." He returned to his father's body and hefted him onto his shoulders before trudging to Lauren's bedroom.

Lauren could hear the series of knocks and bangs from the room. She wondered silently what he was doing, but decided to await his instructions. When he emerged, he could not conceal his pleasure. "Come and see," he said softly. "This's one day he'll not forget, not for the rest of his life." She stared blankly ahead as she followed in his footsteps.

Unprepared for what she saw, Lauren simply stared for a long moment. Could her brother have done this? she wondered. On her bed lay Rex Mitchell, flat on his stomach. His blond hair, crew cut, stuck out in all directions and his body, limp and lifeless, was naked. Her father's wrists and ankles were tied securely to the bedposts, stretched tight and exposed before them. Lauren was speechless;

Darren turned to seek her face. His arm stole around her shoulder. "Well?"

"Oh, Darren, I can't believe it," she said, breathlessly. "*I can't believe you did this.*" She stared at her father's sprawled figure. "Oh, Darren." Her astonishment melted into hysterical giggling.

"Lauren," Darren begged, himself laughing with her, "get a grip on yourself." He held her up, she was so consumed by it. "C'mon, now, *stop it.*"

"I can't!" she gasped as she coughed from laughing so hard. "I just *can't.*"

"I know," her brother admitted. "I just couldn't leave without showing him that he doesn't control us anymore." He looked deeply into her eyes as she sobered. "C'mon, let's go." He pulled at her arm, but she did not move. "*C'mon, Lauren.* Let's get out of here before he wakes up."

"What could he do?" she asked softly, more to herself than to him. "Huh?"

Mischief was in her smile as she faced her brother. "What could he do, Darren? Huh? *What could he do?*"

Darren saw the devilry in her eyes. "Lauren Mitchell, what are you thinkin'?" She explained herself, and he protested but to no avail. His sister wanted her share of the revenge.

The steady tick of the mantle clock was the only sound in the house. The Mitchell youths sat with eyes transfixed on their bound father. They were waiting for that precious moment when he would awaken. Darren held fast to Lauren's hand. He could feel the nervousness in her clammy grasp. He reassured her often with a smile.

Lauren was solemn; her mind set upon one thing. She was ready and quite willing, eager even, to vent her anger on her father. She was also patient enough to wait until he was conscious. She wanted him to *know* it was *her*. Leaving him physically beaten would not be enough. She wanted to hear his pleas for mercy and deny it.

Lauren was mad with hatred.

When Rex began to regain consciousness, he felt groggy, as if he'd been asleep for days, or even years. He tried to move, but couldn't. His confusion was only momentary; he burst wide-awake. Lifting his head, he tried to roll over. Then, he felt the sickening sensation of being so vulnerably naked.

"What th' hell—" he grumbled as he struggled to free himself. "What's goin' on, here?!" He frantically turned his head from side to side.

Lauren rose to her feet and walked slowly to his bedside with sweet satisfaction welling in her chest. "What's the matter, *Daddy*?" she nearly whispered, tongue dripping with sarcasm.

Rex's head jerked around to face her. "Dammit, Lauren! What's goin' on here? Untie me!" He pulled on the twine, but it held tight. Darren had done his job well.

"*I don't think so*," she cooed. "I like you just where you *are*." She stood like a statue, his eyes blazing into hers.

"Lauren," he spoke slowly, "get me th' hell up from here! *Now*! Let me **loose**!" Darren watched in silence. He had never seen his sister like this; he felt her anger and feared it.

"Are you *afraid*, **Daddy**?" she asked, a grin escaping. She moved her face close to his. "Huh? Could you be afraid of *me*? Of little *Lauren*?"

Rex sputtered with fury. "I'm not 'fraid o'you, you worthless pile o'shit! You're nothin', Lauren. *Nothin'*! You never have been," he sneered. "Now, get me up from here 'fore I really show you who's the boss here!"

Darren was surprised at the laughter that escaped her lips. She sobered before she addressed him, again. "You've told me that so many times it means nothing to me. *Nothing*." She glanced at Darren before she continued. "I know how you feel about me, *Daddy*, but those days are over. They're over *forever*." She moved her head so close to his that their noses almost touched. She gazed into the pale eyes that had sent shivers down her spine so many times. "*No one will ever tell me what to do ever again.*"

"*Lauren—*" Darren began, but was cut short as she went on, oblivious to him.

"I'm not afraid of you, any more," she spoke slowly. "I don't have to be. Yesterday, you had me locked up in this room." She motioned around her. "But, today, I hold the belt in *my* hand and *I* will do my pleasure, not *yours*." It was then that Rex saw the weapon she fisted. It was stained with her blood of over a month before. She had searched the house while he slept until she found it.

Rex's eyes grew wide with terror. He had never been more frightened in his life, though he'd never admit it to anyone. He simply took a deep breath and threatened her, again. "Go ahead, Lauren. *Go on,*" he said through gritted teeth, "and then what? Where will you go? You're only sixteen. I'll have the cops lookin' everywhere for you. Then you'll *come back to me*, Lauren, and I will do my *worst*."

Darren stopped breathing. He was too mesmerized by the scene to move. He only hoped that everything worked out. If that were true…if Lauren had to come back…he couldn't stand the thought of it.

"You don't scare me, old man," she replied. "I will be safe, safe from you and all your abuse. I'll *never* come back here."

Rex's heart pounded in his ears. His arms ached from the position they were in. He tried to move, but it was of no use. "Damn girl, you know better than that," he spat. "You know *me* better than that. I'll hunt you down *like a dog*. I'll see to it. Jus' try me."

Lauren's laughter was too much for him. As she cackled, he became enraged. The bed shifted on the floor with his movements. Sobering, she peered down at him, the same scornful look she had gotten from him so many times.

Lauren grasped the stained belt in her left hand and raised it high above her head. Facing her, he tensed with her intention. He sucked in his breath as she brought the first one, quickly and powerfully.

Amid her father's curses, she repeatedly lashed him, bringing her arm high and low with agile ability. She raged on and on, with little regard to his screams or pleas for mercy.

Darren was frozen in the corner. Holding his hands to his ears, he blocked out the obscenities that only made his sister strike harder. She stopped only when she tired, not because she felt it could ever be sufficient. Throwing the weapon to the floor, she sneered, "There, you *son-of-a-bitch*, take that."

Flushed, angry, and exhausted, she reeled to face the ashen Darren. He found his strength and grasped her by the upper arm. "C'mon, Lauren, *let's go*," he urged. Her tear-filled eyes looked up into his face and she nodded. Stepping from the room and closing the door, they heard only the croaking curses of their father.

"Wait," Lauren said, halting suddenly. "There's something else." Her pleading eyes convinced her brother to let her go. She quietly entered the room and the sickening stench of fresh blood assailed her nostrils. She covered her mouth with her hand and walked to the dresser. In a drawer, preserved, was Macy.

Lauren carefully picked up the headless doll she had loved for so long. She held it to her chest, placed a parting kiss on the ragged dress, and then walked to her father. As she placed the object on his pillow, her eyes met his. She saw tears in the pale stare she received.

Quickly, she turned and strode from the room. She remembered to lock the door behind her and rejoined Darren at the front door. As she bent to grasp the handle of her bag, she saw it. With a startled cry, she ran to the bathroom. She washed the crimson stains from her hands and face and dried them with a towel. With a lump forming in her throat, she hurried to her brother.

Darren smiled and hugged her. "It's all right. We're going to be all right." She nodded, numbly, and followed him. The playful summer rays jumped into the doorway, and he closed the door behind them.

"When does our train leave for Edenton?" she asked, calmly.

"In half an hour," he replied as they stepped onto the sidewalk. "Uncle Malcolm said he'd be waiting for us there."

"Good." Lauren breathed a sigh of relief. She wrapped her free hand around Darren's waist. They strode down the street to the station...to freedom...to a new life.

Tables of the Heart

"Forasmuch as ye are manifestly declared
to be the epistle of Christ ministered by us,
written not in ink, but with the Spirit of the living God;
not in tables of stone, but in fleshy tables of the heart."

II Corinthians 3:3 KJV

.

For Wanda Summers & Tracy Watson

CHAPTER 1

The seats jostled in the passenger car as the train swiftly moved toward its destination. The sweltering heat inside the cramped quarters made Darren's head swim. His sister was at his side, silent. Lauren's hair was combed down onto her shoulders, her bangs falling low on her forehead. The ocean-blue eyes were glassy, bloodshot, and staring just beneath them. Fists were clenched in her lap. She had not spoken since she and Darren had left the house...their home.

As she rode, Lauren envisioned Rex's helpless form as it had been laid prostrate before her. She recalled the flood of anger that had consumed her and the heady feeling that her brand of justice had brought. The revenge she had meted out to him, still hot and smoldering, burned deep within.

Tears found their way to her eyes once again, though, as she thought of their mother and the inevitable discovery of their beaten father. She feared that with their escape, Rex would only turn more violently on his wife; and Helen would be too weak to withstand the onslaught. The summer scene blurred in the window. Lauren gazed, not really seeing, and breathed slowly. Her emotionless exterior hid her inner turmoil. The explosions inside of her heart and mind shook her to the very core.

Darren was subdued by her mood. Though she said nothing, he felt the tremor in her body. They rode for another quarter hour, and her silence maddened him. He needed to talk to someone so badly; his own mind buzzed with anxiety. What had they done? What was going to happen to them? Who would protect them, now?

Darren turned his body toward hers in the seat beside of him. She jumped as his hand landed lightly on hers atop the armrest. He forced a smile. "Are you okay, Lauren?" She nodded, slowly. "Are you *sure?*"

Lauren's lip trembled, and she tried to cover her mouth with her hand. Tears welled up in her eyes and overflowed onto her hot cheeks. A large sob escaped as she whispered to him an echo of his own thoughts. "Oh, Darren, Darren, what have we done? *What have we done?*"

He swallowed hard as her head fell onto his shoulder. He grasped her firmly. "I know, I know," he whispered into her ear. Though curious passengers looked their way, the two teens were oblivious to them. When she regained her control, she lifted her head and peered deeply into her brother's eyes. "Darren, do you realize what we did today? We ran away! From our *mother!*" She added in a hushed whisper, "My God, we tied Daddy up and *beat him!*" Her eyes widened as she exclaimed, "What is he gonna do to us when he gets *loose?*"

Darren took a deep breath. "Don't worry, Lauren. Everything is gonna be all right. He's not gonna take you back. *I'll see to it.*" He squeezed her hand. "Besides, he won't get loose for a while. Momma was going to make a day of it, remember?"

Lauren nodded. "Yeah, I guess so." She turned back to the window, her mother in her mind's eye. What would Helen think of them? "I just can't believe what I did. Oh, God, I can't believe it. I did it—what I always wanted to do," she spoke slowly, turning back to him. "Oh, Darren, there was so much blood." Her voice fell. "*So much blood.* God, I can't believe it was me. It was *me.*"

Darren's pulsed quickened as she reminded him of the morning horror. He had witnessed the terrible scene when his sister lashed their father bloody. Now, only a couple of hours later, he peered into the same eyes which had gazed into their father's, grasped the same hand which had held the weapon, and comforted the soul which had been—and quite honestly still was—consumed with anger and hatred.

Like his sister, neither could Darren believe what had transpired that ill-fated morn. Running away to their relatives had been his plan. He'd done everything so carefully that nothing should have gone awry. He now asked himself, why had *he* tied him up? Why didn't he *stop her*?

Oh, what had they done?

❦   ❦   ❦

Rex Mitchell's exhausted and beaten body lay still upon the small bed. His arms and legs ached from the twine that held them securely to the bedposts. The wet, sticky blood slowly ran down the sides of his torso onto the flowery sheets.

His head pounded as if a jackhammer was going at top speed on his skull. Mouth parched, he only croaked curses. Rex's face was damp with the tears that streamed from his cold eyes. Tired from his angry outbursts, he now lay in great physical pain. The dripping blood tickled as it trailed over his body. The leather instrument had left wide, angry red welts. Some of these were sliced open from which the blood had spurted and sprinkled the sheets. Any muscular movement sent piercing pains throughout his body, so he lay very still.

Rex's mind, however, was racing in circles. He still could not fathom the tragedy that had befallen him. He retraced the morning in his mind...all had been well. Lauren was locked safely in her room, Helen was shopping, and Darren was watching television with him. The next thing he knew, he was stretched naked upon Lauren's bed and soon felt her wrath. What had happened in between?

His mind, weary from the morning, finally slipped into slumber. He dreamed of the reunion; he would have a chance to settle the score with his children. As the clock chimed one o'clock, he was unconscious.

❧   ❧   ❧

The station in Edenton bustled with excitement. It was three o'clock; the bulk of the trains were still to arrive. Malcolm Preston sat with arms folded, concealing his nervous energy. He was alone; Carolyn was at the farm preparing supper. She, too, was filled with anxiety over the arrival of their niece and nephew. Both prayed for the teens' safety; they had no idea what had transpired.

Darren had called them almost a month before this appointed day. He had hurriedly explained that they were coming for a visit and needed *help*. That emphasis combined with the plea for secrecy from their parents let the elder couple know that something serious had happened. He promised to tell them everything when they arrived.

The Prestons had quickly answered in the affirmative, not knowing what to expect. Twice they had almost called Helen, but had stopped before the dialing was complete. They would simply wait and see for themselves what had prompted the escape. Lord, what would they discover?

❧   ❧   ❧

Darren gently prodded Lauren's arm. They had arrived in Edenton and were about to stop. She yawned and continued to stare forward. The passengers slowly rose to their feet and retrieved their baggage from the overhead compartments. Both bags in hand, Darren allowed his sister to step in front of him. He followed her down the aisle to the door. Side by side, they stepped from the train steps

and searched for their uncle. Their eyes swept the lobby until his figure caught their attention. Both cleared their throats and proceeded
toward him.

Malcolm rose quickly as their pale faces met his. He looked deep
into their eyes, fearful of what they could tell him. He forced a smile.
"Did you have a good trip?"

Darren nodded. "Yes, it was fine."

Silence.

"How are you, Lauren?"

Silence.

"I think we better go," Darren suggested, softly.

The distinguished lawyer nodded and grasped one of the bags the
young man held. "The car is over here." He led the way as Darren fell
into step behind him.

Lauren numbly followed, her mind not registering on anything
real. Red rimmed from her crying, the pale blue pigment of her eyes
gave her a hideous countenance. Her limbs were as limp as her hair,
hanging at her sides without any movement save from walking. She
hardly noticed that her brother often peered over his shoulder at her.

The ride to the farm was as silent as the conversation in the station. No one spoke. Darren held Lauren's hand tightly in his. He
wished he knew what was going on in her head. Malcolm drove
steadily toward his home, his mind filled with questions.

Helen Mitchell arrived home late in the afternoon, about four-
thirty. Arms filled with groceries, she pushed the front door open
with her foot and hurried inside. She made three trips to the car to
get it all to the kitchen.

The house was strangely quiet, she thought, for a Saturday afternoon. Rex usually had the TV on or Darren was outside practicing
his pitching. She had neither seen nor heard either of them. She
dropped her purse on the table and began to put away the groceries.

It was at least half an hour later that she decided to check on Lauren. She assumed her husband and son had gone somewhere and left the girl in her room. She quietly strode to the bedroom door and tried the handle. It was locked, as usual.

Helen remembered where a spare key was kept. But when she quickly searched the bureau top, she found nothing. She stepped back into the living room, her hands on her hips, thinking. "What'd he do with it?" she asked herself in a whisper. She peered around the room and spotted it on the television. She got it and walked to the door.

CHAPTER 2

Carolyn Preston sat on their front porch, waiting. She had paced herself into a frenzy and finally forced herself to sit. Todd had gone riding, and Marilyn was playing upstairs in her bedroom. She was alone in her worry.

As the faint sounds of the approaching vehicle could be heard, she turned her ear toward the winding lane. She smiled. "They're finally here." She rose and lifted her hand to shade the evening sun from her eyes. A cloud of dust swirled behind the car as it pulled to a stop. She anxiously walked down the steps to the sidewalk.

Malcolm's expression was enough to communicate that something was wrong, terribly wrong. His usually youthful face was drawn tight. He ran his fingers through his graying hair and turned to offer his help with the luggage. Darren helped his sister from the car. He allowed his uncle to carry their things.

Carolyn's periwinkle eyes peered into those of Lauren as their faces met. In them, she saw much pain and anguish. She knew, then, that it was far worse than they had ever imagined.

Helen held to the key with a clammy grasp. She knew that Rex would not approve of her caring for Lauren, but she simply couldn't help herself. The opportunity was much too great to ignore. The key slid into the lock with ease. She turned it slowly, hoping not to startle the young girl. She carefully grabbed the knob and creaked the door open.

Her eyes fixed on the sleeping figure. She was frozen, mesmerized by the view. She grew weaker and weaker as disbelief flooded her consciousness. The light from the hall filtered inside the dark room, revealing her husband's bound body. She stared for a moment, just to verify that it was, indeed, her husband who lay so still.

Rex's usually light skin was marred with crimson strokes. Crusted blood covered his naked body, revealing the cruelty with which he had been attacked. The sheets were stained, as well, from the blood that had run down his sides in streams.

Helen's eyes filled with tears as she stood. She felt as though her heart stopped, her breath only a luxury. She could not believe what her eyes beheld. Nervously, she looked to his chest. She strained to see whether he was still alive. Faintly, she could perceive the rise and fall of his ragged breathing. Finally able to wrestle her mind free of its immobility, she mustered the strength to move.

Quietly as she had entered, she stepped back into the hallway and closed the door. She turned the key and walked to their bedroom, closing the door behind her. What was he going to do? To Lauren? To Darren? She fell to her knees beside of the bed, weeping uncontrollably from the horror of the scene falling all around her.

"*Oh, God, oh, God,*" she called in a coarse whisper. "Oh, my God, what is going to happen to us?" The tears ran down her cheeks onto her neck and hair. Her shoulders rocked back and forth with her sobs. "Oh, what will he *do*?" She gazed up to the ceiling, her face etched with her fear. "It must have been them…who else would have *done* such a thing? What is he gonna do to them when he gets them? My God, he'll *kill* them. I know he will. I know it. He'll *never* get over this…oh, God, he'll never forgive them."

She fumbled for the nightstand; tears blurred her vision. She finally grasped the familiar bottle, and with quivering hands, swallowed two of her pills. She collapsed a while later, completely unaware of the world.

❧   ❧   ❧

Malcolm led the guests upstairs to show them their rooms. Darren would use the spare room at the end of the hall. He smiled and began to unpack his bag. Lauren was given Kathy's old room; the elder cousin had her own apartment, now, near the university. She walked behind her uncle without a sound and stepped inside. He smiled at her reassuringly and closed the door. She set her bag on the floor.

Lauren's eyes swept the room. Oh, what memories were there! She spotted the dollhouse, just as it lived in her imagination. She peered into the small structure; the dolls were happily going about their business of whatever it was the last person chose for them to do. She closed her eyes and the scenes replayed in her mind. The young Kathy excitedly showed her the latest addition, and she had marveled.

Lauren's eyes filled with tears. Oh, what she had been through…what she had endured…and envied. She was, again, so angry with her father. Her blood raced through her veins. She could see him, glaring at her with those eyes, *those eyes!* The cold eyes which had pleaded for her to stop…the eyes from which she saw tears fall as the headless doll was placed on his pillow…the eyes which had looked upon her with distaste, scorned her very existence…she saw the eyes which had terrified her for so long.

Lauren stood like a statue in the silent room. Her own eyes, blue and piercing, stared forward, seeing the past. Her heart thumped in her chest like an African drum. Would Rex come after them? She was certain he would try. What would he do when he did? With those thoughts her body went limp, and she collapsed on the bed, weeping quietly.

The door slowly opened, revealing a reddish-brown blur of hair. It was Marilyn, the ten-year-old. She tiptoed across the room to get a glimpse of the visitor. "Lauren?" she whispered.

"Who's there?!" she answered with a start. "Who is it?" She bolted upright.

"Me, Marilyn," the girl answered with quickened pulse. "Gosh, it's just *me*." She looked at the tear-stained face of the young woman. "Whatcha cryin' about?"

Lauren sniffed and lay back onto the pillow. "Nothing, just leave me alone."

"It's got to be somethin'," she continued.

"I said, leave me alone," she repeated with a hint of exasperation.

"C'mon, you can tell me."

"No!" Lauren shouted. "No, I don't want to tell you! I don't want to tell anyone! Do you understand? Huh? I don't want to talk to you!" She breathed heavily. "Get out, just get out!" she screamed and pointed to the door.

By this time, Carolyn had arrived. She watched the enraged girl as she lashed into her sometimes-irritating daughter. Marilyn was in shock; she had never been verbally flayed in her life. She tore her mind from the shock of it to respond to her mother's urging. "Marilyn," Carolyn whispered. "Marilyn, come here." The girl forced her stiff legs to follow the impulses from her brain. She stepped into her mother's arms for a comforting embrace. Carolyn then closed the door to the room and led her daughter to the kitchen. It would soon be time for supper.

Mother and daughter were completing the meal when Todd returned from his ride. He was of medium height, smart, and possessed the most beautiful velvet brown eyes imaginable. His hair was the color of his father's, chocolate, and cut precisely in the same fashion. His shirt was wet from sweat, and his face was flushed. "Hi, Mom," he said as he kissed her on the cheek.

"Oh, Todd Warren, get washed up. It'll be time to eat in a few minutes." Carolyn laughed. "You can get as filthy as your father fooling with those horses."

Todd smiled, mischievously. "It seems to me that it was *you* last year who came back from a ride all covered in—"

"That's quite enough, thank you," she cut in with *the look*. "Don't be late." He grinned and lightly mussed his little sister's hair as he left the room. After he had gone, Carolyn tried to explain to her daughter that Lauren was their guest and needed her privacy. Therefore, Marilyn was not to enter her room without an invitation. The girl dutifully nodded at her mother's instructions.

Meanwhile, Todd entered his father's study following his quick bath. Malcolm had called to him from the doorway and now, he sat opposite his father. He explained that Darren and Lauren were their guests and under stressful circumstances. He was to be hospitable, as always, but considerate, too. The fourteen-year-old nodded as if he understood it fully. He didn't, nor would he for a long, long time.

CHAPTER 3

The Preston family and their two guests gathered around the table for the evening meal. Malcolm and Carolyn were nervous, Todd and Marilyn were anxiously interested, and Darren and Lauren were painfully withdrawn and silent. All bowed their heads as the blessing was offered.

The simple meal was larger than either of the Mitchell children had seen in a month or more. Darren quickly filled his plate and hungrily began to eat. Others joined him. But, Lauren did not move to help herself at all. Carolyn took her plate and placed a meager portion on it, hoping the teen would taste it. Lauren did not touch it.

Marilyn and Todd talked excitedly. He had seen a wild turkey on his ride and shared the tale with her. She listened attentively. But, Malcolm and his wife ate silently. Both were worried about the days ahead of them. Would they ever know what had really happened? Would Rex and Helen contact them? Their minds were filled with questions to be answered all too painfully, very soon.

Finally, Lauren could take no more. Her head pounded and she felt as though it might detach from her neck. Eyes dry and scratchy from her crying, she could yet feel the hot tears about to pour forth again. She stood, pushed back her chair, and left the room. All turned and watched her leave. Darren started to follow her, but Carolyn motioned for him to stay. She, herself, rose and strode from the room, her face wrinkled with worry.

Lauren's face was wet with tears by the time she reached the bathroom. She bent over the commode, heaving. Only a pale, thin liquid would come. She still struggled when her aunt arrived.

"Oh, Lauren," she consoled. "Oh, Lauren." She placed a cool cloth on the teen's forehead and handed her a towel with which to wipe her mouth. Lauren was flushed, mentally and physically exhausted. The aunt pulled her upright and embraced her. Carolyn held her for a long time. She thought of Kathleen, her eldest, and how many times she had held her so. She squeezed her niece and whispered her love.

Lauren continued to cry. Never had she felt so loved and unloved at the same time. Flashes of her memory filled her blurred vision. She saw her father bound and bloody, her mother crying. *Oh, what had she done?*

Carolyn carefully pushed Lauren from her chest and smiled. "Come, now, and get some sleep. Hmm?" Lauren could have lived inside of those kind, ocean-blue eyes and soft smile. She nodded and followed. Her aunt unmade the small bed and helped her unpack her bag. When she was ready to undress, Carolyn bid her a good night and left.

❧   ❧   ❧

When the meal was over, Todd excused himself to go to the stables. He had some organizing to do. He secretly wondered to himself why his cousins were in such a state of mind. Marilyn assisted her mother clear the table and began working on the dishes. Carolyn watched with anticipation as Darren followed his uncle to the study. She hoped to soon know all that had happened.

Malcolm seated himself on an old sofa he kept in his study, one that had belonged to his grandmother. He motioned for the young man to join him, and Darren sat nervously. "Well, Darren, I guess it's time you tell me what's going on. Why did you call us, now, after all this time?"

Darren swallowed hard. "It's a long story, Uncle Malcolm, a real long story." His uncle nodded for him to continue. "Well, it goes back as far as I can remember…"

❀   ❀   ❀

Carolyn placed the last dish in the drain board and dried her hands on the towel. Turning to her daughter, she smiled. "Well! Thanks, Marilyn, for your help." She hugged her tightly.

"Anything else?"

"No, thank you," her mother answered. "I appreciate it."

"Okay, then." She stepped toward the door. "I'll just go talk to Lauren."

"No!" Carolyn answered a bit roughly. "No, Marilyn, that's not a good idea. She needs her rest."

"But, I want to ask her somethin'!"

"What?"

Marilyn shifted her feet. "Uh, well…"

"That's what I thought." Carolyn shook her head. "Now, go on and play or read and leave your cousin alone. All right?" The young girl slowly nodded and left the room. Carolyn breathed a sigh of relief. She walked to the hall and ascended the stairs to her bedroom not far behind her youngest. She planned to prepare her Sunday School lesson for the morning.

❀   ❀   ❀

"…and that's what happened today," Darren finished with a sigh. He had control of his tears, but his hands shook. "I just had to get her out of there, Uncle Malcolm. That's why I called. I didn't know that this would happen."

Malcolm's countenance was frozen in expression—*horror*. He turned from his nephew and covered his face with his hands, weeping bitterly. "*Oh, God…oh, God…*" he cried, softly. Darren's face was tight as he fought to keep from emotional collapse. The shudder he felt was from his uncle's sobs. He was completely helpless to comfort him.

※   ※   ※

Carolyn was working quietly when the screaming made her jump. Who was it? She got to her feet and ran into the long hallway. Immediately, she halted.

It was Lauren. She was standing outside her door, wild with anger. Marilyn was rigid in her shadow. "Don't you understand? Huh? *Don't you*?!" Lauren exclaimed. "I don't want to talk to you. Leave me alone! I ain't got nothing to say!"

Marilyn was crying from terror. "I-I'm s-sorry, Lauren. I-I'm s-sorry."

"Sorry isn't good enough!" she snarled. "Leave me alone!" She collapsed onto the carpet, crying. "Just-leave-me-alone," she whispered. "*I just want everybody to leave me alone.*"

Carolyn rushed to her daughter. Grabbing her by the upper arm, she forced her attention. "What're you doing, young lady?"

Marilyn's eyes widened. She stumbled across the words. "I-I w-was jus' tryin' to t-talk to—"

"What did I tell you?" Carolyn's voice was tense. No response. "Marilyn? What did I tell you about talking to Lauren?"

Marilyn's face pinched. "You, you told me not to," she whimpered.

"Exactly right," Carolyn responded. "And you disobeyed me." She released the daughter's arm and placed her hands on her hips. "Go get your pajamas on, and I'll be there to tuck you in."

"But, Momma, it's not dark yet!" she protested.

Carolyn's eyes peered into those of her daughter. "Marilyn, I suggest you do as I asked you, young lady. You're in enough trouble as it is." Her stern look assured that she meant business. Marilyn's tiny face twisted again as she pouted. She walked slowly to her own bedroom as instructed. She glanced back at her mother only once, catching the frigid stare.

Carolyn helped Lauren to her feet and gently took her to her bed. She pulled the sheet up to her chin. "Are you all right?" Lauren nodded. "Sleep well, now." She leaned over the bed and kissed her forehead ever so lightly. Lauren breathed a sigh of relief and closed her eyes.

❦   ❦   ❦

"My Lord, *why*? Why to these *children*?" Malcolm Preston's anguished cry was aimed at the ceiling as he paced in agitation. "*Why*?" His chest felt as though it would rip apart. The guilt at having been cautious while they were tormented was almost more than he could bear. Finally grasping hold of his control, he turned to Darren. "Oh, son, I am so sorry, so *sorry*. Can you ever *forgive* us?"

Of all the requests, it was the last Darren had expected. For a moment, he did not answer; he was so stunned. The image of his uncle's bloodshot, piercing eyes would never leave him, he thought. "*What*?"

"Will you ever forgive us?" Malcolm repeated. "We did nothing, nothing to help you. No matter what we suspected, we did *nothing* to—"

"But, you *did*, Uncle Malcolm," Darren interrupted. "You gave us something to look forward to every year—Thanksgiving. It was something to live for every day."

"But, Darren, I—"

"And, now, you have given us the very best," he went on. "You've allowed us to come here when we need you the most. I never forgot that promise I made—to call if I ever needed you. I'm just so thankful you didn't refuse."

Malcolm ran his fingers through his gray-streaked hair. "Years ago, Darren, years ago—that's when you should have come here. I should have gotten you out of there *years ago*."

"How could you?" Darren asked, softly. "We would have denied it and so would Momma. It would have only made things worse. We'd never have got to come back here, and we needed that so bad. What else *could* you do?"

Silence.

"Uncle Malcolm, we've got to put our past behind us, now. We've got to concentrate on the *future*." Darren took a long breath. "And, that's where you and Aunt Carolyn come into all this. *We need your help*."

Malcolm sat in his large swivel chair and leaned on the desktop. "Whatever it takes, Darren, whatever may come, I'll see to it that Rex Mitchell *never* hurts either of you *ever* again. That is a solemn *vow*."

No longer could Darren deny his tears. They fell shamelessly.

CHAPTER 4

$\mathcal{T}$he dark room was humid, so thick with moisture it was hard to breathe. Helen's mind was groggy and unfocused as she pushed herself up from the floor. Her head felt like it was being smashed by a sledgehammer, heavier than an anvil. She sat, head in hands, trying to recall what had happened. What was she doing there on the floor?

The faint, muffled cries that had awakened her from her drugged slumber stirred her memory. She *did* remember; oh, how she'd love to *forget*. She got to her feet and slowly made her way to the locked bedroom door. It was after nine o'clock at night; she'd been asleep for hours. Stumbling to it in the darkness, she paused to find the light switch in the hall. Blinding her for a moment, she stood still as her eyes adjusted. Her hands trembled as she rubbed her face to help the blood return.

The curses from behind the door were aimed at her. She nervously inhaled, fearing the confrontation that lay ahead. She mustered all of her courage and turned the handle.

The lamp on the dresser burned dimly, casting shadows on the walls. The bed was unmade and ready for nighttime visitors, but the couple had more important matters on their minds than a good night's sleep. Neither could sit for very long without getting up and pacing. Carolyn finally rested on the dresser seat opposite her husband who continued to make a path through the master bedroom. She held a tissue to her face, absently wiping the tears that continued to fall. She'd not been able to believe all he had to share with her.

"Darren had to give up baseball season to come here," Malcolm was saying. "He's not sure if they will give him a scholarship, now." He glanced at his wife. "And, Lauren did not even complete the last two weeks of school. She missed her exams."

"Can she take them at the high school, here?" she asked. "I mean, they won't fail her, will they?"

"I think I can arrange it," Malcolm replied with a sigh. "I know the principal really well." He sat heavily on the bed. "The scholarship, I'm not sure."

"He won't really need one," Carolyn pointed out. "After all, if they accept our offer then—"

"Darren is a stubborn young man, dear," her husband said with a weary smile. "He doesn't want to take from us without earning it."

"Isn't there some way he could, then? There's more than enough work to do."

"I'm sure I can find sufficient to keep him busy."

Silence.

"There's only one true difficulty."

Carolyn's brows lifted. "And, that is—?"

Malcolm met her squarely in the eye. "Rex." Both swallowed hard at the mere mention of his name.

❧   ❧   ❧

The door creaked open and light filtered inside the musty quarters. Helen covered her mouth with her hand. The stench of urine nearly took her breath away. She flipped the light switch and his head turned with a start. "Wh-who's there?"

"It's me, Rex," she answered, stepping into his vision.

His eyes were mad with anger. He peered up into her face. "God, Helen, it's 'bout time! When th' hell did you get *home*?"

She swallowed hard. "Uh, not long ago. I fell asleep."

"Fell asleep?!" he shouted. "Goddamn, Helen, I'm layin' here dyin' and you're *sleepin'*?" He put his face into the tear-stained pillow to muffle his cries of pain.

"Are, are you all right, Rex?"

"Oh, my God," came the muffled reply. He raised his head unbelievingly at his wife. "Sure, Helen, I'm just great. Why don't we go down to th' Dip for a cone o'ice cream? Huh? And, while we're at it, let's take us a little trip, maybe go for a horseback ride!"

"Rex, I didn't mean—"

"Dammit, Helen! How's it look like I feel? Huh? Damn, I'm in pain, here! I've been beaten by your damn kids like a dog and all you can say is, '*Are you all right*?'! Goddamn, but you're a dumb ass!" Again, his head hit the pillow. Every movement, even to speak, proved too painful a venture. He breathed slowly and evenly, trying to ease the throbbing sensations.

Helen wiped the tears from her eyes. "Rex, I'm sorry. I'm sorry." She stood like a statue. "What can I do to help you? Just tell me."

Rex lifted his face from the bed and took a deep breath. "Well, it sure as hell would feel a lot better to be untied, Helen." He gave her a calm stare. "Didja hear me? Get me outta these ropes!"

She nodded. "Okay, Rex, okay. I'll get a knife." She stepped hurriedly from the room and returned in a moment. Very carefully, she cut the twine that held her husband prisoner. His wrists and ankles were rubbed raw from the rope; they were swollen and painful. She tried to massage them for him, but he groaned.

"Rex, you're gonna have to lay still," she instructed, "until I can clean you up. It looks pretty bad."

He groaned, again. "God, I feel like hell," he whispered. "Oh…"

Helen listened to his story, what she could decipher of it, as she prepared to cleanse his wounds. She got a pan of warm water and a soft cloth. Luckily, she had some salve left in the cabinet from Darren's baseball sliding accident and a bit of bandage, too.

Rex made little sense of the events. He, himself, knew little of what had happened aside from the beating. That his children had been the perpetrators, however, he was certain. He settled any doubt in Helen's mind about that. "I'll kill Lauren if I ever get my hands on her," he vowed as he tried to shift position. "She'll regret the day she did this to me. I'll see to it!"

Helen was silent as she immersed the cloth in the water. She slowly wrung it out and prepared to begin the task. "This is gonna hurt, Rex. Be ready," she warned.

"Be ready, *hell*! How am I supposed to get ready for—*a-a-o-o-o-w-w-w*!"

"I told you," she said quietly, as she pressed the rag on his shoulder.

"Aw, damn that hurts!" Rex whined. "Be careful, woman! Remember who this is!"

"I'll remember," Helen answered without emotion. She continued to remove the dried blood from his welted body. She was astounded by the damage done to him. There was hardly a spot unmarred by Lauren's leather weapon. The marks had risen, swollen, on the edges and were sliced open as if with a scalpel. The oozing sores were crusted with blood and fluid. It nearly turned her stomach.

The smell of the blood was enough to choke her, but mixed with his urine, it was unbearable. She held one hand to her mouth and used the other to do her nursing. Rex screeched curses at her and the children from the pain she inflicted from the cleansing, tensing from the scraping of his torn flesh. His head pounded, even to the aching of his teeth.

Finally cleaned, medicated, and bandaged as much as possible, he rested. Helen gave him one of her pills, and it soon rendered him unconscious. She did not want to risk his reopening the wounds that had begun to heal.

CHAPTER 5

*L*auren was awakened early Sunday morning by her aunt. She was informed that breakfast would be ready in half an hour, and she was expected to be present. There was another surprise: she would be attending a church service for the first time in her life.

Though she complained to Darren that she only wanted to hide in the bedroom, she accompanied the family to their church of many years, Edenton Baptist. She wore one of Kathy's old dresses, and her brother borrowed one of Malcolm's sport coats. The six of them rode in austere silence and arrived in time for Sunday School.

Both the Mitchell teens and Todd sat in the youth class while Marilyn was with the children and her mother. Carolyn had taught since before her husband had returned from the war; she never tired of telling young people about the Lord. Malcolm, too, was a teacher (for the adult men) and a deacon. They were joined by Kathy who came from the University across town.

The Prestons were well-known in their church, as were some of their closest friends, the Derebournes. One of Malcolm's old army buddies, Cary Derebourne III, owned Edenton Bank and Trust, as well as half of the city. It had been his father, in fact, who had turned his own law firm over to Malcolm. They were old money, but generous, too.

Cary's wife, Blanche, greeted Carolyn, and she stopped a few minutes to talk. Mrs. Derebourne had raised two sons, Cary IV and James; the younger had been missing in action for more than four years now over the Pacific. The heir to the fortune had yet to marry, and he had strayed from the family business of law and banking to manage the large property holdings and dabble in real estate. Since both he and his father kept the Preston Law Firm as their retainer, the three of them saw much of each other. Church, it seemed, was the only place they had to visit unofficially, and they enjoyed the time of fellowship.

The service was uneventful, and the Preston group left quickly. Both Malcolm and Carolyn knew how uncomfortable it might make their guests and did not want to ruin what they were sure was the Mitchells' first experience in a sanctuary. She had prepared a nice meal for them and it only took a few minutes to warm it up upon returning to the farm.

Kathleen assisted her mother and asked only a few questions about the presence of the cousins. She was answered curtly with a promise of explanation at a later time. They had not yet discussed their offer with Darren and Lauren. Their acceptance must come first.

It was later that same afternoon that Helen decided to call her sister. She continued to feed Rex her medicine so that he did not move from the bed. He had not eaten in over a day; he was never awake long enough. Carolyn was alone in the den when the telephone rang. She answered and stammered a hello when she recognized the voice. "H-hello, Helen."

"Carolyn, I n need to talk with you. Rex is asleep."

"What is it?" Carolyn's voice was remarkably calm.

"It's about the ch-children." Pause. "Darren and Lauren have run away." Long pause. "Have, have they b-been there?"

Carolyn cleared her throat. "Why do you think they'd come here, Helen?"

Helen nervously watched the bedroom door where Rex slept. She didn't think he could walk, but she'd take no chances. She lowered her voice. "Uh, well, you're *family*, Carolyn. Where else would they go?"

The Preston matron paused, unsure of what to say next. "If they were here, Helen, what would you want me to do?"

Helen's sigh of relief was evident. "Oh, thank God," she whispered into the receiver. "They are there, *aren't they*?" No response. "Please, Carolyn, tell me. They're my *children*." She began to cry.

Carolyn's pulse pounded in her ears. "Yes, Helen, they're here."

"Oh, thank God, thank God," she cried. "Oh, Carolyn, are they safe? I mean, are they all right?"

"Yes."

"Let me talk to them."

"No."

"What?" she asked, astounded.

"No."

"What do you mean? I can't talk to my own children?" her voice rose, slightly.

"Not now," Carolyn replied evasively. "They can't come to the phone." She paused. "What do you want me to tell them?"

Helen held the phone without answering for a long time. "Tell them we want them to come home," she said, softly. "Tell them that I'm not mad at them, and Daddy will promise not to be mad. Okay? Will you tell them we miss them?"

Carolyn almost dropped the receiver. She recovered quickly, her anger causing her voice to become frigid. "Of course. Is that all?"

"Y-yes," her sister answered, hesitatingly. "Carolyn? You all right?"

"Oh, I'm fine," she sneered, unable to stop herself. "Just fine. You take care, Helen." She slowly lowered the phone and broke the connection. In a few minutes, she was crying silently in her bedroom.

It was some time later that Malcolm found his wife, the tear-stained pillow at her side. She lay across their bed, the aforementioned pillow hugged tightly against her. With her eyes shut, she did not hear him enter.

He immediately slowed his step as he approached her. Carefully sitting beside of her prone body, he comforted her with his expression. "Are you all right, dear?" She had turned her head to see who had found her. She nodded, negatively. "What's wrong? Is it the children?"

Overcome by her fresh tears, she did not answer for a moment. "Oh, Lord, Malcolm, those poor children." She blew her nose in a handkerchief. "Their young minds so scarred by—"

"I know, I know," Malcolm interrupted as he placed his hand on her shoulder. "But, we'll do all we can to erase the terrible memories they have. I promise you that."

"It's not just them, though," she spoke softly as she brought herself to a sitting position beside of him. "I know *we* care about them, but their *parents* do not. I mean, how could they allow all of that to—" She broke off as she sobbed, falling to his chest. "Those are her children, Malcolm, her *children*. How could she let him—?"

Malcolm's body tensed as his eyes filled with tears. He could feel his wife as she shuddered inside of his embrace. He hated to see her hurt like this. "Oh, Malcolm," she whispered, "Helen's my sister. I've known her all her life and yet, I'd have never believed that she would be like this." She swallowed hard. "She called me a while ago."

Malcolm quickly released her and pushed her from him so he could look into her eyes. "When? What did she say? Does she know—I mean—that they're here?" The alarm was clearly in his voice.

"Yes, she knows they're with us."

"Well, what did she say about, about what happened?"

Carolyn smiled, wryly. "She didn't."

Malcolm stood and took a few steps away from the bed before turning to face her, again. "You mean, she said nothing about it? About Rex?"

"No," Carolyn answered softly. "She said only that they had run away, and they were worried about them. Oh, and, of course, they weren't mad at them."

"Not mad?!" Malcolm laughed in disbelief. "What kind of fools do they think we are? Do they actually believe we don't *know* what's happened?"

"I don't know." Carolyn shrugged her shoulders. "I just can't believe this is happening. I mean, I knew something was wrong when Darren called us and asked if they could come. But, I never could have imagined anything as horrible as this." She rose and walked to her husband. "I love you, Malcolm Preston. I truly do. But," she looked directly into his eyes as she spoke, "so help me God, I would kill you if you ever hurt one of our children like—"

Her husband squeezed her tightly, cutting off her sentence. "This hurts me, too. I can't imagine treating anyone's child like they have been, especially our own."

"My own *sister*, Malcolm," Carolyn reiterated. "My own sister!"

"Shh," he soothed as he held her close to his chest, her auburn hair tickling his chin. "Don't think about it, or you'll go crazy."

There was a brief pause before she responded. "They must never go back there, Malcolm. They must never return to that hell."

"No, my dear, they will not. This house must become their home. They will become one of us." Both prayed silently that their hopes would become reality.

CHAPTER 6

*H*elen lay exhausted on her bed, ragged from waiting on him. It had been only a week, and Rex was slowly recovering from the beating inflicted upon him, courtesy of his only daughter. The wounds were still painfully sore and swollen. He was forced to spend his days and nights face down on the bed, unable to even sit up and watch television in the living room. His wife was his constant nurse and receiver of profanity. She waited on him without complaint. He was unconscious from her drugs each night when she cried herself to sleep.

Malcolm used the respite to collect information for their case. He researched precedents related to their dilemma; they were few in number. He interviewed Darren several times throughout that first week, but never Lauren. In fact, they had yet to fully explain their intentions to her, though she assumed at the least they would protect her from her abusive father.

Darren spent his days on the basketball court when he was not doing odd jobs for his aunt and uncle. Todd would be a freshman in the fall semester and wanted to try-out for the team. He solicited Darren's help and found a ready coach. It did much for his mental health to escape, if only for a few hours, the stress of the uncertain future. He still had no word about a scholarship.

Carolyn had perhaps the most challenging assignment, Lauren. She was determined to be a good surrogate mother for the troubled teen. Although the younger was polite and sometimes helpful, she made no move to get close to her aunt. Carolyn's prayers were dominated by this simple request, peace for Lauren.

❧   ❧   ❧

It was a late Thursday night in July of 1961, a couple of weeks since the escape, that Malcolm received the call at his office. He was working late on some documents for a friend. His own practice, Preston Law Firm, had been established ten years before this. Sitting there at his massive desk, his hair was messy, and his eyes were tired. He had spent most of the day in court with little relief. It was a weary response he spoke into the receiver. "Malcolm Preston speaking."

"Jus' th' man I wanted to talk to," a cold, bitter voice responded. "I called your house, but Carolyn said you'd still be at your office."

Malcolm revived. "Yes, Rex, I've been expecting your call." His voice was steady, though his hands were not. He felt his heart begin to pound, and he cleared his throat nervously. "What's on your mind?"

"Goddamn, Malcolm, you know what's on my mind!" The prestigious lawyer mentally braced himself for the spiked conversation. "You've stole my damn kids from me!"

"I didn't steal them, Rex. They came for help," he replied, calmly.

"Help? What kinda help do they need from you? Shit, they're not worth anything to anybody but us!" the irate man screamed. "You got enough kids without mine."

Malcolm took a deep breath. "Rex, we've done nothing but protect them from harm these last few days. It was their choice to come here. We haven't made them do anything."

There was a long pause as Rex geared up for his final blow. "I want them back, Malcolm. They're comin' home with me and Helen."

Perspiration broke out on Malcolm's brow. He felt the tightness of fear in his chest as he heart ached for them. "No, Rex."

"What do you mean, no? Hell, they're mine! I raised them up, kept food in their bellies and clothes on their backs all their life, and now you say they're not comin' home?! Damn, but they will! Hellfire and damnation, Malcolm, they're my kids!"

Anger replaced his fear as he answered. "No, Rex, they're not going with you. Darren is of age and Lauren—"

"Is comin' home!" Rex finished for him. "You can't tell me that shit, Malcolm. I know my rights. Lauren's only sixteen, and she's comin' home—to *me*."

Silence.

"You may see her, Rex, but that's all. And, it has to be at my office."

"When?"

"Saturday at twelve."

"I'll be there. You can count on it," he spat as the receiver was slammed down on the machine. Malcolm gathered the last few papers from his desk and placed them in his briefcase. With a quick and confident step, he left the office and headed home. He was the bearer of tidings all would be interested to hear.

❀   ❀   ❀

Saturday morning a nervous Darren stood in the bedroom with his sister. He was dressed in a new navy suit, and Lauren had a dress to match it. Carolyn had taken them on Friday to the shopping center in Edenton. "Are you all right?" he asked softly as he stroked her hair. He was peering at her reflection in the mirror. Her pale countenance showed well her anxiety, and she tried to smile for him.

"Yeah, I'm all right. You know *me*." She turned and grasped his hands in hers. "*You know me*—" she began as tears filled her eyes.

"Yes, I know you, Lauren," Darren answered as she buried her head in his chest. "I do love you so." He ran his fingers through her long, blond locks. "Oh, Lauren, what a day this is!"

She pushed herself from him and looked into his face. "Oh, yes, what a day...one where I might be on my way back to Hadesville with *Daddy*." Her lip began to tremble as she spoke. "Oh, God, Darren, I'll have to see him today. I'll have to *see* him and maybe even go—" Her voice broke.

Darren grasped her head in his hands and lifted her face to him. "Don't talk like that, Lauren. Uncle Malcolm is prepared for today. He's gonna take care of us. You gotta believe that and be strong." He smiled reassuringly. "Promise?"

She forced the small smile in return. "Promise," she whispered. They joined hands and walked to the car together.

CHAPTER 7

"You still won't come?" Malcolm's eyes peered into those of his wife of almost twenty-two years.

"No," she answered softly, looking away. "I can't." There was a bit of silence before she continued. "I can't face her today, Malcolm. She's my sister and I must love her, but she is wrong. She's signing their death warrant by wanting them to go back there. I just can't see her today." Her fingers twisted as she wrung her hands.

"I know, Carolyn," he replied, "but the children need you. They need to know you support them. Please—"

"No!" Carolyn exclaimed, reeling, her sapphire eyes blazing. "Malcolm, I will not go!" She took a quick step toward him. "My prayers go with you, but I can't."

"But, Carolyn—"

"No!" her voice rang loudly in the large bedroom. "I tell you, I won't!"

Malcolm took a deep breath. "Putting your foot down, eh?" His near-smile made her want to smack him. "You know I hate it when you—"

"So help me God, Malcolm, I'll hurt you," she warned.

He laughed, letting some of the tension between them ease. "I'm sure you'd try." He ignored her growl. "It's just that I think we might need you—"

"I don't know what I might do," she interrupted him, solemnly. "I don't know what I would do to her." The mental images of her sister flashed through her brain, renewing her anger. "I just don't think I'd be able to control myself."

Malcolm sighed and pulled her into a strong embrace. Her head rested on his shoulder, and the tears fell onto his dress shirt. "All right, dear. It's all right. I understand," he comforted. "I'll tell them." He felt her head nod and kissed her lightly on the cheek as pulled her from him.

"Thank you, Malcolm."

"For what?" he asked with a smile.

"For giving in," she replied curtly.

"I didn't give in," he informed her. Her questioning expression made him explain further. "I just don't see any reason I should have to defend you for murder next week."

❦   ❦   ❦

It was a quarter before twelve that the Prestons arrived at the law firm. Malcolm escorted them to his inner office. Being Saturday, no one else was there. The meeting would be held in the small conference room. Darren held to Lauren's hand as they sat on the couch in their uncle's office. Neither said much. Nervousness had complete control of their minds; fear gripped their hearts.

Malcolm was unusually distant and fidgety. He, himself, had no idea what the meeting would bring to them. He prayed silently for peace, a lasting peace for the children who had known nothing but chaos all of their young lives.

A short, few minutes later, Malcolm answered the knock at the front door. Darren and Lauren strained their ears to hear what was being said, but only murmurs reached their anxious ears. Both teens jumped as the door to the room they were in opened to reveal Malcolm's calm figure. "Come with me, Lauren. Rex is waiting in the conference room." His kind eyes reassured her of his support.

Lauren brushed her long, blond bangs from her eyes and forced a smile for her brother. He squeezed her hand as she stood to leave him. "I love you," he whispered. She nodded.

As Lauren stepped into the hallway, she saw her mother. Helen stood by the secretary's desk, pale and emotionless. Lauren choked back a sob and followed her uncle. Malcolm motioned that Helen could wait in his office with Darren. She reluctantly agreed. Stepping into the room, she sat opposite her son in a wooden chair. Darren's chest tightened, and he coughed.

Meanwhile, Malcolm opened the door to the conference room and allowed his niece to enter first. She walked inside the doorway and stopped cold. Her blond locks again blurring her vision, she raised her hand to smooth them away. As she lifted her head, her pale eyes met those of her father.

They stood, transfixed, for a long moment. Lauren felt a single shiver run up her spine at the glare. Of all the years she had been peering into the devilish blue eyes of Rex, she had never seen such an expression as in that moment. A hatred, burning, smoldering, and blazing as if stoked like a fire, raged within them. It was a look not so unlike the one she had given him just a few weeks before as she had whipped him with many a bloody stroke.

Malcolm was speechless. He watched them as they tortured one another by their silence. He prayed even more fervently for success. His musings, however, were broken by Rex's offensive.

"Well, little Lauren," he grinned slyly, "how things have changed. Eh, little girl?"

"Yes, things have changed," she spoke softly. "I'm not a little girl any more, *Rex*."

"'Th' hell you ain't! I'm your *daddy*," Rex sneered. "You're jus' a baby, Lauren, a baby! And, you're comin' home with your mama and me. So, be ready, little girl!"

"I'm not going with you. Not today, not ever."

He took a quick step toward his daughter. "Damn girl, I'll show you who says what you'll do and not do—"

"Hold it there, Rex," Malcolm raised his hand in interruption. "We've come to talk. Let's keep it at that."

Rex smirked. "Yeah, we'll talk, for now." He stared into Lauren's eyes that showed her fear. She was nauseous. "So, what's to talk about? She's my kid and we're goin' home. There's nothin' else to say."

"Much more, Rex," Malcolm began, "much more. You'd better sit down." Rex did so tentatively and Lauren choking back a smile, relaxed a bit, memories of her recent victory coming to the forefront of her mind. Malcolm opened the briefcase on the table. "These are papers that will give Carolyn and me legal guardianship of Lauren. Darren is already old enough to be on his own, therefore—"

"Damn!" Rex exclaimed. "I knew you'd pull some of this legal shit on me." He slammed a fist on the table. "No, Malcolm, no! She's my daughter, dammit, and she's goin' home with us. Do you hear me? *With us!*"

❦   ❦   ❦

There was dead silence in the office where Helen and Darren sat. Both held their hands in their laps, their eyes on the floor. Neither knew where to begin. Finally, Darren found his voice.

"I'm sorry. We never meant to hurt you." Tears dripping from his face fell onto the floor. He looked up into his mother's weary face as he knelt in front of her. There were tears in her eyes as well.

"Oh, Darren," she whispered, "my Darren." She embraced him and held tightly for a long time, oblivious to the fury of the inner room.

❦   ❦   ❦

"Rex, be reasonable. We can give Lauren everything she needs. She'll go to college—"

"No!" he screamed. "You think because you got money you can wave it in front of her nose, and she'll follow you like a puppy and do everything you say. Well, you're wrong! *She's not the kid you think she is.*" Rex turned his powerful gaze to the girl of sixteen who was tossed in the balance. "You don't know who you're wantin' to help. *But, I do.*" Malcolm was silent. He, too, was mesmerized by the dancing pupils of the man's eyes. "She's made her bed and now she's gonna lay in it, Malcolm. She started this and I'm gonna finish it. She's gonna get what she asked for, dammit, or else!"

Malcolm faced Lauren. Though she was ashen, her hands trembling from nervous energy, she managed to motion for him to leave the room. At her uncle's silent protest, she confirmed her decision. With heavy heart and curious mind, he stepped from the room, being mindful to not be too far from the door should she call for him.

❦   ❦   ❦

Darren still cried on his mother's shoulder as she gently pushed him from her. He peered into her red eyes and felt something being thrust into his hands. He looked down and saw an envelope from Edenton University. Hastily, he tore it open, hands quivering. He unfolded the crisp letter and read it quickly…a scholarship! For the fall semester! His grin was welcomed by his mother who was wiping her nose with a tissue.

Helen whispered into his ear, "Hide it, Darren. You're father doesn't know I dug it out of the trash and brought it to you. He'd kill me." Darren solemnly folded it and placed it in his jacket pocket with an unspoken thank-you.

＊   ＊   ＊

As the door to the conference room quietly closed behind Malcolm, Rex smiled in apparent victory. "Well, come to your senses, eh, little girl?" He pushed his chair back and stood, placing a hand to his belt buckle. "Knew better, didn't you? Well, at least, you will when I get through with you."

Lauren stood, as well, silently gathering strength. She could see the bloodshot veins in his eyes. He rolled his tongue over his teeth and smoothed his short, blond crew cut with his hand. "You know, Lauren, all these weeks, all I could think about was *you*. Just a little whore who got what she deserved and then turned on her old man. Yeah, turned on him, her own *daddy*." He was so close, now, she could feel his hot breath on her face.

"Thought you were pretty smart, eh, Lauren? Takin' advantage of your old man like that? Yeah, pretty damn smart. Well, it don't seem so damn smart, now, does it? *Does it?*" he snarled as he grabbed a fistful of her hair. "Huh? What 'bout, now, Lauren? How smart does it feel, now?" He slung her hard from him. She grabbed the side of the table to keep from falling to the floor.

Rex's hollow laugh filled the room. "How th' hell did you think you'd get away with it, Lauren? Huh? What'd you think you was gonna do? Run to Malcolm? He can't do nothin', Lauren, not a damn thing. So, you'd better get that straight right here and now." His figure moved closer to her, and he gave her a cocky grin. "So, whatcha gonna do now, huh? What th' hell you gonna do, now?"

"*This*, you bastard!" she gritted through clenched teeth as she shoved him with all of her strength to the floor flat on his back. He gurgled with the pain from his tender sores being pressed onto the marble floor. She gave him no chance to retaliate; she pressed her knees onto his shoulders and enclosed her hands around his throat.

"Listen to me, damn you, and listen well," she said menacingly. "I'm never going back with you. So, get that straight right now. *I'm never going back with you.*" She lifted his head and pounded it against the floor to make her point. "Either you sign those papers, or I'll-make-you-wish-you-had."

Rex sputtered in fury. "Damn girl! Let me up from here!" He was so angry with himself he could have died. "I'll never sign those papers, dammit, never!"

"You will or you'll be sorry you didn't," she warned, again. "I'll take you to court and then, then old man, they'll hear it all—every bit of it."

"Of what? You got nothin' on me!"

"What about my whole life? You beat me more than that one night, you *bastard*!"

"Jus' a man takin' care of his kids! No one will blame me for disci-plinin'!"

"Maybe not, but they'll sure as hell be interested in the rest! Oh, won't they though!" She laughed with her sense of power, leaning close to whisper in his ear, "I'll tell them *what we did*. That we stripped you naked and tied you down. That I took your *belt* and then—"

"*N-n-o-o-o-o-o-o*!" Rex wailed from the depths of his being. "Never! No one is gonna know 'bout *that*!"

"They will before I'm through," Lauren cooed. "They'll know every single detail—*everything*." She peered into the eyes that showed only fear, now, a cold, hard fear.

"No," Rex whispered between gasps of pain, "I won't let you." She tightened her grip on him. "I'll let him have you, you little slut. He can *have* you."

Chest tight with emotion, Lauren released him and carefully got to her feet. She had the pen and document ready by the time her father limped to the table. With a shaky grip, he signed them.

It was over.

CHAPTER 8

❀

$\mathcal{M}$alcolm turned with a start at the slam of the conference room door. Rex, sweltering with fury, moved quickly in search of his wife. He held the legal document in his fist. "Helen, dammit, where are you?"

"Comin', Rex," she called as she hurried from the inner office. Darren did not follow immediately. Had his sister won, or lost everything?

"Sign this damn paper. We're goin' home," Rex spoke through gritted teeth.

Helen did as she was told. "What 'bout Lauren?" asked his wife, hesitantly.

"Stayin' with them," he sneered as he glared at the astonished Malcolm who breathed a sigh of relief. "Let's get th' hell outta here." In a matter of minutes, they were gone. Darren rushed out of the office and stared at his uncle in disbelief.

"It's over." Both turned and saw Lauren emerge from the conference room. Her face glistened with fresh tears. "It's finally over." Her brother wept as he embraced her.

Darren shared his good news during the ride home. Edenton University had offered him a baseball scholarship for the champion Edenton Colonels. He would be provided with room, board, and books, but the tuition was his responsibility.

Malcolm assured the young man that it would be no problem. Darren insisted upon working on the farm for the money, and his uncle agreed. For the first time in his life, his goal of teaching high school and coaching baseball was attainable.

Puffy, white clouds were scattered across the sky that next morning, Sunday. It was as though nature, itself, were celebrating. The humidity had declined, and a light breeze blew on Lauren's pale shoulders. All gathered in the car dressed in their best garments and went to church. Darren smiled a lot and his sister tried to be as cheerful. Although she was thrilled with the success of the previous day, she was still much troubled by the upheaval in her life. She'd told no one what happened in the conference room; she kept that to herself.

Lauren had only reluctantly agreed that morning to attend the services with her new family. She had no desire to go to the church; however, she was soon to learn her preference meant nothing. Church was not an option. Though rankled by their insistence, she chose to fight that battle another day.

❦   ❦   ❦

The summer months passed more quickly than any of them imagined they would. Darren spent his time divided between work and play. Todd enjoyed having a private coach and learned well. It kept the soon-to-be college man occupied and not worrying about his sister.

Lauren rarely ventured from her room. She had been allowed to use Kathy's old hi-fi and listened to all the records that were there. Her aunt had taken her to town and purchased a wardrobe that would suffice until winter. She thanked them with little more than cold indifference.

In fact, except upon rare occasions when bothered by Marilyn or besot with memories, the sixteen-year-old showed little emotion.

She was distant and nearly untouchable, if not for her brother. He was the only one in whom she would confide.

❧   ❧   ❧

Kathleen Elizabeth Preston completed her pre-law coursework in early August. She had already been accepted by Vanderbilt in Nashville, Tennessee, and would move there to complete her degree. The family gathered the night before her flight for a farewell dinner at the farm.

After they had eaten, the spacious living room filled with family. Kathy, on the couch with her father, laughed merrily and spoke of his days in law school. On the opposite of the room sat Carolyn with her arms snaked around her youngest, Marilyn. They, too, were enjoying themselves.

Lauren sat by herself, thinking of all that she witnessed. It was obvious, actually always had been, that the eldest Preston was a daddy's girl. Kathleen was not unkind to her mother, but the relationship was different. Perhaps it was her major—law—that bonded her to her father so closely; Lauren did not know.

The youngest seemed partial to her mother; Marilyn was at her feet most of the time. Since her father worked so much and spent the other spare moments supervising the boys on their work on the farm, she saw relatively little of him. Besides, Carolyn had always said there was no mistaking Marilyn for being anyone's but hers. She reminded her so much of herself during those young years.

Where did that leave Todd? Lauren wondered. At the moment, he was engaged in conversation with Darren, his idol. They worked together both on and off the court and had become good friends. He seemed quite happy, she supposed, receiving equal attention from both. Not that the girls didn't—it was just different, somehow.

As Lauren peered about the pleasant scene, she thought of her own family, her real family. When had they ever even sat together, much less talked and had a good time doing it? *Never*. She felt the familiar tightening of her chest as she mentally pictured her parents. They had caused her so much harm in her sixteen years. Could she ever be able to forgive them and move on? She doubted it.

❦   ❦   ❦

Lauren was scheduled to attend Edenton High as a junior that September, provided she complete her exams the first week, the ones held over from the previous year. She would be joined by Todd, who was a freshman. Both would ride the bus with the youngest, Marilyn, a fourth-grader. And, Darren went to college. It was that change which proved to be of such an impact to Lauren.

The entire family, excluding Kathy who was already in her new apartment, stood on the front porch the day Darren would leave for school. Todd "high-fived" his friend and wished him luck. Little interested in the tearful affair, Marilyn darted across the lawn after her new kittens. Carolyn reminded him to be careful in the selection of his new friends and teammates and to call often. He promised that he would.

Malcolm sat in the car; the clothes were loaded and the dormitory awaited them. He had already assured the young man of the tuition money and spending cash for the first month. He would drive Darren to the University and give him assistance.

Lauren was the last to say her goodbyes. Her eyes were red-rimmed with tears having cried most of the night. "I guess this is it," she said, softly.

"Don't say it like that, Lauren," he replied with a grin. "You make it sound like I'm dyin'."

"I feel like you are," she answered, unamused.

"Don't be silly," he urged as he hugged her close. "C'mon, get hold o'yourself."

Again, her tears rolled. "Oh, Darren, please," she begged, "*please*, don't leave me. You promised you never would—"

"I'm not leaving *forever*," he insisted, pulling her away from his shoulder and looking into her eyes. "I'll be back every month and call as much as I can." She was unimpressed. "You've got them to take care of you for me," he said, motioning to their relatives. "Don't worry, everything is going to be *fine*."

"No, it's not," she said in a whisper. "They're not *you*. They won't understand. They don't know what—"

"Yes, they do understand," Darren broke in, "and they are going to do everything right by you. You'll see." He wiped the tears from her cheeks. "You have two wonderful parents, now, and—"

"They're not my parents," she pointed out in an angry tone that surprised him. "They're only my guardians. They'll give me a place to stay and that's all."

Darren sighed. "They'll be more than that," he promised. "And, besides, we're never really separated—you and me." Puzzled, she just looked at him. With a smile, he lifted the locket from around her neck. "This binds us together—our bond. Every time you see it, remember that."

Lauren grasped his hand over the silver locket. "I will, *Darewin*. I promise." He choked back a sob of his own as he wrenched free of her grip and stepped into the car. She watched the car disappear into a swirl of dust from the driveway.

CHAPTER 9

Carolyn Preston was busily setting the small kitchen table when she heard her niece's quiet step on the stair. It was early morning of the first day of school. Hot pancakes and syrup awaited the students.

Lauren's fragile figure slowly came into view. She wore a pale pink dress that Darren had chosen on their shopping outing before he left for college. The locket dangled around her neck, a good luck charm. She appeared tired even though she'd been the first to retire the evening before.

"Good morning," Carolyn greeted her. "It's good to see you ready so early. I dare say Todd and Marilyn will be another ten minutes." She smiled warmly. "I always have a special breakfast for the first day of school," she went on, since her niece did not respond. "It sets the year off right." Lauren merely nodded.

Silence reigned as the two sat at the table staring at one another. There was so much that Carolyn wanted to say, but just didn't know how to begin. She wanted to reassure her, to make her feel at home. Would she ever be able to convey her love to the teen?

"I want you to have a good time today, Lauren," she finally spoke. "I know it will be different—and difficult. But, this is a new beginning, a new start. Don't forget that." Lauren lifted her head and peered into the deep blue eyes of her aunt. At times, she reminded her of Helen. But, oh, how different they were…

"I'm so scared."

It was only then that Carolyn noticed the tears in the girl's eyes. "Oh, Lauren," she whispered as she rose and stepped toward her niece. Her outstretched arms were met by Lauren's fragile body. Both cried. By the time Marilyn and Todd arrived for breakfast, Carolyn and Lauren had control of their emotions. Malcolm soon joined in the celebration, and for a treat drove them to school.

❖   ❖   ❖

Darren's letters came like clockwork each week. He wrote of professors, tests, and cafeteria food. He was obviously enjoying himself and doing well. His notes of love to Lauren were her life-line. She needed him as she always had.

Lauren's start in school that fall was not as successful as her brother's. She declined joining any clubs or becoming involved in extracurricular activities. Despite her guardians' urging, she merely did her time and came home.

The bus ride, itself, was a whole new experience. At home, she had walked to school. Now, however, living in the country meant a long ride to and from the school. While Todd sat with his own friends, Marilyn sat with her. The constant presence of the fourth-grader was resented by the withdrawn teen, and she pushed the child further and further away emotionally.

Meanwhile, Darren adjusted well to college life. He and his room-mate, Thatcher McKinley, a first-baseman, would play together during the spring season. He was like a plant just being allowed to sit in the sun after a long vacation in the closet. Darren bloomed.

Perhaps it was that Lauren had not shown any interest in school that her behavior in mid-October shocked her guardians. Maybe it was the fact she'd hardly spoken to them in the nearly four months she'd been in their home. Whatever the reason, an ordinary Friday evening turned sour for the Preston household, and Lauren was at the center of it.

The third football game of the season was at home. Todd arranged to spend the night with a friend so he could attend. It was the rivalry game with nearby Greenfield High and promised to be a doozy. Lauren decided at the last minute she, too, would go to the game.

She came downstairs wearing a tan skirt and sweater in Edenton green. Her hair fell to her shoulder blades, a shimmering gold. Marching into the living room, she faced her aunt and uncle. "I'm ready to go," she announced. Marilyn, at the piano, glanced up from practicing the dreaded lessons.

"Go where, dear?" Carolyn asked, confusion clearly on her face. Malcolm looked up from the evening paper.

"To the game," she clarified. "We play tonight in half an hour."

Carolyn looked at Malcolm; Marilyn ceased her pecking. Clearing his throat, the eldest began, "Lauren, you haven't made any plans with us. We didn't say you could go to the game."

"But, Todd went," she insisted quickly.

"True enough," Malcolm went on, "but he checked with us before leaving." He paused. "Who was going to take you?"

Lauren's surprise quickly turned to anger. "I thought *you* would drive me."

"But," he pointed out, "you didn't ask, Lauren."

"I didn't think I had to," she replied stiffly.

Malcolm turned to Carolyn who motioned for Marilyn to leave the room. She did so, reluctantly. Lauren watched her cousin's exit with growing indignation. "Sit down, Lauren," he instructed her, "and we'll talk about this." Warily, she did so.

"Lauren," Malcolm began, again, "your aunt and I realize that you are a young woman and capable of making some decisions for yourself. We truly understand your need for independence. After all, we were once your age, too." He paused. "However, we also deserve to be respected."

"I do respect you."

"Respect includes consideration for others, Lauren," he pointed out. "You did not consider us in your decision. You chose to attend whether or not we would be willing to cooperate with you. That was inconsiderate."

Carolyn added, "We are responsible for you, now, Lauren. You are like one of our children and—"

"No!" Lauren interrupted quickly, jumping to her feet. "I am not one of your children. I've left my real parents and become an adult, so don't think you can treat me like that." Her face flushed red with emotion. "I won't be under anyone's control, *ever*."

"You are our ward and you *will* obey us," Carolyn strongly insisted, her own temper rising. "We are not treating you like a child, but giving you the blessing of caring and loving parents who act responsibly in their care for you. Whether you always agree with us or not, we will be respected!"

"Well, I don't agree with that," Lauren replied coldly. "You can't order me around like a two-year-old. You can't even control that fourth-grader who drives me insane. Surely you don't expect to control *me*." She laughed, albeit nervously. "I appreciate all you've done; I really do. But, when I left home, I said that nobody would ever tell me what to do again. *Ever*." Lauren's eyes turned a deep blue and burned into the hearts of her guardians.

Carolyn Preston was not accustomed to being spoken to in such a manner from a mere teen. She walked across the room and stood directly in front of her niece. The same eyes that had blazed in her direction were now aimed at Lauren. The matron peered down into the angry expression of her niece.

"Listen, young lady, and listen *well*. As long as I am responsible for you, you will *obey* me. I will allow you to participate in activities that I deem appropriate for you. But, I will not allow you to show disrespect for me." She took a long breath. "I *love* you, Lauren, more than you can know. I only want what is best. We are here for you and will help in any way we can, but our feelings and wishes must be respected and taken into consideration."

Malcolm quickly added, "If you had only asked us, Lauren, we would have made plans for you. It was just that simple. But as it is—"

"It's what?" Lauren asked with an ill-timed sneer.

"As it is," he replied sharply, "we deny you this privilege. You did not ask, rather, you demanded to go. Because of your disrespect, you will not go tonight."

Hot tears blurred her vision. Lauren's fists, clenched tightly at her sides, were white with her grasp. "So, that's it, huh?" She turned to the door and took a couple of quick steps before reeling for the final blow. "I hate you for this. I really do." In a moment, she was gone from the room.

"Lauren! Lauren, come back here!" Carolyn called. At no response, she started for the door, herself. Malcolm stopped her.

"Let her go, now, dear," he said, softly. "Give her some time."

"Time?" Carolyn looked at him eyes wide with surprise. "She's had enough time to see the truth, Malcolm. What I ought to give her is—"

"She'll come around," he interrupted with a worried frown, even as the back door slammed shut.

Carolyn sat in her chair with a sigh. "We hope."

Malcolm resumed reading his paper.

CHAPTER 10

*L*auren softly stroked the nose of Comet, the gentle horse she had come to love. Tears fell from her cheeks in streams. "Oh, maybe *you*'ll understand," she whispered, "understand more than anyone." She then secured the saddle and bridle. Mounting, she grasped the reins and rode from the stable into the pasture.

Meanwhile, Marilyn poked her head inside the living room where her mother sat, pondering. Malcolm had gone to his study to work on a few papers from the office. It was his way of worrying without letting his wife know it. The girl quietly entered and sat opposite the reflective woman. "Mom, you busy?"

Carolyn's eyes met those of her daughter. Her face was still solemn. "I don't suppose. You need me for something?" Her voice revealed her fatigue.

"Well, kinda," the nine-year-old said. "I was wonderin'. Is Lauren in trouble?"

Carolyn laughed in spite of herself. "Now, I don't see that it's any of your business, one way or the other." She gave her daughter a sly look. "Eh, young lady?"

"Well," grinned the girl, "I was jus' wonderin'."

"Yes, and you'll continue to wonder," he mother replied. "Now, I believe it's your bedtime."

Marilyn grimaced. "Oh, yeah."

"Pardon?"

"Oh, yes, ma'am," she corrected.

Carolyn patted her shoulder as she rose from the couch. "See you in the morning, sweetheart. Pleasant dreams."

"You, too, Mom," she nodded and kissed her mother's cheek.

"I'll try," Carolyn said without confidence. "I'll try."

※   ※   ※

It was a knock on the front door that awakened the sleeping Carolyn who lay on the sofa. It was eleven o'clock, and Lauren had not yet returned to the house. Despite the fact Malcolm had assured her that the teen would, she simply could not go to bed not knowing. She jumped from her fitful slumber and hurried to the front door. "Lauren?" she asked, hopeful, as she swung it open.

To her surprise, Darren stood on the other side of the threshold, his smile quickly fading. "Aunt Carolyn, what's wrong? Where's Lauren?"

His aunt wearily motioned him inside the foyer. "Oh, Darren, come in. It's so good to see you."

"Who is it, dear?" Malcolm's voice called as he entered in his bathrobe. Before she could respond, he smiled and welcomed his nephew. "Darren! What a surprise!"

The college freshman again posed his question, this time with trembling lips. "Where is Lauren? What's wrong?" Malcolm and Carolyn exchanged glances.

※   ※   ※

"Where would she have gone?" Darren asked as he peered into the faces of his relatives. They were seated at the kitchen table discussing the situation. "Does she have friends here?"

Carolyn shook her head sadly. "Not any that we know of. She keeps to herself." She placed her hand on his. "She's all right, Darren.

She likes to ride and has gone for a while. My mount, Comet, is gone. He's the one she prefers. She'll come back soon."

Darren wondered about that. He had already explained to them why he'd shown up unexpectedly on the doorstep. Having a queasy feeling he couldn't shake, he had taken the bus to the nearest station and walked to the farm, only to find his sister missing. If he ever got his hands on her...

"I thought I heard something just then," Malcolm interrupted his thoughts. All three walked to the window facing the stable nearby. "Look!" A figure led a horse inside the dimly lit barn and the door closed behind her.

"See?" Carolyn whispered. "I told you. She just wanted to be left alone."

"I'm going to talk to her," Darren said firmly.

"No," his uncle disagreed. "Leave her alone tonight. We know she's safe, now." At Darren's pleading eyes, he added, "She'll learn that we're here for her, always. Give her time. You can talk to her in the morning."

"Yes, sir," Darren answered as the trio walked from the room, extinguishing the lights. Only moments later, the lurking figure stole into the kitchen. After locking the back door behind her, she hurried to her warm bed.

❋   ❋   ❋

Darren's tired figure, fully dressed, stood outside the door to his sister's bedroom. It was early, only six o'clock. He could wait no longer, so he knocked. A shuffling of drawers was heard. He knocked, again. "Leave me alone!" she shouted, angrily.

"Please—" he began.

"I said, leave me alone! I want nothing to do with you!"

Darren took a deep breath and slowly turned the knob. The door creaked open to reveal a flushed and angry girl. "Not even me?" he asked.

The look of astonishment on Lauren's face was incredible. She sat on her bed, open-mouthed. She could not believe her eyes. "Darren," she whispered.

"You remember me?" he asked with a smile. "I thought maybe you'd forgotten."

"Oh, Darren," she said as she rushed to place her arms around him. "Oh, God, it's so good to see you. I've missed you so much."

"It's only been two weeks," he replied, even as the stray tears fell onto her golden hair. "But, I've missed you, too." Darren pulled away from his sister and motioned for her to sit on the bed. She pulled her robe around her nervously, sniffling from her late excursion. "Lauren, I want you to tell me about yester—"

"But, I don't—"

"No buts about it, Lauren," he said sternly. "We're going to talk about it, now." She lowered her head and stared at the floor. His voice became harsh. "Lauren, it's no use tryin' to deny it. I already know most of it, any way." Her eyes were wide as she raised her head to seek his face. "But, I want to hear it from you. What did you do?"

Lauren felt his burning stare. "I-I don't know," she said, evasively.

"Aw, c'mon, Lauren!" he exclaimed as he jumped to his feet and crossed the room. "Tell me the truth. What is goin' on here?" When she did not respond, he sighed. "It's me, *Darren*. Tell me, Lauren. Tell me what's goin' on inside that head of yours." With his expression bearing down on her, she began to cry.

❧   ❧   ❧

Malcolm and Carolyn prepared breakfast for their family together. He offered to cook the bacon and sausage, and she happily agreed. The biscuits, however, were her domain. Both had been awake for the greater portion of the night worrying about their ward. A few minutes later, Marilyn bounded into the kitchen, full of energy, as usual. "Hi, Mom, Dad!"

"Good morning to you," Malcolm replied with a smile. "You're up awful early for a Saturday, aren't you?"

"I guess," she answered shyly. "I just thought I'd get up. That's all."

"Uh-huh," Carolyn drawled.

"Just thought you'd get up, eh?" Malcolm asked with a smile as he crunched a piece of bacon between his teeth.

"Yes, sir," Marilyn replied slowly. "That's all." She sat in an empty chair. "So, what's goin' on around here?" Her hazel eyes darted from one parent to the other.

Carolyn cleared her throat, loudly. "Whatever are you talking about, dear?"

The child had withstood all she could. "About Lauren!" she exclaimed, exasperated at their teasing. "Where was she last night? She didn't go to bed!"

Her parents exchanged glances. Malcolm spoke first. "And, what were you doing in her room last night? You have been told, I believe, not to disturb her."

The young girl blushed and squirmed. "Well, uh, I was worried about her and went to check." Her auburn hair was awry and she attempted to smooth it from her face.

"Yes," her mother added, "and I'd already told you to go to bed."

"Y-yes, ma'am," she stammered. "But, I wanted to see if she was all right." There was silence as the adults considered her plea. Her mother responded.

"Marilyn, I know that you are curious about your cousin," she began, "but you must obey our wishes. Lauren is trying to adjust to her life here, and it's not easy. She needs her privacy. Please let us deal with the problem."

"I assure you," Malcolm added, "that, in time, Lauren will want to spend a lot of time with you. She loves you; she just doesn't know how to show it. Okay?"

Marilyn considered her parents' advice. "Just want to know, is all," she insisted. "Curious."

Carolyn laughed. "Yes, we know, but, uh, you remember about the cat?"

Marilyn returned her smile. "Yes, ma'am," she giggled. "I gotcha."

CHAPTER 11

"*I*'m sorry, Darren, so sorry," Lauren cried into her hands. "I want to tell you. I really do."

Darren felt his chest tighten and swallowed hard. "Oh, Lauren," he said softly as he sat by her on the bed. "It's okay. Just tell me what happened."

She sniffed and wiped her nose with a tissue she'd gotten from the bed stand. "Okay, okay." She turned and looked at him with eyes red and swollen. This was not the first time she had cried today, he thought. "I decided to go to the game at school, you know, football." He nodded. "Well, it's the first time I felt like doing something extra. So, I got dressed and went downstairs. I thought Uncle Malcolm would take me. I knew that Todd was gonna be there—"

"But," Darren interrupted, "you didn't ask." She shook her head. "Why not, Lauren? Why didn't you just ask?"

Her anger flared. "I didn't think, Darren, okay? I just didn't think. I thought he'd take me. So what?"

"So what?" her brother asked in surprise. "So, you shouldn't have thought it, that's what! What do you think they are? Slaves?"

"No!" she replied fiercely. "I just thought they'd been so good that they would. That's all."

Darren shook his head in disbelief. "You've got this thing all wrong, Lauren. They haven't said they'd let you do whatever you want and when and pay for it besides. C'mon, Sis, give me a break!"

Lauren roughly removed herself from the bed and pranced to the other side of the room. "Whose side are you on, huh?!"

"Yours!" he answered as adamantly as she'd posed the question. "I'm on your side, Lauren. I want what is best for you, plain and simple."

There was a long pause as she regrouped. Darren held his breath as he waited. She stepped toward him before beginning her argument. "When we left home, Darren, we did it to be *free*. We wanted to be free from anybody telling us every move to make. Ain't that what we did? Ain't that what we *wanted*?"

Darren slowly stood. "Lauren, we left home to get away from *him*."

"Yes, and what he did was control us. We wanted freedom!"

"Not to do what we pleased! God, Lauren, you're talkin' crazy. This is crazy!"

"I am not crazy!" she screamed back at him. "And, don't you ever say that I am. You hear me?" Her eyes danced.

"Lauren," he said gently in an attempt to calm her, "please listen to me. Uncle Malcolm and Aunt Carolyn have been very good to us, better than anyone ever has. They are sacrificing to let us come here. I'm in college, and you're safe! C'mon, let's at least be thankful for that." He waited for her to agree with him; she did not. "They are good parents, Lauren. We knew that or we wouldn't have come here in the first place. Why fight them? All they want to do is help you."

"And, tell me what to do!" she exclaimed. "Like, like I was one of their kids!"

"Well, you are in a way."

Lauren looked at him sharply. "*I am not.*"

"Yes, you are, Lauren. They're your guardians. You knew that when you got Daddy to sign that paper. By law, they are legally responsible for you just like a parent. Like it or not, you're one of their children."

"No!" she spat as she reeled away from him. "No, Darren, I will not like it. I don't need more parents." She turned with a glare. "I'd think we'd had enough of those." Silence filled the room. Both were transfixed by her words. Emotions ran through them like lightening.

Darren took a deep breath. "I am only going to say this once, Lauren, so you better listen up," he warned. "Daddy treated us like dogs, not children. He had no thought for our well-being, our happiness, our hopes—none but his own. He terrorized his wife until she could not even be a mother to us. We haven't had parents, Lauren. We had an *existence* and that was all.

"We've had the good fortune to escape once and for all. We were able to come and be with people who loved us, who *cared*. They have done more for us in four months than our parents did in our *lives*." His voice trembled as he spoke from his heart. "They deserve our love and respect. Whether or not you can love them, Lauren, is up to you. But, you will show them respect and obey them because as far as I am concerned, they are your parents. I'll support any decisions they have concerning you. Don't doubt it."

Darren gripped his sister's shoulders and peered down into her shocked expression. "All they want is for you to be happy and you can't even see that. All you care about is *you*, what *you* have been through. What do you think about me? Huh? I've had to watch you beaten to within an inch of your life over and over and—" He stopped, the tears choking him. "Well, you can give that up, Lauren. *Give it up*. That pity thing isn't going to work, okay? It's *over*. Do you understand? Over!"

Lauren's face had become beet red. "I can't believe you!" she exclaimed furiously. "You're siding with them against me. Your own *sister*!" She raised her hands and shoved him from her. He retreated a few steps. "I don't have to respect them because *you* tell me to."

Darren swiped at the tears creeping from his eyes. "In all the years I can remember, I never knew you to smart-off or be disrespectful to Daddy. No matter what he did, how hard he hit you, how mean he was—you *never* showed him disrespect. It was always yes, sir, no, sir. You never disobeyed his direct order. Yet, you feel no regret for having done those things to the only people who have ever cared for us." He had grown angry and impatient.

"What's the matter, Lauren? Do you only respect someone who holds you in utter fear for your life? What's it take, a good beating to get your attention? Huh? Is that it? Would you be more agreeable if you thought Uncle Malcolm would knock you across the room if you looked at him the wrong way? Is that the problem? 'Cause, if it is, I can take care of that *myself*!"

Lauren's eyes grew wide with fear as Darren quickly removed his belt from his jeans. Her heart pounded inside of her chest. What in the world had come over him? "D-D-Darren, have you g-gone crazy?" she stammered.

"No, just smart," he replied convincingly. "Now I know how to deal with you." He shook his fist full of leather at her. "This is all you understand? Fine. Get ready!"

Lauren fell backwards on the floor as she moved away from him. "D-Darren, please, listen to me. Don't d-do this, p-please," she pleaded as she crawled back to the wall. "I'm s-sorry!"

Towering over her, he ordered. "Get up." Her hands trembling, she warded him off. "Get up," he repeated. Slowly, she obeyed him, keeping her back flat against the wall. Her eyes never left his hands.

Lauren watched as he carefully doubled the belt into a loop and grasped it tightly in his right hand. Raising it high, he made the motion to bring it down across her thigh. She sucked in her breath as he released. A second before he struck, his arm stilled. The belt hung harmlessly from his fist. Slowly she opened her eyes only to meet his gaze.

"I was right, Lauren," he told her. "You've never known life without it." He paused and swallowed hard. "Life doesn't have to be this way. Uncle Malcolm and Aunt Carolyn don't want you to live in fear. Not that you shouldn't be afraid of their punishment, but rather *choose* to obey. They only want your respect and love. Is that too much to ask? Is it really that great a sacrifice?" His eyes pleaded for her agreement.

"I can't believe you did this!" She pushed him away as she moved to the window. "I-I can't believe you did this to me. God, what were you thinking? I could have died just then. *God!*"

Darren turned toward her, begging for her understanding. "Lauren, please listen to me. *I love you.* I'm only trying to help you see that you're wrong. You *must* obey them. It will bring happiness to you. I *promise!*"

"Yeah, right," she smirked. "That's easy for you to say. You're not *here.* You get to do whatever *you* want. Sure, it's easy for you to say so."

"Well, I've said all I know to say," Darren admitted. "I've done my best to help you, and you refuse to listen. All I have to say now is that they are your guardians; they can make your life happy or miserable—it's your choice. There's nothing you can do about it except for one thing."

His pause made her turn and step closer. "What thing can I do?"

"Go back to Daddy," he replied with a straight face. "I'm sure he'd be real excited to have you back."

Lauren's eyes were blazing as she returned to the window. She spat, "Goddamn you, Darren!" Caught in her anger, she did not see nor prepare for his blow. She had forgotten that he still clutched his weapon; and in less than a second, he released all of his strength into a lash on her backside. His aim was as accurate as his fastball.

The sound of it hit her even before the pain. She squealed as she reeled to face him. "How dare you?!"

Darren's teeth were clenched tightly. "You deserved that and a lot more," he said, sternly. "I just can't bring myself to finish it." Without another word, he stormed from the bedroom, her wails erupting behind him.

CHAPTER 12

*I*t was Carolyn who met Darren's angry figure in the hall as he exited his sister's bedroom. Both froze in their tracks. Lauren's sobs could be heard from within. Carolyn's eyes were fastened upon his hands, knuckles white from the grasp of his belt. Chest heaving from his exertion, he swallowed.

"Darren, is everything all right?" she asked, voice quivering.

The anguish in his eyes assured her that it was not. "No," he mumbled. "It's not all right." The tears he'd held back squeezed out onto his cheeks. His aunt reached for him and pulled him close.

"Let's go somewhere and talk," she suggested. She felt his nod on her shoulder. Slowly, she led him to her bedroom down the hall.

Lauren lay sprawled on her bed, weeping. Overcome by her brother's unexpected action, she questioned herself. Did he not love her anymore? How could he say such things? How could he *hit* her? After all she'd been through? And, perhaps most importantly, if Darren was against her, what was she going to do, now? She cried some more.

❦   ❦   ❦

Darren seated himself on the bed, watching his aunt as she did the same. She carefully removed the belt from his clammy grasp and laid it beside her. She sadly peered into his eyes. "Tell me what happened, Darren."

The young man sniffled and coughed from nervousness. "Uh, well, that's not easy," he began. "God, it's hard to do."

Carolyn grasped his hand and squeezed it hard. "Darren," she said firmly. "I must know what is going on. I can't help you or Lauren if I don't know. Please, you can trust me." She smiled. "I promise."

❦   ❦   ❦

In the meantime, Malcolm, Todd and Marilyn waited impatiently for breakfast to be served. The father tapped his spoon against the saucer. "What in the world could be keeping them? Didn't your mother go to call them?"

"Yes, sir," Todd answered as he poured himself a glass of milk. "I thought that's what she said."

"So did I," Malcolm agreed as his stomach growled. "I'd better see what's keeping them." He rose.

"No, I'll do it!" Marilyn shouted. "I'll be right back!" She dashed from the room.

"That child will never slow down," her father said with a laugh.

Marilyn's head bobbed up the stairs into the hallway. She then walked softly, on tiptoe. Listening at Lauren's door for a moment, she opened it a crack and peeked inside. Lauren was sitting at the dressing table brushing her hair and talking to herself. "I can't believe him. How dare him hit me! His own sister!" She paused and Marilyn tried to close her mouth that had dropped open. "To think I've trusted him and he's turned on me like this. He hit me with a *belt!*" With renewed anger, she slammed the ivory handled brush on the table. "Damn him to hell!"

Marilyn's ears burned with her cousin's language as well as the events revealed. Her mind was racing with questions when, suddenly, she felt a frigid shiver run up her spine. Her heart sank as a familiar hand was placed on her shoulder. She let the door open wide as she released her hand on the knob.

Lauren turned furiously toward the doorway at the precise moment her hand released the perfume bottle she clutched in her left hand. "Dammit, Darren, leave me alone!"

It was with sickening horror that she watched the bottle smash against the doorframe, sending shards of glass into her aunt's face. Carolyn screamed and tried to cover her bloody wounds with her hands.

"Oh, God!" Darren screamed as he filled the doorway. "Lauren! My God, Lauren, what've you done?!"

❧   ❧   ❧

Mere moments passed before Malcolm and Todd arrived on the scene. Carolyn's scream and Darren's outburst had brought them at a flat run. Marilyn was hysterical, clinging to her mother, and Lauren was uncontrollable. "What's going on here?" Malcolm exclaimed as he rushed to his wife's side. "Are you cut badly?"

"No," she said softly. "They're only scratches, I think." With his arm around her, they walked to their bedroom with Marilyn in tow. He instructed Todd to bring clean cloths and a pan of water, as well as some ointment. Malcolm placed Carolyn on the bed and tenderly cleaned her face. The amount of blood had deceived him; she wasn't terribly hurt. The wounds to her heart were worse than those of her countenance.

Todd watched the proceedings in silence. He wondered what would become of their home if things were to continue like this. His sister was crying, as much for herself as her mother. After all, it had been in the midst of a reprimand that the accident had occurred.

Malcolm remained calm, but worry lurked beneath the surface. "Be still, Carolyn," he said gently. "Let me make sure you're okay before you sit up." Having cleaned the blood from the cuts, he saw that no stitches would be required. Neither would she have any scars as reminders. He was thankful for that.

"Where's Marilyn?" Carolyn asked quietly, peering up into her husband's face.

"I'm here, Momma," she answered. She moved from the foot of the bed to within reach of her bandaged mother. Malcolm placed pillows behind his wife's back to sustain her sitting position.

"Marilyn, why were you at Lauren's door?"

Her daughter squirmed. "I, uh, was looking for you. Daddy told me to see what happened. You know, why you didn't come back down for breakfast."

Carolyn looked to her husband who nodded that it was so. "I see," she said slowly. "But, when you saw that Lauren was alone, why didn't you leave?"

Marilyn thought for a moment. "Uh, well, I was. I just got there when you did. I was just about to go."

"Oh." She threw a glance at her husband. "Did you knock?"

"Huh?"

"Ma'am," Carolyn corrected.

"Oh," Marilyn blushed. "Ma'am?"

"Did you knock before you opened the door?" she repeated.

The girl swallowed nervously. "No, ma'am."

"You didn't knock?" Carolyn asked, again. Marilyn nodded that she hadn't. "I see. You sneaked inside without knocking to see if I was there. And, just as I showed up behind you, right?"

"Right," Marilyn answered with relief.

"Wrong," Carolyn said flatly. "You did not." Her eyes penetrated her daughter's heart even as Malcolm's stare joined hers.

"But, but I did!" Marilyn insisted.

"No, you did not," Carolyn stated more firmly. "Darren and I stepped out from this bedroom several minutes before you knew we were there, my dear. I was watching you." At this disclosure, Marilyn tried to slip away from her mother's reach. "Don't move another muscle, Marilyn."

The young girl's tears returned. "But, Momma, please—"

"Hush, Marilyn, and hear me out." She paused while adjusting her sitting position. "We have already discussed your behavior concerning Lauren. This morning, in fact, you were told not to bother her at all. You should have knocked and asked if I was there, or called to me from the hall. I would have heard you."

Marilyn's head dropped, but her mother grasped her chin to make her meet her eyes. "Instead, you sneaked up the stairs, opened her door, and spied on her. And this is the result." Carolyn pointed to her wounds.

Marilyn choked back a sob. "I'm sorry, Momma, but you don't know what she said! She was talkin' to herself and she said bad words and that Darren hit her with a belt! I couldn't leave; it was too scary."

Malcolm gave his wife a sharp look. She nodded that it was true, then returned to her daughter. "Marilyn, it is none of your business what happens between Lauren and her brother. Things are rough right now. She shouldn't have said those things nor thrown the bottle. But, Lauren will have to answer for that herself. You must answer for your actions, no one else's."

Malcolm added, "Your mother is right. Whatever Lauren does or does not do is no indication for you. You do what you know is right; you act as we've taught you. Come tell us if you're concerned about something she's said. Don't be disobedient just because she is. Do you understand what I'm trying to explain?"

"Yes, Daddy." She dropped her head. "I won't disobey you again."

"Good," her mother said with a smile. "I love you too much to watch you do otherwise." She pulled her close. "I love you so much."

"I love you, too, Momma."

"What about me?" Malcolm inquired.

"I love you, too, Daddy," she said with a grin, leaping from the bed to hug him.

Malcolm squeezed her tightly. "I love you, Marilyn. And, I want you to understand that we don't do this to hurt you, but to help you see that you must obey us. Hmm?" She peered tearfully up at his looming figure with a healthy fear. "So, as punishment for disobeying us, you will not go to Ann's house this weekend as we'd planned. Understood?"

Relief swept her features. "Yes, sir," she agreed. "May I go, now?"

Malcolm nodded, and she left quickly. He turned to his wife. "So, tell me. What happened this morning?"

Carolyn sighed.

CHAPTER 13

*L*auren watched apprehensively as her brother neared. She brushed the tears from her face and wiped her nose on the sleeve of her robe. "Please, Darren," she begged as he came steadily toward her. "Please, don't hurt me, please. Darren, I'm sorry. I didn't mean to!" Darren's expression did not change as he knelt. She scooted across the floor away from him. "Please, Darren, please don't." She flipped her bangs over her forehead.

"Lauren." She stopped, still pleading silently with her eyes. "For God's sake, what do you think I'm gonna do?"

She coughed. "Well, I, uh, don't know," stammered the teen. "I don't know. What *are* you gonna do?"

"Better yet, Lauren. What *should* I do?" His eyes bore into her soul.

"I see." Malcolm had listened calmly through the grim description his wife had made of the morning's events. It was only eight o'clock.

"He is very upset about her behavior," Carolyn stated of Darren. "He wants her to be happy."

"I know." Malcolm brushed his hand across his face. "We all do."

"I explained to him that he doesn't need to feel responsible for her actions. She must learn that choices have consequences, and we will be the ones to decide what they are at the appropriate time." She paused. "He must be a brother to her, not a father."

Malcolm agreed. "We must do our best to help her understand how much we love her and that she really is a part of our family, now. I mean that in every sense—on all levels—including the discipline we provide our natural children."

"It is so different from what she has experienced all her life, Malcolm." His wife pointed out the obvious. "It's not going to be easy, for any of us."

"I know," he replied with a sigh. "I know."

❦   ❦   ❦

Darren continued to stare at his sister. "Well?"

"Please don't make me answer that, Darren."

"Why not?" he asked without hesitation. "You, above anyone, should know the answer to that question."

She shifted her position and pulled her robe tightly around her. "I guess so, but I don't." She waited for him to suggest something, but he didn't. "Darren, I'm sorry. I shouldn't have thrown the bottle. I'm sorry."

"And?"

"And, what? I said, I'm sorry!"

"Is that all you have to say?"

"What else can I say?"

Darren snorted. "That's what I figured." He rose from the floor and reached for her hands. "Come here," he instructed. She reluctantly was lifted to a standing position. He motioned toward the bed and they sat. He took her hands in his. "Lauren, I don't understand you anymore. You're different. You're so full of anger and hatred that you can't see the *love*. Please, talk to me."

She swallowed the lump in her throat. "I don't know what you mean."

"Yes, you do." He paused. "You cursed me this morning with the most vicious tone I had ever heard from you to me. You hated me at that moment, *really hated* me." He pulled her face toward his. "Didn't you?"

She tried to avoid his eyes, but couldn't. "Yes, I hated you, and even more when you hit me. You've never hit me before."

"You'd never deserved it before," he returned quickly.

"I did not," she said, pouting. "I didn't deserve that." She paused, the tears blurring her vision. "It was because I was mad at you that I threw the bottle. I didn't know Marilyn or Aunt Carolyn was there."

"So, I was the only target in your mind," Darren said thoughtfully. "That's good to know." She threw him a devilish look. "Lauren, you've been acting like a spoiled child, although I can't imagine where you learned how. We certainly knew nothing about it."

"C'mon, Darren. Lighten up on me."

"When you lighten up on the rest of us," he snapped. "You've been treating them like they were put here to serve you. Well, they're not. Okay? They're not."

"It really bothers you that I'm not happy with them, doesn't it?"

"Of course it bothers me," he replied with a sigh. "They saved us, Lauren. They deserve all the respect and love we can give. Period." He rose from his seat and looked back down at her. "And we will. I promise you that. You won't treat them like dirt, Lauren. Not after all they've done."

Her sizzling blue eyes glared back at him. "And, just how do you plan to manage that, if I don't agree?"

"Don't find out," he warned, teeth gritted. "Promise me you'll try to do better. Please, promise me that."

"I'll try."

"Good," he smiled and kissed the top of her head.

She laughed, nervously. "Well, what else was I supposed to say? For all I know, you got a club or something. Can't be too careful around you, now."

He returned her humor. "Yes, well, you've gotten lucky with me, Sis, but you haven't talked with *them* yet."

Her smile faded. "With who?"

"Who do you think? I can't imagine them being too thrilled with your behavior at the moment. Can you?"

"I forgot about them," she gulped. "Oh, God."

❦   ❦   ❦

The breakfast was cold by the time the Preston household had a chance to eat it. Carolyn was served in bed despite her protests. Todd and Marilyn invited their cousin on a trail ride, and he accepted. Lauren was left alone with her guardians. The uneasy silence that followed the departure of the riders was broken only by Malcolm's invitation to a conference in the master bedroom.

Not knowing what to expect of them, Lauren was apprehensive to say the very least. She followed her uncle's large frame down the darkened hallway and into the room where his wife awaited them. She was told to sit in the chair by the dresser, facing them. It was Carolyn who spoke first.

"It's necessary that we discuss what has happened," the woman began. "It can't be avoided." Lauren tried not to focus on the obvious injuries she had caused, but she could not keep her eyes from settling on her aunt's face. "Your behavior and attitude toward us have us quite worried and Darren, too." She glanced at her husband as he sat beside of her on the bed. "Is there anything you'd like to say first?"

When the teen did not answer, Malcolm cleared his throat. "Very well, Lauren. We will begin." He grasped his wife's hand and held it reassuringly. "We realize that your life here is vastly different from your old one. It is truly a new beginning. One, I might add, that you *chose*. You must understand that although you are not like Kathy,

Todd, or Marilyn, indeed cannot be, you are as close as anyone ever will be to us. We love you and want nothing more than your happiness."

"And, because we love you," Carolyn picked up, "we expect you to show us an equal respect. If you choose not to do so, then we will make life miserable for you through whatever means we deem necessary. We can give and take away, Lauren, without ceasing to love and provide for you."

Silence.

"Yesterday," Malcolm said, "you made a decision without consulting us. We cannot function as a family like that. We are responsible for you and must know where you are and what you're doing. Otherwise, how responsible would we be?" No response. "Not only your not considering us, but your attitude following our rejection of it left us troubled. We will not tolerate such disrespect. Do you understand that?"

Lauren nodded without a sound. He swallowed hard. "Now, I don't know all that happened with your brother this morning, but I do know that Marilyn overheard some pretty strong language you were using when she was standing at your door."

Lauren's face flushed red as she asked, "What did she tell you?"

"She told us enough to know that you were not speaking as a lady should," Carolyn explained. "We don't use foul language in this house. We can communicate without resorting to filth to accomplish it." She cleared her throat. "In fact, I believe it was being spoken as a perfume bottle left your hand aimed at me."

"I wasn't aiming at you, Aunt Carolyn," Lauren said softly. "It was meant for Darren. I didn't know anyone else was there."

"I see," her aunt said slowly. "Nevertheless, let me make this clear to you. You do not resort to physical attacks in this house for whatever reason. You are not to hit or throw anything at anyone ever again. Is that understood?"

"Yes."

"Yes, ma'am," Carolyn corrected.

"Yes, ma'am," Lauren repeated through gritted teeth.

"Good. Then all that remains is your punishment," the matron said evenly, locking eyes with her husband.

Malcolm nodded and met Lauren's wide-eyed expression. "For the next two weeks you will be denied the pleasure of riding Comet, Lauren. When you come home from school, you will complete your assignments and then help your aunt in chores around the house. Is that clear?"

"Yeah," Lauren replied with a sigh.

"Yes, sir," said Carolyn.

"Yes, sir," Lauren corrected. "Is that all?"

"I think that should be sufficient," he replied, misunderstanding her request.

"No, I mean, can I go, now?" she clarified.

"Yes," he said calmly. "You may go." The couple watched her exit with fearful hearts. They had hoped for a more penitent apology. They had gotten none.

CHAPTER 14

Time passed rather quickly for the Preston household that October and November of 1961. School continued, as usual, and no other incidents occurred. Thanksgiving came and with it the return of the college students to the farm. Darren had not had a chance to visit since the month before and looked forward to the long weekend. The letters he had received from his sister insisted she was doing well, but he was anxious to see for himself how she fared.

Kathy, too, came home for the holiday. She flew in the same afternoon as Darren, and they arrived almost at the same time. It would have been like "old times" except that Rex and Helen were absent. Darren thought of the years he had longed for the annual trip to the farm. This year was that dream come true…multiplied a hundred times. Darren embraced his sister upon alighting from the car. Malcolm had driven to the University to get him. "Hey, there," he whispered in her ear. "It's good to see you."

Malcolm and Carolyn greeted their long-legged Kathy when she arrived half an hour later. Her dark eyes matched her hair that was pulled up in a distinguished bun. She grinned as she hugged them both. It had been months since she'd seen them last. Todd and Marilyn patiently waited their turns at welcoming their sister. Soon, everyone had said their hellos and moved into the living room to catch up.

Kathy told of her life in Nashville and law school. She was having a marvelous time despite having to work many hours researching as an assistant in the criminal law department. She had met a young man, as well, of whom she had grown fond. His name was Joseph Smithers, and he was an engineer working on an additional degree. They had seen one another for two weeks, now, though nothing serious had yet developed.

Darren, too, had stories to share. He excitedly spoke of his classes and his on-campus job at the intramural building. He helped to keep an eye on the gymnasium and checked-out equipment. It gave him lots of opportunities to practice and stay in shape.

Perhaps the most valuable asset he had gained, however, was the friendship with his roommate, Thatcher McKinley. The latter was a business major who was an all-star first baseman from out-of-state. His father being dead and his mother too far away to visit on weekends, he spent much of his free time with Darren. The two of them were close.

Everyone rose early the next morning and ate a light breakfast prepared by male members of the family, in part to ease their conscience. After all, the women would spend all day cooking the feast for tomorrow.

Malcolm took Darren and Todd with him on a ride over the farm while Marilyn played with her dog, Sherlock. Kathleen assisted her mother with the dishes that required a number of hours in the refrigerator. Lauren helped, as well, though she remained distant in their conversation. Somehow, she always felt like a fifth wheel.

Dinner was served on Thanksgiving in the early afternoon. All were seated and Malcolm provided the blessing. Lauren and Darren exchanged small grins, remembering those times that seemed so many years ago. Everyone enjoyed the fellowship.

It was not until early the next morning that the phone call came. Lauren, being closest to the receiver, answered it. "Hello?"

The voice on the line was shaky. "H-hello? Who's s-speaking?"

"Lauren."

"Oh, hello, Lauren." The startled person paused. "It's Momma."

The receiver hit the floor with a clang. Carolyn jumped and peered into her niece's pale complexion. "What's wrong? Who is it?"

The girl stammered, "I-It's M-momma, uh, on the phone."

Carolyn tried to hide her surprise. "Oh," she said softly, walking to the phone. "I'll talk to her." She bent and grasped the receiver. "Helen, is that you?"

"Yes, yes, it's me," came the mumbled reply. "Is Lauren okay?"

"Yes," she answered. "She's fine. She just wasn't expecting to hear from you is all." She forced a smile for the ashen teen who could not return it.

"I was just, uh, calling for the holiday, you know." There was silence. "Did ya'll have a nice dinner?"

"Yes. Yes, we did. And you? Did you, you and Rex have a good holiday?" Carolyn stammered.

"Oh, yes," her sister answered, absently stroking the faint bruise on her cheek.

"Good," Carolyn replied flatly.

Helen cleared her throat. "Well, uh, Carolyn, just wanted to call. Tell Lauren and Darren I said, that I—"

"I'll tell them you love them, Helen."

"Th-thank you." The line went dead.

❦   ❦   ❦

The Prestons celebrated Christmas together with their new family members for the first time in 1961. Both Kathy and Darren were home for two weeks, and the younger siblings were out of school, as well. It was a wonderful, peaceful time.

The family attended services on Christmas Eve, which fell on a Sunday, at their church, Edenton Baptist. Malcolm and Carolyn smiled as they filled a pew with their family. The music was truly of a Christmas spirit that filled them. All, that is, except for one.

Lauren did not feel comfortable there, despite the months she had attended with her guardians three times per week. There was something about the whole affair that she didn't like, something that bothered her down deep inside. She couldn't quite put her finger on it, but it was there, churning just the same.

Darren, on the other hand, seemed to enjoy the time he spent in church. Although he did not attend while at college because of his schoolwork, he never missed a service when he was at the Preston home. Perhaps he just felt it was expected and never thought about it much. Either way, it irritated his sister that he never complained.

Both Kathy and Todd had made professions of faith and were baptized; Marilyn had yet to make a decision. Their parents were quite proud of their commitments to God and their trust in Jesus Christ. They hoped and prayed that their new charges would also seek Him.

As a newly ordained deacon, Malcolm had the honor of assisting with the Lord's Supper ceremony that morning. His heart ached as he noticed both of the Mitchell children passed the metal plates to the next person. He silently renewed his own commitment to help them find Christ and His unconditional love.

Christmas morning brought many smiles to all. Marilyn busily examined all that Santa Claus had deemed worthy of her. Carolyn and her daughters prepared a special breakfast of ham and eggs for the lot of them. All ate hurriedly, anxious to open their presents. The shiny wrapped packages brought new clothes for each of the family members. Squeals of delight went up in every direction. Todd boasted a shotgun, Marilyn a porcelain doll, and Kathy a leather briefcase. Malcolm and Carolyn purchased each other a small gift.

The greatest burst of emotion came from Lauren. Her brother had saved for weeks to buy her a dainty, onyx dinner ring. She was delighted, as he was over the EU sweater she had gotten for him. Tears of joy were shed by everyone.

However, not all tears that Christmas morning were expressions of happiness. Helen Mitchell sat in her bedroom clutching the card she had received in the mail the day before. It was signed simply, *Lauren*. There was no tree, no child, and no Christmas cheer for the thirty-eight-year-old woman. Rex was still asleep from his drunken stupor of the previous evening. She wept bitterly before swallowing her pills.

CHAPTER 15

$\mathcal{T}$he new year, 1962, rolled in with a bang. Blizzard weather caused school closings for over a week. Freezing rain and sleet left ice over three inches thick on everything exposed. The Preston Law firm remained closed, as did most businesses in town. Temperatures fell below zero for several consecutive nights. Fortunately, the Prestons had stored wood for the winter and did not suffer as many others.

Lauren spent most of the time in her room. A troubled young woman, she searched for that part of herself, a void, which eluded her. For a sixteen-year-old with her whole life ahead of her, she felt as though she had already lived enough for two people. Perhaps, she was correct.

At least Darren was at school, safe and content, on campus. Edenton University did not close for the weather, which allowed him to concentrate on his studies rather than worrying over his life and future. Unlike his sister, he had a tangible goal to achieve and was making progress toward realizing it.

January slipped by in relatively quick fashion. Once school was in session, the young students were kept busy. Lauren found herself challenged with an algebra course that she enjoyed. Chemistry was another matter, however. If she passed, it would be by the good grace of her instructor.

Had Edenton High offered psychology she would have been a class-A case study. Though at times Lauren appeared recovered from her tragic ordeal, there was much reconciliation still to come. No one, not even Darren, could have guessed just how far from normalcy she really was. Well, at least, not until after the pivoting event in February.

It was the fourteenth, St. Valentine's Day. Lauren carefully set the card she had received from her brother the day before on her dresser and placed her precious locket beside of it. She sat for a long time, just looking at them, the tokens of his love and care. She missed him so much. Finally, she convinced herself to get out of her room and occupy her mind. As she left, Marilyn approached her in the hall. "Whatcha doin', Lauren? Goin' somewhere?"

Lauren's eyes narrowed. "None of your business, Squirt." She had no time to waste on her pesky cousin. "Get outta my way."

The girl stepped aside, yet followed. "C'mon, Lauren, let's do somethin' together! It's Valentine's!" Her auburn hair hung to her shoulders and bobbed with her head. "Wanna play Monopoly?"

"Nope."

"Checkers?"

"Nope."

"Watch TV?"

Lauren stopped quickly and turned. Her cousin bumped into her, then jumped back a foot. "Listen, Marilyn. I don't wanna play with you—*period*. Got it? Just leave me alone." She, again, began her descent.

"Please, Lauren?" she begged.

"No!" Lauren screeched as she whipped her hand around behind her and pushed the child. Marilyn lost her balance and fell two or three steps. She began to whimper and clasped her knee. Lauren peered down at her with cruel eyes. "That'll teach you to leave me alone when I say to, won't it?"

Marilyn's face pinched into a scowl. "That hurt, Lauren!" She sniffed. "I'm gonna tell Momma on you!"

"I don't care," Lauren answered coolly. "Go ahead." She walked past with an air of unconcern. Marilyn watched her don a coat and walk outside. When she disappeared from sight, the ten-year-old stood and called her mother.

"Now, calmly, tell me what happened," Carolyn instructed her youngest.

Marilyn took a deep breath. "I was jus' talkin' to her when she pushed me down the stairs!"

Her mother sat for a moment in silence. "Were you talking to her or pestering?"

"I was talkin'" she insisted, "but, she might have thought it was pesterin'."

"I see." Carolyn hid a smile. "Now, you know that Lauren is not very patient when you keep asking her things. Right?" Her daughter nodded, dejectedly. "Then you must stop doing it."

"But, she pushed me!"

"And, she shouldn't have," Carolyn went on. "I will talk with her about it later. But, for now, you need to remember that when she says no, she means it." She pulled her daughter close for a hug. "Leave her to herself today. She obviously wants to be alone, and we will honor that. Got it?" she said with a stern expression.

"Yes, ma'am," Marilyn agreed.

Meanwhile, Lauren was in the cold stables trying to distract herself by petting Comet, her favorite. She was determined not to allow herself to be caught up in the past, but somehow she could not avoid it. Finally, she pulled up a small, wooden nail keg and sat.

Her mind flooded with painful memories. Scenes replayed in front of her closed eyelids. They took her back, years back, to the horrors of her childhood. And, as always, they took her to the images of her father. She could see him, small but powerful, making all cower to his every desire. His spiked hair revealed angry eyes wrinkled in fury. His mouth, uttering obscenities to every party, never ceased. His arms were flung in every direction, wild with anger.

She then saw herself, terrified and helpless. Fearing his every flinch, every change in the intonation of his voice, she was small again in body and spirit. She was merely a toy to be exploited and abused. She could feel the dirty looks and condescending words coming from his twisted mouth. Suddenly, she felt as dark and sinister as he was. Weeping profusely, she fell to a kneeling position. The sobs jarred her from deep within.

Amidst all of her pain, she saw yet another picture, another time—Valentine's Day, 1950. Her father had brought gifts for Darren and her, candy hearts in a plastic container. It had been his only kindness. She saw him in her mind as he had been that day, handsome and emitting sparks of love. Oh, where had that man come from? Where did he go? Where was he now? Why had he come at all?

Lauren cried as she talked to herself. "Why? Why, Daddy? Why did you do it? Why then and never again?" She hugged herself. "I had forgot. The only thing you ever did for me, the only thing."

Marilyn lurked in the doorway. Checking over her shoulder, she knew they were alone. What was this her cousin was talking about? Why was she crying so? She made not a sound as she listened to Lauren's moans.

Lauren was oblivious to the intruder, engulfed by her memories. Her cries turned suddenly to uncontrollable giggles as she remembered Rex as she'd beaten him with every ounce of hatred she felt…then as she'd pounced on him that day in her uncle's office. She sobered. "Oh, God, I still can't believe that I did it. To Daddy, to *Daddy*…" she said softly.

"What did you do?" Marilyn's voice rang out in the hollow stables.

Lauren lifted her head ever so slowly and faced the young girl. Her eyes were mere slits of sapphire, burning into the soul of the wide-eyed, curious child. With a disgust overwhelming her, she got to her feet. Marilyn swallowed nervously. "I-I'm sorry, L-Lauren," she stammered. "I-I'm sorry, L-Lauren!" She took a step backward.

"You will be," Lauren hissed. "I promise you." She took three quick steps toward her cousin before the younger escaped. Marilyn ran as quickly as her legs would allow and Lauren could only watch as the back door slammed shut.

CHAPTER 16

A flushed and frightened young girl stood panting inside the kitchen. Her mother turned with a start as the back door slammed. "Oh!" Carolyn exclaimed. "What're you doing?"

The younger tried to catch her breath. "Nothin'," she answered carefully.

"Well," her mother sighed, "could you please do it a bit more quietly?"

"Yes, ma'am," she replied and eagerly started out of the room.

"Oh, Marilyn?" The girl stopped. "Did you see Lauren anywhere? I wanted to speak with her about this morning."

Marilyn's eyes stayed on the floor. "Uh, no, ma'am, I didn't see her," she lied. "I was jus' lookin' for Sherlock." She remembered, then, to remove her coat and hang it on the rack by the door.

"Okay," her mother said with a smile. "I thought you might have seen her. I guess she's gone for a walk or something. I hope she wore her jacket."

"I guess," Marilyn replied.

"Well, any way, thank you," Carolyn said with a nod. "That's all I wanted to know. Go play, now. I have some cleaning to do in the den."

"Thanks, Mom." She darted ahead of her and ran upstairs.

Plopping down upon her bed, she mused aloud, "I wonder what she was talking about? What did she do to her dad that was so bad, anyway?" She rolled onto her back. "Gosh, she sure looked mad. I just wonder…" She lay thinking for a few minutes before making her decision.

Quietly, she rose and walked into the hall. She stole to her parents' bedroom—empty. She crouched near the stairway—only the faint humming as her mother worked. Finally, the coast being clear, she tiptoed to Lauren's bedroom and knocked. No answer. With hardly a sound, she slipped inside and closed the door.

For a few minutes, she just stood peering at everything in the room. The bed had been hastily made and things thrown underneath. The closet door was ajar, revealing few garments. The chest of drawers was covered with a crocheted runner and topped with a framed picture of Darren and school papers.

However, the items of greatest interest were atop the dresser. Marilyn quietly sat on the stool. Glass bottles of perfume and pieces of jewelry were scattered. She fingered the onyx ring, placing it on her thumb, before discarding it with the others.

It was the card, propped ever so neatly, that she found to be irresistible. She carefully picked it up and began to read. It was a simple valentine with a personal message, "I love you always, Darren." She smiled to herself. As she replaced the card trimmed in pink lace, she saw the locket.

Her interest renewed in jewelry, she used her fingernail to open the silver encasement. With a gasp, she peered into the tiny faces of the young Mitchells. Both Darren and Lauren were represented, although they were much younger then. Marilyn strained her eyes to glean all she could from the faded photographs.

With hands shaking, she closed the locket. "I wonder how this would look on me," she said aloud. "I know! I'll try it on just for a second." She held the chain over her head and slipped it on. She admired herself in the mirror. "Not bad," she complimented with a giggle. "I better put this back and get outta here before Lauren or Momma catches me in here," she said, sobering.

Marilyn had lifted the necklace from her neck when she felt the snag. Her untamed mop of hair had grabbed hold of the chain. "Oh, no," she whispered to herself. "It's stuck." Her heart raced and she began to jerk on it, her hands sweaty from nervousness. "Oh, gosh, I can't get it loose!" Becoming more and more anxious to be free of its grasp, she gave a hearty tug. It broke loose—truly broke—and fell in two separate chains. The heart-shaped locket hit the floor.

And, Lauren was standing in the doorway as it did so.

Marilyn whirled around on the stool, searching for the missing piece. Her eyes scanned and stopped on two booted feet. With sickening realization, she slowly raised her head and locked eyes with those of her cousin. She gasped, "Lauren!"

"What th' hell are you doin' in here?!" She slammed the door shut behind her.

The girl stammered, "I-I was jus' lookin' at your stuff…I-I didn't mean nothin'! Please, I'm s-s-sorry!"

"Not as sorry as you're gonna be!" she snarled in return. "Look what you've done! My locket!" Lauren quickly retrieved the metal object from the floor. Her eyes, filled with tears, rose again to those of her terrified adversary.

"I-I'm sorry 'bout that!' Marilyn repeated. "I'll get you another one. I promise!"

"You can't get another one, you little idiot!" Lauren screamed. "Damn you, you broke my locket! It's the one Darren gave me so long ago…" her voice trailed off into silence.

Marilyn was frozen to the stool. Of all the months they had been in the house together, it was the most upset she had ever seen her elder cousin. Considering some of the past events, that was an achievement. She simply waited, wide-eyed.

Lauren again turned her attention to the mischievous child. With cold confidence, she laid the locket and the chains she wrenched from the girl's fists on the dresser. Marilyn's face was pinched in a scowl as her cousin suddenly grasped her arm. "Please, Lauren. Don't tell Momma!"

"Don't worry 'bout that," Lauren spat. "I'm gonna take care of this *myself.*"

"Let me go, please!"

"I'll let you go, all right," she sneered, "when I'm through with you and not before!" She marched her toward her bed and shoved her facedown.

"Wh-what are you, you doin'?" the child asked in a loud whisper. "L-Lauren? Wh-what are you doin'?" The teen did not answer. Her eyes were sweeping the room. Landing on the dresser once again, she smiled. Yes, the brush would do nicely. Lauren made three brisk steps toward her dresser. Marilyn's head twisted over her shoulder as she rolled over. She saw with horror as her cousin grasped the ivory handled hairbrush from the set on the tray. "Wh-what are you gonna d-d-do?"

"What I should've done a long time ago," Lauren answered flatly. "You're just a spoiled brat who keeps her nose in other people's business. Now, you'll think twice before you get it in to my stuff, again!" She moved quicker than the child who made a last attempt at escape. Lauren's arm caught her by the waist. She was more powerful than Marilyn had imagined for she threw her to the bed with little trouble. In a matter of a few seconds, Lauren had her cousin into the desired position.

Grasping her weapon fiercely in her left hand, Lauren began to mercilessly beat the ten-year-old. Screaming curses at the top of her lungs, she made swing after swing whisk through the air with remarkable agility. Lauren, herself, was amazed by her strength and accuracy; she felt so powerful. The child's pleas for release were drowned in the fury of it all. Her anger raged far beyond her control, now.

Lauren continued without thought of the consequences. She forgot all else in existence save that Marilyn be punished for her interference, once and for all. Tiring from her physical exertion, she loosened her grip. Slight as it was, it provided enough incentive for Marilyn to wriggle free. Face wet with tears and sobbing uncontrollably, she crawled to the door.

"You're not goin' anywhere," Lauren spat. "So, get that outta your head right now!" She quickly moved toward the girl, her sweaty grasp clinging to the handle of the brush. "Come 'ere!" Lauren laid hold of her with her right hand and raised her left to bring another blow just as the door swung open. She sneered, "I'm not through with you, yet!"

A voice boomed from the hall, "Oh, yes, you are!"

Carolyn Preston stood transfixed in horror and determination.

CHAPTER 17

*L*auren froze in her stance, her heavy hand of justice still mid-air. Marilyn was crying without any sign of stopping. "Let her go," Carolyn instructed firmly. "*Now*, Lauren." The sixteen-year-old removed her hand from the child's back and Marilyn quickly got out of her reach. She managed to get to her feet and stood in the hall. Lauren breathed deeply from her physical activity. Eyes narrowed, she clutched the brush.

Carolyn mentally tried to calm her racing heart. She prayed for the strength to control her anger. She swallowed before addressing her daughter. "Go to your room, Marilyn."

The child sniffled between sobs. "But, Momma," she whined, "what 'bout her?"

"*Go to your room*," her mother repeated slowly. "I'll be there to speak with you in due time." Her expression held much meaning for the disobedient child who broke into tears for a different reason. Tentatively, she walked to her room across the hall.

Carolyn then turned her attention to her niece. She was amazed at the display of temper the teen had shown. Now, it was time for a demonstration of her own. She stepped into the doorway and peered down at the squatting figure.

"Give it to me." Lauren looked confused; Carolyn clarified. "The brush. Give it to me." She held out her hand to receive it.

Lauren gritted her teeth, rising, and slipped a few feet away from her aunt. "*No.*"

Carolyn took another step and closed the door behind her. "Lauren," she spoke ominously, "give it to me, now. I will not ask again." Her eyes, like Lauren's, were deepening in color to a midnight blue. She felt the blood rush to her head as she spoke.

It was noon at Dodge.

"I said, *no,*" Lauren replied. "I won't give it to you." She retreated a couple steps. Her ankle bumped the bedpost and she glanced down to assure herself of her position in the room. She watched, the chills creeping up on her, as her aunt proceeded to come.

Carolyn now stood within arm's length of her niece. With palm outstretched, she waited. Her eyes never left Lauren's face; her stare was cold and determined. "Lauren, let's not make this any worse than it already is. I suggest you cooperate with me. I'm *not* going away. You will do as I say, one way or the—"

"No!" Lauren screamed. "I *won't*! You're not going to punish me because of that brat! I gave her exactly what she deserved, and I'd do it, again. I'm not going to pay for her crime!"

"Lauren, you will not speak to me with that tone of voice, young lady. I will not allow it. I will give you a chance to voice your opinion as long as you treat me with respect." Her temper, already aflame, was soon blazing.

"What do you mean by that? Huh? That I don't respect you? Well, what about *me*, huh? That damn kid broke my locket! What about that?!"

"I do not appreciate your language," Carolyn informed her.

"And, I don't give a damn what you appreciate!" Lauren spat. "Did you hear that? I don't give a shit!" She waved her weapon as she spoke, coming closer to Carolyn's face with each movement, "Ya'll let that kid drive me nuts and don't do nothin' to stop her. I bet—I bet—that's the first whippin' she ever got! God, I bet it was!"

Carolyn's face was drawn tight. She fervently prayed, now, for self-control. Never had she been addressed in such a manner by any of her children and she wasn't about to let it begin with her ward. Her silence was wrongfully assumed to be a weakness by Lauren, and the younger trudged on.

"Yeah, I bet it was! God, never get a whippin'! I can't imagine!" She paused, the apparent puzzle coming together. "No wonder she's a damn brat! Hell, I might be, too, if I'd never been stopped!"

"There's no one to say that you're not one," Carolyn replied coolly. "Is there?"

Lauren's face sobered and she lowered her voice. "What're you tryin' to say? That *I'm* a brat?" No response. She laughed. "Well, at least somebody tried to do something about it. You and Uncle Malcolm sure as hell ain't done nothin' with her!"

"And, I suppose your father is the one we should consult in this matter, eh? Is he the expert?" She paused, the words taking their effect. "Did you do what he would have done today? Is that where you learned it? Got your experience *first-hand*?"

Lauren was silent only a moment. "No! I mean, no, not him—"

"Really?" Carolyn continued. "I thought that's what you just said—*somebody* tried to do something with you. Is that what he *did*?" Her eyes held the compassion that Lauren refused to receive.

The teen's confident face peered into her aunt's. "At least, at least he *stopped* me. You haven't done that," she spat venomously, "*have you*?"

The poisoned dart hit its target; Carolyn felt the prick. She smiled, determined. "No, Lauren," she said calmly, "*not yet*." She held out her hand once more.

Lauren looked at her aunt's empty palm and then her face. "You *want* this?" She grasped the brush more tightly. "I'll give it to you on one *condition*." She raised it to her right shoulder in preparation to backhand the woman. As her arm began to move, Carolyn braced herself but did not move.

"The moment you hit me, Lauren, you forfeit your right to be treated as a young adult. You'd be nothing but a foolish child." Lauren hesitated before moving it again in her aunt's direction. Carolyn warned, "Go ahead, Lauren, and see what you gain."

Silence.

Without changing her position, Lauren inquired. "So, what're you gonna do, anyway? Slap my hand?" She laughed. "Oops, goodness, no! That might hurt me!"

Carolyn held her face as straight and emotionless as she could muster. "You've misjudged us." She waited for a response, but got none. "You see, we do punish our children with the rod when they are disobedient. Just because you haven't seen us do it, doesn't mean it hasn't happened. We don't put it on display; it is done privately." She glanced around them. "Well, Lauren, such as we are, now." The effect on her niece was evident.

Lauren swallowed hard and tried to act as though the thought unaffected her. "Like we are, eh?" she smirked. "You wouldn't be thinkin' of tryin' it?" She laughed. "I mean, that'd be crazy. I wouldn't let you."

Carolyn was finally on the offensive. "As I said, Lauren, the moment you hit me you give up your right to be treated as a young adult. You would be only a foolish child and treated as one. Do you understand me?"

Lauren laughed nervously. "Yeah, you'd try to whip me if I hit you. That it?"

"I didn't say *try*," Carolyn replied smugly.

"Yeah, but *I* did," Lauren said as she brought the blow. It was, as Carolyn had hoped, aimed too high and allowed her to duck without a scratch. Lauren had swung so hard that her body twisted with the miss, and in seconds, Carolyn had wrenched the brush free from her hand. She twirled her niece around, off balance, and with steady aim, popped her a good one with it.

Lauren yelped, tripped, and flung herself onto the half-bed. Carolyn stood over her with a confident air. "I warned you, Lauren, not to try me." Her lips were set in a tight line. Lauren set her teeth to keep from cursing. She glared from her vulnerable position at the woman who had bested her. "Get up, Lauren. Stand up." No movement was made. "Lauren, I will not tell you again."

When her eyes set on the ivory in her aunt's hand, Lauren found her incentive to obey. She slowly rose to her feet and unconsciously rubbed the stinging spot. "*What?*"

"It's ma'am."

Lauren threw back her head defiantly. "Yes, *ma'am?*"

Carolyn tried to smooth the anger from her face. "Lauren, we will not tolerate what happened today. You are not to punish Marilyn for *any* reason. You come to me. I'll take care of my daughter. On that, you can rest assured." She paused. "And, should you do so, despite this warning, I shall repay you *measure for measure*. Do you understand?" Lauren nodded slowly. "Neither will I be treated like this ever again. I love you too much for that."

"You don't love me," Lauren said through gritted teeth. "Or, you wouldn't have hit me." Her cold eyes bore into her aunt's soul.

Carolyn's eyes misted with tears. "It is *because* I love you that I smacked you. You've been entrusted to my care, and I've made a commitment to God to train you as best I can. I will not let you show disrespect for me." She searched for understanding in her niece's eyes, but found none. "It's also because I love you that I forbid you to go see Darren next weekend as we had planned. Instead, you'll stay home and do some work for me." Lauren gasped with horror. Not see Darren? The trip she had looked forward to for weeks? Not go? Not on her life!

"No!" she exclaimed, backing away. "No, I can't let you do this. I want to go!"

"*You will not go, Lauren.*"

"But, why?" she asked, bewildered. "*Why* can't I go? It has nothing to do with today. Nothing!"

"It has everything to do with today, my dear," Carolyn sighed. "You knew not to strike your cousin, and you did, anyway. You were disrespectful to me and even tried to strike me! No, you will not go, *period*. Discussion over."

"It's not over! Listen to me, today has nothing to do with going. How could it?"

"As your guardian, I have promised to provide you food, clothing, and shelter. That I can do here. Privileges such as this trip are at my discretion. They can be given and taken away; your behavior determines which. Your decision was made today." Carolyn stood firm.

Lauren was still shocked. "You can't do this to me," she pleaded. "Please, let me go. Don't do this to me."

Carolyn smiled gently. "I didn't do this to you, Lauren. You did this to yourself." She turned to leave.

"Wait!" Lauren exclaimed. Her aunt looked back at her. "What can I do to change this?"

Carolyn looked at her sadly. "Nothing can change the decision about this trip. However, future outings are up to you. Think about how you can change your *behavior* to ensure those." She smiled. "That should keep you busy until suppertime." She stepped into the hallway and closed the door behind her.

CHAPTER 18

Carolyn slowly opened the door to her youngest daughter's bedroom. She hung her head inside and scanned the room. Marilyn lay on her stomach across the bed with her eyes closed. Her breathing was heavy and without rhythm. She jumped as the door closed. "Momma!"

"Yes, it's me," Carolyn answered softly. Her daughter's eyes locked onto the object she clutched from her confrontation with Lauren. Marilyn carefully lifted herself from the bed with a wince. "M-Momma," she asked, "why have you g-got that?"

Carolyn followed her daughter's gaze to her right hand; she was surprised to see she still had it. "Oh, no reason," she replied. "I just forgot to put it down." Marilyn released a sigh of relief that did not go unnoticed. "Not that I shouldn't use it," the mother went on with finger pointing accusingly. "You certainly deserve it."

Marilyn was clearly repentant. "I'm sorry, Momma. Really, I am."

"I guess so," the woman agreed as she sat on the edge of the bed. Her daughter remained standing. "I guess you would be." She laid the brush beside of her. "Anything you want to tell me?"

Marilyn nodded and cleared her throat. "I didn't mean to lie to you today. I was just so scared. I promise! I know Lauren told you 'bout the stables and I'm so sorry."

Carolyn was confused. "What about the stables?" she asked. "And, lying to me?"

Marilyn swallowed hard. "D-Didn't L-Lauren tell you?"

"No."

"Oh." She stepped backward. "Oops."

Carolyn shifted her position and glanced at the brush for Marilyn's benefit. "What happened in the stables today that you lied about?" she asked sternly.

Sweat trickled down the neck of the nervous child. "Well, uh, this morning I was lookin' for Sherlock—"

"Was that all you were looking for?"

"I was hopin' to see Lauren," she admitted.

"Was this before or after we talked about the stairs incident?"

"After."

"You mean, *after* I told you to stay away from her today? To leave her alone?" Carolyn's eyes bore into Marilyn's hazel jewels.

"Yes, ma'am," she answered with dread.

"I see." Carolyn crossed her arms. "Go on."

"Well, I went outside and over to the stables. That's when I heard her talkin' to herself. Somethin' about her daddy and somethin' she did to him. I didn't know what it was, so I asked her."

"You asked her?" Carolyn was astonished.

"Yes, ma'am. But, she got real mad at me and I was scared. So, I ran inside."

"When I saw you," Carolyn finished.

Marilyn nodded. "I didn't want to tell you that I'd been near her, so I told you I hadn't. I didn't mean to lie about it, but I didn't want her to find out I told, either."

Marilyn's eyes pleaded for mercy. "I see." Her mother paused. "So, how, might I ask, did you break her locket?" Marilyn took another two steps backward. Carolyn drew in her breath at the implication. "Tell me."

"I went to her room just to look around," Marilyn began, the intensity of her mother's eyes burning into her, "when I saw her card from Darren on the dresser. I looked at it and then picked up the locket." She paused. "I, uh, decided to put it on over my head. It got tangled in my hair and I jerked it loose. But, it broke. That's when I saw Lauren was there."

"She saw you break it?"

"I, uh, guess so. I don't know how long she was there. But, she got real mad, madder than I ever saw her."

"And, that's when she spanked you with this?" Carolyn asked as she grasped the handle. Marilyn nodded fearfully. "How many times did she hit you?"

Marilyn shook her head. "I don't know." Her lip trembled. "Lots."

Carolyn's heart ached for her child. "Come here, Marilyn." Dragging her feet, she did so. "Turn around." The girl reacted with terror.

"No! Please, no, Momma," she begged. "Please don't. I'm sorry! I won't do it again, I promise. Please, it still hurts. Please, don't spank me for—"

Carolyn dropped the brush on the bed and grasped her daughter's shoulders. "Marilyn Preston, listen to me," she commanded. "You deserve a spanking, as you well know, for disobeying me and lying on top of it. You knew better than to do what you did. There's no excuse, is there?" Marilyn tearfully nodded, her lip trembling. Carolyn, still holding to her, gave a grim expression. "However, you have already experienced enough punishment today as a result of your misbehavior. Lauren performed my duty without my permission, and she is being punished for that. Do you understand me?"

Marilyn nodded, gaining control of her hysterics. Her mother was not finished. She continued, "I am not going to spank you again, tonight. But, you will work two Saturdays for me to earn the money to have Lauren's locket chain fixed. Understood?"

"Yes, ma'am."

"Good." She paused. "Now, I need to look at you to see if you're bruised. Turn around so I can check you." Marilyn did as her mother instructed. Carolyn gasped as she pulled the girl's panties down to reveal what she had suspected. Marilyn would be sore, but there was nothing to be done.

❊   ❊   ❊

Carolyn put the telephone receiver down with a soft click. She released a sigh of relief. Tiny tears crept out the fine lines of her crow's feet. She covered her mouth with her hand and sobbed.

Malcolm was thoroughly shocked by her account of the morning's events. His wife had been compelled to call him at the office and speak with him about her decision. He had comforted her as much as he could and promised to be home as soon as possible.

CHAPTER 19

T he soft knock at the door aroused the napping Marilyn from her sleep. "Come in," she called softly. Through her blurred vision, she saw the tall figure of her father. "Daddy."

"Yes, it's me," Malcolm spoke as he sat on the edge of the bed beside of her. She leaned on one elbow, lifting her body from its sprawled position. He sat for a long time without speaking. His wait made Marilyn's mouth grow dry with anxiety. Finally, he began. "I hear we had a bit of trouble today."

"Yes, sir."

"Suppose I hear it from you?"

"All of it?"

"All of it—from the very beginning."

"The whole thing," she reiterated.

"*Marilyn*—"

She swallowed the lump in her throat. "Yes, sir..."

❦   ❦   ❦

The Mitchell house was empty and chilled. Rex had gone early the morning of the fourteenth and left little firewood for his wife to burn. Since she was forbidden to touch the fire, she simply froze. Helen sat in the living room bundled in an afghan she had crocheted some years before. With two layers of clothing and three pairs of socks, she was relatively warm. Sometime in the afternoon, she drifted into a light sleep.

It was the rush of cold air and the pain in her arm which jarred her awake later that evening. She jerked into consciousness. "Rex!" she exclaimed. "What in the world are you doin'?" He grinned as he whisked the last of the afghan from her and threw it to the floor. Her wrist snapped as it pulled from the entanglement and she squealed.

"Aw, shut your complainin'," her husband muttered. "C'mon." He motioned his head toward their bedroom. At her refusal, he pointed the second time. "C'mon, Helen."

"Oh, Rex, not now," she stammered, teeth chattering. "It's cold in here. Put some wood in the stove."

He laughed. "Won't be cold for long." He rolled his tongue over yellowed teeth. "I'll make that fire for ya, but not in the stove." He chuckled as she blushed. "C'mon, Helen," he added with less humor, "let's go, *now*." He stood waiting for her to move. With obvious reluctance, she timidly walked past him into the bedroom. He rewarded her with a slap to her backside that *she* returned with one to his *face*.

Rex Mitchell was so stunned, he didn't move for a full ten seconds. His wife, as shocked by her own behavior as he, instinctively stepped backward with a sickening realization. Her husband strode through the doorway after her and slammed the door shut. Helen screamed. His grin had curled into a sneer.

❦   ❦   ❦

Carolyn placed the last of their dinner on the table. Dread of calling Lauren to the meal was a rock in her stomach. Todd had already left for the Valentine's Dance with one of his friends; the rest of the family remained. She walked slowly to the kitchen and stood at the sink, gazing at the pasture. Her knuckles were white as she held the basin. She was attempting to grasp hold of her emotions. Emitting a small scream, she turned with a start.

"Oh, Malcolm!" she exclaimed. His arms open, he hugged her close. Tears fell onto his chest. "Oh, Malcolm, it was awful, just *awful.*"

"I know," he answered softly. "You did the right thing, Carolyn, the right thing."

She pulled away to look into his eyes. "*Did I?*" Her anger returned. "Are you sure I shouldn't have let her have it? Do you *know* what she did? What she did to our little girl?" Carolyn's bold blue eyes pleaded with those of her husband.

He fully understood her anger and hurt. "I know. You told me, and so did Marilyn."

"And, you *still* think I shouldn't have?"

"It's over," he insisted. "We can't go back and prevent it, now. I wish we could." Fresh tears rolled down his wife's cheeks. "And, we can't blame ourselves for this. We know why she did it. We *know.*"

"But, does that make it okay?" his wife asked. "Do we *ignore* what she has done? You don't know how she talked to me, Malcolm!"

"We must do whatever necessary to help Lauren recover from the abuse she has suffered," he pleaded gently. "We can't expect her to be healed overnight."

"Our child will not be healed overnight."

He fought back the tears in his eyes. "I know." Silence. "Marilyn wants to eat in her room tonight. I told her she could." His wife nodded her approval. "That leaves the three of us."

"What are we going to do with her? What do we say?"

Malcolm took a deep breath. "You've denied the trip to visit Darren. That'll hurt. I'll have her call him in my study and tell him what happened after supper."

"She won't do it."

Malcolm's eyebrows rose. "You don't think so?" He smiled. "You underestimate me, my dear."

"Do I?" she said with mock innocence.

"Yes, you do," he answered as he placed a kiss on her lips. "And, you should know better." He smiled mischievously. "I can handle Lauren. You go on to the table. We'll join you." She nodded and left the room.

❀   ❀   ❀

Lauren lay on her bed, lightly sleeping. Her exhausted body was still, save for her steady breathing. She had cried for a solid hour after her aunt's departure and finally lost consciousness. Her greatest fear at the moment was her brother. What was Darren going to say to her? *What would he do?* She shuddered at the memories of October. That incident certainly paled in comparison to this one. What would he say, *now?*

She awoke to a bold knock at her door. She groggily raised her head and called, "Come in!" Malcolm's strong figure emerged from the hall and closed the door behind him. The look of seriousness on his face made Lauren's heart skip a beat. She slowly rose from the bed and stood with hands trembling. "Uncle Malcolm."

"Lauren."

Silence.

"I've come to call you to supper. Your aunt has baked a ham for us. She's expecting you."

A bit of anger deep within the teen stirred. "I'm not hungry."

"You'll come to the table."

"No, sir, I'm not hungry."

"Lauren, you will come to the table with us whether you eat or not. *Now.*" He stepped back from the door and motioned with his hand. "Lauren—"

"I said I wasn't hungry—"

"And, I said, you'll come to the table," Malcolm interjected. "I can understand, however, why you would not want to face your aunt after what happened today."

"You know what happened?" Lauren asked fearfully as she instinctively placed her hand on the tender spot left by her aunt's lick.

The uncle swallowed hard. "Yes, I know all about it." He paused. "We'll discuss that later. It's time for supper, now. Come with me."

Lauren hesitated for only a moment before following her uncle. With quivering knees, she descended the stairs. She dreaded seeing her aunt's face, those piercing eyes. How would she ever withstand the duration of dinner?

❦   ❦   ❦

When Helen regained consciousness, she was alone. The horrors of the past few hours were only vaguely present in her mind. She lay on the bed she had shared with Rex Mitchell for twenty-two years in a puddle of her own blood.

The last clear memory was of her slapping her husband's face. Her fear returned as she recalled his slamming the door and shoving her to their bed. As he ripped her clothes from her body, he yelled curses at her. The smell of whiskey choked her as she pleaded for mercy and forgiveness. After he had stripped her, he had brutally raped and beaten her weakened body. In his drunken rage, she was powerless, and he was deaf to her cries. At some point she had blacked-out, but she couldn't recall when.

As she tried to move, the agonizing pain hit her. She gasped and fell back onto the pillow that had somehow made it beneath her head. Tears fell out of her eyes and ran down onto the sheets. Even the sobbing brought her pain.

CHAPTER 20

"Hello, Lauren," Carolyn spoke softly as her husband and niece entered the room. The girl did not answer, did not even look up. Carolyn smiled ruefully at Malcolm. "Supper is ready." She motioned for them to sit. Malcolm was at his usual spot at the head, his wife at the opposite end. Lauren slid carefully into her seat and made no attempt to communicate. The adults bowed their heads and she followed suit.

"Father, we come to You tonight asking Your forgiveness of our sins. Thank You for sending Your Son, Jesus Christ, to make that possible. We ask that You bless the food we are about to receive to the nourishment of our bodies. In Christ's name we pray, Amen."

Lauren sat silently as her guardians ate their dinner. Malcolm shared his day with them, although only his wife gave him an ear. The conversation, although strained, was kept going throughout the meal despite the hostile member of the group. Finally, Carolyn could stand no more. "Not hungry, Lauren?"

No answer.

"Lauren?" she repeated.

Silence.

"Lauren," the deep voice stated gravely, "your aunt asked you a question. Answer her."

Lauren lifted her head and turned her blazing eyes toward Carolyn. "I told him I wasn't going to eat before he made me come down here. I want nothing from you." Her tone was vicious and her sharp tongue cut to the bone.

Malcolm calmly placed his fork on the table and wiped his mouth with a napkin. One last glance at his wife, he pushed his seat away from the table. "Come with me, Lauren," he said, clearing his throat.

The teen turned and looked up at his hulking figure. She could not hide her surprise. "Wh-what? Wh-where are we g-goin'?"

"Never mind that, young lady. Come with me." His voice was cold.

"N-Not until you t-tell me—" she began.

Her uncle grasped her shoulder and squeezed. "I told you to come with me."

"Ow!" she exclaimed. "You're hurting me!"

"I'll not tell you, again," he warned, only slightly loosening his grip.

Lauren sensed his seriousness and decided not to test his determination just yet. "All right," she conceded. "Where to?"

"My study," he answered briskly. The fearful expression on her face lasted only for a moment. It was replaced with resolution to victory. Carolyn watched them depart with the sensation of an impending battle.

Malcolm closed the door behind Lauren as she entered the small study. He silently motioned for her to sit on the couch, and he followed. "Why did you come here, Lauren?" His eyes bore into her startled ones.

"What do you mean?"

"I mean exactly what I said. Why did you come here? For what purpose?"

Lauren shifted nervously on the cushion. Clearing her throat, she slowly answered. "I thought you knew what happened. I thought Darren told you about…that."

"About what?"

Lauren's palms were instantly sweaty. "Uh, about why we left," she said, her tongue pasty. "About Daddy."

"What does Rex have to do with it?"

"Everything!" she exclaimed. "He has everything to do with—"

"So, you left because of the abuse," Malcolm interrupted.

Lauren's eyes slowly met her uncle's steady gaze. "Yes." She paused in disbelief. "But, I thought you just said you didn't know—"

"I said I wanted to know why you *came here*, not why you *left there*."

Fury swelled within her chest. "It's all the same thing!" she exploded. "Why put me through this if you know?!" She rose from the couch and took a couple of steps before reeling. "What th' hell is this all about anyway?"

Malcolm was on his feet in an instant. Two quick steps and he towered over her. The fear was obvious in her expression as he raised his hand to slap her. *But, he didn't.* He simply watched as her face steeled for the smack and she waited. When the assumed blow did not come, she stepped back from him in disbelief. He slowly lowered his arm and then walked back to his seat on the couch. "Disappointed?"

His question seemed ludicrous to her. "What?"

"Are you disappointed?" he asked, again.

"Why would I be—?" she began.

"It seems you intend on forcing us to punish you," he interrupted with a sigh. "Is that really what you want?"

Lauren was nearly speechless. "No, never that," came her response in barely a whisper. "Why would you think—"

"Sit down and listen to me, Lauren," he instructed. She did so. "I don't want to hurt you, neither does Carolyn. We've never wanted that for you. In fact, it is because of your experiences that we have been so tolerant of your behavior." She kept her eyes on the floor. Feeling her long, flaxen locks on her shoulders, she was uncomfortably warm in the small room. All he needed was a lamp to complete the interrogation, she thought. Despite the urge, she listened without retort.

Malcolm went on, "If you were a child, Lauren, there would be no question about my response to your behavior. A child's willful, intentional disobedience must be punished with the rod, and I would comply with a ready hand. Never doubt it." His face was complete seriousness. "However, you are not a child."

"No," she agreed with a hint of agitation.

"Although, I do approve of your aunt's action today. If any teenager deserved a good lick, you did and more." Lauren's fiery eyes quickly met his in an angry stare. "You disagree?"

"Yes, I do!" she exclaimed. "She had no right to hit me!"

"And, by what right did you hit Marilyn?"

"That's not the same thing."

"No, it isn't."

Lauren's mouth dropped open. "You agree with me?" she asked, astonished.

"Oh, yes, my dear, I do." He took a deep breath. "While connected events, they are not, by far, the same issue. You see, Lauren, you had absolutely no right to beat Marilyn as you did, but your aunt had every authority to spank you if she chose."

Lauren grew red in the face. "That is not what I said, you bast—"

"Hold it there, Lauren!" her uncle warned.

"Hold it, shit!" she replied venomously. "I won't let you treat me like this. I'm not a damn child!" She rose in preparation to leave. "You want to fix somebody? You go fix that kid of yours. She's the one who needs this, not me!" She turned to the door. "God, you ought to thank me for what I did!"

Malcolm also rose, the fury clearly etched on his face, "Sit down, Lauren." She looked him straight in the eye and did not move. "Lauren, sit down." Still, no movement. "Sit down!"

She sneered, "You gonna make me?" Without even so much of a grunt, Malcolm roughly cradled his niece in his arms. She screamed as he dropped her into a chair with a dull thud. "Ow, you hurt me!" she wailed.

"And, that's only a taste of what you'll get if you move from that chair," he warned as he crossed the room. The air was still and quiet for several minutes...the wide-eyed teenager awaiting the judgment...the judge deliberating the decision...and calming himself.

"We're going to end this, Lauren," he began with a frightening tone. "Whatever it takes, whatever I must do to convince you, we'll see it done. I promise you that."

CHAPTER 21

*T*he distinguished lawyer walked slowly to his desk and pulled open the bottom file drawer. With hardly a second glance, he grasped the object for which he searched. He closed the drawer with his foot and stepped back into Lauren's view. She swallowed the fear in her throat. Determined not to cower to him, she waited for his explanation.

Her uncle sat on the small couch opposite her, laying the object on the cushion to his right. He folded his hands on his knee and exhaled. "Lauren." His voice was again soft and thoughtful. She peered at him with interest. "I cannot claim to understand how you feel, how you must have felt growing up with your father. That is an existence with which I cannot possibly identify. In fact, it pains me even to think of it." He paused and watched the tears come to her eyes. "But, what I can do is tell you about mine."

Lauren shifted on the hard, wooden chair and rested her arms on the sides. What was this, a stroll down memory lane? "My father was a schoolteacher, high school science. A serious man, he was, thoughtful and cautious. He could also be the most caring, kind, and playful man in the world. One moment, he was lecturing us about the digestive system, the next he was chasing us about the yard playing tag. He was all matter of men to me."

"So, what's this got to do with today?"

"I'm getting to that," Malcolm assured her with a slight grin. "As I said, he was serious about many things, and perhaps, the most serious when it came to obedience. Oh, was he serious, indeed." He laughed softly as Lauren squirmed. She did not like direction this story was taking…

"I remember once when I was eleven, Pop told me to feed the livestock. Well, my brother Amos was ill, and it was his chore. But, I still didn't want to do it. So, I didn't." He stopped, collected the details of his memory, and continued. "Amos, not knowing that I was supposed to do it, went himself. He was on his way back to the house when my father caught him. He knew, then, that I had not done as he asked. So, he came to me."

At this point, Lauren could not stand a moment more. "All right, so I get your point. You were punished. Fine. What else?"

Malcolm straightened in his seat. "For one, I'd like you to show me some respect by hearing me out, young lady." He glanced down to his right and she only smirked. "When Pop came to my room," he continued, "he asked me if I'd done the task, and I said, 'Yes.' He simply told me to follow him. When I realized we were going to his workroom, I knew I was in trouble.

"Pop was calm, saying nothing, but reaching into his desk he pulled out this." He now lifted the object he had taken from his own desk. "It was an old paddle he had used in his schoolroom until a student brought him a new one. As you can see, it had names on every inch and dates—signatures of those who had felt its bite. It wasn't the first time I had seen it or felt it, but he had never let me sign it."

Lauren's mouth was parched. She wanted to close her eyes or look away, but she couldn't tear herself away from the worn piece of oak that her uncle held so tightly in his fist. She dared not take her gaze from it for a second. Wishing she were anywhere but in that room, she listened on.

"He set it on the desk and said, 'Son, tell me the truth.' And, I did. He listened as I poured out my soul to him. I was crying so hard I could barely speak. Not once did he scream, yell, or berate me for my excuses. He only listened." The steady tick of the clock on the bookshelf was the only break in the cold silence. "My knees trembled as I finished my story and waited for him to speak. Finally, he sat in his chair and motioned for me to do the same in the one opposite him. As I did, he looked at me with the saddest expression I had ever seen. He cleared his throat and said, 'Son, I am so sorry you chose to disobey me.'

"I remember trying to keep the tears from falling, my head shaking. He explained that I had to be punished so I would not make the same mistake, again." Malcolm rose from the couch taking the paddle with him. He walked a few feet across the room and turned to face his niece. "He had me put my hands on the desk and he walked behind me, carrying only this." He lifted the smooth object. "Lauren, it was the last time my father ever whipped me...the last time." He peered into her blank stare. "I never wanted to disappoint him like that again. Ever."

Lauren sat stiffly, awaiting the punch line. There simply had to be more to it than that, she reasoned. She was right. Her uncle cleared his throat once again. "Do you know what he said to me when he finished?"

No answer.

"I love you, Son." Tears crawled out of the wrinkled corners of his eyes. "I love you," he repeated. "He held me, dried my tears, and told me that he loved me." There was a long pause. "Did your father ever tell you that he loved you, Lauren?"

Silence.

"Did he?"

Silence.

"*Lauren, did he ever tell you that he loved you?!*"

"No, no, no!" she screamed. "God, no! He's never loved anybody in his whole, sorry, damned life! No, he never told me that he loved me!" Malcolm said nothing as he handed her a handkerchief. She blew her nose and wiped the angry tears from her eyes with the back of her hand, sniffling.

"Your father never told you that he loved you," he restated. "I suspected as much." He lifted the paddle and held it just under her nose. "Look here," he instructed, pointing to the faded, ink-scratched name crudely engraved in the wood. "Do you see that? What does it say?"

Lauren strained her eyes. Faintly, she could make out the majority of the letters. "You. It's your name." She peered up at him. "So, what?"

Swallowing his temper, his eyes bore into hers. "I signed it the night I told you about. I asked to sign it."

"Why?"

"I never wanted to forget it," he stated simply. "And, I never have."

"But, what's it got to do with me?" she asked.

"I wanted to explain to you that discipline doesn't have to be abusive. It has its place."

"You're not going to—"

"I didn't say that," he interrupted quickly.

"You didn't say you wouldn't, either," she shot back.

"No," he agreed.

"But, you said I wasn't a child, anymore," she reminded him. "You said you would if—"

"I said it would be simple if you were a child," he explained, "not that I wouldn't use it."

Silence.

Lauren posed her question thoughtfully. "What do you want from me?"

"Love."

"And, if I don't love you?"

"Your respect, if nothing else." The pain she caused by her last question hurt badly. "Love would include that."

"Fine then," she responded. "I do respect you."

Malcolm actually laughed. "No, Lauren, you do not." At her shocked expression, he explained, laying the paddle on the desk. "Why, you respect Rex Mitchell more than you do me."

"I-I do n-not!" she denied.

"Of course you do," he said. "You would not have dared to speak to him as you have me, tonight. Would you?" When she did not answer he went on. "You see? What do you suppose would have happened if you'd said to him, 'You gonna make me?'"

She hesitated. "What does it matter?"

"I need his advice," Malcolm responded quickly.

"His advice?"

"Yes, indeed. You told your aunt today that he stopped you and we haven't. Should we consult him?"

"No!" she screamed. "I-I told you we left because of him, the way he treated us. Why do you think we—"

"Again, Lauren, that is why you left. What I want to know is, *why* did you come *here*? What do you expect from *us*?"

Silence.

"Well, whatever you envisioned, let me make something clear. We cannot allow you to act as you did today, Lauren. Whatever commitment we made to you is secondary to the ones of our own children. Marilyn will not be exposed to your abuse. We must protect her." The teen's pulse quickened. "Quite simply, Lauren, you would have to leave." He stared directly into her eyes. "You would have to go home."

No one moved. No one spoke. Dreadful silence.

CHAPTER 22

*T*he clock ticked rhythmically. Lauren felt faint. Visions of her father as he had left the law office that last day flooded her consciousness. "I can't believe what you just said," she choked.

Malcolm remained stoic. "Believe it, my dear. I mean it."

"You'd make me go back? Home? To *him*?" Her eyes were tear-filled and pleading. "Do you know what that would *mean*?"

"I know what it would mean to both of you," he answered slowly.

"Then, surely you're not serious about it. I mean, you couldn't do that to me."

"If my family is in danger, Lauren, I will protect them through whatever means necessary."

"Sonofabitch!" Lauren exploded as she erupted from her chair. "Damn you and your fancy words!" Her face flushed as her bottled anger uncorked. "You tricked me!" she accused with fists clenched. "You said you'd protect me, forever! Now, you threaten to send me back to him? Just because I gave that little bitch a whippin'?" Her hair fell around her angry, youthful face. "Damn! Damn you to hell!"

"*Lauren*—" her uncle began.

"Lauren, nothing!" she screeched. "Don't start that shit with me! I'm sick of it, sick of hearing you begging for my respect," she spat. "What kind of a man are you, anyway? Huh? You break your promise and expect me to fall on my knees and ask forgiveness? Hell, that'll be the day!" She got as close to his face as she could. "I hate you, *you goddamn sonofabitch*!"

Malcolm had not seen one of her tantrums until now, and unfortunately for him, it had to have been the worst. Philosophy and child psychology fell by the wayside. Whatever reservations he had once had were now gone. As she turned to leave him in his controlled fury, he acted.

Lauren was surprised, to say the least, to find herself being hoisted off of her feet and tossed across the large, wooden desk; paperweights and bookends scattered with a crash. "Wh-what are you d-doing?!" she gasped. He did not answer. Blindly, he searched for the paddle he had discarded and finally seized it. She fought to free herself of the uncomfortable position, but he held firm. Just as he prepared to bring the first lick, he was distracted by his wife's voice. "Malcolm? Malcolm!" Carolyn called from beyond the door. "*Malcolm*, what is going on in there?" The screams and thuds of the struggle had brought her running. "Is everything all right?"

"Leave us, Carolyn," he shouted in response.

"Aunt Carolyn!" Lauren called. "Help me! Please! He's gone *crazy*!"

Carolyn froze. "*Malcolm?*"

"Go on, Carolyn! I can handle this!" With that last assurance to his wife, he brought the first blow to his unsuspecting niece. The sound echoed through the room. Carolyn did not move. Was that what she *thought* it was? Surely he had not...Malcolm let another lick fly...he had! She couldn't believe her ears.

Lauren cursed him, earning her another swift stroke from her uncle. He, himself, was silent as he swung. He concentrated so his aim was true to the squirming figure. The tears Lauren had fought so hard to keep from falling trailed down her cheeks in hot streams. She gritted her teeth together to block the pain from her mind. Hands grappling for a hold, she seized the rim of the desktop and held on for dear life.

Carolyn finally found the courage to slip inside of the room, despite her husband's instructions not to interfere, and risked his rebuke. She was amazed at the scene before her. Saying nothing, she merely watched the drama unfold. Malcolm paused, his palms sweaty from the exertion. He knew that she must be in considerable discomfort by now. "Are you ready to show some respect for me?" he asked boldly, not releasing his grip, even for a moment.

No answer.

"Lauren?"

Silence.

Targeted swing.

Silence.

"Are you ready, Lauren?"

Silence.

Another blow.

Quiet sobs.

"*Lauren.*"

It was Carolyn's voice. Malcolm turned, and she walked to the opposite side of the desk so she could face them both easily. "Lauren, please listen to him. We want to help you. We can't do that if you won't let us." She pleaded with tears in her eyes. "This only brings you pain. Please, accept our authority as your guardians."

Silence.

Malcolm looked to his wife, strong and confident. She nodded. He swung, again.

Sobs, louder, now.

"Lauren?"

"Yes," came a quiet whisper.

"Yes, what?"

"Yes, I'll…listen…to you," she choked. "Just…please, stop." Malcolm sighed and released his grip on her. It was a moment before Lauren carefully lifted herself from the desk. Her knuckles were white from grasping the edge so tightly. Face ashen, her eyes were red and swollen. She tried to wipe the tears from her eyes and face with her hands.

Malcolm laid the warm paddle on the desk, and his wife moved to his side. He swallowed hard. "Sit down, Lauren."

She sniffled. "I-I'd rather n-not," she stammered.

"Very well," he replied, understanding perfectly her condition. He squeezed his wife's hand and walked back to his top desk drawer and opened it. When he had gotten the bar of soap, he walked to within his niece's reach. "The next time you curse in my presence—or even if I hear of it—I will, personally and with great pleasure, wash your mouth out with this. You want to act as a child, we'll treat you as one. *Do you understand me?*"

"You wouldn't—" she began.

"You bet he would," Carolyn assured her with a weary smile. "Why, to this very day, the smell of Ivory makes Kathleen Elizabeth vomit. Ask her sometime. She can't even see a commercial without gagging."

"I asked you, do you understand?" Malcolm repeated.

"Y-yes, sir," she stammered.

"Good." He tossed it atop his desk and returned his attention to her. "Lauren, we love you more than you know, more than you can even understand. We want only the best for you. But, we must have your respect."

"Respect both for us and our instructions," Carolyn explained. "We want to be parents to you, Lauren. To do that, we must think of you as one of our own. We would never allow any of our children to treat us in this way, and we won't let you." She forced a smile. "We love you too much to see you act like this. We really do."

Lauren listened carefully, then threw a wicked stare at her uncle. "What about sending me home? What was that, a bluff?"

Malcolm sighed. "I meant every word of it when I said it, Lauren. The only problem is that I loved you enough that I could stand the thought of whipping you more than sending you back to Rex to be beaten, or even killed. After all, if you were to be spanked, at least it was done because you deserved it and by someone who loved you." He paused. "You're a part of this family, now. Nothing will change that. So, if you choose to defy us, rest assured you will be miserable. That is a solemn oath." Lauren nodded that she understood.

Carolyn exhaled loudly. "It's been a long, busy day. What do you say to getting some sleep?" Lauren breathed a sigh of relief. She turned to go but stopped suddenly. "Is something wrong?"

The teen's eyes met those of her uncle. "May I sign it?" she asked, softly.

He smiled. "Of course, my dear. Of course." Carolyn, not understanding, watched intently as her husband handed their niece an ink pen and the old paddle. In her best handwriting, Lauren signed her name. As she turned again to leave, he placed his arm around her shoulder. "Remember, I love you."

The Preston couple watched as their niece nodded obligingly and exited. Neither spoke as Carolyn began picking up the debris from the floor and he put the paddle back where it belonged. With a weary, assuring smile, Malcolm led his wife to their bedroom. They only paused as they passed the door to Lauren's room, her soft cries coming from within. It pained them to know of her hurt, but it was done, now. Each kissed their youngest good night, who feigned sleep, and then prepared for bed.

Marilyn had, in fact, just gotten back into bed before her parents arrived. She had waited for her cousin to return from supper for almost two hours. She'd nearly given up when she heard the elder's slow steps and snubbing sobs. Peeking from behind her door, she had watched Lauren go inside.

There was no doubt in Marilyn's mind as to the reason for her tears. She had gotten into big trouble. Deciding against getting a closer look, she turned toward her own bed and heard her parents approaching. She dove for the covers and they found her there, snoring loudly.

CHAPTER 23

$\mathcal{M}$alcolm was already in his pajamas and beneath the sheet and quilt when his wife emerged from the bathroom. She sat on the dresser seat and brushed her hair. "Malcolm?" she asked. He rolled to his side and looked at her reflection in the mirror. "I thought you said I did the right thing today," she said softly.

"I did," he agreed.

"Then why did you do it?" she asked, looking at him in the mirror. "I mean, what was the difference? Why couldn't I have—?"

"That's not why I paddled her," he said quickly.

"It's not?"

"No."

"Then, why?" She set the brush on the tray and turned around to face him. "I don't understand."

"What happened today with Marilyn was terrible," he agreed. "But, had our daughter not disobeyed you, it would not have happened." He sighed. "And, as much as I hate what Lauren did, I will have to admit one thing. Marilyn will probably remember that lesson much more clearly than if either of us had taught it to her."

"But, *Malcolm*—"

"I know, dear," he assured her with a smile. "I don't like it one bit." He groaned. "I planned to have her call Darren, you know, but she was so nasty to you at supper and then with me—well, even worse."

"She lost her temper, then?"

"You could say that." He laughed. "I've never seen anything like it."

Silence.

"She deserved the paddling, Carolyn," he stated gravely. His wife nodded, sadly. "I would have done no less with one of our own."

Carolyn took a deep breath and joined him in their bed. "It was a hard one," she commented quietly.

Malcolm, still on his side, looked into her face that stared up at the ceiling. "No harder than the one Kathy got for shoving you," he defended, "or, the one Todd got last year for—"

"I know, Malcolm," she interrupted, exhaling. "I just hate it, that's all."

"So do I."

Silence.

"I tried to avoid it, you know," he went on. "I even told her about Pop and his—"

"You didn't tell her that same old story about the chores, did you?" his wife asked with a groan, rolling to face him.

"What's wrong with that story?" he asked, defensively.

She shook her head. "I swear, you've told the kids that so many times, I know it backwards and forwards. Don't you have another one?"

Malcolm propped himself up on his forearm. "All right, *Mrs. Preston*, the next time I need an example of disobedience and punishment, I'll call *you*." His eyes danced with merriment in the feigned anger he saw in hers. "Of course, it may take you half an hour to decide which one of yours you wish to share. I can't help it that I was such a good—"

"*Malcolm Allister Preston*," she interrupted with a mock frown, "how dare you suggest that I was an unruly child!"

"I wasn't talking about your childhood, dear," he teased. "Why, it was just last week—"

He was silenced as her lips took his.

✳   ✳   ✳

Darren was not at all pleased. "What do you mean, you're not coming?" His face showed well his worry. "Why not?"

Lauren nearly dropped the receiver, but looked into the eyes of her aunt who stood nearby. It was early the next morning. "I'm just not."

Darren was not convinced. "C'mon, Lauren, tell the truth. I know you've been looking forward to this visit for weeks. What happened? What have you done?"

"Nothing."

"Nothing?"

"Right," she answered, hopefully diverting him. "I just decided not to come." Carolyn frowned at her. "I thought maybe I'd come next month. Is that okay?"

"No."

"Wh-what do you mean, no?"

"I mean, *no*. You're not coming unless you tell me what happened."

Silence.

"Lauren, are you going to tell me?"

Silence.

"Very well," he sighed. "Let me speak to Aunt Carolyn for a minute."

Lauren thought her heart stopped beating. "Uh, no."

"Why not?"

"She's not here," she lied. Carolyn's mouth flew open.

"Fine. I'll come there, myself."

"What? Come here! Why?"

"To get to the bottom of this."

"No!" she protested more loudly than she wanted. "You don't need to do that," she pleaded, the thoughts of October flooding her.

She didn't need another argument with Darren like that one. No, she thought ruefully as she placed a hand tentatively on her sore back-side, certainly not in this condition. Before she could respond fur-ther, however, Carolyn had taken the phone from her.

"Darren."

"Aunt Carolyn?"

"Yes, Darren." She paused, glancing at the nervous teen at her side. "We need to talk."

"Finally, I'll get some answers," he said with a sigh.

A weeping sixteen-year-old left the room as the receiver was placed on the holder. Her aunt had told Darren everything. He had been livid and insisted on speaking with her; her ears still burned.

Darren vented his anger to Thatcher, his best friend and room-mate. "Can you believe her? Cussing her uncle?"

Thatcher laughed. "Yeah, sisters."

Darren stopped his pacing and turned to him. "Yeah, sisters." He smiled in spite of his agitation. "But, this one! Oh, *brother!*"

Thatcher's sandy blond bangs fell around his face. His periwinkle eyes shone. "*Brother*—get it? Not *sister*?"

Darren returned his humor. "Yeah." They both laughed.

❦   ❦   ❦

Marilyn was unable to attend church services that morning. The bruises her cousin had made were dark purple and sore to the touch. She lay on her stomach reading her Sunday School lesson. Carolyn stayed with her so Todd would not miss.

Although Lauren was experiencing pain of her own, she attended with her uncle and cousin. She knew better than to complain when Marilyn was in such a condition because of her. The day passed with-out further incident.

CHAPTER 24

Spring training began in March for the Edenton University Colonels. Thatcher, an all-star first baseman, was allowed to start—almost unheard of for a freshman. Darren began the season as a relief pitcher. By mid-April, the Colonels held a winning record and stood third in the division. Darren had started only one game, but he had won it. The manager was pleased with the performance of both. Their futures were promising.

*　　　　*　　　　*

Lauren awoke early the morning of May 4, 1962. She wrapped her terry cloth robe around her and stole to the bathroom down the hall. She washed her hair, which was now mid-way down her back, and quietly returned to dress. Wearing her riding clothes, she emerged from the room just before dawn; no one else was awake. She tiptoed down the stairs to the stable.

"Morning, Comet," she whispered, stroking his soft nose. "Ready for an early ride?" She smiled as she brushed him thoroughly. Placing the blanket just so, she then tossed on the saddle. She secured it and retrieved a bridle from the wall. In only a few minutes, she was astride, grasping the reins in hand. She guided him out of the barn and onto the countryside. She needed some time to herself. It was her birthday.

❧   ❧   ❧

Helen Mitchell sat at the breakfast table quietly sipping her morning coffee. Tears fell onto her apron as they dripped from her chin. Her mind was years away, seventeen years, in fact.

The morning of May 4, 1945, was clear in her memory. She had worked until the early hours getting Rex's work clothes ironed for the week. He had told her to have them finished by the afternoon, and she hadn't. He had been so angry, she begged him for another chance.

Helen had put Darren, who was two, to bed and worked as hard as possible. Four o'clock the next morning, Rex found his wife unconscious in the living room. Rushing her to the emergency room, Lauren was born six hours later.

Now, here she sat, seventeen years later and in no better situation. In fact, it was worse. At least she'd had her children then; now, she had no one, except Rex. She stopped her crying at the sound of the front door opening. Her husband returned from work. She hurriedly wiped the tears from her eyes with a tissue and blew her nose. Rex, tired and irritable, entered. "Got any coffee?"

"Yes, on the stove," she replied.

He walked around her and looked her in the face. "What's the matter with you?"

"Nothin'."

"Then why you cryin'? Huh? What's gotten into you?" His scowl did not invite confidence.

"Nothin', Rex," she stammered. "I was jus' thinkin' about today. You know what today is? His expression was blank. "Lauren's birthday. She's seventeen."

"Is that why you're snivelin'? 'Bout that damn girl?" He snorted. "God, what th' hell you care 'bout her, anyway? Huh? She sure as hell don't care about you, does she?"

"I guess not," she whispered. "I guess not."

Rex laughed and poured himself a cup of coffee. He sat and took a long gulp. "Damn woman, sure know how to ruin' a mornin'."

Helen later closed the door to her room and walked to her bed. Opening the lid of her pill bottle, she poured the contents onto her palm. She grasped the glass of water on the bed table and quickly downed them all. With a weary smile, she lay down and went to sleep.

❧   ❧   ❧

Lauren rode across the fields of her uncle's property. She liked the feel of wind in her hair and the thrill of the ride. She had her destination already in mind, the pond. It was certainly a day to be thinking on a lot of things.

She slowed her horse to a walk at the first sight of water. She often went there to ponder and relax. She loved to dip her feet into the cool water and wade in as far as she dared without soaking her clothes. Somehow, she always felt alone there, totally alone.

She brought Comet to a halt at the edge of the clear water. She dismounted and tied the rein to a small apple tree. Stretching her muscles, she sat on the soft, green grass. She closed her eyes and listened to the birds. Oh, heaven.

Lauren lay basking in the bright sunshine, her hair falling back to the ground. She had remembered to bring a blanket with her, this time. She stretched out upon it and attempted to catch a few rays.

❧   ❧   ❧

Malcolm knocked at Lauren's closed door. "Lauren?" he called. No answer. They had missed her at breakfast, and he decided to check on her. "Lauren?" He slowly turned the knob and entered. Her bed was already made and a piece of notebook paper was propped on the dresser. He retrieved it with dread. It read: Gone for a ride. Needed some time to think. Be home later. Lauren. He smiled.

❧   ❧   ❧

The ambulance siren wailed through the streets of Hadesville. An ashen Rex Mitchell held to the sides of the seat as he looked upon his wife's silent figure. The paramedic worked fervently to keep her alive until they reached the hospital.

Her husband discovered her drugged body when he had started to bed later that morning. He would have thought nothing about her being asleep if not for the empty bottle on the floor. When his efforts to revive her had failed, he called for help. He only hoped they were not too late.

❧   ❧   ❧

"Have you studied for that history exam, yet?"

"No," Darren answered with a groan. "I haven't even thought about that one. Wow, it's gonna be a dilly!" He peered over his pile of notes at his roommate.

Thatcher sat at his desk, typing a term paper due on Monday. "Well, I won't have to worry about it, if I don't get this paper done. It's a third of the grade."

"I know," Darren laughed. "That's why I did mine last weekend." Thatcher only glared in return.

CHAPTER 25

$\mathcal{R}$ex sat nervously tapping his foot in the emergency waiting room. His arms were crossed to keep his hands from shaking. His wife had been there an hour, yet there was no word from the doctor. What if she didn't make it? He tried not to think of life without her. Who would take care of everything? Never before had he even considered the many things she did for him each day, until now, at what appeared to be the end.

"Mr. Mitchell?" a voice called.

Rex's head jerked upright and he stood. "Yeah?"

A man in a white coat approached, presumably, the doctor. His look was serious. "Mr. Mitchell, your wife is in critical, but stable, condition. We were able to rid her body of most of the medication she took." Rex breathed a sigh of relief. "However, she is still very ill. We suggest you contact any other family members of the situation, just in case. I'm sorry. We're doing all we can."

"Thanks, Doc," Rex replied as the man strode away. He once again sat on the vinyl chair and buried his head in his hands. He struggled with the decision whether or not to call the children. He thought for a long while.

❈   ❈   ❈

Lauren lay stretched out underneath the small apple tree that grew beside the pond. The emerald green water sparkled in the warm sunshine. Oh, what she would give for a swim! She hadn't worn her swimsuit, but she decided not to let that stop her. After all, she did have a blanket with which to dry herself. Looking all around her, she decided that she was, indeed, alone. No one would be in the fields today. What could it hurt?

In the sparse shade of the tree, she hurriedly undressed, leaving her clothing in a neat pile. Quietly, almost as if she thought someone might hear her, she slipped into the cool water with a gasp. The Prestons were fortunate in that a hidden spring fed fresh water into the pond, giving it a clear, clean feel. It was heavenly.

❈   ❈   ❈

Carolyn answered the ringing telephone. "Hello? Carolyn Preston, speaking."

"Uh, Carolyn, it's Rex."

She drew in a quick breath. "Hello, Rex."

"The, uh, reason I'm callin', is about Helen. She's in the hospital."

"The hospital?" Carolyn's voice showed her alarm and suspicion. "Is she all right? What happened?"

"Well, she's pretty bad, but they think she's gonna be okay. They just wanted the family to know."

"But, what happened? What's wrong with her?"

"Well, she took too many of her pills," he paused. "Looks like she meant to."

Silence

"I see," Carolyn said, slowly. "What do you want me to tell Darren and Lauren?"

"Tell 'em that their mother is in the hospital 'bout dead cause they left her and broke her heart. Tell 'em that, not that they'll care."

Click.

Carolyn replaced the receiver and left the room. It was mid-morning and her husband was still in his study. She wanted him to call Darren. She, herself, wanted to find Lauren and explain the situation.

Lauren swam for an hour. Feeling a bit pink from the sun, she decided that she'd better get dressed and ride home. She stepped from the water and shielded herself with the blanket. In a few minutes, she was dry and fully clothed. She brushed her hair back off of her forehead. She had not done as much thinking as she had planned. But, she had relaxed and that was important. Feeling better than when she had left, she rode home.

🍁　　　🍁　　　🍁

Darren dropped the receiver on its hook, bringing a startled stare from Thatcher. "What's wrong?"

"Momma," he answered flatly. "She's in the hospital."

"Is she gonna be all right?"

"Yeah, I think so."

"Good," Thatcher reassured. "Everything will be okay."

"I guess." Darren was not so easily convinced. He knew there was more to the story than he was told. But, he wasn't sure whether he wanted the whole truth or not. He simply accepted it as another event in his life from which he should detach himself.

🍁　　　🍁　　　🍁

Lauren was just as stoic a receiver of the news. "Will she live?"

Carolyn swallowed. "They think so, dear, but nothing is certain."

"You say it was an overdose?"

"Yes."

"Accident?"

"Not sure. They think it was purposeful."

To her aunt's surprise, Lauren smiled. "Can't blame her, can you?"

❧   ❧   ❧

Two weeks after Helen's attempted suicide, school was dismissed for the summer. None could have been more thrilled than Lauren. She had marked the days on her calendar for she knew that Darren, too, would be home soon.

Thatcher McKinley visited the Preston farm for the first time later in the month. He had accompanied Darren and would go on to see his mother after the weekend. It would prove an important moment in his life. From the moment he stepped onto the porch, Lauren was mesmerized by him.

Tall, like Darren, Thatcher possessed good looks. His hair was the color of hers, platinum blond. Piercing with inquisitiveness, his blue eyes soaked in all of his surroundings. But, his smile...it was the smile that melted her so. It was a lazy, shy grin that was so boyish and yet, so sophisticated like her uncle. She simply stood and stared. "Well, is that any way to treat your brother?" Darren's voice boomed in the silence, bringing Lauren from her trance.

"Oh!" she exclaimed with a little scream. "Oh, Darren! I'm sorry!" She rushed to him, his hands laden with baggage. He dropped his bags, and they embraced.

Tears glazed Darren's eyes. "Oh, Sis, it's great to be home." She hugged him tighter. "I love you."

"I love you, too," she whispered.

He pushed her gently from him and looked her in the eye. "You haven't been causing any trouble lately, I hope?"

"Who, me? I'm never any trouble!" His look was serious. She smiled. "I've been a good girl...lately."

"Lately."

"Um-hmm." She hugged him, again. "C'mon, let's go in and not talk about this anymore. Okay?" She grasped his hand and began to pull him toward the front door where the rest of the family waited.

"No."

She stopped. "Why not?"

He gave her his most stern expression. "Because I have company that you've ignored." He motioned his head to Thatcher, who was watching curiously. "Huh? How 'bout saying hello?"

"Oh! You scared me!" Lauren pushed him. He laughed. "Sure. Is this your roommate?" Her cheeks flushed red.

"This is Thatcher McKinley," Darren spoke formally. "And, yes, he's my roommate. The one I've told you about." Thatcher stepped toward her and offered his hand. "Oh, and Thatch, this is my little sister, Lauren."

The two smiled and shook hands. "Nice to meet you, Lauren." She nodded, unable to speak, again. He laughed. "So, where's the rest of them? Did they hide 'cause they heard I was coming?"

"Oh, no," Lauren said as she found her voice. "They're inside waiting for us. We can go in, now." Darren picked up his bags and followed them.

Thatcher was often a visitor to the farm that summer. He enjoyed spending time with Darren outside of school, riding the horses, helping out, and seeing Lauren...*especially* seeing Lauren. He was intrigued by her strong spirit. He just had no idea how tough it could be.

❦   ❦   ❦

"You are not going to do such a thing. Surely!"

"Why not?"

"Because it's not *proper*." Carolyn's voice was tense. "Especially with Thatcher here!" She stood in Lauren's bedroom, hands on her hips.

"What's *he* got to do with it?" the younger pressed on.

"Everything! It's not right for a young lady to display herself in one of those things in the first place. It leaves way too much in the open. Why, if I'd known what you were going to buy, I never would have—"

"Oh, Aunt Carolyn, don't be silly! It's just a *bathing suit*! For heaven's sake!" She pleaded with her eyes. "Don't tell me Uncle Malcolm has never seen you in one!"

Carolyn's eyes narrowed. "What your uncle has and has not seen me in is certainly none of your business, young lady. And, it has nothing to do with this discussion, which is over."

"No one's gonna be there but me. The pond is way out there—"

"You are not going to swim in that pond! Not with the boys all over the farm!"

Lauren caught herself just before she confessed to having done it many times in the past. Changing course, she attacked. "But, I need a tan!" she begged. "The summer's almost over and I'm white as a sheet! What will they think at school?"

"Lauren, it is June. The summer is not over. And, you are so fair, you'll only burn! Come now and be reasonable."

"I am being reasonable!" she shouted.

Carolyn took a deep breath. "No. You are not going to swim in that pond. *Absolutely not.*" Lauren knew that tone of voice. The argument, short as it was, was over. She had lost. Slowly, she placed her new suit in the drawer. Her aunt walked from the room. Lauren watched her exit and grinned. There was more than one way to get a tan before the fall term. And, she knew just how to do it.

Half an hour later, she was mounted on her favorite, Comet. She had rushed through the kitchen, hoping not to draw attention. She drew a quick breath as she recognized her aunt's voice. "Lauren?"

She turned the horse's rein and faced her. "Ma'am?"

"You're not going swimming, are you?"

"No, ma'am!"

"Just for a ride?"

"Yes, ma'am!"

"Well, be careful!"

"Yes, ma'am, I will!" Lauren smiled and rode out of the barnyard. Her aunt shook her head. She ascended the stairs to Lauren's bedroom. To her relief, the swimsuit was just where it should have been. Carolyn laughed at her own mistrust and returned to work.

❦   ❦   ❦

Lauren arrived at the pond thirty minutes later. She tied the horse and smiled. The sun was shining brightly in the center of the cloudless sky. The water sparkled and rippled as she tossed a stone in its middle. Carefully, she took the blanket roll from the saddle and spread it out on the soft grass. Darren and Thatcher were mending a fence in the far field. They wouldn't be there to bother her. Marilyn was with her father in town. What was there to threaten?

With surprising boldness, she stripped to the skin and swam, keeping her hair well out of the water. Afterwards, she lay down on the "bed" she had made. Being careful to roll over every few minutes, she did not burn, although she was a bit pink. She dressed quickly and rode back to the house in time that her aunt would suspect nothing. She was quite pleased with her deception.

Daily trips to the pond assured Lauren of an average tan by the time school started. When questioned, she merely pointed out that riding gave her a lot of exposure to the sun. If they had only known how much *exposure* she meant...

CHAPTER 26

*T*he fall semester brought class rings, invitations, and senior pictures. It was quite an expensive venture, but her guardians spared nothing. They had dedicated themselves to her and were determined to see her with only the best.

Lauren's last year at Edenton High passed quickly. Just as her brother's had been eventful, hers would be filled with surprises. As usual, it was her willfulness that got her into compromising situations, but no one could have convinced her of that truth.

*   *   *

It was Valentine's Day, 1963. It had been a year since that fateful confrontation with Marilyn and the chain of events that ended with Lauren's spanking. Her behavior was improved, but of course, not perfect.

The snow had fallen two days before, closing school. Although a welcome respite at first, Lauren had bored of being cooped up…especially with her young cousin. She lay on her bed reading her card from Darren. It had just arrived in the morning mail. Despite the cold, she was warmed by his kind words. She knew how much he loved her.

"Lauren? Are you up here?"

She recognized her aunt's voice. "Yes, Aunt Carolyn, in my room!"

Her aunt's slender body slipped through the door. Her hair was only beginning to gray, and the soft wrinkles around her eyes sometimes made her seem older. She smiled. "There's something for you downstairs. They just brought it. Come and see." She beckoned to the door.

Lauren followed with interest. They descended the stairs quickly and entered the dining room. There, setting on the table, was a vase with a tender rose. The teen looked at her aunt, then at the card. With trembling hands, she opened the tiny envelope. It read, "Just to say hello and Happy Valentine's Day. Thatcher." Her heart leapt! She blushed crimson.

"So, who's the admirer?" Her aunt's voice brought her back to reality.

"Uh, they're from Thatcher, Darren's roommate."

"O-o-h," Carolyn said slowly with a smile. "Your sweetheart?"

Lauren blushed, again. "Don't know," she stumbled. "I'd like him to be, I guess."

Carolyn laughed. "I see. Well, you'd better take it to your room. You'll enjoy it more there." Lauren nodded and did just that.

❧   ❧   ❧

Darren had thrilling news that spring. He had been selected as a starting pitcher for the Colonels! He and Thatcher were now playing together more often. Another scholarship fell his way, and he was able to plan for an entire summer at the farm instead of a regular job. That made Lauren very happy.

It was during that season that Darren and Thatcher became involved in a Bible club for athletes. Some of the team members had invited them to a meeting and cookout. They had had a wonderful time and became regular members. For the first time in his life, Darren really considered the existence of God and his relationship to Him. He'd been to church numerous times with the Prestons, but he still had not given it much thought. It bothered him, and he decided to talk to his best friend.

The two of them were walking back across campus from a meeting. They had been silent, deep in thought. Darren ventured, "What do you think about all that? I mean, God and all?"

Thatcher did not look up. "I don't know, man. I mean, what's it mean for me, *personally*?"

"Could it be that we've missed it? I mean, all my life been without something and suddenly need it? Or, realize I've needed it all along? Is that possible?"

"I guess so. But, if you've missed it, buddy, I have, too. I've never gone to church or anything. I don't know much to tell you."

"Yeah, me neither," Darren responded. They continued in silence.

It was a beginning...the darkness before the dawn.

❦   ❦   ❦

It was late March of 1963 and the University was on Spring Break. Darren brought Thatcher to the farm with him. Malcolm had agreed that he and Darren would be able to work there during the week for a little extra spending money. Thatcher's mother had gone to Oregon to visit with her mother, and he had nowhere else to go. And, besides, Lauren was there...

During their stay, a dance was being held in town. Darren had asked a girl from his math class to go, and Thatcher asked Lauren. She was elated. She spent two hours getting ready. When she emerged, all eyes were on her. "Wow, you look great," Thatcher exclaimed.

"Yeah, pretty snazzy," added Darren.

"Thank you." Her cheeks flamed red.

Malcolm was the next to speak. "Ya'll be careful and don't get hurt, okay? And, get her home by ten. Hmm?"

"Ten?! Can't I stay until eleven, at least?"

"Ten," her uncle repeated.

"But, why?"

"Ten."

"But, why can't I stay later? I want to!"

"Ten, Lauren, or not at all."

"Yes, sir," Thatcher answered for her. Malcolm smiled as her date grabbed her by the arm, a protest dead on her lips, and exited. "We'll see you by ten! Promise!" he called as he closed her car door. Lauren was still mumbling to herself, but thanks to Thatcher, she was getting to go. Another word and she'd have been in her room, grounded.

The dance was enthralling. Thatcher and Lauren met Darren and his date, Susan, at the concessions. They sipped punch, then danced for hours. However, at nine-thirty, Thatcher excused them and began the drive home. Lauren pouted.

"I've had a really nice time, Lauren," Thatcher said as they drove. "It's been nice getting to know you. I've heard so much from Darren."

"Not too much, I hope," she quickly said with a frown.

"Oh, enough," he replied with a grin. She relaxed, a little. "So, what are you gonna do this summer after graduation?"

She paused. "Haven't thought about it much. I guess I'll get a job somewhere. You know, something good."

"But, not college?"

"No," she said emphatically. "I've had all the school I want. Just give me a good job, period."

"Oh." Thatcher didn't voice his disappointment. He had been hoping she would be coming to EU the next fall. He grinned at her; she blushed. They entered her home ten minutes early. Carolyn smiled and welcomed them.

CHAPTER 27

*T*he following month, the Prestons were thrilled to discover that Darren and Thatcher would be joining them for the weekend—the last days of Lauren's spring break. She had lain around all week, doing nothing, the epitome of Senioritis. The boys arrived late on Friday night, full of smiles and warm hugs. Lauren was always glad to see her brother, but Thatcher did hold the controlling interest in her attention. He embraced her and laid a soft kiss on her forehead. She turned all colors.

Marilyn, sulking, strolled into the living room. With the boys there, she would be noticed even less. And Lauren, well, she would be gloated over. If there was anything Marilyn couldn't stand, it was her older cousin basking in attention. Who did she think she was, anyway?

Everyone stayed up later than usual catching up on everything…baseball, studies, Lauren's graduation. Malcolm asked if they would help him mend a few fences, and they agreed, teasing him that he always found work for them to do. Lauren would be alone, and Marilyn would assist her mother in preparing Sunday's meal.

Malcolm, Darren, and Thatcher were already gone by the time Lauren awoke. She tumbled from her bed and staggered down to breakfast. Carolyn informed her that the men had eaten quickly and gotten started on their way. They had a lot of work to do.

"You just relax and enjoy yourself, today, honey," her aunt told her. "We'll do something together tonight, all of us. Okay?" She nodded. "Don't worry. Marilyn is going to help me, so you won't have her to bother you. Just have a good time. Graduation will be here soon."

Lauren nodded her agreement and grabbed a biscuit. "Thanks, I *will* have fun today." She walked slowly up to her room, the plan turning over and over in her mind. The men in the far fields…Marilyn and Aunt Carolyn in the kitchen…yes, it would work well. She hadn't had a chance all week because of her cousin. This was the perfect opportunity.

She dressed quickly and brushed her long, blond locks with the ivory-handled brush on her dresser. She pulled it into a ponytail and secured it with a rubber band. She stroked her face. "I am so pale, I look a fright." She paused and grinned. "Well, we'll take care of that today, won't we?" She strolled from the room en route to the stables.

"Where ya headed?" Marilyn asked as her cousin passed.

"Nothin' to you, Squirt."

"Lauren." It was her aunt's voice. She hadn't seen her in the kitchen.

Lauren cleared her throat. "Uh, riding, Marilyn. I'm going riding."

"Can I go with you?"

"Uh, Aunt Carolyn—"

Her aunt nodded and she exited. Carolyn turned to her daughter. "Marilyn, dear, I need you here with me. How else could I get it done?"

Marilyn's face was sour. "But, why does *she* get to go? Why ain't she got to stay and help?"

Carolyn sighed, "Because I'd rather have you." She grinned, but Marilyn was not convinced. "Perhaps if we finish early, I'll let you ride out and find her. How's that?" Marilyn smiled. Now, that's motivation!

Lauren rode swiftly, her ponytail flopping on her back. The sun was high and covered by only wisps of clouds. A breeze, just enough to tickle, flowed. It was a perfect day for sunbathing. And, she knew just the right spot. She pulled Comet to a halt a few feet from the edge of the cool water…too cool for swimming, yet. The small tree she used to tie him was just budding with no leaves. Virtually all around her was grassy pasture. She was at an oasis…heaven.

With nothing to fear, she carefully folded her clothes as she undressed. The saddle roll made a wonderfully soft blanket. She inhaled deeply and stretched out in the basking sun. With only thoughts of Thatcher dancing in her head, she rested.

❦   ❦   ❦

Rex Mitchell lay sleeping on the couch. An empty whiskey bottle lay on the floor just out of reach. Trailing from his mouth down the side of the cushion, his vomit cast a horrible stench in the room.

Helen was in her bedroom, unconscious. She had not stirred in several hours from the blow she had taken to her head. Rex had lost his job and, obviously to him, she was to blame. After all, it was for her hospital stay and recovery that he had missed so much work time. And, he made her pay for it.

❦   ❦   ❦

"God, I can't believe I forgot my sunglasses," Lauren mumbled to herself. "I can't stand this sun in my eyes." She tried to shield them, but it was no use. "Well, I guess I should roll over, anyhow. This being my first time this year, I'd be sure to blister. And, I can't afford that," she thought with a shiver. She lay on her stomach and hid her eyes. The warmth was magnificent. She dozed quietly.

❧   ❧   ❧

"Whew! I'm glad that's done!" Marilyn exclaimed as the turkey was placed in the oven. "Now, what do we do? Slowly roast it until mornin'?"

Her mother nodded with a smile and licked her lips. "Yep. And then, we EAT it!" She grabbed her daughter and hugged her tightly. "Oh, thank you, dear. You were so much help to me!" She stepped over to the clock. "Wow! It's almost one o'clock! We've been working a long time."

"Yes, ma'am." She paused, trying to judge her mother's good will. "And, uh, you said that I could, uh—"

"Yes, Marilyn, you may go," her mother said with a laugh. "Go find your cousin and tell her to come back to the house. She needs to straighten her room and help with supper. The men will be back for that, you know."

"Yes, ma'am!" she called as she ran to the stables and saddled her gentle mare, Blue. In a matter of minutes, she was on her way to find Lauren.

CHAPTER 28

❀

"**D**amn!" Lauren swore as she stood. "Damn! I fell asleep!" She surveyed the damage. Not too bad...not so much she couldn't cover it up...somehow. She was definitely rosy-pink. "I can't believe I did this," she muttered. She was just about to begin dressing when she heard it.

Horse hooves...coming toward her...closer...and faster.

"My God! Darren! Or, *Thatcher*!" There was no time to do anything but jump...into the pond. With a splash, she felt the icy water surround her. She inhaled quickly and stifled a scream. Her teeth began to chatter. What was she going to do? What was she going to say?

She watched with sickening realization as the horse drew closer. The dirt bellowed up from behind the rider. Lauren's blood boiled, despite her chilly surroundings, when she determined it was her adversary. Marilyn.

Marilyn the Nosy. Marilyn the Soon-to-be-Deceased.

The young girl's hair fell to her shoulders as she stopped and dismounted. Her mouth was agape at the sight of Lauren's head protruding from the water. "Are you swimmin'?"

"No, dammit, I'm not swimming," Lauren spat.

"Um-mmm-mmm, I'm gonna tell Daddy what you said—"

"Go ahead, you little monster!" fury spewing out her mouth. "What th' hell are you doing here? I thought you were helping Aunt Carolyn!"

"I was, but we got finished. She said I could come with you."

"Damn, damn, damn," Lauren muttered aloud. What was she going to do? Could the child be bribed? "All right, Marilyn, what do you want? What will it take to get you to keep your mouth shut?"

Marilyn considered this. What an opportunity! It hardly took a moment for her to form a list. "Uh, I want you to be nice to me and call me Miss Marilyn. Oh, and clean my room, every day. And, uh—"

"Whoa!" Lauren exclaimed. "Stop right there. I'm not going to do all that! God! It's just this once, Marilyn! Help me!"

The child slowly looked around her. She smiled. "Okay, Lauren. I won't tell…but, you got to come out of the water first."

"What?"

"Come out of the water," she repeated. "So, I can tell Thatcher *all* about ya." She giggled. "I'm sure he'd like to know."

Lauren had had enough. "Dammit, Marilyn, that's all I'm gonna take from you! You do like I say, or else!"

"Else, what?"

"Else, else," she sputtered. "I'll take that brush to you again!"

To Lauren's surprise, she laughed. "No, you won't. You got in big trouble last time."

"No, I didn't," she lied.

"Oh, yes, you did," Marilyn taunted. "I heard you cryin' when you went to bed that night. Didn't I, Lauren?"

Lauren was silent. The girl couldn't be threatened. Oh, Lord, what was she gonna do? She needn't have worried; her cousin had it all worked out. She watched as Marilyn carefully rolled the blanket and placed it back on the saddle. When she crammed Lauren's clothes into the saddlebag, it was too much. "What th' hell do you think you're doing?" No answer. "Marilyn, what are you doing?"

There was no response as Marilyn untied Comet and held to his rein. Lauren watched with horror as her ten-year-old cousin snapped her riding crop to her horse and witnessed him run away into the nearby woods. "What-in-the-hell—"

"Momma told you not to be laying out in the sun, didn't she?" No answer. "Didn't she? Not even in a bathing suit?" No answer. "Boy, will she be surprised!" She fell into a fit of laughter.

Lauren stammered, "But, he won't come back here...he'll go home...to the stable."

"Um-hmm."

"But, what will they say? My horse without me?"

"They'll just say he got away from you and you're walking back. You'll have to do that, you know, walk back...alone...in the dark or...in the daylight. Up to you."

"You little bitch! I hate you! You'll be sorry for this!"

"I'm gonna tell Daddy what you said!"

"I don't give a shit!"

"See you later, Lauren. *Have a nice walk.*"

"You know I *will* come home, don't you? You do know that? And, when I do, I'm gonna—"

"Be in BIG trouble," Marilyn finished for her as she mounted and spurred her horse toward home.

Lauren watched the dust until it settled. She looked down at herself, naked in the water. What in the world was there to do? To stay in the water meant disaster. To stay on the bank was worse; she might be seen. And to go home—the worst. For Marilyn was right about one thing, she was in deep trouble there.

❦   ❦   ❦

"Where's Lauren?"

"Couldn't find her," Marilyn lied.

Worry wrinkled across her mother's forehead. "Really? You didn't see her?"

"Nope."

Carolyn cleared her throat.

"Oh, uh, no, ma'am."

Hours passed.

"I can't believe this is happening to me," Lauren moaned. She was crouched in the crystal water, trying to shield her most vulnerable parts from the scorching sun. She held her arms out of the water and tried to judge their color. Already, they were reddening. "Oh, God, I'm gonna be redder than a lobster." She sighed.

In time, though, Lauren had a plan. As soon as it was dark enough that she would not be easily seen, she would walk home to the stables. Comet would be there…and her clothes. She would dress, carefully, and make up some story about him getting away from her. Yes, she was certain it would work.

Hours passed.

"Well, boys, that's about it," Malcolm said with pride as he wiped his forehead with a towel.

"Yes, sir, we got 'em all, I think," Darren said with a smile. "And, it looks like it's about supper time, too," he added as he peered into the setting sun.

"Now, that's what I've been waiting to hear!" exclaimed Thatcher with a grin. They all laughed and started the tractor. It was time to go home. They'd hardly gotten the equipment stored when they heard the frantic voice from the backyard.

"Oh, Malcolm, I'm so glad you're here!" Carolyn yelled as her husband approached. "It's Lauren! She went riding this morning and only Comet came back! I sent Marilyn looking for her, but she couldn't find her!"

Darren and Thatcher immediately responded. "We'll go." In a matter of minutes, both had saddled horses and mounted, "Don't worry, Aunt Carolyn, we'll find her."

Lauren had just emerged from the pond, dripping wet and feeling some quick pain from her burns, when she heard it, again.

Horses...coming her way...and fast...with flashlights! She dove headfirst into the cold water and slowly surfaced gasping in agony.

The voices sounded familiar as she strained her ears. *Oh, no.* Darren...and *Thatcher!* The last people she hoped to see were there to rescue her. Oh, no, not them, she fervently whispered.

"La-aure-en? La-aure-en?" Darren called as Thatcher flashed the light in all directions.

"What's that over there?" Thatcher inquired.

"Oh, that's the old pond," Darren responded. "Wait, I thought I saw something move." With hardly a sound, they rode closer. Try as she might, she could not hide forever. The light hit her full in the face and she blinked.

"Lauren?"

"Darren?"

"Lauren, *is that you?*" he called as he dismounted and rushed to the bank. Thatcher was close behind with the flashlight. "What in the world are you *doing?*"

"Uh, swimming?"

Darren turned and looked at his companion, then back at his sister. "Try again."

"I, uh, was sunbathing and thought I'd take a dip, and, uh, while I was in, Comet got loose and ran away."

"Yeah, he got home...hours ago."

"Oh, really? Has it been that long?"

"Um-hmm. And, do you mind telling me why you didn't just walk home?"

"I, uh, well, Darren, uh," she stammered nervously. "Why can't we just go home? Please, I'm tired."

"Oh, all right. I guess we'll get the whole story later." He paused and turned to Thatcher, shaking his head. "C'mon, Lauren, let's go. You've worried Aunt Carolyn long enough. You can ride with me." He held out his hand. She didn't move. "Well? C'mon, you said you were ready to go!"

She blushed (as much as one can with a sunburn such as hers). "Well, uh, I'm not *quite* ready." He looked at her in confusion. "You wouldn't happen to have some other clothes, would you?" she whispered.

"What?"

"Clothes. I need some clothes."

"Clothes!" he shouted, bringing Thatcher's full attention. "You can get dry clothes at home! C'mon!"

"I *need* clothes."

He peered into her eyes. "*Don't tell me—*" He looked over his shoulder at his roommate and then back at his sister. "You don't have anything on, do you?"

She shook her head. Thatcher laughed. Darren stood, hands-on-hips, in complete shock. "I can't believe this." He pushed Thatcher to his horse. "We'll ride together and she'll take mine. Here, hold this." He handed him the rein and pulled his t-shirt off. "Here, Lauren, I'm leaving this by the tree. You'll have to make do with this. I'm not giving you my pants."

He and Thatcher mounted and waited. They listened as she emerged from the water and pulled the shirt quickly on. She gasped and tears sprang to her eyes at the pain in her back. I must really be cooked, she thought.

"Ready?" Darren called.

"As I'll ever be," she retorted with a grimace. "How are we gonna do this?"

"Get on my horse. We'll stay in front and you follow. Got it?"

The mere thought of riding horseback to the farm made her shiver. As if her day hadn't been rotten enough...she rode with a scream held in her throat. If she ever got her hands on that Marilyn...

CHAPTER 29

*T*he shrill call of the whippoorwill rang in Lauren's ears as she rode behind the men. The coolness of the night swept around her; she shivered. The painful sunburn caused flames of fire to whip up all around her body. She now questioned the wisdom of curling up in that water all day, exposing her back to the worst of it. Hot tears filled her eyes as she suppressed the urge to scream.

Darren and Thatcher rode silently in front of her. Both had minds whirling with questions. What in the world was she doing out there? Had she lost her *mind*? Did anyone else know? Neither could believe that a lazy Saturday afternoon could have had such a wicked turn of events.

When the soft lights of the barn and house came into view, Lauren cringed. Retribution was at hand. Marilyn was going to pay...but was she, too, going to regret her actions? What price would be required of *her*?

"Lauren!" Darren called back to her. "You stay behind. We're gonna ride ahead and make sure nobody sees you. I'll send Aunt Carolyn to take care of everything."

"No!" she begged. "Please, I can take care of myself—" She stopped short, for he had already spurred their horse. She steeled herself for whatever lay ahead.

"Darren? Is that you?"

"Yes, Uncle Malcolm, it's me and Thatcher."

"Where's Lauren? Why are ya'll both on old Blue?"

Darren pulled the horse to a halt and both dismounted. He laughed, in spite of himself. "She's coming behind us. We gotta get inside." Confusion crossed his uncle's features. Before he could ask, Darren answered. "She's not in any condition for us to see her. Well, at least, we, uh, men shouldn't be here. Aunt Carolyn will need to help."

At that moment, Carolyn stepped from the back screen door. "Oh, thank God, Darren. Ya'll are back." She paused. "Where's Lauren? You didn't find her?!"

"Oh, uh, yes, ma'am," Thatcher reassured. "We sure did that!" He chuckled, and Darren elbowed him in the ribs. He choked back his giggle and added, "She's comin' behind us. See there?" He pointed to a figure in the distance.

"Well, is she all right?" Carolyn inquired. "And, where is your shirt?"

"Lauren needed it." Darren said quickly. "Well, I guess I'll let her explain. We better get in." He motioned to the other males. "You'll want to stay, Aunt Carolyn, and tend to her." With a puzzled expression still on his aunt's face, Darren and the others entered the kitchen and began eating their cold supper.

Carolyn strained her eyes to see the approaching horse and rider. "Lauren! Lauren, come here! Stop fooling around! We've been worried sick about you!" Lauren urged her horse to pick up his pace. She grimaced as she bounced in the saddle. In a moment, she was in front of her aunt.

Carolyn peered up at the young girl. The lights from the top of the barn shone down on them. Was she seeing things, or was Lauren wearing Darren's t-shirt? "Are you ready to tell me what's going on here?"

"Not really," she answered slowly.

"Well, you'd better be getting ready!" her aunt exclaimed, feeling a growing sense of intrigue. "I want an explanation, young lady, and *now*." Lauren felt a pit in her stomach, like the day had just gotten worse—something she didn't think possible. She sat as straight as she could without moving. Carolyn looked at her closely. "Get down off that horse and bring him into the stable."

Lauren's heart skipped a beat. "Right now?" The look of anger on her aunt's face answered her question. There was no stalling; it was time to face the music. Fearing the pain caused by movement, she slowly dismounted on the opposite side of the horse. She prayed that Darren's large shirt would hang low enough to cover her. She gasped as fiery flames leapt up her body. Carolyn watched the teen stiffly lead her mount into the stable. The tentative step and erect posture gave a first clue as to the problem. The aunt followed, her suspicions roused even further.

Once inside, Carolyn took the rein from Lauren's hand and put the horse into his stall. "You can brush him down later," she said calmly as she latched the door. Lauren stood, waiting, with her blood coursing through her veins. She felt so exposed in only the over-sized t-shirt she had borrowed. How could her aunt *not know*? Carolyn, breathing deeply to calm herself, turned once again to her niece. "All right. *Now*."

"Now, what?"

"Tell me what happened today, Lauren. I want the truth. *All of it*."

Lauren swallowed hard; her throat was dry. "The truth." She paused, wishing she could look anywhere but into the eyes of her aunt. The disappointment had already settled there. "I went riding like I told you."

"*And?*"

"And, I went down by the pond. You know, the one with the spring? There's a tree there."

"I know what it looks like. Been there many a time. What were you doing there?"

"I, uh, went there to be alone."

"Obviously."

Lauren began to feel the sweat on her brow. This wasn't going to be easy. "And, I, uh, wanted to get some sun."

Silence.

"I decided to s-sunbathe."

Silence.

"D-did you hear me?"

Silence.

Carolyn took a deep breath before answering. "Yes, I heard you, Lauren. I just can't *believe* that I heard it." She placed her hands on her hips and stared. "Do you mean to tell me that you were sunbathing today? In that *swimsuit*? With the *boys* here? In the *fields*?"

Lauren swallowed, trying to get some moisture to return to her body. What she wouldn't give for some refreshing water. That pond didn't seem too bad, now. "No, ma'am," she answered weakly.

"No?" Carolyn watched with disbelief as Lauren nodded in the negative. "Are you telling me I *didn't* hear you say you were sunbathing today…by the pond?"

"No, ma'am, I didn't say I wasn't *sunbathing*. It's that I wasn't in my—"

"Wasn't what?" Carolyn's voice grew louder. "How else could you be sunbathing, but in your—" She stopped, mid-sentence. Incredible. *Surely not.* Carolyn took a step toward her niece and ran her eyes down the teen's figure. "Don't tell me that you weren't in your swimsuit, Lauren. Don't tell me you were, you were, you were—"

"Nude."

"*Naked!*"

"Aunt Carolyn, please, listen to me—"

"Listen! To what? Your excuses? No!" Her face grew crimson. "I cannot believe I am hearing this! You, *intentionally*, left the house this morning to go lay in the sun—*naked*—in the field! By the pond!

Where the boys might well have come! Not to mention, your *uncle*! What were you *thinking*?"

Lauren had never seen her aunt so angry. Not even that day she had beaten Marilyn had she looked like this. "I-I was j-just tryin' to g-get a t-t-tan," she stammered.

"A tan!" her aunt exclaimed. "*I'll* give you a tan! I'll *tan* your hide for this!" In an instant, Carolyn walked to the stable wall and selected an old riding crop.

Lauren's mouth hit the floor as her eyes set upon the leather-covered rod. "Aunt Carolyn, no! Please, don't! *Please*—"

"Turn around, Lauren! Turn around!"

"No! Please, Aunt Carolyn, you don't understand!"

"I understand *perfectly*! You blatantly disobeyed me and got caught in the act. You have *disgraced* yourself—why you even rode home with your brother and his roommate, *naked*!"

"I wasn't naked, I had on his—"

"T-shirt, I *know*! But, did they see you before? What about *before*?"

"I-I don't know," she stuttered.

"Exactly! You don't know *who* saw you! Who knows?" Her face was flushed red. "Turn around, Lauren. I won't tell you again!"

"Please, can't I at least get dressed fir—?" she started, but seeing her aunt's intended advance, she did as she was told. Gripping one of the boards of the stall behind her, she felt the sting of the first stroke. Searing pain, beyond any other she had ever felt, hit her like a razor blade. She sucked in her breath and gritted her teeth together. At first, she couldn't even scream.

Heartbroken, Carolyn was silent as she swung. Her pulse pounded in her temples, and tears blurred her vision. Clenching the rod with all her strength, she made every stroke one to be remembered. Lauren felt the rush of wind even before the blow. The thin shirt Darren had given her was hardly protection from the harsh leather. Tears streamed down her face by the time her aunt concluded the punishment.

"Turn around, Lauren." The voice quivered both from exertion and tenderness. "*Lauren*—"

The teen obeyed. Sucking in gasps of air, she held her hands to her throbbing bottom. She was shaking and weeping bitterly. "I'm sorry."

"I know."

Silence.

"I d-didn't mean to—"

"Get *caught*," Carolyn finished. Lauren looked at her with surprise, but didn't argue. She was right, after all. "Lauren, I love you," her aunt began, "and I want you to protect yourself and act as a lady should. Not as most do, but as you *should*. Do you understand?" Lauren nodded. "And, I love you enough to punish you when you disobey me. Do you believe that? *That I love you?*"

"Yes, ma'am," she croaked.

"I would not have whipped you, Lauren, except that you are old enough not to treat me as though I mean nothing to you, that I'm someone you can ignore and deceive. I will not stand for that." She peered into the swollen eyes of her niece. "Don't put yourself into a position that is only going to lead to disaster, Lauren. And when you blatantly disobey us, it *will* lead to disaster. That I *promise* you. Clear?"

"Yes, ma'am."

"Good. Now, I want the rest of the story." Her niece's eyebrows rose. "Yes, Lauren, *the rest*. You can tell me. You didn't stay out there all day because you wanted, did you? Comet came back without you...*why?*"

Finally, *revenge*.

At the conclusion of the long tale, Carolyn's face was pinched. Marilyn. Her own daughter had sabotaged her older cousin! Left her there, alone, naked! And, perhaps most importantly at this point, she had *lied* to her mother. It was going to be hard to wriggle out of this one!

Lauren was still standing by the stall when Marilyn arrived. Carolyn, herself, had gone to the house and requested her presence. Marilyn had been upstairs—praying for deliverance. Her prayer was left—unanswered.

Mother had sent for her.

The door to the barn creaked open, revealing a mass of reddish-brown hair. "Come in, Marilyn." It was her mother's voice. She tentatively stepped into the dimly lit room. Her heart stopped as she looked at her mother—and the crop. Her next search was for Lauren. She found her a few feet away, blistered red and glaring. She swallowed hard. "Y-You wanted t-to see me?"

"Yes." Carolyn motioned her closer. "I've heard it from Lauren's point of view. Now, I want yours."

"What about?"

With controlled anger, Carolyn stepped closer and brandished the crop. "Marilyn, you're in no position to be smart about this. I want the truth—*all* of it."

"Yes, ma'am." She felt her pulse quicken. "You remember when you told me to go find her?" Her mother nodded. "I went all over and finally to the pond. That's when I saw her. She was in the pond with just her head sticking out. I asked her if she was swimmin', but she just *swore* and told me to—"

"Swore?" Carolyn asked with raised eyebrows.

"Yes, ma'am! She was swearin' somethin' awful! Wanna know what she said?"

"No!" Carolyn answered with a frown. "I can quite imagine." She turned an icy stare toward Lauren, who was trying to shrink into the floorboards. "Go ahead, Marilyn. What happened then?"

"Well, she tried to bribe me into not telling anybody. But, I didn't take it."

"No, you offered something else," her mother put in.

Marilyn threw a glare at her cousin. Lauren managed a smile in return despite the pain she was experiencing at the moment. "Yes, ma'am, but you know 'bout that, right?"

"Yes, but I'd like you to tell me."

She took another deep breath. "I told her I wouldn't tell, if she came out of the water. So…so…I could tell Thatcher." She felt her mother's burning stare. "I'm sorry, Momma! Really, I am! I never meant to tell him! Honest!"

Carolyn simply prompted, "And when she refused?"

"I, uh, put the blanket and her clothes on Comet and turned him loose."

"Knowing he'd come back here and not to her."

"Yes, ma'am," she answered dejectedly.

"Why? What did you hope to gain?"

Marilyn thought for a moment. "I, uh, knew she wouldn't walk home in the day, cause she thought somebody might see her. So, I knew she'd have to stay there…in the sun."

"And get burned."

A smile escaped. "Yes, ma'am."

"Wipe that grin off your face, Squirt," Lauren said through gritted teeth.

"Enough, Lauren," her aunt warned. "I will take care of this." She turned her attention back to her daughter. "And then, you deserted her."

"Yes, ma'am, I came home."

"And lied to me." Marilyn only hung her head. "And, *lied to me*?" she repeated.

"Yes, ma'am," she barely whispered.

Silence.

"Lauren, get your clothes from Comet's saddle bag and dress."

"But, what about *her*?" she asked, pointing to Marilyn.

"I'll take care of her. You get dressed."

Lauren silently obeyed. She stood behind a saddle rest and tenderly pulled her underclothes on with a short scream. She heard Marilyn's quiet laughter at her expense, and then, Carolyn's decree. "I wouldn't be so humored, if I were you," she said gravely. "Because when I get through with you, young lady, your behind will be as red as hers!"

It was Lauren's turn to laugh. Marilyn's face pinched in a scowl. "I hate you, Lauren! I hate you! This is all your fault!"

"I wouldn't say that," her mother interjected. "You certainly did your share."

Lauren slowly emerged from her hiding, fully clothed once more. She was in obvious pain. "I'm going in, now."

"Go to bed. Your Uncle Malcolm and I will talk with you in the morning."

"Uncle Malcolm? Why?" she asked apprehensively.

"I think he will be quite interested in your choice of words, if I'm not mistaken."

Lauren swallowed the lump in her throat. "You mean he…he won't…will he?"

Carolyn forced a smile. "Without a doubt in my mind." She moved to Lauren's side and gently kissed her on the cheek. "Good night, my dear. I'll see you in the morning." A tender finger wiped a stray tear from the younger's face. "*I love you.*"

Lauren sniffled. "I, uh, love you, too…*I guess.*" Carolyn smiled, knowing full well how she felt; expressing love at a time like that is tough. Lauren quietly closed the stable door as she left. Hoping not to attract any attention, she entered the back door through the kitchen and crept to her bedroom. Thankfully, her brother and Thatcher were already in bed.

Carolyn watched as her niece exited and then faced her daughter. "Well, Marilyn, let's get this done." She motioned with her crop. "Pull your panties down to your knees." Marilyn's eyes popped open. "You heard me, young lady."

"But, but why?"

"You surely did not expect special treatment, did you? Are you any better than Lauren? Don't you think you deserve a good whipping for what you did?" She paused and then said, sternly, "Do it, Marilyn. Turn around, and you better hang on."

Marilyn tearfully obeyed, grasping a board slightly below where Lauren had. As she stood awaiting the first stroke, she thought of what lay ahead. "Oh, shit," she muttered.

Her mother spoke clearly just before the leather struck. "And, I know another young lady who will have an appointment with her daddy in the morning!"

CHAPTER 30

*M*arilyn entered the back door choking back a sob. She walked past Todd, who was in the kitchen for a snack. "Hey! What's wrong? What happened to *you*?"

"Just *shut up*, Todd," Marilyn spat bitterly. "Leave me alone."

"Marilyn, go to bed, now," her mother's voice echoed from behind her.

"Yes, ma'am," she agreed softly.

"I love you."

"I love you, too, Momma."

"Good night, then." The girl nodded and entered the living room. She quietly ascended the stairs to her bedroom. With one last glare at Lauren's door, she walked to her own room and closed the door behind her.

Carolyn still stood just inside the kitchen door. She looked worn. Her tired eyes were red; her eyelids were heavy. "Mom, are you okay?"

She peered at Todd's sweet, youthful face. "Yes, dear, I will be." She sighed. "Could you do Mother a big favor?" He nodded. "Would you make sure all the horses are taken care of? I think we've neglected some."

He smiled. "Sure, Mom."

"Thanks, dear. I certainly appreciate it. I don't think they've even been unsaddled." She took a few steps.

"Uh, Mom?" he called. She stopped and turned. "Do you want me to take that back for you, or do you have something else in mind?"

With a puzzled expression, she followed his eyes to her hand. The riding crop…she still clutched it. With color rising in her cheeks, she stated, "Oh, uh, yes, you can take it back. I don't think I'll need it any more tonight." He smiled and reached for it, but she stopped him. "Then, again, perhaps I will. Thanks any way." He shrugged and left her alone.

❧   ❧   ❧

Lauren was in her room considering her dilemma. She had already locked her door and carefully undressed. Standing in front of her full-length mirror, she peered at her blistered body. There was not a speck of her left untouched by the scorching sun. Her skin felt as if it had been stretched tightly over her bones like a drum and secured. Even the slightest movement proved too painful a venture.

Looking over her shoulder, she affirmed her suspicion. The worst damage had been done to her back, being exposed to the rays at a much better angle. It seemed as though all the blood in her body had surfaced and settled just under her skin. Memories still painfully vivid, she turned to see her lower body. Her buttocks were scarlet with darker, deep red-purplish crisscrossed marks where the crop had struck. The stinging sensation had not subsided. She could feel the lashes, even now. She tried to ease the pain with her palms, but her skin was sensitive even to the lightest touch. It was as though her whole body was swollen and her skin bursting from her. She cried, anew.

❧   ❧   ❧

A knock.

"Malcolm?"

"Yes. Come in." He had been expecting her. She stepped inside his study, instrument fisted, and sat heavily on the couch. She turned her sapphire gems on him. He was seated at the massive desk. His expression was nothing but seriousness as he focused on the crop and then on her face. "I'm sorry, I'm just too tired for a ride tonight."

"*Malcolm*—"

"Oh, I know, honey," he said with a grin. "I'll make up for it next time."

She did not share his humor, no matter how she adored it, usually. "I'm being serious."

"All right, so what's happened? You look upset." He glanced at the crop to make his point. "It hasn't been pleasant, I assume?"

"Since when is dealing with our children's disobedience *pleasant*?" Carolyn fought the urge to cry and lost. She dropped the rod on the floor, burying her head in her hands. "Oh, Malcolm, I was so upset, so *upset*. I shouldn't have acted then…I should have *talked* to her…" she broke off, and he quickly sat beside of her.

Holding her in his arms, he asked, "What has she done?"

"You won't believe it," she mustered.

He smiled, slightly. "Try me."

"She was sunbathing out by the pond today, naked—"

"*Naked!*" he exclaimed, rising quickly, and letting her fall to the seat cushion. She pushed herself up. "In the field? *Today*!?!" She nodded in the affirmative. "I can't believe it!"

"Neither could I," his wife agreed, looking up at his figure, her hands outstretched in amazement.

"What did you do?"

Her eyes peered into his pale face. "I whipped her," she said, motioning to the fallen object, "with the crop."

Silence.

"Malcolm?" No answer. "*Malcolm*?"

A soft laugh.

"You used the crop, eh?"

"Yes."

Silence.

"Malcolm? What're you thinking?"

He grasped her shoulders, held her up long enough for him to sit down and placed her head in his lap. "I'm thinking that it must have been mighty painful if she's as sunburned as I'd think she'd be after spending the day outside *naked*." He gazed down into her concerned face. "Eh?"

"I suppose." She paused. "I really didn't think about it."

"I bet *she* did."

Silence.

He began to gently stroke her hair that had fallen around her face. "Carolyn, answer me this. Did she *deserve* a whipping?" he asked soberly.

"Yes," she answered wearily, I believe she did."

"And did you assure her of your *love* and tell her *why* she was being punished?"

"Yes."

"Had you *told* her not to sunbathe?"

"Yes, Malcolm."

"Good," he assured as he bent to speak directly in her ear. "Then why are you stewing about it? You did exactly what you should have done—would have done with one of your own."

She had to smile at that. "That is for certain." She turned her head and winked. "Without a doubt."

He gently pushed her into a sitting position and faced her. "Marilyn?" She nodded. "Well, I guess I better hear it all. Lord, I should have known." Carolyn took a deep breath and began the story. Malcolm sat calmly through the whole ordeal. He flinched when she told of the obscenities used. When she had finished, he sighed. "Well, now I know you did the right thing," he said with conviction. "And, I'll take care of the other in the morning. But for now, I think we should get some sleep. What do you say?" He stood and offered his hand, but she did not reach for it.

"I was angry," she mused, as much to herself as to him. "She'd never seen me so angry before—"

"Perhaps she needed to," he offered.

"Perhaps so," she agreed quietly. "I don't think Helen ever punished her. You know, like that."

"I doubt anyone has," he said, adding, "*with that.*"

Carolyn glanced at the crop. "You know what I mean, Malcolm."

He sat, again. "So, what makes you think so?"

"The way she looked at me," she said, remembering Lauren's eyes, those pleading eyes. "It was like she was in a nightmare."

"She *was*," he answered with a grin.

She elbowed him in the ribs. "Oh, just thinking about it," she said with a shiver. "I guess Rex took care of everything. You know, in that way."

"Um-hmm."

"I scared her, Malcolm, really scared her. Not even that night in here—she was different. It was almost like she was expecting it." She paused, seeking his face. "Not that she wanted it, but accepted it. Like we always were as kids. You know? Dreaded it, but knew we deserved it. Even like one of our own. She was just like mine. I love her like she was mine."

He smiled as he put his arm around her. "I know. So do I."

Silence.

"Malcolm?"

"Yes?"

"Did I over-react? I mean, she was already so embarrassed and everything. Perhaps I shouldn't have—"

"Carolyn." He pulled her against his chest. "If you were challenged enough by her behavior to take a crop to her—well, she must have deserved it. I trust you." He hugged her tightly as she groaned. "I do love you so much, you know."

"I know," she whispered as she wiped the tears from her eyes. "I love you, too, sweetie." He grinned and kissed her cheek before he stood, bringing her with him.

"Now, are we ready for bed?" She nodded and stepped to the door. "Uh, Carolyn?" She turned and saw that he had picked up the crop. "What do you want me to do with this?" She only laughed and shook her head at his teasing. He was impossible.

❦   ❦   ❦

Lauren pulled the covers back on her bed revealing the cool sheet. She had decided that clinging clothing would only irritate her, so she would sleep nude. With tentative movement, she lay down on her stomach…and cried herself to sleep. About midnight in her fitful slumber, however, she rolled onto her back, pressing her hypersensitive skin to its brittle limits.

"Oh, shit!" Lauren hissed as she came fully awake. "Oh, God, that hurts." As quickly as she could, she pushed herself off of the bed. She stood, stiffly, hardly breathing. Tears trickled out of the corners of her eyes as she squeezed them shut. Heat generated from her body in cruel waves. She felt as though she'd been set ablaze.

She finally decided, once again, to go to sleep—or at least attempt. She crept to the side and slid onto the top as easily as she could. With a muffled cry, she buried her head in the pillow. Morning was still hours away.

❦   ❦   ❦

"Good morning, Mrs. Preston." Thatcher entered the kitchen dressed in slacks and a nice shirt.

"Oh, good morning, Thatcher! I hope you slept well?"

"Yes, ma'am. I guess fencing does that to you." She laughed. He sat in a chair at the smaller kitchen table. "Can I ask you something?"

"Of course," she answered curiously. "Something wrong?"

"No," he answered slowly. "I was just wondering about Lauren."

"What about Lauren?" Carolyn asked, evenly.

He sighed. "I kind-of like her, that's all," he said slowly. "But, I just don't know her very well. What's she like? I mean, really like?"

Carolyn fought the smile. "Perhaps you could talk to Darren about that. He's known her longer than anybody. They're quite close."

"I guess so," the young man concluded. "I'll do that. Thanks."

"Anytime." Carolyn let her grin escape as he stepped out the back door. Interested, was he? She bet he *was*…

✿   ✿   ✿

A knock.

"Lauren?"

Silence.

"Lauren? Are you up yet?" No answer. He grabbed the doorknob and turned it. Locked.

Another knock. Louder, now.

"Lauren!"

"What do you want, Darren!?!"

"To talk."

A pause. "What about?"

He took a deep breath. "You know what about. Last night!"

"No."

"Please?"

"No."

"Lauren!" There was exasperation in his voice.

"Not now, Son." Darren turned with a start. Malcolm had come up behind him. "We'll talk."

"Yes, sir," Darren answered grimly as he tapped the door. "Lauren, I'll see you later." He turned and followed his uncle. Lauren breathed a sigh of relief. She had only just risen and not dressed. Now, if only she could get herself excused from breakfast…

Malcolm intently watched Darren's face as he concluded his explanation. In the expression, he saw shock, hurt, and anger. "I'm sorry, Uncle Malcolm. I just can't believe she's being like this. She knows better. She was never like this before."

"Perhaps she was too frightened to be like this before."

"I *know* she was!" Darren agreed. "Do you know what Daddy would have done to her? My God, look what he did when he just *thought* she had been less-than-ladylike! He would have killed her!"

Malcolm shifted uncomfortably in his seat. "I don't think she'll continue, Darren. She's beginning to adjust. We must be patient *and* firm. She needs to know you love her and want only the best for her—just like we do. We must convince her that we're all working on her side."

Darren thought for a long moment. "You know, this whole situation is like nothing we've ever experienced. On our side? We didn't even think it was possible." There were years of pain in his eyes.

Malcolm swallowed the lump in his throat. "I know, Darren. I know."

❧   ❧   ❧

Being Sunday there was always much to do before the services. Everyone gathered for an early breakfast. Well, *almost* everyone. Darren and his uncle entered and took their places. "Good morning!" Malcolm called as he sat. "Where's Lauren?"

All looked around, only just noticing her absence. He glanced at his wife. "I'll go get her," she said softly as she excused herself from the table. All waited patiently for her return.

CHAPTER 31

*H*elen Mitchell held an ice pack to her cheek. The bluish-purple bruise was swelling, and her eye was almost closed. Her husband was asleep in their bed, alone. He had kicked her out, literally, upon retuning home the night before. Crawling her way to the living room, she had slept miserably on the couch.

Without any money coming in, Helen wondered where he was getting all that whiskey. Obviously, someone was buying it for him. Or, he was doing something on the side. Illegal? *Perhaps.*

For *certain*, Rex Mitchell would never cease to amaze her.

Carolyn boldly knocked on her niece's door. "Lauren? We're waiting for you at breakfast."

Silence.

"Lauren? Are you there?" she asked as she tried the locked handle. "Lauren? Let me in!"

No answer.

"Lauren!"

Soft click.

The door opened slightly, and Carolyn entered.

Lauren was standing by her dresser with her bathrobe gently pulled around her. Her hair, still damp from the pond, hung on her shoulders and around her face like silent seaweed. She looked like something called for that couldn't come—*literally*.

"*Lauren*," her aunt said firmly, but softly, "you need to come down for breakfast. We're all waiting on you."

"I'm not eating," she said flatly.

"You know the rule. You come with us whether you eat or not." She paused. "I thought you wanted as much time with Darren as possible, hmm?"

"Not really," she mumbled. "Couldn't I be excused? Just this once?"

"For what reason?"

Silence.

"Lauren, I asked, for what reason?"

"I don't want to go."

"Not good enough."

"But, I don't want to! I can't!" Her eyes were wide and pleading.

"Why can't you?"

Silence.

"Lauren, answer me."

"I-I just can't," she stammered. "I can't sit there and—"

"Sore, eh?"

"Huh?"

"Sore?"

Silence.

"Yes, ma'am," she said with controlled anger.

Carolyn walked closer to her. "And who do you blame for that? Marilyn?"

"She-she *is* the cause of it!" the teen sputtered. "She left me there!" Eyes blazing, she added, "And, *you* certainly didn't help matters any."

"I see. Now, it's me, too?" her aunt asked. "Do you not agree you deserved everything you got yesterday? Did she drag you out there?

Or, was that on your own?" Her aunt quickly stepped even closer. "If you hadn't been out there disobeying me, it would've been impossible for this to happen. Right?"

Silence.

"Be honest with yourself, Lauren."

Silence.

"I know," she said simply, head drooping.

Silence.

Carolyn moved to put her arm around her, but Lauren gasped and stepped from her. The elder silently extended her hand and the girl grasped it. "Breakfast is waiting." Lauren accepted this defeat without comment and began to exit with her aunt. "Try to hurry. Church this morning, you know."

Lauren stopped instantly. "*Church*? Surely, you don't expect me to go to—"

"With bells on," her aunt finished, struggling to keep a straight face.

CHAPTER 32

$\mathcal{B}$reakfast was only the beginning of Lauren's troubles. She descended the stairs like an elderly woman. Carolyn waited at the base of them. "I'm coming," she groaned.

In a few minutes, they entered the dining room. All eyes turned and glued on the young woman. She felt their burning stares. "Good morning, Lauren," her uncle ventured. "Glad you joined us."

"Morning," she replied dryly.

"Looks like you got some sun," Todd said with a smile. "You look like an Indian." He held up his palm toward her. "How!"

"*How* 'bout my fist in your mouth, Todd?" she growled.

"Touchy, touchy!" he laughed, "Guess I'd better drop the subject." Malcolm and Carolyn exchanged glances. Thatcher hid a smile. Darren sat silent. Marilyn fidgeted.

"Uh, have a seat, Lauren, and I'll say the blessing," Malcolm said quietly.

Lauren nodded and pulled out her chair beside of Darren. She looked down at the thick cushion that had been added that morning, then glanced at her aunt who met her gaze knowingly. With silent gratitude, she tried to sit ever so slowly, inhaled quickly as the pain hit her, grimaced, and finally rested all of her weight.

All bowed their heads and Malcolm prayed. The breakfast of sausage and eggs was enjoyed by all, except Lauren who fasted. After everyone had been served and eaten a helping, she asked to be excused from the table. "No," her uncle said firmly. "I want to speak with you and Marilyn as soon as your chores are done."

After the meal, the young men left the table to get dressed for church services. Carolyn and the girls cleared the table and washed the breakfast dishes. Malcolm awaited them in the study.

Carolyn held the door open as the young girls stepped inside the room. Marilyn, with much apprehension, was first. She stopped at her father's desk, fearing the worst. Lauren was immediately behind, slowly walking, and dreading whatever was to be said or done. She simply wanted to get the whole experience behind her.

Carolyn closed the door and stood behind the transgressors. She waited for her husband to speak; it was his turn to express his displeasure. He stood, as well. "I've been informed of yesterday's events," he began calmly. "And, to be honest, cannot believe that it ever happened." He looked at his niece. "To think you would risk being *purposefully* disobedient to us about something so trivial. It's not like getting a suntan is a life or death situation. After all, you've never even expressed an interest before—"

"Wait," his wife interrupted. "She has wanted to before. It was last year." Lauren's gut wrenched. *Oh, God.* This wasn't happening. It couldn't be. Not *now*. Carolyn paused, thinking. "As a matter of fact, you were very compliant with my decision last year. You never argued with me about it, but once that I remember. And, when you looked so dark, well, it seems I remember questioning you about it. Didn't I?" No answer from the teen. Suddenly, it dawned on her. She placed her hand on Lauren's shoulder and pulled her around with a squeal. "You've done this before! Haven't you?"

Silence.

"Lauren," she said, growing increasingly serious, "you have, *haven't you?* Tell me the truth."

Silence.

Malcolm and Marilyn had not moved. Both watched the scene between 'mother' and 'daughter' with fear for the latter. Neither said a word. "Lauren Ann Mitchell, *so help me God*, if I have to—"

"Yes," she whispered.

"Yes, *what*?"

"Yes, I've done it before." Her eyes welled up with tears. "I'm sorry—"

"How many times before? Once? Twice? How many?"

Nothing.

"*Lauren*—"

"I don't know," she finally mustered. "Too many, I think."

"Think! I *know* it was too many! *Once* was too many!" Carolyn exclaimed. "I don't believe this!" She searched Malcolm's face, and he intervened.

"Lauren, we're quite surprised by this. She has trusted you, and you've let her down. You disobeyed her, deliberately and without regard to the consequences." He paused. "What have you to say for yourself?"

"I'm sorry."

"Sorry!" Carolyn exclaimed. "You haven't even thought sorry, yet!" She stepped closer and added, "My dear, if you ever lie to me again or do something like this, I'll make last night seem like a tickle! Do I make myself clear? *Do you understand me*?"

"Y-Yes, ma'am," she stuttered.

"Good." She turned to the smiling Marilyn. "And that goes for you, too, young lady. Don't think I've forgotten your part in this little affair."

She frowned. "Yes, ma'am."

Malcolm straightened and placed his hands on top of his desk. His youngest daughter peered up at him fearfully. He cleared his throat. "*Marilyn*."

"Yes, s-sir?"

"I am very disappointed in you." She dropped her head. "What you did yesterday is unspeakable. You deserted your cousin and left her defenseless. Did you not consider what might have happened to her?"

The girl looked up at him. "What do you mean?"

"Well, for one, she could have had a sunstroke—passed out and drowned. Or, maybe been snake bitten. Did it not occur to you there are snakes all around that pond?" Lauren swallowed hard. No, it hadn't occurred to *her*...and she was glad it hadn't. She would have died with the thought. Marilyn stood silent. "You didn't, did you?" She shook her head. "Exactly. You subjected her to danger you were not even aware of. You could have killed her."

"Daddy, I didn't mean to hurt her—"

"The hell you didn't!" Lauren exclaimed.

Malcolm gave her a sharp look. "That's enough from you, young lady."

"Yes, sir," she whispered.

He returned his gaze to his daughter. "What do you mean you didn't mean to hurt her? Why else would you do it?"

"I mean, I didn't mean to *really* hurt her, like die or something. I just wanted to play a trick on her. See her get it for a change."

"See her get it," he repeated. She nodded, embarrassed. "So, was it worth it?"

"*No, sir*," she said with conviction.

He looked over her head at his wife and back to Marilyn. "I also understand you chose to use profanity last night in front of your mother."

"I didn't mean it toward her—"

"You shouldn't have meant it toward anyone!" he interrupted. "You know better than that." He looked at Lauren who was shocked by the revelation. "I blame *you* for this, Lauren. She's heard you use this type of language." Lauren said nothing. "I also understand that in addition to a moment ago, you were swearing yesterday at her at the pond. Do you have anything to say for yourself?"

Silence.

"Lauren?"

No answer.

"Very well, I shall take care of this."

Malcolm frowned and opened his desk drawer. Lauren sucked in her breath and held it there. Marilyn had no idea what was going on. She looked curiously at her father who was searching for something; she knew not what. In a moment, he straightened, the object in his hand. He peered at his two charges. Glancing at his wife, he said, "Water."

Carolyn nodded and stepped from the room. Marilyn looked at Lauren who watched her uncle's every move. He was very serious. "Marilyn, sit down in that chair." She obeyed without question. "Lauren, stand over there." He pointed to the wall on the other side of the desk.

"Why?"

His look silenced her further inquiry. She obeyed. Carolyn returned with a small pan of warm water. She set it on the edge of his desk and stood beside of him. "I hope that this soap takes all the filth out of your mouth, and I never have to do this again."

Marilyn's eyes widened. "But, *Daddy!*"

"Not another word, Marilyn," her mother warned.

Lauren watched with dread as her uncle submerged the bar of old soap from his drawer and lathered it. Marilyn began to cry. When the translucent bubbles dripped from his wrists, he stepped to where she sat. Carolyn stood behind her and held her arms to the chair. "No!" she screamed as he neared her. "No, *please!*"

His face was strained with emotion. "Open up, Marilyn." She cracked her jaws slightly. "Wider—and Marilyn—if you bite me, you'll regret it." She clung to the chair with a vise grip. Gagging and sputtering, she succumbed to the treatment, silently vowing never to be subjected to it again. She was heaving when she left the room. The suds on her chin were evidence of her experience. She had solemnly accepted her father's admonition and left her older cousin with a glare.

Carolyn's face was drawn tight with her inner turmoil. She hated doing this. She detested the thought of punishing those she loved, but she disliked their disobedience even more. She wiped her face with her hand and motioned to her niece. Lauren slowly walked to the chair. Malcolm nodded. Gingerly, she sat with a frown.

"Now, Lauren," her uncle began. "I want you to know that I am so disappointed in your example for Marilyn. Whether you agree or not, she looks to you. She watches everything you say and do—and she's following. I don't want her to fall into the same paths of disobedience you have trod." She nodded with hidden disgust. "You seem to believe that you can do whatever you like—say whatever you like—and we'll let it slide. We won't."

Carolyn peered down at her and for a moment, looking so much like Helen that Lauren stared. Her mother's sister…how different they were. Carolyn was so strong, Helen so weak. Her aunt spoke firmly. "Lauren, we will not tolerate your use of profanity under any circumstances. We have been patient because we know that it was normal at your other home. But, it's not here. *Ever.*"

"And, to help you remember," Malcolm broke in, "I am going to make good on my promise to you." He held up the soapy bar. "The next time you feel an urge to curse, perhaps you'll taste this, instead."

Tears crept out of the teen's eyes. Carolyn grasped her arms and held them, unknowingly twisting the skin as she did so. "Oh, sh—" she began, but Malcolm finished for her by thrusting the soap into her mouth.

Gurgling with fury and revulsion, she tried to fight him. Her teeth closed on his hand, and he calmly warned, "Open wider, Lauren, or you'll wish you had." She hesitated only a moment before Carolyn pressed harder on her arms. She yelled, which sufficed him. She silently cursed him for his brutality and her own ignorance. Why had she done it again this morning? Why remind them?

When he had finished, he dropped the bar in the pan of water. She was spitting flakes in his direction, but not on purpose. Carolyn held to her a moment longer and then allowed her to stand. Her uncle turned with a humored grin. He peered into her eyes as closely as he dared and warned, "Next time, I swear I'll make you eat the bar." Lauren glared and tried not to swallow. The acrid taste made her physically sick. She thought perhaps she'd vomit. With his next instruction, she almost did.

"Lauren, go upstairs and get ready for church. We leave in an hour."

"But, I don't want to—"

"Get dressed, Lauren," her aunt said from behind her. "I'd hate to take you in your robe."

"You wouldn't dare—"

"Try me."

Lauren turned toward her aunt, the dry suds flaked on her chin. "I'd be *indecent,*" she smirked. "For a woman who couldn't stand the thought of sunbathing, I'd think that'd be the last thing you'd do! Why, that preacher just might see me—"

Malcolm's unexpected spank with his hand cut her short. She had forgotten he was behind her. Eyes opening wide with surprise and feeling the stinging pain on her sore behind, she gasped, "Damn!"

Carolyn's eyebrows rose, and her eyes met those of her niece. Anger and exasperation were evident on Malcolm's face. He roughly grabbed her by the arm and placed her firmly in the chair. She squealed. "Don't even think of begging for mercy, Lauren," he said through clenched teeth. "Your pleas fall on deaf ears." Her mouth gaped open, unable to say anything. He turned with the bar of soap once again in his hand. "Open up, my dear, nice and wide." No choice in the matter, she tearfully obeyed.

CHAPTER 33

L auren opened the door to her bedroom. She was weeping, stran-
gling with saliva she dare not swallow. She had coughed and
gagged until she felt sick to her stomach. She could almost forget her
sunburn...almost.

In an hour, all stood in the foyer dressed in their Sunday best.
Thatcher and Darren both wore ties, looking very handsome. Broad-
shouldered and tanned, they were a young girl's dream. They waited
for Lauren who was the last to appear. Clothed in the lightest sundress she owned, she descended. Her golden hair was washed and
gleaming in the rays through the open front door. Her eyes were a bit
puffy, but darting sapphire jewels to her admirer. Her skin was shiny
red and obviously burned severely.

"Ready?" Malcolm asked with no expression in his voice. All nodded and followed him to his car. Marilyn rode in the front with her
parents. Lauren and the boys were in the back. It was a tight fit, especially uncomfortable to Lauren who needed her space. She gritted
her teeth together to keep from saying anything.

The ride was as silent as the grave. No one was in the mood for
conversation. All minds were whirling with questions, each with a
different set depending on their knowledge of the facts. One thing
was for certain, none knew it all, except perhaps, for Lauren. And,
she wasn't about to share anything with anyone.

The Preston group filled a pew that morning. Malcolm and Carolyn were seated in the middle; Todd, Thatcher, and Darren on one side, the girls on the other. Lauren could have sworn she felt the burning stares from the congregation. Do I look that bad? she asked herself. She tried to ignore them. After all, her aunt was right beside of her and the 'monster' on the other. She could take no chances.

Lauren flinched each time the congregation was asked to rise and then be seated. If they only knew what that did to her...they'd be sorry for making her come. Wouldn't they? She *wondered*.

The pastor took his place at the pulpit and opened his Bible. Lauren inhaled deeply. Finally, the service was going to begin. The sooner it was over, the better. "Open your Bibles to Revelation chapter twenty, verses ten through fifteen, if you will." Carolyn opened hers and handed it to Lauren. The latter looked up in surprise, but said nothing. She glanced down at the Scripture. Terrific, she thought. *Hell.*

By the time she got over the surprise at her misfortune, the preacher had begun. "*...and shall be tormented day and night for ever and ever...*" Forever? "*...And I saw the dead, small and great, stand before God; and the books were opened; and another book was opened, which is the book of life...*" Book of life? What's this fairy tale? She gave this to me to scare me, she thought. "*...and they were judged every man according to their works. And death and hell were cast into the lake of fire. This is the second death. And whosoever was not found in the book of life was cast into the lake of fire...*"

Oh, God, she thought, lake of fire. She could almost feel it, now...or was that sunburn? She wasn't sure which. "*...if you'll turn with me to Matthew chapter twenty-five, verse forty-six, we'll hear the words of Jesus...'And these shall go away into everlasting punishment: but the righteous into life eternal...'*" The righteous...peace...comfort...safety...heaven.

The Pastor's words drummed into Lauren's head. Hell...damnation...rejection...everlasting punishment. Could it be true? Was it possible? Her mind was troubled as he expounded on his message. As the pastor droned on, Lauren Mitchell felt as though she was literally catching on fire. Her entire body ached and stung with pain as she squirmed through the sermon. She didn't want to hear this…not today…not the way she felt…she didn't want to be there…yet, she couldn't help listening when her troubled mind would allow her to focus, a few seconds at a time.

"…But, for the righteous," the man continued, "there is life eternal, peace with God. Turn with me again to Revelation, chapter twenty-one, verse four. To those who have been saved, it says, '*And God shall wipe away all tears from their eyes; and there shall be no more death, neither sorrow, nor crying, neither shall there be any more pain; for the former things are passed away.*'" No sorrow…no pain. "If there is any among us today who has not been saved by the loving grace of our Lord, Jesus Christ, let him come forth at the invitation and trust in Him, today as we sing—" All rose and hymnals were opened.

As the congregation sang, "Softly and Tenderly", Lauren clung to the pew in front of her. "If only I could believe it was true…if only I felt…no, no," she thought. "This is crazy…I know this is crazy…no, no, no…they're not going to trick me like this…" In half an hour, they were on their way home. She'd resisted…refused…rejected. Was there ever to be any hope for her?

CHAPTER 34

*D*arren and Thatcher returned to the University later in the afternoon. It was a tearful goodbye for they would not be able to visit again until summer vacation. Lauren denied her brother a hug but did allow him to kiss her cheek. He grinned, laughing all the way, as he and Thatcher waved goodbye and were soon long gone in Thatcher's old '54 Ford.

After lunch, Lauren spent the day in her room. No one had bothered her, and that was for the best. She lay stretched out on the bed without the torture of clothing. She needed some time to consider some things and heal from her wretched condition.

That night, typical of sunburns, the pain grew worse with a vengeance. She would later look back to that time as one of pleasure considering what was to come. At the time, however, all she could think of was one thing—school. Vacation was over, and she knew well that they would never let her stay home. That night, she dreamed of the taunts and ridicule she might face.

Her aunt's knock came awfully early the next morning. She groaned as she lifted her naked body from the bed and stumbled to the mirror. No change. Worse, perhaps? "Oh, God, I just can't go," she mumbled. "I just can't." Nonetheless, she dressed and left her room, every step a painful one.

Marilyn was in the hall, as well. "Morning, Lauren!" she said brightly.

Lauren glared. "Get away from me," she snapped. "I don't want you within ten feet of me from now on, got it?"

Marilyn found her command humorous and laughed as she ran down the stairs. "C'mon, Lauren! Can't you walk any faster than that?" Lauren bit her tongue and swallowed the retort she said only in her mind. Merely shaking her fist, she descended, silently vowing revenge for that remark. Someday...*someday*...

Lauren stepped onto the school bus cautiously and sat in the front. The lurch and bumps did nothing for her comfort. Her skin was tight and flaming. She breathed deeply and willed herself not to scream. Marilyn sat as far back as the young children were allowed. On the seats just behind her were the teenage boys. Some of them secretly liked the quiet Mitchell girl and inquired about her. "Hey, Marilyn," they whispered. "What's with Lauren? Why ain't she sittin' back here?"

Marilyn's devilish eyes twinkled. "You *really* want to know?"

"Yeah," they replied with sly grins. "Tell us."

Marilyn looked ahead at Lauren's back. She smiled. Boy, was she gonna regret tattling on her...

Lauren had no idea what caused the ruckus in the back of the bus. The teen boys were cackling and falling over each other, faces red and eyes wet with tears. She saw her cousin, sitting quietly, face forward. Oh, well, she thought, I guess I'll hear about it later. Oh, would she!

Marilyn exited the bus with the other elementary school children. She smiled at Lauren as she passed. "See ya!" she said as she slapped the elder's shoulder. Lauren was too surprised to answer. She held her breath until the light throbbing subsided. Oooh, that child!

But, it was a different expression Marilyn saw on Lauren's face that evening. Looking into her eyes, she saw anger, burning and smoldering with hatred. The young girl rushed by her and sat as she had that morning. Lauren did not turn around. The bus was unbearably hot, and she was sweating. She could feel it running down her scorched back, making her blouse and skirt cling to her. *She wanted to die.*

Marilyn was soon to discover what had happened at school. Those boys had made the rounds that morning to every male in Edenton High. Not a one was unaware of Lauren's apparent dilemma. They had heard her rosy-red sunburn had no tan lines—*none whatsoever.* Todd, who'd not gotten the full story 'til now, finally understood everyone's strange behavior at home.

Laughing and catcalling, their taunting had followed her to every class. Of course, it didn't take long for the girls to find out what was going on, as well. They were appalled and humored. While they felt she was disgraced, they silently admired her courage and daring.

Poor Lauren had been watched all day; every move was an event. She felt like a bug in a jar being passed from one observer to another. She had never been more embarrassed in her young life. And, all day she had thought of only one thing—*Marilyn.* It had to have been her. Who else knew? And, would have told? Only the redheaded monster with whom she lived. *And, would she pay…*

Marilyn walked in the house and immediately went to her room to do her homework. Lauren followed slowly behind, taunts still ringing in her ears. She went to Marilyn's room and entered without knocking. "Lauren! Wh-what are you doing in here?"

"You told them, didn't you? Didn't you!"

Marilyn braced herself. "Told what to who?"

"You know what I'm talking about, d-d-darn it!" she exclaimed. "You told them!"

Marilyn felt safe, now. Lauren hadn't even cussed her. She must be afraid of something, she reasoned. So, she smiled, confident. "Yeah, so what?"

"So, what! So, what!" Lauren was livid. "Why did you do that? Why?"

"To get you back."

"*For what*? You're the one who hurt *me*! If anyone should be mad—"

"You told on me."

"You did it!"

"But, you didn't have to tell!" She stepped back. "I got a whippin' cause of you!"

"Look what I got!" Lauren retorted. "It wasn't my fault you deserted me," she hissed.

"Yes, it was."

"How?"

"You're mean to me all the time. And, and, you hit me. Hard."

Lauren smiled with the memory. "Yeah, and you deserved it, too. I just might do it again."

"Don't try and scare me, Lauren. I know you won't. You're afraid of what Momma and Daddy would do."

"Yeah, and I might just tell them about this. What about that?"

"Don't, Lauren."

"Why not?"

"Because I'll tell those boys tomorrow what else happened."

"What do you mean?" Lauren inquired with growing apprehension.

"About you gettin' a whippin' from Momma," she replied quickly. "And, about the soap. You gettin' your mouth washed out. I bet they'd love that!"

"You little...you little..."

"What, Lauren? A little what?" she taunted.

"Monster," Lauren growled. She would just have to come up with something else...something subtle...*something where she wouldn't get caught*. She was trying to determine the easiest method for murder—one with a lot of suffering. Finally, she sputtered, "You are d-dead meat, Marilyn. D-E-A-D. G-got it?" Her cousin paused and then laughed, again. "Listen to me! I'm gonna kill you," she said with a lowered voice. "*Kill you.*"

"Go ahead and try," she taunted, "and you'll be the sorry one. Just think, you got a whole month of school left...a whole, long month...and they'd all know...*every one of them.*"

Lauren swallowed hard. It wasn't worth it. Not, now. She gave one last look filled with hatred and turned to exit. "I won't always be in school, Marilyn, remember that. I *will* graduate." She faced her gloating cousin. "And, then, I'll get you. *I promise.*"

❦   ❦   ❦

After surviving the fourth day of her torment, Lauren realized the full extent of the damage to her skin. She had been forced to go to school as usual and exposed to the heat on the bus. Without adequate ventilation, large blisters formed on her to the extent she couldn't sit or even lie down comfortably. The least attempt at movement caused such agony, she cried.

When she did not come to supper even when called, Carolyn went to investigate. She knocked. "Lauren? You in there?"

"Yes!" the teen replied in horror. "Don't come in! I'm not dressed." She lay on the top of her bed, trying to withstand the fiery punishment she'd endured for several days. "Please excuse me from dinner."

"We'll wait for you to dress," her aunt answered with a laugh. "We're not *that* hungry."

"I'm not coming down at all," she explained further. "*Please,* excuse me—"

"What's wrong, Lauren?"

Silence.

"I'm coming in to   "

"No!" she screamed. "You can't!" She moved to stand and gasped in pain. Her sobs erupted.

Carolyn's heart pounded in her chest. "*Lauren?* Please, tell me what's going on."

Silence.

"I can't help you if you won't—"

"You helped me, all right," she wailed. "I'm dying here!" She tried to get a grip on her heaving sobs; even that made her hurt.

Carolyn's face pinched into a scowl. "I don't understand. What did I do?"

"You made me go to school," Lauren whimpered. "And, now I can't even walk!" She sucked in her breath. "I'm blistered all to hell!"

Her aunt visibly stiffened. "I'm coming in right now."

"No," the younger stated with apprehension. "I told you I am not dressed—"

"I've diapered you, Lauren. For heaven's sake—"

"A lot has changed since then," the teen answered quickly. "I don't want you—"

"You have to the count of three to be on that bed so I can take a look at what you're complaining about," her aunt warned. "One…two…three!" With that, she entered the forbidden sanctuary. Lauren retreated to the bed and fell on her stomach just in time. She closed her eyes, pretending that it wasn't really happening. She heard her aunt's gasp from the other side of the room. "*Oh, Lauren!*"

Carolyn moved quickly to her niece's side and just stared at the damaged skin. There was no doubt that the girl was in severe pain. How she'd made it this long was something to admire. "Pretty bad, eh?" Lauren asked, dryly.

"*Oh, Lauren,*" her aunt agreed. "You are blistered as badly as I've ever seen." She felt the tears spring to her eyes as she noticed her part in the faint crop marks. "Don't move. I'm going to get something from the cabinet." She returned within moments with a spray antiseptic which was supposed to numb the pain from burns. She applied it liberally and left her niece to rest. She returned to her supper with no appetite.

Lauren missed two days of school lying on her bed waiting for the blisters to burst and then peel. Little tan was left underneath to add insult to injury. As much as it would have pained her to admit it, she was eternally grateful to her aunt who was so kind to her those agonizing days.

CHAPTER 35

*I*t was during this time that an unexpected event occurred. Darren and Thatcher had both been involved with the Christian Athletes Bible club on campus that spring and looked forward to meeting with them during the summer. But it was during the first night of their weekend crusade in April that it happened.

Darren sat in the metal, fold-up chair on the grass beneath the tent. The preacher, an evangelist, was speaking on salvation and something clicked. It was so obvious that Darren felt stupid for it not occurring to him before now. For the first time in his life, he understood what everyone had been trying to tell him. All are sinful and remain so until cleansed by the saving power of God…the precious blood of Jesus…the sacrifice…the Savior.

He found himself walking up the aisle before he even knew he had stood. The voices of the congregation as they sang *Amazing Grace* buzzed in his head while he moved steadily toward the man in the gray suit. The man knelt with him and they had a quick discussion. Darren answered yes to all his questions and bowed his head.

He prayed earnestly for Jesus Christ to come into his heart and make him a new person…born again…into the Kingdom of God. When he raised his head, he found tears streaming down his cheeks and an overwhelming smile on his face. It was then he noticed another person at his side—Thatcher. He had followed his best friend's example and was kneeling, as well.

The song ended and they stood. The closing prayer was offered and everyone came to them with hugs and kisses. Darren and Thatcher both recognized many of the faces from the team as well as other students they knew. All were proud of their decisions.

On the way home, they were talking at once, hardly making any sense at all. It was a joyous two young men who entered the Preston home that evening. Malcolm and Carolyn both cried with happiness; their prayers had been answered. Marilyn looked on with envy of the attention. Lauren said nothing.

Darren tried to witness to Lauren, but he failed miserably. He was surprised at her apathy and downright rejection of anything he had to say. She attended church every Sunday, yes, because she *had* to go. She had no desire to be there.

※   ※   ※

Lauren turned eighteen on May 4, 1963. It was on Sunday, and she spent it leisurely at home (after services, of course). Her aunt and uncle gave her a cake and a new summer outfit. She was pleased and thanked them profusely.

Marilyn was terribly disgusted. She had tried everything to provoke her cousin into trouble, but nothing had worked. Now, she was eighteen and too old to be punished by her parents, or so she believed. She had no way of knowing for sure. Kathy was the only example by which for them to judge, and she kept her secrets to herself.

Lauren Ann Mitchell became a high school graduate on May 15, 1963. She posed for pictures with her brother who had just taken finals, himself. Thatcher was also in attendance, so she was very happy. All the Prestons attended, of course, including Kathy who was in for a visit from Nashville. Todd and Marilyn watched with envy.

But, it would not be long until they, too, would walk the stage for a diploma.

Darren sat there in his seat thinking about his own graduation. Lauren had not been there. She was locked in her room, beaten and hurting. He wiped the stray tears from his eyes. He had never really expected to see her graduate. He had honestly believed a funeral would occur before then. They had been so fortunate, he thought, for they had survived it all.

Lauren was hired as a clerk at Sears and Roebuck in the town of Edenton, just a block or two from her uncle's law office. She was able to ride with him each day to work which made for some interesting conversations.

Although the verbal taunts had ended that first week after spring break, Lauren still felt like she was being talked about in class. It certainly had not made her last days of high school a pleasant time. Marilyn well remembered Lauren's promise, and for a time, looked for mischief around every corner. Finding none, she finally decided that her cousin had mellowed—or forgotten. When it finally *did* happen, she didn't even suspect that it was a nightmare designed and orchestrated by her cousin. Revenge…nothing could be sweeter…or more deadly.

And, Lauren had forgotten just how dangerous it could be…

CHAPTER 36

*I*t was blessed springtime, June 1963. Darren and Thatcher were out of school for the summer and seeking employment at home. Thatcher, however, returned to his mother's home only for tragedy to strike soon after. He found his mother one morning unconscious in her bed. She had suffered a stroke sometime in the night. He called an ambulance, but she was already gone. He later took comfort in that she didn't suffer.

Naturally, he called his best friend, Darren, and asked Malcolm for advice. He was in a predicament he had not foreseen. They arrived within a few hours by train. "Thank you," Thatcher said, greeting them at the terminal. "I just don't know what to do." His usually jolly face was swollen from his crying, and he looked exhausted.

"Come on," Malcolm suggested. "Let's get you home so we can discuss things." The twenty-year-old nodded and directed them to his car. They rode the few miles in silence.

Thatcher McKinley certainly had a problem. He had no money, not even for the burial expenses. The house he had grown up in was rented, and he owed the bank a loan for his tuition. Even the best of jobs would not be able to keep him in school and assume responsibility for his debts. "What am I going to do?" he asked, wearily. "I don't know what to do."

Malcolm sighed. It *was* a dilemma. "Don't worry, Thatcher. We'll work this out."

"But, it's not your problem," the young man pointed out. "I wouldn't have called, but I have no one else. I just don't—"

"We're glad you called," Darren put in. "I would have been mad if you hadn't."

"Thanks." Silence. "Can you see any way out, Mr. Preston?" he asked.

Malcolm thought carefully. "Let me think for a moment, Thatcher. I just may have it." The two young men exchanged glances as the lawyer left the small dinner table and found a phone.

Malcolm did, indeed, find a solution for the young McKinley business major. One of his oldest friends, Cary Derebourne III, a very prominent member of the community and a fellow deacon of their church, was not only the president, but he was the founder of Edenton Bank and Trust. The two of them had served in the army together during the war and remained close. In fact, it had been Cary's father who had given Malcolm his first job.

The Derebournes were a family of lawyers until Cary chose business. His father died soon after the war ended and left him with a massive inheritance. He used it to establish the most successful banking institution in the city. Though he and his wife, Blanche, had two children, Cary IV and James, only the young Cary remained.

Twenty-eight and determined not to be a banker, he had gone into real estate and was doing well. James, who was lost at sea at twenty, had been a great loss. He was expected to assume the head of the family business. Cary III had despaired long ago of having someone he trusted to succeed him. It was his knowledge of this that led Malcolm to believe he could persuade his old friend to give Thatcher the chance of a lifetime. In exchange for the funds he needed to take care of his responsibilities and his education, he would agree to work for free the next two years as the elder's protégé. Malcolm was not disappointed.

The rest of the family joined the others for the funeral. Lauren offered her condolences. She knew what it was like to give up your mother—even a bad one—and hers was to a living death. She felt so sorry for him.

With the end of the spring semester, Darren returned to the farm. He had a part-time job in town during the week. Thatcher, too, came to stay there during those months, and shared a room with his best friend. He spent the weekdays in the bank learning the trade. He would never be able to repay Malcolm for his good fortune.

Darren and Thatcher convinced Malcolm to let them work as farm hands on the weekends to pay for their room and board. They cleaned fencerows and took care of the horses. This allowed Todd, who usually saw to those chores, to attend a two-month course at the University he had been offered due to his grades in school. He would stay on campus—his longest vacation away from his parents.

Darren and Thatcher stayed in the guest room just down the hall from Lauren. They had stored most of their "room stuff" in the barn and kept only their necessities in the house. When the new term began, they would have to move back to campus.

Although Lauren worked in town each day, she and Thatcher spent quite a lot of time together. They took long rides on Sunday afternoons and talked about many things. Each enjoyed the other's company and felt comfortable with the relationship.

She admired his seriousness, and he delighted in her spirit. He had never met another young woman quite like her—she was an original. He was handsome, athletic, and kind. He was her dream come true.

However, their relationship almost came to an abrupt end in July. Neither could have known about the other's intention and fell into the web woven for another. A silent war was raging between Marilyn and Lauren, and Thatcher was an innocent by-stander caught in the crossfire.

It was a hot and sticky day, the kind that almost smothers the life right out of you. The humidity was dreadful, the temperature the highest of the season. A cloudless sky made the sun seem even bigger and brighter than it was. And this was *the day*...

Lauren sat relaxing in her room. It was Saturday, her day-off from work. She had little intention of even stepping out of the house. Darren had gone to town on an errand and would be gone all afternoon, Thatcher was clearing a fence in one of the fields, and Malcolm was working in the office. That left Carolyn, Marilyn, and Lauren at the house alone. It was a combustible arrangement.

Marilyn was outside, enjoying the day when she ran around the old corncrib. It was a structure that hadn't been used in some time and was generally avoided. Malcolm thought it dangerous and planned to tear it down in a couple of weeks. It was then that she saw the wasp nest. It was huge, hardly even believable, attached at the tip-top corner of the doorway. She stood and stared.

Carolyn was mopping the front foyer when Lauren came down. "Just going to the kitchen for a snack," she said as she passed.

"All right, dear," her aunt acknowledged without looking up.

Lauren strolled to the kitchen and stood at the sink. Peering out the window, she thought she could see a figure. Was there something near the crib? It was too far to tell. So, she stepped onto the back porch and held her hand to her forehead. Yes, she could barely see her.

Marilyn.

Lauren smiled to herself. No one was supposed to be around there. She glanced over her shoulder and checked. Nothing. She quietly hurried across the lawn and hid just behind the oak tree. As she peered around it for a better look, she gasped.

Marilyn was wild. Her arms were flinging in all directions, and she was screaming. The house, however, was too far away for her to be heard clearly. Then, it happened.

Marilyn dodged for the door, the small one leading under the crib where the beanpoles and other equipment were stored. As her cousin watched, the eleven-year-old, not thinking clearly or she would have run toward the house, crawled to safety to await the calming of the wasps. She had been stung several times already and was going to avoid any others.

The "room" she had chosen was terribly hot and small. She felt as though the sides were closing in on her, but she dared not move or make a noise—anything that would send them down on her, again. She had just grown as comfortable as she could have been when the door shut...and locked.

Marilyn's eyes opened wide with fear. She crawled to where the opening had been and pushed. No use. The latch on the outside had fallen across and secured her. She wanted to yell, but she could hear the slight humming of the already angered wasps overhead. So, she was silent. In fact, she was so absorbed in her dilemma, she didn't even see Lauren stealthily returning to the house. She never knew that anyone had been there...and locked her in.

Lauren stood, panting, in the kitchen. She rubbed her throbbing hand; she'd been stung. Taking some baking soda from the drawer, she made a paste and applied it.

"What're you doing?"

Lauren jumped. "Uh, I was getting something to eat, and a wasp got in here. I got stung."

"Oh, let me see it," her aunt said sympathetically. "Well, it looks like you've done all you can for it. Did you kill it?"

Lauren blushed. "Uh, no, ma'am, it got away."

"Oh, well." She opened the back door and poured out her dirty water. She looked all around. "Seen Marilyn lately?"

"Not since breakfast."

"Oh. Wonder where she is—"

"I, uh, don't know. You want me to look for her?"

"Oh, no," her aunt said with a smile. "I'm sure she's okay. She's just out running around. I'll look for her later." She patted her on the back. "You enjoy your day-off, all right?"

Lauren grinned. "Yes, ma'am." Carolyn didn't have any idea how much Lauren would enjoy this day...her day of revenge...a day of justice.

❈   ❈   ❈

Marilyn lay still on the dirt floor, crying silently. The welts from the stings were throbbing with sharp pain, and she could do nothing to help herself. She only prayed that she would get no more before someone found her.

Thinking of the black snake, the one her father had killed just the week before, preyed on her mind. What if one was here? Lying beside of her in the darkness? She cringed with the thought and wept. She was terrified and alone, so dreadfully alone, and vulnerable.

❈   ❈   ❈

Lauren went to the living room and passed the time with a book staying in plain view. The last thing she wanted to do was go outside. She needed a tight alibi, and her aunt was a perfect choice. As long as she stayed indoors, she could not possibly be blamed for it. And, one thing she knew for certain...she didn't want to be caught in this one. She could only imagine what would they do to her if they ever found out.

Hours passed.

Sweat poured from Marilyn's forehead. The weather had been so perfect, she thought, until one is stuck out in it. The crib seemed to absorb the heat she was trying to avoid. She tried to move into a more comfortable position, but there wasn't much room. She covered her face with her filthy hands and tried to breathe more slowly. Finally, in spite of her terror, she fell asleep.

The light darkness of the summer months had fallen when Malcolm and Darren returned to the farm. Inside what seemed to be a tranquil house, there was turmoil. Carolyn was sitting in the living room, weeping, with Lauren at her side.

"Carolyn, what's wrong?" her husband asked as he rushed to her.

"Oh, God, Malcolm," she exclaimed. "We can't find Marilyn! I tried to call you, but you'd left. We don't know where she is, and we've looked everywhere! Lauren and I looked all around the house and...*everywhere*. I've called and called..." her voice drifted as she broke into a fresh wave of tears.

Malcolm's face drew tight. "Darren, get a horse saddled and search the lower fields. I'll look around here." Both left quickly.

Lauren held her aunt's shoulder. "Don't worry, Aunt Carolyn. They'll find her. I'm sure she's okay," she comforted as the mother wept.

CHAPTER 37

Darren found her. He was riding by on his way to the fields when he heard her crying. He called her name; she answered. In a matter of minutes, he located her and yelled for his uncle. Malcolm and Darren pulled her from the cramped quarters, filthy and exhausted. Cradling her in his arms, her father carried her into the house. Carolyn met them at the door. "Oh, thank God! Is she all right?"

"I think so," her husband assured. "She just needs to be cleaned up."

"Hi, Momma," Marilyn whispered.

"Hello, darling," Carolyn said softly as she pushed her wet hair from her forehead. She looked at Malcolm. "Carry her upstairs to her bedroom. I'll wash her and find out what happened."

Thirty minutes later, Carolyn and Lauren sat on the bed with Marilyn, freshly washed and looking much better. "I was over by the crib when the wasps came at me. I didn't know what to do. They were stinging me and it hurt! So, I ran over and crawled in the door."

"It was open?" her mother inquired.

"Yes, ma'am. I got inside and they left me alone."

"But, then what happened?" Lauren asked with mock concern.

"I don't know," she answered slowly. "The door shut and then it wouldn't open. I couldn't get out, and I was afraid to say anything. I was afraid they'd come back." She shuddered at the memory.

"Well, at least you're all right, now," her mother comforted. "I guess you'll stay away from there from now on. Hmm?"

"Yes, ma'am!"

Carolyn smiled and kissed her forehead. "I love you."

"I love you, too, Momma."

"Get some sleep. You'll feel better in the morning."

"Okay."

Lauren and her aunt left quickly and stood in the hall. "I wonder how the door shut," Lauren mused. She was playing her part to the hilt.

"I don't know," the elder answered. "Maybe the wind?"

"Maybe so," her niece agreed. "Well, whatever it was, she's fine, now."

"Yes," Carolyn said thankfully. "And, Lauren, I appreciate your concern for Marilyn. I'm glad the two of you are getting along, now." Lauren forced a smile. "Well, I'm going downstairs and talk to Malcolm."

"I think I'll go to bed, now. It's been a long day."

"Yes, it has," Carolyn agreed with a weary smile. She patted her niece gently on the shoulder. "Good night, Lauren."

"Good night, Aunt Carolyn."

Lauren watched her aunt disappear down the hall and the stairs, then entered her room, safe, at last. She fell onto her bed, thoroughly pleased with herself. She had gotten even. All those pranks…the tales Marilyn had told at school…all the embarrassing stares…she had paid for them, dearly, Marilyn had. Lauren had made it a day her cousin would not soon forget,

❈   ❈   ❈

Darren sat at the kitchen table, worrying. "Where could he be? Do you think he's hurt?"

Malcolm sipped his coffee. "He's all right. He probably lost track of time and got caught in the dark."

"I hope so."

At this moment, Carolyn arrived. "Isn't Thatcher back, yet? I expected him an hour ago."

"So did I," Darren answered with a frown. All sat silently for a few moments.

"Is Marilyn, okay?" her father inquired.

Carolyn sighed. "Yes, I think so. She was more scared than anything. Who could blame her? Left all alone under a rickety old building with wasps already around? Maybe *snakes*? Makes me shiver just thinking about it."

"Wonder how she got locked in like that," Darren mused aloud. "I mean that latch was perfectly set. Almost like someone—" He stopped short. "You don't think—"

"No," Carolyn answered quickly. "Lauren has been with me all day in the house. Besides, she has been so good to me this afternoon when I was frantic—and to Marilyn, too. She couldn't have. I don't think she would've."

"No, I guess not," Darren agreed with a blush. "I guess she'd be mad at me for even suspecting her. I shouldn't have, you kn—"

He was interrupted again by Carolyn. "Thatcher! Here he comes, now!" All turned and watched as the lantern light bobbed up and down. They opened the back screen door for him. He stepped inside.

"Where have you been?" Darren asked anxiously.

Thatcher laughed. "Oh, I've been around. I worked all morning on that fence—you know the one I told you about—and then I came back here and—"

"Why, I didn't see you today!" Carolyn exclaimed.

He laughed, again. "Well, I got here with just enough time to grab the tool that I needed and walk back to the spot I'd found. It took longer than I thought it would. That's why I'm late." He sat heavily in the remaining chair. "So, anything exciting happen while I was gone?"

The three laughed nervously. He stared at them. "Well, obviously it did. What was it?" Carolyn proceeded to tell him of Marilyn's adventure, search, and rescue. He listened carefully, with a frown. When she had finished, he asked, "Did you say the door was open when she ran to get in?"

Carolyn looked at him seriously. "Yes, why?"

"Well," he shrugged. "I guess someone opened it, again, before Marilyn got there."

"What do you mean? You *closed* it?"

"No, I saw Lauren latch it today on my way back for that tool. She closed it and went back in the house. I was glad because I was afraid something was going to happen in that old thing." He paused. "Wonder who opened it, again?"

Carolyn's heart nearly stopped beating. She looked up at Darren, whose eyes met hers, and then at Malcolm. She said slowly, "*I don't believe it.*"

Thatcher looked at her quickly. "You don't think Lauren locked her in, do you? She wouldn't—"

"Don't say that," Darren interrupted.

"I can't believe it," Carolyn repeated. "It all fits. Everything *fits.*"

"What do you mean?" her husband asked, a pit growing in his stomach.

Carolyn eerily smiled as she explained her deduction. "Today…I came into the kitchen…Lauren had been stung by a wasp…she said it was in here…in the *kitchen*…but it wasn't." She swallowed, "Oh, she was so cool about it…she lied so easily to me…all day…*all day she lied to me…*" Her smile had faded into steely determination and she rose.

Malcolm got to his feet. "No, Carolyn. I'll take care of this," he said solemnly. "I'll—"

"*No*," his wife corrected. "She's mine first, Malcolm. I'll have my way *first.*"

"Carolyn, your *temper*—"

"I'll watch my temper, Malcolm, and this will be one day Lauren Ann Mitchell will remember for the rest of her life." With a sure step, she left the room before her husband could comment further, three pairs of eyes watching her exit.

Judgment had come.

CHAPTER 38

*G*aining fury with each step, Carolyn walked swiftly up the stairs and down the hallway. She only paused at her daughter's door, her heart aching for her child. Marilyn had been through so much that day...so much...all because of Lauren...*and her lies.* Mission renewed, she strode to Lauren's door and without knocking, entered. Her niece had just gotten snuggled beneath the sheet. At her aunt's entry, she sat upright. "Aunt Carolyn! What's wrong?"

Silence.

* * *

"Lauren's going to kill me," Thatcher finally mustered. "She'll never forgive me for this." He looked up at his best friend and his employer.

Malcolm took another sip of his coffee. "Yep, she's going to be rather disagreeable."

Darren had been silent, but found his voice. "It's not your fault. You just told the truth. No one can blame you for that."

"*She* can," Thatcher reiterated. "Lauren will blame me for telling on her."

"You didn't tell on her, son," Malcolm said slowly. "She was the one who did it and then lied about it. You're not to blame for that.

Lauren'll be angry, yes, but she has enough sense to realize that *she's* the only one to blame."

"I hope you're right, Mr. Preston. I sure hope so." There was silence as the three drank their beverages. In fact, it was *deathly* quiet until...

"*No-o-o-o-o!*" came the scream. All in the kitchen turned just in time to see the two coming at them through the door. "You're *hurting* me! Let me go!"

Carolyn held her niece by the ear and was dragging her behind. "*Hurt* you? I haven't even gotten started, yet!"

"Ple-e-ase!" Lauren's muffled cry wailed. "What is going *o-o-on?*"

"*Carolyn*," Malcolm mustered, rising.

Choosing to ignore him, Carolyn did not answer as they passed the petrified boys at the table. Their eyes bugged and mouths fell open. Barely able to turn their heads, they watched as the mother dragged her charge out the back door...off the porch...and to the barn. The girl's cries lingered and then stopped as the door to the stables was slammed shut.

Silence, once more.

Thatcher looked around at Malcolm's face. "She'll never forgive me." Darren nodded in agreement. "*Never, never, never.*"

Malcolm slowly returned to his seat, a silent prayer for his wife's patience uttered.

❧   ❧   ❧

Carolyn yanked the teen into the barn and shut the door behind them. Lauren was bent double, trying to prevent her ear from being pulled completely off her skull. Her head ached and throbbed with the pulse of her heart. With a shove, her aunt released her, sending her reeling.

Lauren tumbled, trying to catch her balance and finally stood upright. Her short nightgown fell just below her knees, which were trembling. She looked at her guardian with tear-filled eyes. "Wh-what is g-going on? What did I d-do?"

Carolyn said nothing. Her graying light auburn hair was brushed back from her face; and her eyes, deep blue like her sister's, gleamed in the dim light. Her face was flushed red, her heart racing. She was too angry to speak.

"Aunt Carolyn," Lauren whined as she held to her sore ear. "What's going on?"

"Don't give me that," her aunt warned. "I've heard enough of your lies today."

"Wh-what lies? What are you talking about?"

Carolyn quickly retrieved a riding crop from the shelf. Calmly as her heart would allow, she strode to the terrified teen and backed her into a corner. Brandishing it wildly, she screamed, "The *truth!*"

"I *am* telling th—" Her aunt let a lick fly, but Lauren dodged at the last moment. "Aunt Carolyn, please!" Seeing her intentions, she begged. "Please! No-o-o-o-o!" Two more followed, one catching her thigh. "All right!" she agreed. "Please just stop!"

Carolyn looked deeply into her niece's eyes and she took a step backward. Her hands shook with her fury. "Tell me what happened, Lauren. I want to hear it all. The whole, dreadful lot of it."

Silence.

"A-Aunt C-Carolyn?"

"*Yes?*"

"I s-still don't know what you mean."

"Yes—you—do!" she insisted as a stroke to the stable wall accented each word. "Tell me what you did to Marilyn!"

"N-nothin'," Lauren mumbled as she tried to soothe the stinging pain in her leg. "I didn't do nothing to her! I *promise!*" Her eyes pleaded. "I was with *you!*"

Carolyn could not believe her ears. Did the girl really think she would believe her lies, *even now?* What kind of fool did she take her for? She took another step closer to her niece. Her eyes, glazed with unbidden tears, bore into Lauren's very soul; their noses almost touched.

Carolyn's voice, deceptively calm as the July winds, spoke slowly and clearly. "Lauren, I doubt you *fully* understand just how upset I am at this moment. If you did, you would thank your God I am as controlled as I am. Because I *assure* you, before we leave this barn you will confess to me what you did today. And then, *then*, my dear, I will *personally and with great relish* whip the blood from you! Do you understand what I am saying? *Do you really understand?*"

Lauren's face felt hot and her legs were weak. Oh, God, she *did* know. She knew…about Marilyn. O*h, God*…what would she *do*?

"Lauren! Answer me!"

"Y-yes, ma'am," she stammered. "I-I understand."

"Good." Her face was drawn with tight lines around her frowned mouth. "I'm ready to listen."

Lauren hesitated. "But, w-why d-do you think I did—"

"Thatcher."

"*Thatcher?*" Lauren repeated with obvious shock.

"Thatcher."

"What's *he* got to do with it?"

Her aunt's voice was cold. "He came back to the house today for a tool. He saw you latch the door to the crib. Only he didn't know my daughter was in there."

Lauren's blood turned to ice. *Thatcher.* She had forgotten about him…hadn't even considered…*oh, God*…her fate was sealed. She stole a glance at her aunt's fists; both were clenched, one around the handle of a very supple *switch*, if you will. Lauren swallowed hard.

"*Oh.*"

Silence.

"My patience is growing *thinner*," Carolyn informed her as she lightly tapped the crop against her own leg. Transfixed with horror, Lauren watched. Did her aunt *really* mean to—? "*Lauren!*"

She snapped back to attention. "Yes, ma'am?"

"You are not making this any easier, my dear. And, believe me, you haven't much room to grow *worse*."

"All right," she said, swallowing the lump of fear in her throat. "I was standing in the...in the...kitchen when I saw something by the...by the crib. So, I went out the back door and over to the tree. I knew then it was M-Marilyn."

"What was she doing?"

"F-fooling around, I guess. But, but, then she started swinging her arms and ran under the crib...through the d-door."

"Did you know what was happening?" her aunt asked evenly.

Lauren blushed. "Y-yes, ma'am. Wasps were all around there. I guess she was getting stung."

"Fifteen times," Carolyn added.

Lauren felt her blazing eyes in her heart. "I ran over and c-closed the door where she couldn't see me and l-locked it shut. Then, I came b-back inside."

"And, noticed you were stung?" The teen nodded. "And, lied to me? Both about the wasp and not seeing your cousin?"

"Yes, ma'am," she barely whispered.

Silence.

Carolyn's eyes glazed with tears as she said, "You left her there knowing she was in pain, scared, and trapped—as hot as it was today. She could have died under there, Lauren! What would you have done then? Nothing? *Just like today*!?!"

Silence.

"*Lauren*? What would you have done? *Cried* at the funeral? What would you have said, then? *What*?"

Silence.

Carolyn's voice lowered. "I think I know." Her niece waited anxiously. "You would have comforted me just like you did today, *denying everything*. You would have *lied* to us all...and been a *murderer*."

Lauren swallowed, again. "I'm sorry—"

"Oh, yes!" her aunt agreed. "*You will be*!"

"Aunt Carolyn, I didn't mean to hurt her—"

"Oh, really?" Her aunt smiled sarcastically. "Isn't that what Marilyn said about leaving you to sizzle in the sun?"

Silence.

"But, I-I had a reason for—"

"A reason!" she exclaimed. "There is *no* possible excuse for your behavior! None *whatsoever!*"

"But, you d-don't understand!"

"Oh, I understand *perfectly*, Lauren," her aunt said, her fury evident. "You wanted to hurt her more than she'd hurt you. *Didn't you?*"

Lauren dropped her head shamefully. "Yes, ma'am."

"*Good.* Then you'll understand exactly how *I* feel when I say that I want to hurt *you* now more than you hurt *her* today."

Lauren's head jerked up. She was peering into very cold eyes.

❋   ❋   ❋

"What do you think she's gonna do to her?" Thatcher asked fearfully.

"I don't know," Darren answered looking over at his roommate. "Can you see anything?"

Thatcher stood peering out their bedroom window. The safety light was bright enough to show the outside of the barn, but nothing on the inside with the door shut. "No." He flopped down on the bed. "I wish I knew what was going on."

"So do I," Darren agreed. "Although, we may not really want to know, after all. I don't think Uncle Malcolm would have asked us to leave if he didn't see real trouble."

Thatcher nodded. "Uh-huh."

"I wonder where he was going," Darren mused. "He seemed worried."

"Yeah," Thatcher agreed, "and *that* worries me most of all."

❦   ❦   ❦

"Didn't you know you'd get caught? Didn't you *know* you could not possibly get away with it?"

Lauren shifted her feet nervously on the floor. "I didn't think anybody saw me."

"What did you think would happen to you if we *did* discover it was you? What'd you expect us to do?"

Silence.

"*Lauren*? What did you expect?"

"I-I d-don't know. I didn't think I'd get caught this time. I thought I'd gotten her back for all the things she d-did to me—"

"All the things *she's* done? What about everything *you've* done to *her*?" her aunt accused.

"She told everybody about my sunburn!" Lauren exclaimed angrily. "Everybody at school laughed at me!" Tears threatened to fall with the painful memories of her humiliation. "They all stared and stared—"

"Why didn't you tell us?"

"She threatened me."

"Threatened you? How? What could she do?"

Lauren sniffled. "She said...she said she'd tell them about me...about me getting whipped and my mouth...my mouth washed out."

"And, you believed her?" The teen nodded. "You didn't think we would have stopped her? Done something?"

"I decided to get her back myself after graduation."

Her aunt stared. "And, today was it? Your *revenge*?!"

Silence.

Carolyn stepped closer and Lauren gulped. "You locked my hurting and scared little girl in a hot crib all day for your petty *revenge*? When you could have *told* us what she'd done? *Knowing* we would have punished her?"

"I wanted to get her back myself," she admitted bravely. "I wanted her to know that she couldn't do that to me."

"She didn't know it was you!" her aunt exclaimed. "None of us knew! You lied! Covered it up! No one would ever have known!" She paused. "You couldn't possibly have hoped to accomplish anything but a devious punishment only you would know who caused. All for your *satisfaction!*"

Silence.

"I'm sorry."

Silence.

"Do you think that makes everything *okay*?" Carolyn asked icily. "That your *apology* will erase her pain? Can go back and keep her from being locked in there for hours, too terrified to even scream for help? *Do you really think 'I'm sorry' takes care of all that?*"

Silence.

"*I didn't think so*. I suggest you get yourself prepared." Lauren's mouth fell open while she waited for an explanation. What did she mean by getting prepared? What was she planning to do? *Surely*, she wasn't going to—"I said, get ready, Lauren. *I meant it,*" her aunt's voice rang loudly in the lofty barn. "*Now.*"

"I-I don't understand," Lauren stated simply.

Carolyn's expression was chiseled in stone. "*I told you what I was going to do,*" she said clearly as she brandished her rod. "I suggest you get yourself bent over that hay bale before I do it for you." Lauren's pulse thudded in her ears. The woman couldn't be serious…she was *eighteen*! She was too old for this! What had come over her aunt?

"But, but I'm eighteen!"

"So, you are. Bend over."

"But, I'm too old for this! You have no right—"

"*I have every right!*" her aunt exploded. "As long as you live in our home, you will act according to our rules. You have broken them all today with malice and forethought and I can think of no one who deserved a whipping any more than you do at this moment." She paused and held up the crop. "In fact, you deserve a horsewhipping, but I think I'll make do with this."

Lauren's mind raced. She couldn't allow this to happen to her. "No, no," she began. "Please! You can't do this!" she exclaimed even as she dashed toward the door.

CHAPTER 39

"Any change?" Darren asked from the bed. Attempting to read a magazine article, he'd read the same paragraph four times. Thatcher stood with his mouth hanging open. Darren stared at him. "Hey, buddy, what's the matter?"

Thatcher motioned with his hand for him to come to the window. "You're not gonna believe this." He pointed to the barnyard.

"Oh, my God," Darren whispered.

❀   ❀   ❀

Lauren made it just beyond the door before Carolyn got to her. Grasping the teen's arm with her left hand and holding her within reach, the woman swung with her right. Lauren screamed as they made a circle in the barnyard, illuminated by the light from the pole. Neither knew that both Thatcher and Darren watched from above. They stood, mesmerized, not speaking.

Luckily for Lauren, her aunt's aim was hindered in the struggle, and she remained untouched despite Carolyn's determination. She fought with all of her strength to escape her aunt's grasp, but the hold was sufficient. They continued to ring-around-the-rosy in the barnyard, the niece pleading for mercy as the intended strokes whistled close in the hot, night air. "Please! Please, *stop!*" the girl screamed, sending her plea through the second story window where her brother and beau stood.

"The barn, Lauren! Get back in the barn!" Carolyn yelled.

"All right, *all right!*" she called. "I'll go, just stop! Please, stop!"

Carolyn paused and pushed her toward the barn door. Lauren heaved violently as she stumbled back into the stables. Her aunt, face flushed with exertion and anger, slammed the door behind them.

The young men watched as the door was closed and the night was once again, silent. Slowly, they turned and looked at each other. Thatcher mustered, "I don't believe I just saw that."

"I do," Darren said solemnly. "Lauren has pushed too far this time."

"And, I helped shove her over the edge," Thatcher said with a groan. "Now, I *know* she'll never forgive me."

"Forgive you?" Darren asked, a nervous laugh escaping. "You'll be lucky if she ever even *looks* at you." Thatcher nodded sadly. "You keep watch. I'm going to find Uncle Malcolm."

❧   ❧   ❧

Carolyn walked to her niece with a deliberate step. Within a foot of her, she stopped and motioned with the crop. "Do as I told you, Lauren. Don't make things worse than they are. *Another stunt like that and there won't be enough of you left to take back in the house.*"

"Please," Lauren softly begged, the tears slipping down her cheeks. "Please, *I'm sorry*...please!" Carolyn emotionlessly gestured once again for her to turn around. "Please, don't do this to me, *please*..."

"*I'll do it and enjoy it,*" Carolyn gritted between clenched teeth as she pictured in her mind her bedraggled daughter who was pulled to safety and the pain Marilyn had endured. "*You'll regret this day for a long, long time,*" she added as she quickly approached.

A small scream escaped Lauren's lips as her arm was roughly twisted when Carolyn attempted to position her. But, it was not until Lauren's knees buckled and the crop was drawn back for the first vicious stroke that Carolyn's hand was stilled. For in that moment, she looked for the first time into the cowering, terror-filled eyes of her niece and saw on Lauren's face an expression that had not been uncommon to her; after all, Rex Mitchell had seen it each and every time he had ever raised his hand to strike her. Carolyn then realized what she had almost done, what she had so desperately *wanted* to do…and hated herself for it.

Lauren watched in dumb disbelief as her aunt's face, so recently contorted with rage, drained of color as she walked backwards, shaking her head at the horrible thing she had envisioned. Blindly almost, she stumbled to the stacks of hay bales to her left and fell to her knees, crop slipping from her weakened grip. "Oh, *Father*," she exclaimed pressing her palms over her eyes, "have *mercy* on me!"

Quietly at first and then bursting into wailing tears, she pleaded for forgiveness. "*Oh, God*, how could I do it? How could I have been so *angry*?" she asked, her throat raw. "I've never been that *furious*. God, please, *help me*." Her weeping soon became sobs of grief as she remembered the horror of the day and the cold, cold fear that had gripped her heart when her child was lost.

"I was so scared, Lord, so scared that she had been taken from me. I couldn't bear it, I just *couldn't*." Her neck was slick from the streams of hot tears that had flowed down her cheeks. Her nose ran, and she tried to keep it at bay with the sleeve of her dress when her sniffling failed. "My little child, Lord, my *precious little girl*."

Lauren, meanwhile, had remained quite still. Though she wished she could run, as her common sense told her to do, she found that it was as if she were nailed to the spot. Her own tears dried on her cheeks and the rhythm of her breathing returned to normal, even as the petitions of Carolyn grew in intensity.

Never had Lauren seen her aunt so distressed…and vulnerable. Stalwart and proud she had always seemed to Lauren, never this penitent and remorseful. She had seen her cry many times for many reasons, but somehow, this was different. This was for the lack of a better description, *childlike*. For the first time, Lauren thought with a pang of guilt, Carolyn reminded her of Helen, her mother. It was a sight she hoped never again to witness.

Lauren's heart nearly broke as she listened to the painful recount of the day's misfortune and the agony her aunt had suffered those long hours, a situation that she knew was all her fault. Not Marilyn's, not Thatcher's, but hers, *alone*. Not only had she caused Marilyn to be trapped, she had purposefully kept the secret that had tortured this now pitiful woman who was weeping a few feet from her. And, she was truly sorry of it…*truly*.

Finding fresh tears in her tired eyes, Lauren slowly got to her feet. The plank floor was scratchy on her bare feet as she slowly approached her aunt. Her short nightgown, now dirty from her excursion, she pulled around her knees as she knelt down beside of her. A tender hand was placed on her shoulder and simple words spoken.

"I'm sorry."

Carolyn's head lifted and she turned to look upon the niece she'd forgotten was in the room. Her eyes were already red and swollen, but still filled with pain. "*Lauren*," she whispered, "*oh, L-Lauren*."

"I'm sorry, Aunt Carolyn, so sorry I hurt you."

"*Oh, Lauren*." She started to grasp her niece's hand, but instead covered her mouth to keep the sob from escaping. The memory of her raging anger coming again to the front of her mind brought her pain. "Oh, God, *have m-mercy on me*," she breathed once more.

Lauren, not knowing how to comfort her, felt inadequate for the task at hand, but compelled to say *something*. "It's okay, Aunt Carolyn. *Please*," she said, tenderly, "*please, stop crying*."

"I c-can't," her aunt answered, "I can't s-stop thinking about…*you*." She mustered the courage to look into her eyes. "The thoughts I had were…*t-terrible*." A fat tear rolled off of her chin, but she didn't brush it away.

Lauren looked away. "*I did a terrible thing*, Aunt Carolyn. I hurt Marilyn and you and lied to you and—"

"No excuse," her aunt broke in, "none for what I've done—and was about to do. *God, help me*," she whispered, "*there's no excuse*." There was a short silence broken only by the quiet sobbing of the elder. Finally, Carolyn took her hand, forcing her niece to look at her, and spoke with conviction so strong it made Lauren shudder. "*I love you*."

Lauren nodded. "I know, Aunt Carolyn, I—"

"No, *Lauren*, I *really* love you. Like one of my own children, a part of me. I want you to be loved and happy and everything I want for Kathy and Todd and, yes...Lord love her...Marilyn. *I love you, Lauren*, like you can't even *imagine*." She swallowed hard. "That's why I hate myself so much right now."

Carolyn slid down from her knees onto the floor and folded her legs around her as she grappled to gain hold of her emotions enough to speak without crying. "It's *never* easy, Lauren, punishing a child. You *love* them so much. Their cries, their tears, will nearly *rip you apart* inside, but you swallow your grief and do what you know you *have to do* because...because you *love them* too much *not* to." She released Lauren's hand and gripped her own hands in front of her and wringed them. "And sometimes you think, Lord, they're never going to learn, why do I have to keep doing this? Is there some other way *besides* punishment? Of any kind, I mean," she added quickly, "not just physical. Restriction, work, whatever it is you do to teach a lesson, but, you know, there *isn't*." Then, she looked up from her downcast expression to peer directly into her niece's face.

"I love my children enough, Lauren, that I'll *never* give up on them—and that includes *you*. Because *my* parents never gave up on me though Lord knows I gave them reason to." She sighed, remembering. "Papa swore I'd be the death of him. And poor *Mother*! It's a wonder I don't carry the willow switch marks to this *very day*, I was so *well acquainted* with it." She was able to smile despite the silent tears that crept down her cheeks. "I just never seemed to learn either, but they kept trying and one day, well, I guess I just finally *surrendered*." She patted Lauren on the knee, bringing a small grin. "And I didn't just give in to my *parents'* will, Lauren, but to *God's*. And, you know what? *He*'s never given up on me, either.

"Oh, He has to chastise me every now and again," she went on, her lip trembling as the tears threatened to roll, "but He still l-loves me...and *forgives*." Carolyn swallowed nervously, choking back a sob. "I wish you could know that forgiveness and love, Lauren, that *only* God can give you. I can just show you my imperfect love, but He...He can love you unconditionally *all* the time and discipline you *without* sinning as I did tonight." She sniffed loudly. "Oh, I want so *desperately* for you to seek Him!"

Lauren, her own tears now coming to the fore, felt the stirring inside of her heart which ached always for only one thing and that one thing *only*. She looked into the eyes of her aunt, the emotion overwhelming her. "How can God love *me*," she asked quietly, "when all I can think of is **pain**? The hate and anger inside of me that *I can't let go*? It *haunts* me. *Can* He really take that hurt away? Can He make it *all* go away?" The tears did fall and she nearly choked on them. "Because all I want, Aunt Carolyn, is *peace*. That's *all*." She covered her face with her hands and cried, "*I'm just so tired*."

Carolyn could say nothing for a while. She simply opened her arms and pulled Lauren inside of them and embraced her as she wept from the weariness of burdens she had been laden with far too young and for far too long. When her aunt trusted herself to speak, she said, "Oh, yes, Lauren, *He can*. Christ can give you the peace that 'passeth all understanding.' All you have to do is ask for it."

Lauren's shoulders shook as she wept. "Can you show me how to ask? I've never talked to Him before. Not for *real*. Not like this."

Carolyn laughed softly in her joy and leaned down to place a tender kiss on the top of Lauren's head. "Let me introduce you to my *Father*."

In the minutes that followed, Carolyn explained the plan of salvation, the promises of God, to her niece, and Lauren asked God to forgive her and give her the peace she had long craved. The void that had troubled her was filled and the thirst for love and forgiveness was quenched. She was no longer an orphan, but a child of God.

When their tears of sorrow had turned to joy and they had regained control of their emotions, both took deep breaths and sighed, the tension of the long evening subsiding. Carolyn found herself chuckling and Lauren, busily drying her tears, was quick to inquire. "What is it?"

"Well, I think I'm finally calm enough to give you the whipping you deserve for that horrible trick you played today," she began, a bit of devilry in her eye, "but—"

"But, you're not going to, right?" Lauren finished for her. "I mean, I admit I might deserve it, but—"

"*Might* deserve it?"

"Well," the niece stalled, "you're not are you?" The inflection in her voice betrayed her; she wasn't so certain that her aunt would excuse her, even now.

Carolyn rested her hands on her knees that were now pulled to her chest; Lauren sat similarly across from her. "Elizabeth Preston, your Uncle Malcolm's grandmother, told me once that one time in a person's life you should give them a good dose of *unexpected, undeserved mercy* just so they'd have a taste of what *God's grace* is like." She grinned, then. "And at the time, I was awfully grateful for her *interference* and that advice. Tonight you can be grateful I remembered it."

"*You* were grateful? I thought you said it was *Uncle Malcolm's* grandmother, not yours. By the time you met her ya'll must've been dating! How could *you* be grateful to *her*?"

"It's a long story I'll share sometime," Carolyn said with a comic grimace. "*Maybe*."

Lauren laughed, her whole spirit lighter than it had ever been. "Well, if we're finished here, I'd like to go share my news with Darren. He's going to be happy, I think."

"Very," her aunt agreed. "And, yes, we've done all we're going to do here. I may stay a few minutes longer, but you go ahead." Lauren nodded and before she stood, reached for another embrace. "I love you, Lauren," Carolyn whispered in her ear, "so very, *very* much. *Never* forget that."

"*I love you, too*, Aunt Carolyn. And, I'm so sorry about today. I'll never do anything like that *ever* again. I *promise*."

"That's good," her aunt agreed with a chuckle. "You just used up your one free pass." Lauren smiled and slowly stood. She started to leave, but hesitated, looking back at her aunt who had knelt, again. Carolyn, not hearing her leave, added, "I'm fine, Lauren. I just want a few minutes alone. I'll be along shortly." As Lauren turned to leave, however, Carolyn's voice stopped her. "Oh, and, uh, Lauren, if your *uncle* asks about tonight, you don't have to tell him *everything*, you know. What he doesn't know—"

"Won't hurt *you*?"

"Something like that," her aunt agreed sheepishly, not turning around.

"Don't worry, Aunt Carolyn. Your secret is safe with me." Lauren bent and kissed her on the cheek before winking to the person she saw emerging from the shadows. Swallowing a chuckle and smiling inwardly at the surprise awaiting her aunt, she left the stables.

When her niece had gone, Carolyn began to softly sing her favorite hymn with deep conviction and praise. "Amazing Grace...how sweet the sound...that saved a wretch like me...I once was lost...but—"

"*Now am* **found**," a deep voice boomed from behind her in harmony, stopping her cold and nearly scaring her senseless. She reeled, landing with a dull thud on her seat, and *found* herself staring into the solemn expression of her husband.

"Malcolm Allister!" she exclaimed. "You nearly scared me to death!" Her heart pounding, she gasped for breath. "Honestly!"

"Quite the one to be speaking of *honesty*," he observed dryly. "Asking your child to lie to *me* after coming within an inch of whipping her for lying to *you*."

"I didn't tell her to *lie*," Carolyn insisted, her face flaming, "just not to—"

"*Carolyn*."

His wife of nearly twenty-four years sighed. "All right, so how long have you been back there *spying* on me?"

Malcolm did not answer immediately. Instead, he stepped around the stalls and to her silent horror, picked up the crop she had discarded. Looking into her eyes, he said, "Long enough to know you lost your temper worse than you ever have before." He waved it in her direction.

Carolyn started to argue, but the expression on his face caused her useless excuse to be caught in her throat, her defense ending before it began with her throwing up her hands and sighing wearily. Her voice quivered when she finally spoke. "Malcolm, *please* don't lecture me tonight for—"

"You don't *lecture* with this thing, darling," he said, a grin fighting to escape. "Even the horses know better than that."

"*Malcolm*—"

"Oh, don't worry, Carolyn. I know Granny saved you from me once already," he said, his expression stern, "but I asked God and He said it was okay to give you another free pass—*just one more*." His face softened and she knew then that he had seen her repentance and was there only to comfort her.

Carolyn's heart melted in love as he tossed the crop aside and offering her a hand to get to her feet, he took her in his arms and held her to his strong chest. "*Unexpected, undeserved mercy*," she whispered as the peace coursed through her, "what a wonderful gift to been given."

"Yes, *sweetheart*," he agreed. "It certainly *is*."

Truly.

CHAPTER 40

*U*pon entering the house, the first person to greet Lauren was her brother. Mistaking the glistening tears on her cheeks for those of sadness and not joy, he had rebuked her for her thoughtless prank before she could share with him her good news. Words cannot capture the rush of emotion that overwhelmed them both as they stood clinging to each other in the kitchen of the old Preston farmhouse. Darren's joy was unspeakable.

Thatcher, too, celebrated her conversion both for itself and because she easily forgave him for his "catching her in the act" since she escaped harsh punishment. His prayers had been answered twofold. He kissed her on the cheek in Christian love before retiring to his room.

Lauren walked to her bedroom with a small smile on her face and relief in her soul. She closed the door behind her and sighed loudly. Changing into a freshly washed nightgown, she crawled under the covers and stared at the ceiling.

She thought of the whipping she had almost gotten, and she shivered. She thanked God for her deliverance, and then something reminded her of the beating Christ endured before the cross. She'd heard it described many times in church services, but not until now, did she realize that it was her *fault* and His *love* that had held Him there. Tiny tears crept from her hot eyelids as she envisioned the scourging he took, far worse than any Carolyn could ever adminis-ter—for *her sins*. The innocent had paid the price for the guilty. She thanked Him, again, for being such a wonderful, loving, and *forgiv-ing* God. She prayed that she would never forget that he had written His Word—not on tables of stone—but on her *heart*.

Malcolm and Carolyn decided that it was wise if Marilyn was never told that it was Lauren who had trapped her in the crib. Their niece, as well as Darren and Thatcher, were sworn to silence. The boys, also, said nothing to Lauren about what they had seen out of their window that night. She acted as though it had all been just *con-versation* with her aunt that evening, and they humored her by not letting her know that they knew *exactly* what she had faced.

In the months that followed, Lauren softened toward Marilyn, but their relationship would never be a good one. Too much troubled water had passed under the bridge for either to come to a loving for-giveness of the other. After all, Marilyn was yet to make that profes-sion of faith that Lauren had, and therefore, did not posses the love of God that she needed to help her find peace of her own.

Though Lauren struggled to improve relations with her *sibling*, her relationship with Thatcher McKinley grew smoothly into more than just friendship. She'd always cared for him, perhaps even loved him, but feared he would always see her as his roommate's little sister rather than the young woman that she was. She needn't have wor-ried; he was smitten with her.

Nearly a year after that emotional night, spring break came in March of 1964. Darren and his best friend returned to the farm, as usual, for the week and Thatcher finally got up the nerve to ask Lau-ren to dinner, a *real* date. She accepted, gladly, and they left one afternoon before six o'clock. She was dressed in a spring frock with her hair combed down on her shoulders. She had grown tall, five feet seven, and she filled out her new dress nicely.

Thatcher, ever the athlete, was in great shape and tanned from his days in the field. His eyes were almost as blue as hers and were matched beautifully to his sandy blond hair. He wore the sports jacket they preferred at the bank where he worked part-time. They spent the evening in idle chatter and enjoyed the evening. Little could have spoiled it for them. The couple would be inseparable over the course of the next year.

Darren and Thatcher were seniors, as well as Kathy and Todd. She became engaged to her beau, Joe Smithers, and planned to begin at her father's law firm the next summer. The Preston son received a full scholarship to Ohio University and would be majoring in chemistry following graduation, while Darren and Thatcher ended their last semester with a winning record and a division championship. Both were honored as outstanding athletes and scholars by the University. They graduated with honors in May of 1965.

Thatcher went to work as promised at Edenton Bank and Trust. He was an assistant to Mr. Derebourne, the president, and thus able to afford a small apartment in town. For the first time in his life, he was supporting himself with help from no one. Of that, he was so proud.

Darren returned to the farm. He had a degree in history and physical education and hoped to teach and coach. Unfortunately, there were no openings in Edenton. He placed applications in the surrounding counties.

Lauren turned twenty in May, still at home on the farm. She had little, if anything, to do with her natural parents. Aside from an occasional call from Helen, it was as if she had lived two different lives with no connection between them.

It would be a special day, June 11, 1965, at the Preston farm. The entire family gathered for a family dinner after church. Kathy and her fiancé were there as well as the other Preston children, including Todd. Thatcher had been invited, for he was like a member of the family after all the years.

After dinner, when most were relaxing in the living room, Thatcher and Lauren went for a walk through the fields. They did this often, enjoying the peaceful quiet of the countryside. Working in the city tended to do that to you.

They strolled for a long time before either spoke, holding hands. The summer sun was warm, but not hot, and directly above them. The silent breeze was just enough to make the day seem cooler than it was. "Is there something on your mind?" Lauren finally asked. She peered into his nervous, blue jewels. He smiled. "Can you tell me about it?"

He looked afar off and spotted the trees. "Come on, let's go up here, and I'll tell you." He pointed and she hid a smile...the pond...how many memories it held. When they had gotten there, he motioned for her to sit on the grassy area beneath the tree and he followed. He grasped her hands in his and looked into her eyes...those eyes.

He swallowed the lump in his throat. "Lauren?" She nodded. "I love you."

She laughed. "I know that, Silly. You've told me," she said, poking him in the ribs.

"No," he said with a blush. "I mean it, I *really* love you."

"So, you didn't mean it before?"

Lord, there were times when he hated her. "No, Lauren, you know what I mean." He sighed. "I love you like no one else in my life...like no one else *ever* in my life. *I love you.*"

Silence.

"Lauren, do you love *me*?"

Silence.

"Lauren?"

"Yes."

"Yes, you love me, or, yes, I'm listening?"

"Yes, I love you."

Silence.

He released her hand and reached into his pocket. "Enough to accept this?" She blushed with surprise as he extended his arm and handed her the tiny velvet box.

"Thatcher, is this—"

"Open it." With trembling hands, she pried apart the hinged jaws of the ring case. She drew a quick breath as she looked upon the solitaire. "It's not very big—"

"It's beautiful."

"I wish I could—"

"It's *beautiful.*"

Silence.

"Try it on," he said softly. Carefully she removed the golden ring and placed it on her finger. The stone sparkled in the sunshine. Her heart thumped in her chest. "It looks beautiful on you."

"It does?"

"Yes," he answered as calmly as his heart would allow. "Does this mean you accept? Will you marry me?"

Lauren's mind swirled. It had all happened so quickly. Was this what she wanted? Was this the real thing? Was marriage for her? She only had to look into Thatcher's kind face to find the answers. Yes, she loved him, more than she even knew.

Lauren paused for a long moment, considering the proposal. This was her chance for happiness. Or, was it for bondage and…disaster? Had not Helen married Rex? Had she known then what she knew, now, would she have? How would Lauren know?

Lauren knew Thatcher. She believed in him. Trusted him. Loved him.

"Yes," she answered with a smile. "Thatcher McKinley, I *will* marry you."

"Oh, thank God," he whispered with a grin. "I love you." They embraced and kissed, the cool breeze off the water blowing in their faces.

❦   ❦   ❦

As expected, the summer was filled with wedding preparations. Thatcher and Lauren would be married at Edenton Baptist Church where they all attended. Darren would be the best man, Kathy the maid of honor. She had asked Malcolm to give her away. He accepted with a smile.

The wedding date was set for August 30, 1965. Lauren had turned twenty and Thatcher, twenty-two. They were still so young, and yet so matured by their experiences. He worked all summer at his new job and was very well respected. Lauren had also kept her job as sales clerk; she looked to be promoted in the fall.

❦   ❦   ❦

Helen Mitchell sat at the dinner table, slowly sipping her coffee. Her husband sat opposite her. He had choked down a burned chicken leg, cussing as he did so. She avoided any conversation until now.

"Rex?" she asked, hesitantly. He grunted. "Lauren's gettin' married tomorrow." No response. "I was plannin' on goin'." Silence. "I was just wonderin'. You want to come?"

Rex's head slowly rose, grease on his chin. His pale blue eyes glared. "What th' hell did you say?"

"I said, you want to go—?"

"Hell, no!" he exclaimed as he slammed his fist on the table. The glasses shook. "Damn, woman! What's gotten into you? You think I want to see that little whore!?! She's probably been with half of Edenton by now! What's a weddin'?"

Small tears ran out the wrinkles of Helen's eyes. "I'm sorry, Rex. I just thought, since she's your daughter—"

"She's not my daughter!" he screamed, rising from his seat. "She's nothin' to me! Nothin'! Got it?" His wife nodded. He lowered his voice to a menacing tone. "The day she left here she deserted her fam'ly. She don't deserve to be called my daughter."

Helen looked up at him with anger in her eyes, pain in her heart. "No," she said slowly, "she deserves better."

Silence.

"What did you say, woman?"

Helen stood, fists clenched beneath the tablecloth. "I said, she deserves—"

Whack!

Rex's hand flew across the table and her face. She released a short scream as it hit her. He grabbed her by the shoulders and shook her. "You better remember who wears the pants 'round here, woman, or, you'll be out on your ass! Got that?"

Helen was crying. "Yes."

He threw her onto the floor with a shove. She yelled and he pointed his finger at her face. "I'll knock you out so fast you won't know what hit you." He turned and took a few steps before reeling for one last retort. "Clean up this damn mess and get me a beer."

❦   ❦   ❦

The morning of the wedding dawned bright and clear. It was dreadfully hot and sticky, typical weather for August. The participants were all eager and nervously awaiting the service. Carolyn and Malcolm beamed with pride. Having Lauren in their home had not always been easy, but they truly believed it had been worth it.

Helen, Lauren's natural mother, was there, too, sitting alone in the back of the church; she had quietly entered the sanctuary just before the ceremony began. She'd not seen her children since the day she gave up her legal rights to them in Malcolm's office; it had now been over four years. An occasional teary phone call was all they ever received of her.

At two-thirty in the afternoon on August 30, 1965, Thatcher and Lauren McKinley became husband and wife. Helen Mitchell slipped quickly out the door before anyone had seen her as the groom claimed his bride. Covered in rice, the newlyweds entered their "canned" vehicle with wide smiles on their faces and drove away from the church. Their honeymoon would be spent in their apartment downtown.

The adventure their life together would be had only begun.

Afterword

A Message…

This volume is the result of interviews and imagination. I was fortunate in my upbringing to have loving, caring parents who used Christian discipline to shape my will and not crush my spirit. The horrors of Hadesville that I have described are as foreign to me as I hope they are for you. I am saddened to note that some of you may identify with the abuse my Lauren suffered at the hands of her father, or the neglect of her mother. I can offer only my broken heart and unending empathy. I pray that you have found peace through the love of our Savior, Jesus Christ.

A Warning…

Lives are described here as they happened in my mind—not ideally—but as they are or were. Certainly we condemn Rex & Helen and glorify Malcolm & Carolyn, but neither couple is wholly bad nor good—just as each of us has both vice and virtue. The only sure and full truth by which we should judge and act is the Word of God, the Bible. That is your guide, not my story nor my characters. I pray that my examples of those truths are conveyed to you and appropriately demonstrated in this first volume.

A Challenge...

Remember that whatever you have been, or are, or think you'll be—God loves you and it is by His grace that you wake up each morning. Accept His gift of life and use the talents He has given you to glorify Him and lead others to His loving arms. Let us allow the Holy Spirit to be manifested in the *Intents of the Heart*—yours and mine.

About the Author

Lezlie Ann Word grew up on a farm near Dover, TN, in a community called Hurricane Creek with her parents, maternal grandmother, and younger sister, Ginger. They attended a small Baptist church located on the corner of her uncle's farm where she accepted Christ as her Savior at the age of eight during a fall revival. She credits her late mother with encouraging the love of biblical study that would lead her to accept the call of teaching when she was twenty.

At an early age, she developed a passion for reading and at the age of thirteen began her first novel; it remains unfinished. Gifted in academics, she received numerous awards and was valedictorian of her senior class at Stewart County High School in 1989. She attended Austin Peay State University on the Kimbrough Memorial Scholarship where she majored in education and received the Outstanding Achievement in Elementary Education Award in 1993. She completed a Master of Arts in Education for the Reading Specialist degree two years later. Lezlie is currently beginning her tenth year at Dover Elementary School where she has taught fourth grade, seventh and eighth grade literature and language arts, and seventh grade mathematics.

Gathering information and ideas from many sources (some of them personal accounts), Lezlie began writing *Intents of the Heart* while completing her student teaching semester in February 1993 after experiencing the climatic scene at the end of part one in a dream. Five years later, the series was completed and the final editing process began. This volume represents one-third of the complete work; the other two volumes will be quick to follow.

Currently, Lezlie is working on two writing projects. One is a prequel to *Intents* that chronicles the early life of Malcolm Preston, his courtship with Carolyn, and the years he spent at war; the other is a three-volume account of a member of the Derebourne family called *Chastening*. She hopes to see both in print.

On March 17, 2001, Lezlie married Richard Lynn Tyson, the love of her life. She was proud to take his name in all matters but one; she had decided to honor her father (the last of his line) by always publishing under her maiden name. Richard is a full-time youth minister at Harvest Fellowship in Clarksville, TN, where the couple resides.

Any questions and/or comments are welcome and can be sent to: Lezlie A. Word (or, Tyson), c/o Norman Word, 551 Les Ferrell Rd., Stewart, TN 37175.